Great Possessions

'Did you live in America with old Uncle Henry before you came here?' she asked.

'No, I lived in Alleshill.'

'Why have you come to live with us? Haven't you got any family of your own?'

'Yes, I have. Lots and lots of people. Mum an' Dad an' Tommy an' Uncle Bob an' Grannie and my other Grandma and Grandpa in Cogsdene, so there!'

'Why aren't you living with your own Mummy and Daddy?' Sally persisted.

'Do leave the kid alone, Sally,' Guy said.

'They've gone to Australia,' Lonnie said.

'And left you behind?'

Lonnie nodded, unable to speak.

'If she's got all this family, why is she living with us?'

'Because I grew out of the wrong seed,' Lonnie said and dissolved once more into tears.

GREAT POSSESSIONS

Kate Alexander

THE SHERIDAN BOOK COMPANY

This edition published in 1993 by
The Sheridan Book Company

First published in Great Britain
by Hutchinson 1989
Random House, 20 Vauxhall Bridge Road, London SW1V 2SA
Rowan edition 1990

Printed and bound in Great Britain by
Cox & Wyman Ltd, Reading, Berkshire

ISBN 1-85501-455-6

CHAPTER ONE

Lonnie Dunwell met her father, her real father, for the first and only time in the spring of 1921, when she was six years old.

She was fishing for frog spawn in the stream which ran by the side of the road leading into the village of Alleshill in Surrey when the motor car pulled up. Lonnie straightened up, the jam jar on a bit of string dangling from her wet hand. She had never seen the large black limousine before and she gave it a good long stare, especially when she saw it was driven by a uniformed chauffeur.

The chauffeur opened the car door and a tall, thin man got out, moving as if the effort was almost too much for him. Even on that day of spring sunshine he wore a thick overcoat. He had fair hair, lying lankly against his head, and his face was pale and drawn.

A grassy bank sloped down from the road to the shallow stream. Celandines grew there and water crowfoot, pale primroses flowered on the bank and Lonnie knew where to find the shy wild violets. On the other side of the stream the bank was steeper, with a hedgerow along the top where the blackthorn was already in flower and the hawthorn was showing clusters of pink buds.

The man walked to the edge of the grass and looked at Lonnie, standing in the shallow water. When he spoke his voice was low and husky.

'Is your name Eleanor Dunwell?'

'That's right, mister. Has your motor car broken down? My Dad mends them. I can show you the way.'

She looked hopefully at the limousine. A ride home in that would be a real treat and might divert her mother from the scolding she had earned by not going straight home from school, getting her feet wet and, worst of all, encouraging her little brother to join her in mischief.

She was an enchanting child, sturdy and warm-coloured from the gypsy blood she had inherited through her grandmother, but even at that early age there was something different about Lonnie. She had beautiful hands, long-fingered and deft, and narrow feet with high arches and long toes. Her head was finely poised on a graceful neck, and not even the fact that the neck was distinctly grubby could detract from her charm. She was alert and vigorous and intelligent.

As Rupert Humfrey watched, she climbed out of the water and up the bank towards him, her hair straggling down her back in an untidy tangle, her legs and feet reddened from the cold water, her dress, inexpertly tucked up into her knicker elastic, very damp round the hem.

'There's nothing wrong with my motor car,' he said. 'I just wanted to see you. A boy in the village said I'd find you here.'

She looked at him with big brown eyes, considering this eccentric behaviour.

'I used to know your mother . . . and your father, years ago,' Rupert said.

'Before the war? My Dad fought in the war. He was a soldier and he had a gun and killed lots of lots of Germans.'

'He came through all right, then?'

'Without a scratch, thanks be!' Lonnie said, repeating something she had heard her mother say.

'Lucky man! Have you . . . have you any brothers or sisters, Eleanor?'

'I'm always called Lonnie, 'cos that's what I used to say my name was when I was little. He's my brother, him there. Tommy, come out of the water! He's only four, and there's another one at home, but he's just a baby. He's called Jimmy.'

As she spoke she pulled a clump of grass and began to dry her feet. Her stockings went on with difficulty and one of her elastic garters seemed to be missing, but there was nothing unusual about that. She sat down to put on her shoes, calling again to Tommy to come and join her.

'We've got to go home to tea now,' she told the stranger. She considered. 'I 'spect you could come, too, if you wanted,' she offered.

'No . . . no, better not,' the man said, as if to himself. He coughed, a harsh, dry sound, which seemed to hurt him because he pressed one hand to his chest. He still lingered, watching as Lonnie helped Tommy to put on his shoes.

'What did you catch?' he asked, looking at the jam jars.

'Frog spawn,' Lonnie said, holding one of the glass jars up to the light. 'It turns into tadpoles and then they turn into frogs, but Mum'll prob'ly make us throw it away before we get any little frogs.'

Her regretful tone made Rupert smile. She smiled back, impudent and irresistible.

'Gi' us a penny, mister?' she asked hopefully.

Rupert's smile broadened. He felt in his pocket and found half a crown.

'A silver penny,' he said. 'I have to say goodbye now . . . Lonnie.'

'Goodbye, mister.'

Lonnie looked wistfully at the limousine, but it was pointing in the wrong direction, away from the village, and it was obvious that the man had no intention of taking them home in it. She put the half-crown into the pocket of her skirt. It was a pity about that, too. A penny could have been spent on sweets in the village shop, but half a crown was serious money and would have to be reported to her mother, who would confiscate it and dole it out in dribs and drabs, if she didn't decide to waste it on something dreary like elastic garters or a hair ribbon to replace the bedraggled rag which was supposed to be holding Lonnie's hair in place.

'C'mon, Tommy,' she said. 'Time to go home.'

The Dunwells had been living in Alleshill for two years, ever since Joe Dunwell had been discharged from the Army in 1919, having served out his time as a regular soldier a few months after the ending of the war. He had come through it with nothing more than a minor graze from a piece of shrapnel, but he said he had had his bellyful of fighting and he had a different plan for his future. He had got something more out of his years in the Army than the ability to shoot straight: he had become a first-class mechanic.

'I don't know why it is, but I've got a feel for engines,' he explained to his wife. 'There's not many motor cars I can't repair. Lorries, too, and farm implements.'

'Could you make a living at it?' Rosa asked.

'Why not?'

At that time they were still living in Sussex with Joe's parents, in the village where both Rosa and Joe had been born. It was something Rosa had been prepared to put up with while Joe was away at the front, but which could not go on, not with two young children already and more likely if Joe had his way. Joe had a brother, living in Alleshill in Surrey, who was a blacksmith by trade. Horses were disappearing and the shoeing business was not what it had been, but Joe's idea was that he and his brother should join forces. Bob would keep the blacksmith's forge going as long as it was needed and put his metal-working ability at Joe's service, while Joe would start a garage and repair shop. It might be slow going at first, he explained, but if Rosa would be patient while he built up the business, Joe thought that the trade had good prospects for the future.

'I've got some savings,' Rosa said, cautiously, because she had no intention of revealing the extent of her nest-egg, nor the true story of how she had acquired it. 'I've never told you before because, well, it just never happened to come up, but if it'd be any help in setting yourself up I could put in about fifty pounds.'

'Fifty pounds! How ever did you come by that amount of money, lovey?'

Rosa had always known that one day she would have to account for that money and she had her story ready.

'Tips mostly,' she said. 'When I was up at the Hall I

used to help the ladies who didn't bring a maid with them and they often gave me a pound or two. Christmas boxes, too. Mrs Humfrey took to giving me money once I'd become her maid. I put it all by and I've never had much need to touch it.'

'It'll make all the difference,' Joe said excitedly. 'I can get the tools that I'll need and put up the workshop I was thinking would have to wait until I started showing a profit. Are you sure you want to risk your savings?'

'Silly! What's mine is yours, isn't it? Besides, I'm anxious for us to get a place of our own. Being here with Ma and Dad has been all right while you've been away, but we can't go on with it much longer.'

They moved to Alleshill in the summer of 1919. Rosa had the house she wanted, with three bedrooms and an inside lavatory, and settled into it as if she had never had ambitions for a far more opulent life.

A second son arrived, to Joe's delight. They were a contented, happy family, beginning to be prosperous, and if Rosa sometimes gave all of them the sharp side of her tongue that was something that might be forgiven a busy wife and mother. No one noticed that these fits of bad temper came over Rosa whenever Joe was particularly attentive to Lonnie. Joe delighted in Lonnie, she was his 'little lass', and Lonnie adored him, knowing very well that he was her ally when she was in trouble with Rosa for not behaving like a little lady.

On the day when Rupert Humfrey visited the village Lonnie had certainly not been living up to her mother's idea of what was proper. She knew it and was philosophical about it as she and Tommy trudged home with their jam jars full of frog spawn. She had enjoyed herself, it had been good while it lasted, and there was always the chance that she could divert her mother from the scolding that was due to her by producing the stranger's half-crown.

In fact, the money made Rosa crosser than Lonnie had anticipated.

'Where did you get that?' she demanded as Lonnie held out the silver coin.

'A man gave it to me.'

'What man?'

'A man in a car.'

'One of Dad's customers?' Rosa asked, her frown lightening. It was a lot of money to give a small child, but perhaps one of Joe's customers had been feeling generous.

Lonnie shook her head vigorously. 'He said his car wasn't broken down. He just gave it to me.'

'Lonnie asked him,' Tommy put in, not because he meant to make mischief, but wanting to help.

Lonnie gave him a disgusted look, but she recognised that he was too young to realise that their mother would be far from pleased to hear that.

'Lonnie, you never did!' Rosa said. 'Whatever got into you? You know better, I should hope, than to ask anyone for money, let alone a strange man.'

'He wasn't a stranger,' Lonnie put in quickly. 'He said he knew you and Dad. He was looking for me. He asked if I was Eleanor Dunwell. And I didn't ask him for half a crown. I just said give us a penny.'

'You shouldn't have done that,' Rosa said, but she spoke automatically, while she was trying to puzzle out just what had happened. 'What sort of man was he?'

'He was a tall man and thin, like a skellington,' Lonnie said. 'He had a nasty cough.'

'And he had a big black car and a man to drive it, with a cap on his head,' Tommy said, still trying to help.

'Old or young?' Rosa asked.

'Oh, old,' Lonnie said. She thought about it. 'As old as you. He had yellow hair. Mum, can I have a penny for sweets, can I, Mum? It is my half-crown and I did bring it straight home and give it to you. Can I, Mum?'

She was surprised when her mother handed her a penny and gave another to Tommy without even commenting on the wet hem of Lonnie's dress or the mud on Tommy's shorts.

'Sweet shop,' she hissed to Tommy and they ran out of

the house, leaving Rosa to grapple with a memory she thought she had put out of her mind for ever, of a young face, bleached by the moonlight, with hollows under his deepset eyes and high cheekbones.

She was imagining it, of course. Lonnie's visitor couldn't possibly be Rupert Humfrey. Why should he come seeking her after all this long time? And yet . . . Rosa knew that Rupert had come home from the exile in America to which his mother had banished him in order to join the Army; knew, too, that he had been badly wounded. She had never set eyes on him again since they had been forced to part, nor did she wish to. One of the reasons she had fallen in so eagerly with Joe's plan to move to Alleshill was to get well away from the place where Rupert lived. If he had come looking for Lonnie then it was a rotten trick to play. If he ever came again Rosa would tell him so, in no uncertain terms. What right had he to come disturbing the life she had built up, the peaceful, prosperous existence she and Joe had worked so hard to enjoy?

There had been a time when Rosa's ambitions had flown far higher than her present circumstances. She had been Rosa Seward then and employed as Mrs Humfrey's maid. She wanted a diamond ring and a silk gown, a fine house and servants to wait on her, a fire in her bedroom and breakfast in bed, leisure to arrange flowers in cut-glass vases and to sit in the drawing room doing embroidery – all the things she had seen since she had first gone into service at Firsby Hall. And so, in the lovely spring of 1914, she had tempted Rupert Humfrey into making love to her, because she had thought he would marry her.

It was an idyll that had lasted a mere six weeks. Long enough for Rosa to feel sure of her hold over Rupert, long enough for Rupert to work off the frustration of being sent down from Cambridge after an escapade he knew had been childish, long enough for Rosa to become pregnant.

She had told him on one of the nights when she had crept out of the house to run over the smooth, dew-sodden lawn to find him waiting for her in a rustic hut at the

11

point where the grass gave way to trees. He had been eager for her that night, so ardent in his lovemaking that she had no doubt about his response to her news.

They lay in one another's arms, slack and satisfied, wrapped in a rough travelling rug which rasped agreeably against Rosa's bare skin. A shaft of moonlight, entering through one of the cracks in the wooden wall, fell across Rupert's head.

'You look like a ghost,' Rosa said, propping herself up on her elbow and looking down at his face, bleached of colour and full of shadows.

'No ghost,' Rupert said, pulling her down to kiss her. 'Flesh and blood, my little gypsy, as you well know.'

She was a lovely girl, black-haired and sloe-eyed, with a golden skin and a warm flush of colour in her face. Her body was rounded and firm, plump with good living and strong from hard work, and once they had got over the initial awkwardness of her virginity, which was something Rupert had not expected from the readiness with which she had fallen into his arms, she had gloried in his passion.

Gypsy blood, they said in the village. Rupert knew all about that, just as he knew about the woman who had married his father's gamekeeper and borne him this one child, and who now lived alone in a broken-down hut in these same woods. A strange woman, but her daughter was delectable as she leant over him, with her bare breasts brushing his chest.

All the same, she had her limitations, and when she began talking about marriage Rupert was dismayed.

'Darling, I'm only nineteen, you know. I'd need Mother's consent to marry you and, quite honestly, my dear one, she wouldn't give it.'

'She'll come round when she knows I'm expecting your baby. She'd like a grandchild, wouldn't she?'

Not while she still thought of him as little more than a schoolboy, and not like this. A vision of his mother, cool and elegant in the floating silks she affected, came into Rupert's mind. It was inconceivable that she would welcome a child he had fathered on her own maid.

Rupert sat up. Looking for a way out, he spoke the words of every other man in the same predicament.

'Are you sure?'

'I'm two weeks overdue and that's enough for me,' Rosa said. 'I've waited till tonight, just in case it was a mistake, but I thought it was time for you to be told.'

Worried by his silence, she said, 'Rupert, it's going to be all right, isn't it? It was bound to happen, with us carrying on the way we have. I've thought about it and I didn't let it stop me because I love you so much, Rupert dear.'

She had seen it as a way of binding him to her, but now the way he had taken the news was beginning to frighten her.

'We will get married, won't we?' she persisted.

'It's going to be difficult,' Rupert said. 'Mother won't give her consent, not even if I go down on my knees and beg her.'

'Yes, she will. She always gives you everything you want.'

'Not this. I'm sorry, but you have to believe that I know her better than you do.'

There was a long silence as Rosa tried to come to terms with the ending of her dream.

'We could live together until you're twenty-one and then get married,' she said at last. 'It's not what I'd like, but as long as I had your promise I could hold my head high and once it was legal people would soon forget.'

'Oh, Rosa! What would we live on?'

'You've got lots of money,' she said uncertainly.

'I've got what Mother chooses to give me and she'd rather see me starve than living with you.'

'She dotes on you. You can wheedle her round if you try.'

'Not over this.'

Rosa could feel the fear, winding down inside her like a rope until it reached the place where the baby was lodged. He was going to let her down. She had thought that he loved her enough to fight for their future and she had been so sure that he would stand by her that she had shut her mind to any other possibility.

It would have shaken Rosa to know how clearly Rupert saw the working of her mind now that he had been jolted out of his infatuation. She had known that she had him enslaved and she had calculated that any risk was worth the prize of marriage. Not that she had been pretending when she had responded so ardently to his lovemaking; her newly-awakened sensuality had been a delight to both of them. As a mistress she was delightful, but except in this surreptitious way he could not afford to keep a mistress. Or a child.

The child. It was impossible for him to visualise himself as a father. All the same, if there was going to be a child then he was responsible for it. Poor little . . . bastard.

'Rupert,' Rosa said, still trying to coax the response she wanted from him. 'You do love me, don't you?'

He had said it often enough, but now it stuck in his throat.

'Don't worry, Rosa,' he said. 'Whatever happens I'll see you're all right.'

He had no clear idea of what he meant by that, nor could he see any way out of the predicament. He toyed with the idea of confiding in his Uncle Edward, the husband of his mother's only sister and one of Rupert's few male relatives, but Edward Lynton was unworldly to a degree which drove his wife frantic. If Rupert had had a problem with a brood mare he could have been sure of his uncle's sympathetic attention; Edward found human beings less comprehensible.

There was another uncle, a great uncle, in fact, who would have sympathised with Rupert, probably have laughed about the matter, since it was exactly the sort of escapade he had indulged in himself in his younger days, but Great Uncle Henry lived in America, which was a pity because he had enough money to make a protracted loan a possibility.

Rosa could not accept that Rupert's obsession with her had been dissipated between one breath and the next.

What he shrank from was telling his mother, as any young man might, Rosa thought indulgently; so she decided to do it for him. Mrs Humfrey would no doubt be angry and think her precious boy had been trapped, but Rosa was convinced that she could be talked round. Rosa was her protégée – she was proud of the way she had brought the young girl on and to some extent Rosa was even her confidante; Rosa believed that she could be wheedled into consenting to the marriage.

It was a belief that survived until Rosa saw Mrs Humfrey's face after she had understood what Rosa was telling her. Before her eyes, Mrs Humfrey seemed to age ten years. Lines which Rosa's fingers had helped to smooth away were suddenly there, stark on her face; all her colour drained from her cheeks, so that the rouge Rosa had applied stood out like a mask of a clown. Even her hands trembled as she pushed her hair back from her forehead in a distracted movement.

When she realised that Rosa was expecting Rupert to marry her, Mrs Humfrey got up in one swift angry movement and for a moment Rosa thought that the other woman was going to strike her. She flinched and stepped back and Mrs Humfrey seemed to remember herself.

'Never!' she said. 'Of course I can't allow my son to marry you. It would ruin his life.'

'What about my life? And the baby's? Do you want your grandchild to grow up without a name?'

'If it is my grandchild! I doubt very much whether the child is really Rupert's . . .'

'Indeed it is! I've never been with any other man, never!'

'Really? I thought you were walking out with the Dunwells' soldier son.'

'Joe's no more than a childhood sweetheart. He's keen on me, I admit, but he's never laid a finger on me, not in the way of . . . not going all the way, like I did with Rupert, over and over again. He was mad for me, crazy.'

Margot Humfrey put her hands over her ears.

15

'Stop it! I don't want to hear any more. You wicked girl, get out of my sight.'

'I'm not a bad girl,' Rosa said. 'I've done what I shouldn't with Rupert, but it was him persuaded me into it. I've told you, we love one another. Talk it over with him. He knows the baby's his. He'll tell you we've talked about getting married. All that's needed is for you to say yes.'

Quivering with distaste, Mrs Humfrey forced herself to demand Rupert's side of the story. She soon realised that what Rosa had said was true, there was no doubt that the child was his. All the same, whatever the girl might say, it was obvious to his mother that Rupert had no desire to take Rosa for his wife. He was miserably ashamed of himself and his mother's embarrassment at having to discuss his sexual adventure made him shudder, but he did insist on accepting the consequences of his madness.

'It's my responsibility,' he said.

'It would be, if you were of age and had any money of your own,' his mother retorted. 'As it is, I shall have to deal with it. Oh, don't look so miserable, silly boy! I'll see that Rosa's properly treated.'

'I suppose she can go away somewhere?' Rupert suggested. 'We could pay for the baby to be fostered, couldn't we?'

'You're the one who has to go away.' Mrs Humfrey put away the handkerchief with which she had been dabbing her eyes. 'I haven't told you before, because I wasn't sure whether I meant to agree to what he suggests, but I had a letter from Uncle Henry last week. He'd heard about your trouble at Cambridge . . .'

'How? You didn't write and tell him, did you?' Rupert demanded.

'Patsy did.'

'Aunt Patsy's far too eager to pass on bad news about me. What made her think Great Uncle Henry would be interested?'

'Sometimes your attitude is positively *simple*,' his mother said. 'Patsy's as much his niece as I am and with three children to be provided for and only a country vet's income on which to do it, naturally she has an eye on Uncle Henry's money. He seems to have made quite a fortune in America. You must remember, you certainly should, how lavish he was when he visited us for the Coronation.'

'He was generous,' Rupert admitted.

'He took a liking to you and he still seems to favour you. He's written about that tiresome Cambridge business – I must say with a levity I thought quite unnecessary – and suggested you should go and visit him for a month or two.'

Watching her son's expressive face, Margot saw surprise, pleasure and then resentment.

'Why didn't you tell me before?' he asked.

They both knew the answer to that. Because she had not wanted him to go. Now, she couldn't get him away fast enough.

The news that young Mr Rupert was going off to visit his uncle in America spread through the household in rather less time than it took to get his trunk down from the attic. Rosa could hardly believe the disgrace that was about to fall on her. The humiliation would be all the greater because she had set herself up above the other servants and they had resented her superior airs.

Rosa listened without enthusiasm to Mrs Humfrey's plans for her to pretend to take another position and disappear. She was shaken by the pain Rupert's desertion was giving her, quite apart from her fear about the baby. It had been love, in its way, what she had felt for Rupert. She had been intoxicated by the white smoothness of his skin, by the clean smell of him, the faint prickle of gold on his jaw, the educated voice murmuring endearments, the way he had trembled in her arms and begged for her body. He had been experienced, too. Whatever Mrs Humfrey might think, her precious boy had known enough to make his lovemaking an intoxication for Rosa.

She had given him her virginity, so precious, so carefully preserved, the virginity which Joe had wanted and she had denied him. Joe . . . she ought to have stuck to Joe. He would have married her if he'd got her with child, not hidden behind his mother and run away.

Mrs Humfrey, it seemed, was prepared to find somewhere for Rosa to go and to pay her an allowance until after the baby was born. The child, she informed Rosa, would have to be given up for adoption; that would leave Rosa free to start her life again.

Rosa was contemptuous. A whole year missing out of her life, a baby born and given away, and she was supposed to just turn her back on it and start again. There must be some other solution, there had to be.

A brief, unhappy meeting with Rupert, snatched in the corridor with the possibility of someone interrupting them at any moment, convinced Rosa that there was nothing more to be hoped for from him. At that moment, looking at his white, worried face, Rosa saw him for the first time not as the lordly young owner of the great house, the man who was destined to give her the splendid position she wanted, but as a nervous boy, younger than she was herself, unsure of himself, not a strong character, not the man she had thought he was at all. The disillusion was so sudden and so complete that she could taste it like bile in her mouth.

'Just remember this,' she said. 'If you have any feeling in you at all you're going to spend the rest of your life wondering what happened to the child of your body you're throwing on the scrap heap. I despise you, Rupert Humfrey, and I wouldn't marry you now if you went down on your knees and begged me.'

There was only one other person Rosa could turn to. Reluctantly, angry with herself for having to go to her mother and admit her predicament and the miscalculation that had led to it, Rosa walked the path through the woods that led to the hut where Thirza Seward eked out an existence that was a mystery to the local people.

The details of that day when she had finally abandoned her dream of a lady's life were etched on Rosa's memory. She remembered that as she had walked through the net-

18

tles and cow parsley that had filled up the spaces where the trees had been thinned the scent from the weeds had hung heavy in the air and a wave of nausea had swept over Rosa as the child inside her proclaimed its presence, staking its claim on her life, the life she had meant to live so differently.

A black cat stalked out of the undergrowth and turned to look at Rosa with yellow eyes before darting ahead of her down the path towards the house. She saw him leap at the latch, open the door and disappear inside, as if to warn his mistress of her approach. Rosa jumped with nervous distaste as a hen flew cackling into a tree. There was a pig, too, rootling for beech mast and acorns. Rosa shied away from his pink snout and cunning eyes, picking her way distastefully over the churned-up ground.

Her mother had come to the door and was watching her progress with ironic detachment. Rosa recognised that look and regretted giving in to the panic-stricken urge to turn for help to someone who was so much at odds with her ambitions.

'What's your trouble?' Thirza Seward asked, without giving Rosa time for any greeting.

'Why do you ask that?' Rosa countered.

'If you don't want something from me when you come here it'll be the first time since you left home. Besides . . .' Thirza paused and gave her daughter a long, thoughtful look, 'I can feel it.'

'Oh, don't start on that tack,' Rosa said crossly. 'You know I don't believe in your gypsy tricks.'

'You'd better come in.'

She was offended; Rosa could tell that from the swish of her skirts as she turned away. She was taller than Rosa and thinner, straight as a birch tree and without a thread of silver in her black hair. From the back she might have been a young girl, but her face, the skin browned and coarsened by exposure, was marked by deep lines, and her hands were seamed with hard labour.

Outside, the hut, weatherboarded and tarred, with an iron pipe from which a wisp of smoke drifted away, sticking out of the roof at an angle, looked no more than a temporary shelter, but the inside held surprises.

It ought to have been dark, for the windows were small, but instead there was a dazzle of light, reflected from the surfaces of mirrors and brasses which hung on every wall. It was clean, too, and only Thirza knew how much fierce pride went into keeping it that way.

The stove on which she cooked and which also provided her only heat, was blackleaded, with a steel trim which shone like silver. The wooden table had been scrubbed so often that the colour had softened to pale cream. On the shelves against the wall there was a pink and gold lustre tea service which had once been the pride of her grand-mother's wagon.

The floor was of rough boards which had been creo-soted, but Thirza had acquired some white paint and had painted a bold design of flowers and arabesques on the dark surface. In front of the fire there was a rag rug, made of strips of material hooked into sacking in a kaleidoscope of colour. Against one wall was her narrow bed and, flung over it, a red and white shawl of the finest cashmere. It apparently mattered nothing to Thirza that her black cat was curled up on this treasure.

It took Thirza no time at all to find out what was wrong with her daughter. Before the kettle she had moved over to stand on the glowing embers of her fire had boiled, she had most of the story.

To Rosa's fury her mother laughed when she heard who was the father of the expected baby.

'That won't be popular with her up at the Hall,' she said.

'She's sending him away. To *America*! Mum, you've got to help me.'

'A long journey and a strange land, but he'll have to come home again one day. Here, drink your tea.'

Rosa took the fine pink and gold cup, vaguely surprised that her mother had chosen to use her treasured heirloom.

'They say in the village that you do help girls who've

made a mistake. Surely you'll do as much for your own daughter?'

'I've maybe given a helping hand to some I thought stood in need of it,' Thirza admitted. 'There's others I've sent away. Give me your hand.'

'Mum, you know I don't believe in that foolishness!'

'You'd let the doctor feel your pulse, so why shouldn't I take your hand to help me decide what to do?'

Reluctantly, Rosa held out her hand and Thirza took it into her own hardened one and spread it out to look at the palm.

'Such a fine, soft hand,' she said with the same irony she had shown when Rosa first arrived. 'When I put you into service I meant you to learn a useful trade, not the foolery of skin creams and washing another woman's silk knickers. Well, you must put that behind you now. Why did you go with him?'

'Because I thought he would marry me.'

'It would never have answered. It's a mistake to move away from your own kind. I did it when I married your father and my people cast me off.'

'Did you regret it?'

'Not until after he died. Then . . . yes, then I would have given anything to have gone back to the travelling life, but I had you to think of.'

'You were glad to get rid of me when I went into service.'

'You were twelve years old and ready to earn a living. I was glad to be relieved of the burden of living surrounded by people. I've been happier since I came to live in the woods.'

'What about when you get old?'

'I'll cope with that when the time comes. I had one thing you haven't had yet: I loved my man. You were hot for young Rupert, but you were more in love with the life he could have offered you. Silly girl, silly girl. You're clever and pretty and quick to learn, but you're not gentry material.'

She ran her finger over the lines on Rosa's palm.

'There's a lot of money here,' she said.

'Oh Mum!' Rosa pulled her hand away. 'Cross my hand with silver and I'll tell you where to find gold! Don't try those tricks with me. Are you going to put me in the way of getting rid of this baby?'

'No. There's other ways of dealing with it. I thought you were walking out with the Dunwells' soldier son. He's home on leave, isn't he? I saw him in the village and he spoke to me very civilly, which is more than some do. I knew it was because I was your mother. A fine, upstanding, vigorous young man.'

The eyes of the two women met and the thought in both their heads was the same.

'I couldn't do that,' Rosa said in a whisper. 'I've never . . . Joe and I have never made love.'

'Start now.'

'I couldn't . . . he'd know.'

'Not if you're clever. Use your head, Rosa, and then get him to marry you, double quick. You'll do well with Joe Dunwell. He's your sort. With you behind him, Joe could go far.'

'In the Army?' Rosa enquired sarcastically.

'There's trouble in the air,' Thirza said, going off at a tangent. 'I went to Brighton races and spoke to some of the travellers. There's been a killing in some far-off place . . . blood on the stones, they said . . . and there'll be more spilt before long.'

'You'd never think we were living in the twentieth century! Honestly, Mum, it's no wonder the people in the village are suspicious of you. You talk like some old witch.'

'If you've drunk you tea, you can go,' Thirza said. 'You came for my advice and I've given it to you. Put the come-hither on Joe Dunwell, tell him the babe is his and push him up the aisle, fast. It's the best hope you've got to make something of your life.'

It was not difficult to entice Joe into going further than Rosa had ever allowed before. He was elated by his promotion to Sergeant and inclined to be more masterful than he had been in the past. It needed little more than a few extra kisses in the deep shadow of the trees, a failure to slap his hand away when he fumbled at the bodice of her dress, a yielding acquiescence as he lowered her to the ground, a token murmur of 'Oh, Joe, we didn't ought to,' and then he was on top of her and beyond stopping whether she wanted it or not.

Rosa shed a few tears when it was over, for a dream that was lost, for the life of ease she had wanted and the man who would have given it to her.

'Don't cry, my dear lass,' Joe whispered. He wrapped his arms round her and held her close. 'It takes some girls like that, the first time,' he said awkwardly, willing now to share with her a knowledge he would not have admitted to before. 'Did I hurt you, lovey?'

Rosa moved her head against his shoulder, unable to speak, but this time she cried for Joe, for his kindness and decency, and the deception she was practising on him.

'Let me put up the banns,' Joe coaxed. 'You won't say no to me now, will you?'

'Oh, Joe . . . what'll everyone think if we get married as sudden as that?'

'That I've got the prettiest girl in Cogsdene, that's all. Everyone knows I've been courting you for years. Besides, you never know what may happen, me being in the Army. What'd you do if I got sent abroad?'

'Joe! That's not likely, is it?'

'You never know. There's always trouble somewhere. Ireland, for instance, they've been cutting up very rough over there, and there's ructions in the Balkans. I've heard the officers talking about it.'

'We won't get dragged into that! You're pulling my leg, Joe Dunwell.'

'Perhaps I am,' he admitted. 'Give us a kiss, Rosa.'

They lay together, kissing and talking idly, while the darkness thickened about them, until Joe's caresses began to grow more urgent. Rosa put her hand under her bare, warm breast and lifted it towards his mouth.

'Kiss me there, Joe. It makes me feel nice.'

23

This time she did not bother to pretend to hold back as she had, with a cunning that shamed her, the first time, but went with him all the way, her body bucking eagerly to meet his, her thoughts incoherent.

This is good . . . Joe . . . it's wonderful . . . Joe. If it's always going to be like this . . . Joe, Joe hold me, hold me. Suppose it makes me lose Rupert's child, what'll I do then? Marry Joe, that's what. Damn being a lady. This is what I want.

They were married on the twenty-sixth of July and went on a honeymoon to Margate, a highly respectable thing to do which pleased Rosa immensely, only to have their holiday interrupted by the outbreak of the war in which Rosa had not believed. Joe went off to join his unit knowing that he left Rosa pregnant and believing that it was the result of their first union in the woods. In all the horror and confusion of war no one worried about when the baby was conceived and when the little girl put in an appearance in February only Joe's mother sniffed and twitched her eyebrows and even she never doubted that the child was her son's.

As for Rosa, she put it out of her mind completely, almost persuading herself that Joe really was Lonnie's father. Only the nest-egg which her mother had secured for her after an interview with Rupert's mother which had made Thirza laugh and Mrs Humfrey choke with anger – two hundred pounds resting securely in a Post Office account – sometimes reminded Rosa that she had been guilty of deceiving her kind and loving husband.

She had put up with the inconvenience of living with his parents all through the war and had been pleased with the way she and Joe had bettered themselves once the fighting was behind them. One thing she was quite sure about: she was not going to allow any whim of Rupert's to threaten her security. If he tried to get in touch with Lonnie a second time Rosa would warn him off in no uncertain terms.

★

Rupert would have been the first to acknowledge that he had no right to intrude into Rosa's life. Nevertheless he had done it, driven by an overwhelming desire to see the child he had fathered. It had not been difficult to track her down. A casual visit to Cogsdene, an enquiry about how Joe was doing these days, and he was in possession of all the information he needed about the village where they lived and Joe's thriving business.

He had gone out for a drive, to while away his boredom, to get the benefit of the air that was supposed to do him good, and told the chauffeur to take him to the Surrey village where the Dunwell family lived. A stroll past the local school, a word with a couple of children, and Lonnie had been easily located.

He had been enthralled by her. Her beauty, her boldness, even her naughtiness, had all appealed to him. But he had no place in her life. She was a healthy, happy, normal child. That was all he had wanted to know. All he had wanted until he set eyes on her, that is. Now, he longed to see her again and the fact that it was impossible was one more heartache added to a life that held little pleasure for him.

When he got home Rupert was exhausted and his mother fussed over him, just as he had known she would.

'Darling, where have you been? I began to be worried. Is it wise to take these long drives, do you think?'

'I merely sit in the back of the car,' Rupert pointed out wearily. 'It's not exactly a tiring exercise.'

'All I can say is that you *look* tired, foolish one. Where did you go? Somewhere nice?'

'I went to see my daughter,' Rupert said deliberately.

'Rupert!'

Margot looked at him in such a frightened way that Rupert took pity on her.

'Don't worry, I didn't see anyone else. I merely spoke to the child, without telling her who I was, and came away.'

'All the same . . . not a very wise thing to do, darling.

I thought you'd put that old business behind you. You never speak about it.'

'It's been on my mind. I wanted to see her, just once.'

'I was never really convinced that you were responsible, especially when Rosa married in such a hurry.'

'She's mine all right.' Rupert smiled, remembering that vivid little face smiling up at him with complete confidence. 'She's got Rosa's colouring, but even I could see the likeness between us.'

'All the more reason for keeping away from her.'

'I agree. It won't happen again.'

'Good. Come and sit down, darling, and let me give you a glass of wine. The shock you gave me has made me forget what I meant to tell you as soon as you came in. I'm afraid it's bad news. I feel quite sad about it myself, and I haven't seen him since . . . goodness, since 1910. Uncle Henry has died.'

Rupert sat down and took the glass of wine his mother had poured for him. He felt tired in all his limbs, but there was nothing new in that. He tried to feel as upset about his great uncle's death as his mother obviously expected, but the war had blunted his response to death. What was one more, especially when it was an old and ailing man?

Henry Singleton had been the brother of Margot's mother and, in his youth, a constant source of anxiety to his family. It had been a relief when Henry had taken himself off to America. He had gone looking for adventure and had certainly found it, if the news that occasionally reached England could be believed. To Margot her Uncle Henry had been a romantic figure and his rare letters home and the occasional bizarre presents he sent back had been highlights of her sedate childhood. To everyone's surprise, Henry had grown prosperous in his new country; his mining ventures had been successful and he had been concerned in some very lucrative railway schemes. He came back to England only twice, once after his father's death, and once for the coronation of King George V, which was when he had met his nephew, Rupert, and taken a liking to the boy.

'He was good to me when I went out to him in 1914,' Rupert said, remembering the way he had poured out his troubles to his great uncle and the robust advice he had been given.

If the war had not intervened, Rupert thought that he might well have stayed on and gone into business with his Uncle Henry. The old man had made it obvious that there was a place for him if he chose to stay, and Rupert's mother had been only too anxious for him to remain safely in neutral America until the war in Europe was over. It was Rupert who had insisted on returning to England and joining the Army, but at the back of his mind he had the idea that after the war was over he would return to America, if not for ever then certainly for a period of years.

A bullet through his lungs and a whiff of gas had put paid to that plan. He was an invalid and only his mother now clung to the belief that one day Rupert would be completely well.

The thought of her son's health was always in her mind, even now in connection with Henry Singleton's death, so that her next remark was, 'I wish now that we'd visited him last winter instead of going to Egypt.'

'Mummy, darling, the Nevada winters are *bitter*!' Rupert said in amusement. 'At least, where Uncle Henry lived.'

'Really? I thought you said it was all desert.'

'Cold in the mountains, I assure you. Who let you know about his death?'

'Some American lawyers. Oh, darling, how silly of me, there's a letter for you, too.'

She waited until her son had read the second letter and then asked hopefully, 'One doesn't want to seem mercenary, but does your letter say anything about his Will?'

'Nothing specific. They just ask to be put in touch with my legal advisers. Mysterious! I suppose I'd better get George Osbert to write to them.'

'Mine says the same. I must say I'm hoping for a thousand or two. After all, we're his only relatives, except for Patsy and her family, and he did seem terribly affluent, didn't he?'

'He was certainly in the money when I visited him, but he was a terrible old gambler,' Rupert said with reminiscent pleasure. 'He told me he'd won and lost at least two fortunes – in the way of business, I mean.'

'He was a real, old-fashioned black sheep, but I always had an admiration for him. Such a pity he never settled down and married; he must have been lonely.'

Rupert, who had been favoured with some colourful reminiscences about the various ladies who had shared his great uncle's life, maintained a discreet silence.

'I suppose we ought to go into black,' Margot said doubtfully.

'No!'

The violence of Rupert's repugnance startled Margot.

'All right, darling, not if you don't think it's necessary,' she said.

'If you want to go into mourning, wear it for the men who were young and healthy and never came back from France, and the ones who are mangled and torn . . .'

He stopped, catching his breath, and then doubled up, trying to stop a paroxysm of coughing.

'Rupert, dear, don't upset yourself.' Margot hovered over him in desperate anxiety. 'You've tired yourself out with that foolish drive this afternoon. Do you want to rest before dinner?'

Rupert shook his head, fighting to get his breath.

'All right . . . in a minute,' he said. 'Don't fuss, Mummy.'

He sat back in his chair and closed his eyes. Perspiration glistened on his forehead and his breath was still wheezing in his chest.

'I'll go over to see George Osbert tomorrow,' he said. 'As it happens, I already had it in my mind to visit him.'

Behind his closed eyes Rupert was conjuring up the memory of a face, not the face of his great uncle, but the one he had seen for the first time that afternoon, the face of his own beautiful child.

It took some weeks for Henry Singleton's affairs to be sorted out, and the American lawyers were cautious in the information they released. All that was known was that there were legacies for one or two people in the United States, and for Margot and her sister, Patsy Lynton, and that Rupert was the heir to the remainder of the estate. His mother was gratified, his Aunt Patsy was annoyed that her own son and daughters had not been included, and Rupert was no more than mildly pleased that the old man had remembered him.

He was far from well. As much as he could, he concealed his increasing weakness from his mother, not realising that she watched with terror every tiny inch he slipped back. She always insisted that he would be better when the summer came, but as the weather turned warmer and the flowers began to bloom in the gardens round Firsby Hall which had been given over to vegetables during the war, Rupert edged every day a little further away from life.

When George Osbert, who had been the Humfrey's solicitor for twenty years, wanted to see his young client, and wanted it with some urgency in view of the news that had been relayed to him from America, he discovered that even in the short period since Rupert had last paid him a visit his health had deteriorated to the point where it was necessary for George to go to Firsby Hall to talk to him.

When he arrived it was obvious that his appointment had been forgotten.

'Mr Rupert's not been able to get out of bed for a couple of days,' the maid who had replaced the butler during the war informed him. 'Dr Lang's with him now. Mrs Humfrey's in the drawing room.'

'Ask her if she'll see me.'

He was shown into the drawing room and Margot came towards him with her hand outstretched.

'I'm sorry, George . . . it quite went out of my head. Rupert has had a little setback, you see. Dr Lang will be down in a moment . . .'

The hand George Osbert took in his was cold and the fingers clutched his like a claw, tense with fear. He tried to hold on to her hand to reassure her, but Margot took it away and moved to the other side of the room.

'Must you see Rupert?' she asked. 'I'm afraid it's not . . . not terribly convenient.'

'I think I ought to talk to him.'

All the more so if he was as ill as Mrs Humfrey's state seemed to indicate, he thought grimly, but that was not something he could very well say.

'If it's something to do with the house or land perhaps I could . . . I managed everything before he was of age and, of course, during the war. I know as much as Rupert, possibly more.'

'It's more personal than that,' George Osbert said reluctantly. 'I want to urge him to make some alterations to his Will.'

'His Will!' Margot turned on him, her face contorted. 'That's the last thing . . . you do realise don't you, that he's very ill?'

The door opened as she spoke and Dr Lang came in. Margot turned to him, desperate for his verdict on her son and determined to get his support in preventing the solicitor from troubling him.

It seemed to George that Dr Lang was pleased to see him there. He had a premonition that the doctor had bad news to break to Mrs Humfrey and was relieved to have the support of his old acquaintance.

'As I've just heard you say yourself, Mrs Humfrey, Rupert is seriously ill.'

'Are you going to put him into hospital?'

There was a barely perceptible hesitation, and then the doctor said, 'I think we'll leave him in peace where he is.'

The choice of words struck a chill into George Osbert, but he was not sure that Margot had understood the message Dr Lang was trying to convey.

'I'll arrange for you to have a nurse,' the doctor went on. 'Certainly for the night-time, perhaps for the day as well.'

'Yes, yes . . . of course . . . anything you think is necessary,' Margot said distractedly.

She seemed to nerve herself to ask the question the doctor did not want to answer.

'He is going to get better, isn't he?'

'Everything possible will be done, but . . . you mustn't be too hopeful, Mrs Humfrey.'

Margot stared at him, at last realising that he was pronouncing a death sentence.

'My lovely boy,' she said. 'He came through the war . . .'

'Ah, but he didn't. When I saw his medical report I was amazed that he'd survived the two operations on his lungs. You've taken wonderful care of him . . .'

'Of course I have! My only son!'

'The visit to Egypt prolonged his life by perhaps six months . . .'

'We could go again! When he's stronger. I don't mind where we go or what it costs.'

She was stopped by the expression on the doctor's face.

'I'm afraid the time for that is past,' he said.

Margot turned away from him and caught sight of George. It seemed to relieve her to speak to him fiercely.

'I won't have you bothering him about a morbid thing like changing his Will!' she said. 'You must see how it would depress him.'

She pressed her hand against her mouth, fighting for control.

'You're going to have to be very brave,' Dr Lang said. 'Come and sit down. A nurse will be with you by nightfall and I'll give you something to help you get a good night's sleep.'

'Sleep! I don't want to sleep! I want to be with him. Can I go to him now?'

'If you can keep hold of yourself. It won't do Rupert any good to see you crying over him.'

31

'I'm not crying,' Margot said, and indeed the face she turned on the two men was set like stone.

Left alone, the two men turned to one another, and George asked, 'How long has he got?'

'Two or three weeks at the most. He's had a massive haemorrhage.'

'Poor young devil. I remember him being born.'

'Before my time, but I brought him through measles and chickenpox and a broken arm when he fell out of a tree. It would have been kinder if he'd been killed outright in the war instead of dragging out his existence for three more years.'

'It's a dreadful thing to say, but it would certainly have made my job easier if he'd died sooner,' George said.

He was so agitated that he got up and began walking up and down the room.

'Is he still capable of making a Will?' he asked over his shoulder.

'There's nothing wrong with his mind, but I have to warn you that periods of consciousness may grow fewer.'

'I must see him, I must!'

They were taken by surprise when Margot came back almost immediately.

'He's drifting off to sleep, so I left him,' she said. 'George, it's no use you hanging about because I shan't let you see him while he's so weak, and especially not about something as depressing as a Will.'

'Very well, I won't bother you any more today, but you must promise to tell Rupert that I want to see him, and urgently,' George said with an obstinacy that aroused Margot to bitter anger.

'Oh, must I! You take too much on yourself, George. Do you really imagine I'll give Rupert a message that will give him the impression that he's dying?'

She looked from one to the other of the two men, defying them to contradict her, trying to impose on them her need to believe that her son would recover.

It was the doctor who said, 'You have to face that probability, Mrs Humfrey.'

'No! He got better before when he was desperately wounded and he didn't have me to look after him then. I can't understand why you're not sending him to hospital. Another operation . . .'

'I doubt whether any surgeon, having seen his latest X-rays, would risk a third operation.'

'But we could try! You're not doing anything!'

'It's my opinion he couldn't survive the anaesthetic.'

Margot made a futile gesture with her hand, as if she could push away the knowledge that was being forced on her.

Silence fell on the room. The only sound George could hear was the ticking of the grandfather clock in the corner. He was not an imaginative man, but that solemn, steady measurement of time made him shudder with the realisation that it was counting out the life of the young man upstairs. And of us all, he thought. *Timor mortis conturbat me.*

The clock struck the quarter and they all jumped.

'George, I know you're only doing what you think is right,' Margot said wearily. 'But surely Rupert has made a Will. I remember him telling me about it.'

'There is a Will in existence,' George said carefully. He struggled with his professional conscience, then went on, 'Naturally I can't discuss the terms of it with anyone but Rupert.'

'Oh, naturally!' Margot mocked him.

'A solicitor, even a solicitor who's an old friend, can only advise, and if a client insists on having his way nothing can be done about it. But circumstances have changed drastically since Rupert and I last talked and proper provision must be made . . . it's essential that he should reconsider. I've at last had full details of Mr Henry Singleton's estate. He died worth five million dollars and Rupert is his principal heir.'

CHAPTER TWO

Lonnie was frightened. She lay in her narrow bed in the room she shared with Tommy, stiff and cold with terror, while downstairs voices rose and fell and she strained in vain to hear what was being said.

Something was terribly wrong and it was her fault, but no one would tell her what she had done. Mum and Dad were quarrelling, not the quick bicker and snap of everyday life, but dreadful, bitter rows with both of them white with rage. Mum had cried and Dad had hit her. At the memory of his hand coming up to strike her mother across the face with a blow that had sent her reeling across the kitchen Lonnie curled up in a tight ball, clutching the hurt that was like an aching knot in her middle.

Whatever she had done, it was very bad, because there were men who had come to the cottage with cameras to take pictures of her, until Mum had seized hold of her and dragged her inside and told her that she was not to go out.

Dad had got drunk, which was a thing he never did, though he liked his beer at the weekend and Mum had often grumbled at having to keep the Sunday dinner hot until he came in, flushed and cheerful, from the pub. He had fought with some other man and looked like murdering him, until Uncle Bob had taken him by the collar and knocked him out with his blacksmith's fist.

Lonnie had not been to school, nor was she allowed to play with the other children. It was worse than having measles, because this time she didn't know what ailed her, why it was that she had to be kept away from other people.

The sounds from downstairs had died away, but although it must be late Mum and Dad did not come to bed. It was more than Lonnie could bear. With a mixture of courage and desperation, she slid out of bed. Very quietly, so as not to wake Tommy, she crept across the room, opened the door and stole downstairs.

The kitchen door was ajar. Her mother and father were still in there, silent and still, slumped in their chairs in attitudes of exhaustion. As Lonnie hesitated unseen on the threshold, Rosa said, 'Joe . . . all that money. We can't just turn our backs on it.'

'I can. If you want it, go to it, but you can leave me and the boys behind.'

Rosa shook her head and then she caught a movement at the door and turned to see her daughter there, in the nightdress which was already too short for her, her hair tumbling down her back, her eyes wide with strain.

'Oh, Lonnie . . . !' she said, and Lonnie only heard the exasperation behind her exclamation and was too young to recognise the despair.

'Mum,' she said in a whisper, but her mother shook her head and turned away.

'Go back to bed, Lonnie,' she said.

Lonnie turned to the man who had always been her ally, her big, strong Dad, who called her his 'little lass' and could still toss her in the air and laugh at her squeals of delight even though she was getting so tall for her age.

She took one timid step towards him and then another, she who had never been afraid of anything in her life, until she could lay a tentative hand on his arm.

'Dad . . . ?' she said.

He seemed to shudder and then took hold of her by the shoulders, his fingers gripping her to the bone, and stared down into her face. His eyes were bloodshot and his face was suffused with angry colour. Lonnie tried to sustain his fierce look, but her mouth trembled and tears began to come into her eyes.

Joe pushed her away from him, towards her mother, so abruptly that Lonnie stumbled and nearly fell.

'Get her out of my sight,' he said.

The back door crashed to behind him.

'Now look what you've done,' Rosa said. 'Just as I was getting him to quieten down and listen to me.'

'I'm cold,' Lonnie said.

'Of course you are, walking about with bare feet and nothing on but your nightie. Why aren't you asleep?'

'I hurt.'

'Where? Don't get ill, for goodness sake. I've got all the trouble I can take. If only he'd see sense!'

For all the roughness of her words, she took Lonnie on to her lap and held her, feeling that the child was indeed shaking with cold.

'I'll make you a mug of cocoa,' she said.

'Don't want it.'

'It'll warm you up.'

She put Lonnie down and lit the gas under the kettle, standing with her hand on it, lost in thought, until the small voice behind her asked, 'Where's Dad gone?'

'To the pub, probably. If he can stand the other men . . .'

Tears rose up and choked her, and she had to stop. Automatically, she ladled cocoa into a mug and poured hot water and milk on top of it. As she stood, absentmindedly stirring the mixture round and round to dissolve the cocoa, Lonnie asked in an even more subdued whisper, 'Why doesn't Dad love me any more?'

Lonnie waited in terror for her mother's answer, but when it came it settled nothing.

'Oh, Lonnie . . . it's nothing you could understand. Your Dad . . . he's had a shock. He'll come round.'

It was too lame a reply to satisfy Lonnie. Tears began to run down her face.

'I didn't mean to do it,' she said.

'Do what, duckie?'

'I don't know!' Lonnie said, doubled up with sobs. 'I don't know! But I didn't mean it, truly I didn't.'

'Lonnie, Lonnie, no one's blaming you! It's not your fault! It's an old, old story that's come out and upset us all. You're too young to understand. Here, stop crying and drink this nice hot cocoa. I've put plenty of sugar in it, just the way you like it.'

The assurance that whatever it was that had gone wrong

was not Lonnie's fault was only partly reassuring, since it did not agree with what she had observed for herself, but Lonnie was exhausted and she let her mother dry her eyes, she drank the comforting hot liquid and when Rosa half-led, half-carried her up the stairs, she was on the verge of sleep.

The next day part of their dilemma was solved be a terse postcard from Rosa's mother: *'Bring the child to me.'*

'It's not a bad idea,' Rosa said, showing the card to Joe, cautiously because he was surly with the drink he had consumed the night before and the breakfast table was no place for yet another row.

Joe said nothing, but something about his silence encouraged Rosa to go on. 'It'd get the reporters out of the way. They'll never track her down there and, if they do, they'll not get past Mum.'

'Do what you like with her, she's your child,' Joe said, careless of the children's listening ears.

'You'll have to look after the boys. I can get there and back in a day if Lonnie and I are on our own, but I can't manage the pair of them as well.'

Nor would she ask any woman in Alleshill to take in her children for the day. That would mean spreading the news of Lonnie's whereabouts. Besides, she had had enough of their curious, censorious eyes and the unspoken questions that had followed her wherever she went since the newspaper headlines: 'UNKNOWN CHILD INHERITS FOR-TUNE'; 'MYSTERY GOLDEN GIRL'; 'HEIRESS TO AMERICAN MILLIONS LIVING IN POVERTY'. Rosa shuddered. The last two weeks had been a nightmare and to think that Lonnie – *Lonnie* – was worth millions and Joe was obdurate that he would not touch a penny of Rupert Humfrey's money.

The journey from Surrey to Sussex was not long in terms of miles, but it involved a change of trains and a tiresome wait at the junction, nor was the village of Cogsdene on a railway line. Rosa paid a surreptitious visit to the Post Office and drew out enough money to pay for a taxi to the outskirts of the village. She could see that the driver thought it strange that she asked to be dropped in the middle of an empty country lane, and stranger still that she wanted to be picked up in the same place later in the day, but Rosa had no intention of walking down the High Street of the village where she had been born and had married Joe, still less did she want to run the risk of meeting her mother-in-law.

She took the small suitcase she had packed for Lonnie in one hand and held Lonnie with the other.

'Over the stile and across the field,' she said. 'Then we can cut through the woods to Grannie's place.'

The meadow they walked across would soon be mown for hay. The grass was long and sweet and full of wild flowers. Small butterflies rose up in front of them as they brushed the grass aside and a grasshopper leapt up and made Rosa jump. She looked up at the hill which rose beyond the line of trees, to where she could just see the chimneys of Firsby Hall above the heavy summer foliage. Rosa's mouth thinned to a bitter line. That damned fool, Rupert. How could she ever have thought herself in love with him?

Her hand tightened on Lonnie's until the child gave a whimper of protest. Rosa looked down at her daughter and her face softened.

'You'll like staying with your Grannie,' she said encouragingly.

'Yes,' Lonnie agreed, since this was what was expected of her, but what she wanted to know, and did not dare ask, was how long the visit was to last and whether everything would be normal again when she went home.

The sight of the cabin in the woods diverted her from her anxiety, especially when she discovered a hen with a brood of chicks. Lonnie captured one of them as they scurried through the grass in the clearing, and held it, warm, fluffy and cheeping, in the palm of her hand.

'She's happy for the moment,' Thirza said, looking through the window.

'It's more than I am,' Rosa said, but as she leaned back in Thirza's old rocking chair and took the cup of tea her mother was holding out, something in her began to relax. At least there was no need to pretend with Mum. No need to defend herself, either. Mum knew all there was to know about Lonnie's birth and it had been her idea that Rosa should entice Joe into marriage.

'Mum, it's been awful,' Rosa said. 'Joe . . . he was beside himself.' She touched her jaw tenderly. The bruises were fading, but it would take a long time for Rosa to get over the shock of Joe raising his hand to her.

'I don't know what's going to happen,' she said. 'He can't bear to see Lonnie . . . not that he'd do her any harm and at the back of it all he's as fond of her as ever, but every time he sets eyes on her, it reminds him . . . Mum, all that money! Not just thousands, but *millions*! He says he won't touch it, not a penny. It seems so unfair.'

'It's not to be expected he'd want to profit from being made a fool of. As for Lonnie, she can stay with me as long as you like, but I doubt if it'll be allowed.'

'Allowed?'

'They'll put someone in charge of her, to see that she gets a proper education and bringing up. If her up at the Hall wanted to take Lonnie over, would you agree?'

'She wouldn't,' Rosa said with conviction.

'She's Lonnie's grandmother and that might weigh with her. She doted on her son and Lonnie's growing very like him.'

'Yes, I've seen that,' Rosa admitted. 'I thought it didn't matter, as long as no one ever saw them together, but now . . . everyone knows, that's what I can't stand.'

'And neither can Joe. Tell me, what is it you really want most?'

Rosa struggled with the chaos inside her, but at last she said in a whisper, 'To stay with Joe.'

'I always knew he was the man for you.'

'We were happy, until this happened. Everything was going well, just like I planned.'

'You're too set on things going the way you plan, that's always been your trouble,' Thirza said. 'You can't keep both Joe and Lonnie and you'll have to put the thought of the money out of your head: Joe will never touch it.'

With a sigh Rosa admitted the truth of this.

'How can I give Lonnie up?' she protested. 'She's my daughter and I love her.'

'If you stay with her, Joe will keep the boys.'

'No!'

The denial burst out of Rosa, but she knew it was true, and it was unbearable. Tommy, the son Joe had delighted in, who was growing so sturdy and like his father, and Jimmy, that moist, wriggling bundle of delight, how could she part with them? And Joe. She loved Joe, he was as necessary to her as breathing, or had been until Rupert's terrible legacy had come between them.

'If it comes to it, you'll let Lonnie go,' Thirza said, and her certainty was so convincing that Rosa nodded weakly.

Rosa stayed only long enough to swallow a mouthful of the savoury stew Thirza had kept bubbling on the stove. Lonnie, she saw with relief, had recovered the appetite that had been lost in the last couple of weeks and tucked in to the meal with something of her old zest.

'I can see you like your Grannie's cooking better than mine,' Rosa said. 'I'll be off now. Be a good girl.'

She tried to sound normal, but the fierce way she hugged Lonnie and the kisses she pressed on her, alarmed her daughter.

'How . . . how long am I going to stay?' Lonnie asked, at last bringing out the question that had been at the back of her mind all day. 'When can I come home?'

'In a little while . . . I don't know . . . we'll see,' Rosa stammered.

She got up from her crouching position in front of Lonnie, tears running down her face now that she had come to the moment of parting, knowing that her mother was right and she had to make a choice between this firstborn child and the rest of her family.

She went without another word, without saying good-bye to her mother, and the trees swallowed her up.

Lonnie turned to her grandmother, her dark eyes full of questions.

'Why don't we go and see if my other hens have laid you an egg for your tea?' Thirza suggested, holding out her hand.

'Yes,' Lonnie agreed. The palm of her grandmother's hand was hard, much rougher than Rosa's hand, but the grasp of it was comforting.

She made another sortie into her dwindling store of courage and asked, 'Why have I come to stay with you, Grannie?'

'Because it's for the best,' Thirza said.

'No one tells me what's happening,' Lonnie said in a despairing whisper.

Thirza looked at her, so small and unhappy, and saw what no one else had realised, that the truth, if it could be put simply, was not beyond Lonnie's understanding, and would be kinder than the fog of bewilderment in which the child was living.

'Do you know how babies are born?' she asked.

Lonnie twisted one leg round the other, her face pink.

'Before Jimmy was born the girls at school did say that he was growing inside Mum,' she said. 'And she got fatter and fatter and then afterwards she was thin again, so I thought it was true, but Mum only laughed when I asked her.'

'She should have told you. If you're old enough to ask, you're old enough to know. Yes, that's right, the child grows inside its mother's womb until it's big enough to come out. But do you know how it gets inside there in the first place?'

Lonnie shook her head, fascinated by this grown-up talk.

'A seed passes from the father to the mother. That's

why there have to be husbands and wives, fathers and mothers. In your case, another man had already given your mother a seed before she married her husband, and that seed became you.'

There was nothing wrong with Lonnie's intelligence.

'Does that mean that Dad isn't really my Dad at all?' she asked.

'That's right. But your mother didn't tell him and so he always thought you were his own daughter.'

The tears that were once so rare with Lonnie and had recently come so readily, rose to the surface and brimmed over.

'I do want him to be my real Dad,' she said.

'It's not a thing you can do anything about, more's the pity. Your real father died and instead of taking the secret to the grave as he should have done, he left you a lot of money – more than he bargained for, silly young fool. So then Joe knew your mother had lied to him and, being the man he is, he felt bad about it.'

'Will he stop feeling bad, Grannie? Will he let me go back and live with him and Mum and Tommy and Jimmy?'

'I don't know, I don't know.' Thirza fell into a reverie. Almost to herself she said, 'I saw there was money in it and I knew there'd be trouble if Joe ever found out, but I never foresaw the half of it.'

She looked at her granddaughter with brooding eyes.

'Did I do wrong? No. When I see you in front of me, my little love, so beautiful and dainty, I know I was right to let you be born. But you've got a difficult life in front of you, that's for sure.'

For a few days Lonnie ran wild in the woods surrounding Thirza's cabin. Her skin browned to a warmer tone, the colour came back to her cheeks and her eyes lost their haunted look, but her grandmother, hearing the way the child whimpered in her sleep, knew that her misery at losing her place in her family was not far below the surface.

Thirza made no attempt to pamper Lonnie, nor to take

42

any special care of her. She went about her normal life, steady and sure of what she was doing, and left Lonnie to find her own level. Grannie, Lonnie discovered, never bothered about torn frocks or tangled hair, and was not particular about washing hands before meals, which was one of the refinements her mother had imposed on her. The thing about Grannie was that she was always there and that stability meant more to Lonnie than any fancy ideas about hygiene.

Thirza only went to the village shop when she needed to buy food she could not produce herself, but having the child with her meant that she ran out of flour and sugar more quickly than she would otherwise have done. Since one of the objects in having Lonnie was to keep the child's whereabouts a secret, she left Lonnie behind when she had to go shopping.

'I'll not be more than an hour,' she said. 'You can amuse yourself that long. Don't wander away from the house and leave the fire alone.'

'Will you bring me back some sweets?' Lonnie asked hopefully.

'I might. Mind now, be a good girl while I'm gone.'

The clearing round the cabin seemed very quiet after she had left, which was funny because Grannie was not a person who made any noise, yet in her absence there was a gap which made Lonnie uneasy.

She played with the chicks, pursued by the anxious clucks of the mother hen, and then went to look in the rabbit hutch. Grannie had told her that the doe was expecting babies, but although Lonnie put her nose close up against the wire netting and peered into the straw, she could see nothing out of the ordinary, so it seemed they had not been born yet.

The pigsty was empty. Lonnie knew that the bacon she had enjoyed for breakfast had come from the fine fat porker Grannie had reared, and so far he had not been replaced.

Lonnie sat down on the grass and began to string daisies together to make a daisy chain, splitting the stems with her thumbnail and threading the heads through the slits, but her small fingers were not as skilful as her grandmother's and she soon abandoned the necklace she had intended to make in favour of a bracelet round one wrist.

Time passed very slowly. Lonnie was not surprised when she heard someone approaching through the woods, even though, in fact, only half an hour had passed away. Without stopping to consider that her grandmother trod through the trees like one of the wild creatures, without disturbing a leaf or breaking a twig, Lonnie ran towards the approaching visitor.

It was not her grandmother, but a man in a black coat with black and white striped trousers, who carried a hat and a briefcase in his hand, and who looked red in the face and cross.

Lonnie backed away, but it was too late – he had seen her.

'I'm looking for Mrs Seward,' he said. 'Is she here?'

Lonnie shook her head, poised to run if he turned out to be hostile.

'Grannie's gone to the village,' she said.

'Grannie . . . you must be Eleanor Dunwell,' George Osbert said slowly.

George was hot and none too pleased at the way things had turned out for him that day. He had gone all the way to Alleshill to see Rosa Dunwell and her husband and, most importantly, the child who had caused them all so much trouble, only to be told that little Eleanor had gone to stay with her grandmother. It had not been easy to get even that amount of information and George had been irked by the suspicion of two people who had had few dealings with the law and knew nothing about the way it worked.

Out of a sense of duty to his dead client and to this little girl who was also, presumably, his client, he had travelled back to Cogsdene and then trudged along a dusty country lane, over a field and through a thicket of trees. And now here she was, Eleanor Mary Dunwell, the daughter of the late, foolish boy Rupert Humfrey, and heiress, even after converting it into pounds, to millions. George stared at her in disbelief.

Lonnie was wearing a dress of pink and white gingham, which had once had a pretty white pocket, featherstitched in pink by Rosa's clever fingers, but the pocket had caught on a bramble and now hung in tatters from the skirt. Nor was the pink and white gingham particularly clean. George was not to know that it was due to be washed the next day and Thirza would repair the tear with stitches which might not be as neat as her daughter's, but which would be adequate. To him the child just looked dirty.

Her feet were bare, she was as brown as a berry, she wore a bracelet of white flowers round her wrist and her hair hung down her back in a tangle of knots. She looked like a gypsy.

One thing was certain, this situation could not be allowed to continue. George sighed, foreseeing that there would be endless difficulties about settling Lonnie in a suitable place, and that they would all fall on him.

'Will your Grannie be long?' he asked, trying to speak kindly because the child was looking frightened.

Lonnie shook her head. 'She said an hour,' she said helpfully.

'She must have reached the village before I left it or I would have met her on the way,' George said. 'I'd better wait here for her. Is there somewhere I can sit down?'

'You can't go in the house,' Lonnie said firmly. ''Cos I'm not to let strangers in while Grannie's away. I could bring you out a chair, if you like?'

George nodded, amused and like Rupert, charmed by her candid gaze. He watched while Lonnie unlatched the door and fetched out a wooden chair. She allowed him to carry it over to a shady spot under a tree.

'You look hot,' she said. 'Would you like a drink of water?'

'I would,' George said.

It had not occurred to him that he was being offered spring water until Lonnie fetched a thick china mug and carried it to the far corner of the clearing. She knelt down

45

and parted the fronds of green ferns which grew on a dripping rock, until she could hold the mug under the trickle of water which ran from a narrow cleft.

She came back, carrying the mug carefully. George sipped it cautiously, but the water was cold and pure, and very refreshing.

'That's the best drink I've had for years,' he said.

'Grannie lives here because of the water,' Lonnie said. 'She can't abide the stuff that comes out of taps.'

She sat down on the grass in front of George, hugging her knees. Now that she was sure he was friendly, she was pleased to have company to while away the time.

'What's your name?' she asked.

'Er . . . George Osbert.'

'Must I call you Mr Osbert?'

'I suppose . . . yes.'

Lonnie studied him. 'Why do you wear those clothes?' she asked and it was clear that she had stopped herself just in time from saying 'those funny clothes'.

'I'm a solicitor. It's a sort of uniform I have to wear.'

'My Dad wore a uniform when he was a soldier,' Lonnie said. A look of bewildered grief swept over her face. 'He did,' she said uncertainly.

For the first time George began to understand the upheaval that her inheritance had meant to this small girl. He had been so occupied with the legal ramifications, not to mention Margot Humfrey's hysterical outbursts, that he had not had time to think about the child herself.

Because he thought it would please her, he said, 'I saw your . . . Dad this morning.'

When he saw the blaze of joy that transfigured her, George knew he had made a mistake.

'Have you come to take me home?' Lonnie asked eagerly.

'No . . . I just came to see you . . . to talk to Mrs Seward,' George stammered.

He took out his handkerchief and wiped his perspiring forehead. Who would have thought it would be so difficult to face the accusing eyes of one young child?

She seemed to lose interest in him after that, leaving him alone on his chair and going to sit on the ground some distance away. Thirza's black and white cat stalked out of the undergrowth and Lonnie took him on her lap and hugged him to her. A minute or two later Thirza appeared.

It was years since George had last seen Thirza Seward, but even though she had aged since he had sought her out to tell her that under the terms of Patrick Humfrey's Will she was free to live in the cabin in the woods to the end of her life, he would have known her queenly bearing and brooding eyes anywhere.

'I've been expecting a visit from you,' she said. 'You'd better come into the house.'

As she passed Lonnie she dropped a paper bag on the ground by her side.

'Barley sugar,' she said.

Inside the cabin, which George would not have dignified by the name of house, Thirza asked, 'What did you say to upset the child?'

'She asked if I'd come to take her home.'

'Which you haven't, of course.'

'I went to see Mr and Mrs Dunwell this morning,' George said. 'Mr Dunwell is talking of emigrating to Australia.'

Thirza was unpacking her shopping bag, but at his words she stopped and stood completely still. George was shocked by the expression of grief on her face.

'So that's to be my punishment,' she said. 'I'm to lose my daughter and my grandsons, and Lonnie will be taken away from me.'

'She can't stay here,' George said, looking round the confined space.

'She'd be happier with me than with anyone else.'

'Eleanor will have great responsibilities when she grows up. She has to be taught to deal with them.'

'You mean she has to learn to be a lady,' Thirza said, with an ironic twist to her lips. 'What are you planning to do with her?'

'It's a very, very difficult situation. For the moment I'm applying to have her made a Ward of Court.'

CHAPTER THREE

She was Eleanor Singleton and she had, as well as a different name, a new home, an Aunt Patsy and Uncle Edward and three children who called her cousin.

The change of name was Patsy Lynton's idea.

'So much easier to bring her up quietly if she isn't known by the name all the papers have printed. Margot won't hear of her being called Humfrey, so why not give her Uncle Henry's name? She can forget she was ever Lonnie Dunwell.'

Patsy was eight years younger than her sister and had married later, and not so well as Margot, who at twenty had rushed into marriage with a man more than twice as old. Patsy, still living in the house on the outskirts of Cogsdene where the two girls had been brought up, had married the young man who had joined their father in his veterinary practice. At the time of Margot's marriage Patsy had been more interested in her bridesmaid's frock than in Margot's achievement in capturing the local lord of the manor, but in later years it had not been possible to suppress an occasional twinge of envy as she contrasted her own chaotic and impecunious household with Margot's gracious existence.

Henry Singleton's Will had been a blow to Patsy. True, she had got ten thousand pounds, but Margot had received the same and she did not really need it, not in the way that Patsy did. Even before she had known the extent of Uncle Henry's fortune Patsy had been disgruntled that he had left the bulk of it to Rupert, overlooking her own children.

She had grieved over her nephew's death and been truly sorry for her sister, but the revelation that Rupert had fathered a baby on Margot's maid and let the girl pass it off as another man's child had given her a moment of

49

triumph. She was ashamed of her reaction and hurried to put it out of her mind. In any case, it was swamped by the realisation that once again the Singleton fortune had passed her by.

Both Margot and Patsy talked of contesting Rupert's Will, but no one could hold out any real hope of their case being successful.

'I put it to Rupert as forcefully as I could – once you allowed me to see him,' George Osbert said to Margot. 'I begged him to reconsider and change the Will he had insisted on making – and that was against my advice, too – but he just smiled and shook his head.'

'He didn't understand.'

'Dr Lang was there and I asked him whether in his opinion Rupert had understood me. He said Rupert's mind was perfectly clear.'

'Oh, very clever, to bring the doctor into it! Just like a lawyer, protecting your own interests.'

'A necessary precaution, in the circumstances,' George said drily. 'Mrs Humfrey, be reasonable. You'll have the income from the estate . . .'

'And the expense of its upkeep. Do you know what it costs to run this house? And the farms are in constant need of repair. I know - I've had the running of the estate ever since Patrick died.'

'As to that, I think some part of the Singleton income could be used for upkeep, especially if the child were to live with you.'

'I don't want her here.'

'Mrs Humfrey, Rupert asked that in the event of Mrs Dunwell being willing to give up the child you should be her legal guardian. He wanted her brought up here.'

'No.'

'Accept the guardianship. It doesn't mean that she has to live with you, if you really can't bear it. You can appoint someone else to take charge of her. In fact, I think Mrs Lynton would be willing to consider it.'

By the time they all met at Judge's Chambers to decide on Lonnie's future, Patsy had seized on the idea that an allowance would be paid for Lonnie's upbringing. With three children to educate, a husband who was a dear, of course, but not the most provident man in the world, and a ramshackle house in dire need of repair, any addition to her income would be welcome.

Joe Dunwell was unshakeable in his determination to take his remaining family overseas. Faced with that, and Mrs Humfrey's reluctance to house the child, even though she had been persuaded to be named as her guardian, the possibility of placing her in a family where she would have young company commended itself to the judge.

He did make a conscientious attempt to discover the child's own preference, but what Lonnie wanted was something he could not give her.

Lonnie was suspicious from the start about being taken to see that judge. After the way she had been running wild she resented it when her Grannie took it into her head to scrub her from head to foot in scalding hot water.

'You're taking my skin off,' she complained.

'Keep still, child, and bend your head forward so that I can do your hair.'

'The soap's going in my eyes.'

'Then keep them shut.'

Anyone with sense knew that soap got through screwed-up eyelids, easy as easy, but Lonnie, her head streaming with water, was forced to submit to her grandmother's iron hand.

It was even worse when she had to put on a frock that crackled with starch and have her hair twisted into tight plaits.

'I never have my hair done up like this, never,' she protested.

'I want you looking neat and tidy, like a well brought up young lady,' her grandmother said. 'As for me . . . well, they'll have to take me as they find me. I haven't the money to spend on a smart new outfit.'

'Where are we going?' Lonnie asked.

'To see a man who'll decide where you are to live.'

She was following her instinct to be truthful with the

child, but she wondered whether she had done the right thing when Lonnie's eyes grew big and her little face took on the pinched look which had almost disappeared in the last few weeks.

'Can't I stay here with you, Gran?' she asked in a whisper.

'It's what I'd like, my little love, but I can't pretend I can offer you the life they think you need.'

Because of this talk it was a very subdued Lonnie who eventually stood before a man who looked a bit like that one in the striped trousers who had come to see her at Grannie's house. He had a fat pink face and large hands, which he rested on his knees. He meant to be kind and he wanted to do the best thing for everyone, but the truth was that, just as George Osbert had been, he was disconcerted by the worried, big-eyed little creature.

'Well, now, Eleanor . . .' he began.

'I'm called Lonnie,' Lonnie said firmly, because it seemed to her that all these people who called her by her given name were the ones who wanted to take her away first of all from Mum and Dad and now from Grannie.

'Very well, Lonnie,' he agreed. 'Do you go to school?'

'I did when I was at home.' Looking at him hopefully, she suggested, 'If I went home to stay, I could go again, and I'd be ever so good.'

With a smile the judge asked, 'Weren't you good before?'

'Not very.'

'Can you read, Lonnie?'

'Sort of,' Lonnie said cautiously.

'Would you like to read to me?'

'Is it an exam, like the big girls have?'

'Yes, I think we could call it that.'

She took the book he offered her and read, slowly and with a lot of stumbling.

'It's got lots of very hard words,' she said, aggrieved.

'You did quite well. How about sums?'

He was amused by the way her tongue protruded from her tightly-pursed lips as Lonnie concentrated on her figures. A bright child, obviously intelligent, who deserved the best that life could offer her, and he very much wished that it had not fallen to him to decide how and where she should be brought up.

The room was very quiet, so that the sound of raised voices in the corridor outside came quite clearly through the door. Lonnie's head went up. 'That's my Mum,' she said.

She was off in a flash, tugging at the door handle. 'Mum, Mum! I'm here!' She turned to the judge, her face frantic. 'Open the door. Please, open the door. I want my Mum. I want my Mum.'

Before he could make up his mind whether to let her out or not, Lonnie had succeeded in turning the stiff brass handle and had disappeared.

They were all out there, except the little boys, who had been left for the day with Joe's parents.

'Mum!' Lonnie said, hurling herself at Rosa. She looked up and faltered. 'Dad?' she said uncertainly.

Not even Joe in his bewildered anger could withstand her beseeching look. He squatted down to Lonnie's level and in utter relief she went to him and felt his familiar arms round her. Everything was going to be all right after all.

'Can I come home now?' she asked him. With her lips pressed against his ear she offered him the utmost she had to give. 'I love you *best*,' she whispered.

Over the top of her head, Joe's eyes met Rosa's. Their future was already decided and he would not go back on what he had chosen to do. He would forgive Rosa, though they both knew in their hearts that nothing would ever be the same between them again, but he wanted to get right away, to go to a land where he was unknown, where he could forget that a bastard child had been foisted on him. Sweet and dear, loving and loved as she was, Lonnie had got to be left behind to be brought up by people who could cope with her vast inheritance.

'Your Mum and me, and the boys, have got to go on a

long journey,' he said. 'I want you to be a good girl and stay here.'

The tears were inevitable, but Joe never forgot Lonnie's despairing shriek of, 'No, no, no!' as he took Rosa's arm and drew her away. If he had not gripped Rosa's arm until he bruised her she would have turned back.

'It's no use,' Joe said. 'It's got to be and the sooner we go the sooner she'll get over it.'

'My little girl! Joe, how can you be so hard?'

'A new life,' Joe said. 'The boys are too young to remember that they once had a sister.'

' You don't expect me to forget, do you?'

'You'll get news of her; I'll not deny you that. Rosa, they'd have taken her away from you even if we stayed in this country. You can see they're bent on it. This hearing today, it's just a farce. The Humfrey family will get her because they're the nobs and they want to get their hands on the money. That judge will say they know how a rich little girl ought to be brought up.'

Since Joe in his obstinacy would have no truck with Rupert Humfrey's money, there were indeed very few options open to the judge. If it had not been for that factor he thought he would have ordered that the child should remain with her natural mother and her husband, at least until she was older and better able to cope with a separation. As it was, there seemed to be only one suitable home for her, and it was not with the extraordinary-looking grandmother who lived like a gypsy in a rough hut with no sanitation. It was fortunate, in the circumstances, that Mrs Lynton was prepared to take the child.

Patsy took the tearsodden, disconsolate little bundle which Lonnie had become straight home with her from the Judge's Chambers. At the back of her mind Patsy still thought they ought to have put up more of a fight to wrest Uncle Henry's millions away from this unsuitable beneficiary, even though there had been some telling points against their case. Margot had given money to Rosa, as good as admitting – as George had pointed out – that she accepted that the child was Rupert's. Until she had seen Lonnie, Patsy had doubted whether her dead nephew would have had the gumption to father an illegitimate child, but once she had set eyes on the little girl she had to admit that the likeness was unmistakeable. Well, since Margot had given up the fight, with a mixture of distaste and fastidiousness which irritated Patsy, and Patsy could not afford on her own to take the risk of bringing a case that might fail, she would take charge of the child and cash in as far as she could on the responsibility of bringing her up.

Her own children accepted their new 'cousin' with varying degrees of friendliness. Barbara, who was nearly fifteen and read the newspapers, knew very well who Lonnie was and shrank from what she knew with adolescent selfconsciousness. She was thankful that she would soon be going back to the school in Eastbourne where she was a weekly boarder and she was already rehearsing the airy phrases with which she would turn aside any questions from her contemporaries.

Guy, who was ten and at Chichester Choir School, would also be going back shortly. He had a vaguer idea of the reasons for Lonnie's presence amongst them, although he understood with a clarity that would have startled his mother, that she had been fathered by their cousin Rupert.

Only Sally, eight years old and the last child left in the shabby old nursery, was completely in the dark and accepted Lonnie cheerfully as a new cousin, vaguely related to an old uncle who had died in America.

They were a goodlooking family. Barbara, in particular, showed signs of blossoming into a dark whiteskinned beauty. Patsy could see in her a likeness to her own sister, Margot, and not only in looks. Barbara had the same yearning after the elegant life which had taken Margot into an early marriage with Patrick Humfrey. She resented Lonnie because Lonnie represented scandal and because the unwanted child possessed money which Barbara could have put to far better use.

Guy was like Barbara in looks, but he had an independence which set him apart from his older sister. Guy went his own way and, even at ten, made his own judgments. He had been sent to the Choir School because he was naturally musical and had a good singing voice and it had seemed the best way of getting him an education at reasonable cost. Patsy was just beginning to wonder uneasily whether perhaps Guy was taking the musical side of his schooling rather too seriously. She had hoped that he would follow Edward and her own father before him as the local vet, but Patsy had been disturbed recently to hear Guy say, in reply to a question from a visitor about following in his father's footsteps, 'No, I don't think so,' with that note in his voice that meant he was not to be shifted.

It was Sally who was mad about animals. Sunny and good-tempered, she was a contrast to the more intense natures of her older brother and sister, and in appearance, too, she was plumper, rosier and fairer, with untidy curls and round blue eyes.

It was fortunate for Lonnie that it was Sally who was the member of the family with whom she had most contact and, since Sally was young for her age and Lonnie more mature than her six years, they were able to play together quite amicably.

All the same, it was Sally who, because of her ignorance, asked the most difficult questions when Lonnie was first brought to join them.

'Did you live in America with old Uncle Henry before you came here?' she asked.

'No, I lived in Alleshill.'

'Why have you come to live with us? Haven't you got any family of your own?'

'Yes, I have. Lots and lots of people. Mum an' Dad an' Tommy an' Jimmy an' Uncle Bob an' Grannie and my other Grandma and Grandpa in Cogsdene, so there!'

'Why aren't you living with your own Mummy and Daddy?' Sally persisted.

'Do leave the kid alone, Sally,' Guy said.

'They've gone to Orstralia,' Lonnie said.

'And left you behind?'

Lonnie nodded, unable to speak.

'Sally, you've been told to shut up. I do wish for once you'd do as you're asked,' Barbara said.

'Yes, but Barbara – if she's got all this family, why is she living with us?'

'Because I grew out of the wrong seed,' Lonnie said and dissolved once more into the tears she had been holding back.

'Now look what you've done,' Barbara said. 'I'm going to fetch Mummy.'

By the time Patsy arrived, Lonnie was being consoled by a worried Guy and Sally, her tears wiped away with Guy's none too clean handkerchief. Looking at his concerned face and the way he put his arm awkwardly round the shoulders of this new little cousin, Patsy was seized by another of her ideas.

Probably when the time came no one would believe that she had not had it in her mind when she offered to take the child, but she had truly only just thought of it. It was the perfect answer to all their difficulties; it would set Guy up for life and allow them all to live in affluence. Guy and Lonnie must marry. Guy would become master of Firsby Hall. Not until after Margot died, of course, but one day . . . He would be rich and influential. He could go into Parliament. His sisters, too, would make splendid marriages. It would be quite wonderful and all because of her forethought of taking in the little waif no one else wanted.

Dazzled by the dream that had come upon her, Patsy was positively purring as she said, 'Guy, what a kind boy you are. Poor Eleanor, I'm afraid she will be unhappy for a while, but we must do our best to help her to settle down.'

'I'm not Eleanor, I'm Lonnie,' Lonnie said, glaring at her over the edge of Guy's handkerchief. 'I won't be called Eleanor, I won't!'

That was not the way to talk to Patsy, as her children very well knew, but to their surprise she said, with astonishing mildness, 'Very well, dear. You shall be called Lonnie if you prefer it. Just as long as you remember that your last name is Singleton now.'

'Wasn't it always?' Sally asked with interest.

'That's quite enough,' her mother replied, in much more the tone they were used to. 'Why are you all cooped up indoors on such a lovely afternoon? Guy, take Sally and Lonnie outside and play ball with them.'

'I haven't done my piano practice,' Guy said.

'You can leave that for once. I'm sure you're quite as far ahead as you need to be with your music. Now go out and get some fresh air.'

Like her sister, until she had seen Lonnie Margot had clung obstinately to the possibility that Rosa had deceived Rupert, even though she had known in her heart that it was not really so. Her first sight of the little girl had shaken her. She was Rupert come back to life again, except that she was robust in a way that he had never been.

For one moment Margot contemplated acknowledging the child, taking her back to Firsby Hall, and bringing her up as her grandchild, then the old resentment swept over her and she put the idea away. Let Patsy take responsibility for the brat.

She felt weary right through to her bones by the time she got back to Firsby Hall. She climbed the stairs and paused on the first floor landing to look at the portrait of her son hanging there. Gazing at the picture she saw, even more clearly, the resemblance between him and Lonnie. Yet again the question formed in her mind: *Rupert, how could you have done this to me?*

After all the drama that had gone before, the days that followed were empty and quiet. True, the running of Firsby Hall was still in her hands, but whereas in the past she had kept the house going, tended the garden and overseen the details of the estate for Rupert's sake, now she was doing it for the benefit of an unwelcome intruder.

She sent for George Osbert and asked abruptly, 'Did you mean it when you said that there would be money available to help run this place?'

'Any two of Lonnie's trustees – myself, Mr Lynton and the American lawyer handling Henry Singleton's estate over there – can decide to use income – not the capital but the income – for any purpose we think is for Lonnie's benefit. I believe that the upkeep of Firsby Hall, since she will own it one day, is certainly to the child's benefit.

He looked at her over the top of the half-spectacles he had recently taken to wearing and added drily, 'Of course, I wouldn't countenance any needless extravagance.'

'I shan't rook the child, if that's what you're thinking, but if there's money to spare you can find a manager to run the estate. I've slaved all my life for the sake of this place and what has it brought me? I'm forty-nine and I've got nothing – nothing. I've lost my husband and my son and Firsby doesn't even belong to me. Once I'm dead that gypsy's child will probably sell up. Make what arrangements you like, George. I'm going away.'

She went to Italy and the South of France, retracing the route of her honeymoon. It was years since she had thought very much about her dead husband. He had been a kind, thoughtful man, very tender towards his young wife, but once the first few months were over he had not been a lively companion. He had fallen back on the pursuits of his long bachelorhood; the books which were his chosen companions, the field sports which kept him out of doors for hours, the preoccupation with crops and animal breeding which made him popular with the farmers.

Margot had married him because she was well-born but poor, because she had wanted an establishment of her own and this was by far the best offer she was ever likely to get, and because she was flattered by the attentions of a man who had been known as a confirmed bachelor. She had found him attractive and she had been grateful for his courtesy and consideration. There had never been any great passion between them, but there was mutual pleasure and an affection which had been deepened by the birth of their son.

It was a marriage that had worked very well, in spite of the heads that had been shaken over the difference in age between them. When Patrick had died Margot had been sufficiently bereft to make the idea of marrying again repugnant to her. Besides, she had Rupert, just ten years old at that time, and all her affections were concentrated on him.

She was not a cold woman, but her capacity for love, except towards Rupert, was like a muscle that had never been used. His death had crippled her far more than his father's had done. There was no one left. She was alone in the world where nobody loved her and she had no one to love, since she would not allow herself to contemplate loving Lonnie.

Margot did not look on her holiday abroad as a success, but the weeks in the sunshine in beautiful surroundings did restore her health, even though she was reluctant to admit it. Certainly she came back looking better, her pale face touched by the sun, her figure back to its usual svelte lines, without the gauntness that had spoilt her looks since Rupert had been wounded.

She stopped in Paris on the way home and stayed long enough to acquire some stylish gowns which, although they seemed shapeless, were cut with a cunning which draped them elegantly on Margot's body, while the mid-calf length showed off the legs which had been one of her unseen assets, just as the new short hair was more youthful than the heavy knot she had always worn at the back of her neck.

Feeling better than she had for many years and very conscious of her improved appearance, she went back to Firsby Hall and met Miles Bowman.

He was an ex-Army officer in need of a job, as so many were in the years after the war. George Osbert had been impressed by his businesslike attitude and by the understanding he had gained of the running of a small country estate through helping out an aged uncle.

'Unfortunately, Uncle Sam's place had to be sold when he died,' Miles Bowman explained. 'I helped pull the place round in the short time I had before the old man went and we got a better price for it as a result. He left a widow and three daughters, so it was important to do the best possible deal for them. If I'd had the capital I would have bought it for myself. No chance of that, unfortunately, and the new chap will run it himself, so I'm on the lookout for a way to earn an honest crust.'

George had seen him as a straightforward professional soldier, with few saleable skills in civilian life, but he had a clear mind and, although he was no accountant, he understood very well the profits and pitfalls of a country estate with tenant farms.

What George did not see was Major Bowman's resentment at his inability to purchase his uncle's property. If he had been able to raise the cash he could have become what he had always wanted to be, a country gentleman with a stake in the land, instead of the paid employee of an absentee widow.

It came as a surprise, not altogether welcome, to discover when he met Margot that she was not the ignorant parasite he had imagined. Indeed, she had a far deeper knowledge than he had had time to acquire about Firsby Hall and all its ramifications.

'I can see where I must come if I need help,' he said.

'I took over everything after my husband died,' Margot agreed. 'And then, of course, by the time my son was of age for me to hand it on to him he was fighting in the war.'

'George Osbert told me what a sad loss you'd suffered. I'm sorry. War has a long arm and the casualties are still falling.'

Margot sighed her agreement. She had invited him to lunch, without George, and they were drinking sherry in the drawing room.

So far, she liked what she had seen of Miles Bowman. A soldierly-looking man, very spare and upright, with brown hair and a thin dark line of moustache along his lip. George had told her that he was forty-two, but Laura thought he looked younger than that.

'Are you comfortable in the West Lodge, Major Bowman?' she asked.

'Very comfortable, thank you. But, look, I've dropped the "Major". Plain Miles Bowman, civilian, from now on.'

He was a widower, Margot knew that, but to make conversation she asked, 'You haven't any family, have you?'

'Unfortunately not. My wife died some years ago and the child we had hoped for died with her.'

He had married his youngest cousin and the son she was going to bear him had been his best hope of retaining some hold on the family land. He had been fond of her, but some part of his regret at her death was due to disappointment at losing the means of influencing his uncle's disposition of his estate.

Margot murmured conventional condolences, but she was already thinking of something else. With an abruptness that took Miles by surprise she said, 'Has George explained to you the way things are here?'

'He has told me that you have a life tenancy and that the ultimate heir is still a minor – a little girl,' Miles said cautiously.

He had read all the newspaper accounts about Rupert's eccentric Will and the great fortune which had passed to his bastard. It had been something Miles had had to weigh up before deciding to take the job. Not that jobs of a similar nature had been all that thick on the ground. On the whole, he had seen it as something of an advantage that the present incumbent was a widow in need of assistance, while the possibility of a long minority for the child ought to ensure that he had a job for life if he wanted it.

It was not that he intended to feather his nest at Margot's expense, but he wanted stability, a good long pull at the job and, above all, a situation in which he could be seen as being important. He wanted to run everything, to make the decisions, to be the man people turned to for advice.

That was why he had not been entirely pleased to discover that Margot was more knowledgeable than he had expected. She was very much the lady of the manor and unconsciously he had seen himself as filling the role she regarded as her own. He would have to see how it worked out. Certainly he would not relish taking orders from a woman, however charmingly expressed they might be.

All the same, they were pleased with one another by the time lunch was over. Miles was pleasantly deferential while managing to convey, without being in the least bit obvious about it, that he thought his new employer an attractive woman. Margot, conscious of her glossy new appearance, preened herself under his admiring eyes.

That afternoon Margot dashed off a note to George to say that she had found Major Bowman – it was difficult to think of him without his Army rank – charming and obviously competent and she congratulated George on his appointment.

As for Miles Bowman, he went back to the adequate but cramped West Lodge with an entirely new idea in his mind. She was a goodlooking woman. Seven years older than him, but still . . . they were past the age of worrying about trifles like that. She had liked him. He had known just how to get on the right side of her. As her husband he would have the position he craved.

From that time on Margot was under siege and the campaign was conducted with all the cunning of an old soldier. Miles did not hurry her, but it gradually became known in the neighbourhood that Margot had come out of the seclusion she had adopted after Rupert's death, that her new estate manager was a gentleman and a likeable chap and that they could be invited as a couple, if only because it was so convenient for them to go home together after a dinner party.

He did not kiss her until New Year's Eve and then it was in the middle of a crowded party and went unnoticed by everyone except the two of them. Margot, a little drunk, clung to him and kissed him back with a fervour that surprised him almost as much as it shook Margot herself.

He took her home soon after that and in the dark porch of Firsby Hall he took her in his arms again. They swayed together in a long kiss and then Margot broke free with a broken murmur, 'No . . . no . . . I can't . . . Miles, I must go in . . . lovely evening . . . thank you . . .'

'A happy New Year, Margot, my darling,' Miles said, firmly marking their new relationship.

He proposed the following week, gambling everything on her acceptance, because if she refused then he knew he would have to leave the most congenial job he was likely to find.

'I'm honoured, flattered . . . I don't know what to say,' Margot said in a distracted way.

'Say "yes",' Miles urged, taking both her twisting hands in his. 'Margot, you must have seen this coming. I haven't been able to hide the way I feel about you. In fact, it seemed to me I had to speak, even though I wasn't sure you were ready for it, because everyone is expecting it.'

That was important, he knew. People would not be surprised if Margot gave up her long widowhood and he was sufficiently well-liked for her choice to be understood.

'Miles, my dear, we must be sensible. I'm . . . I'm older than you . . .'

'Not enough to matter. If you want to know, I look on you as a charming young girl.'

There was some truth in that. Margot's passionless marriage and years of aloofness had left her singularly untouched.

'I shall be forty-eight this year,' Margot said in a rush.

Since he knew very well that she would be fifty, Miles had to look down to hide his exultation. He'd hooked her! She wouldn't have bothered to lie if she'd meant to put him off.

'And I'll be forty-three – the difference is a bagatelle,' he said. 'Darling, you're not going to let that come between us, are you? I've been alone for so long . . .'

'So have I!'

'I need you, Margot, and I think you need me, too.'

'I do! Miles, I've been so lonely, so miserable. Rupert's Will was such a betrayal. I felt as if all those years I'd given him had been wasted and once I started thinking like that there was nothing left; my life was empty.'

'Let me fill it, darling,' Miles said, recognising his cue.

He took her in his arms and Margot felt again the shock of delight she had experienced on New Year's Eve.

'I feel so foolish, falling in love at my age,' she whispered.

'Silly little woman! I'll make you happy, Margot, I promise I will.'

He kissed her again, with an expertise that owed very little to his almost-forgotten marriage and a very great deal to the other women who had passed through his life.

'As to the way your son left things, I'm glad of it,' he said. 'If you'd been an ultra-rich woman I couldn't have asked you to marry me. As it is – I'm a poor man, my darling, but we're not as unequal as we might have been.'

He thought he had got over that hurdle rather well and Margot murmured her acquiescence without apparently giving a thought to the difference in their fortunes. He meant to go on drawing his salary, even though he was married to his employer – that would give him a certain independence. As for the rest, he would live well, in surroundings that pleased him, with an occupation he liked and a wife who would do him credit.

CHAPTER FOUR

The year when Lonnie was fourteen was the year they were all a little in love with Flynn Branden. He was the son of the lawyer who was Lonnie's American trustee. Lou and Cissie Branden had come to Europe partly so that Lou could see Lonnie and talk to his fellow trustees, which meant, as George Osbert realised if no one else did, that he could charge the trip to the Singleton Trust, and partly for a vacation and a tour which Lou had been promising Cissie for years.

Flynn had come with them because it seemed an opportunity too good to be missed. He had graduated from Harvard Law School and joined the law firm in which his father was a partner. He was twenty-three, clever, ambitious and likely to go far. He would have preferred to visit Europe alone, not tagging along behind his mother and father, but when Lou offered to pay for the trip Flynn realised he would be a fool not to accept.

He had always wanted to see Europe. There was something about it that touched his imagination. When he was a child he had dreamed of knights and castles, tattered banners and ancient wars, and although he now saw himself as a sophisticate, and a cynical one at that, he discovered that he could still be stirred by the sight of Dover Castle, massive on its hill, by Canterbury Cathedral and Westminster Abbey and even, laughing at himself, by Stratford-on-Avon.

Firsby Hall satisfied all his criteria for an English country house. It stood on rising ground, with wooded slopes below it, and the bare sweep of the South Downs rising beyond it. It was not a grand house, but it was serene and beautiful and welcoming. Parts of it were Tudor, but it had been substantially rebuilt in the mid-eighteenth century. The architect was unknown, but whoever he was, he had achieved a look of balance and harmony as pleasant as it was unpretentious, and inside he had employed a plasterer who had given the main drawing room and the staircase sophisticated swirling panels as fine as any in the country.

The Hall had descended through Patrick Humfrey's family for generations, though not always in the direct line. His son had been the last surviving Humfrey and that, although he had never told anyone, was why Rupert had felt a compulsion, almost an obligation, to leave it to his own child.

Margot had not wanted to invite the Branden family to visit Firsby Hall, but George had suggested it and Miles thought it would be as well to impress the American part of Lonnie's Trust with the way she was being brought up.

It was because of Miles that Lonnie was spending her summer holiday at Firsby Hall. Once he had discovered, soon after his marriage to Margot, just how much her sister was receiving for bringing up Lonnie he had not rested until he had found a way of diverting some of the money to Firsby Hall.

Patsy had fought against it. She had grown accustomed to the additional income which Lonnie's arrival had brought and she saw no reason for any change, especially since Margot was reluctant to house the child.

At first, when the quarterly cheques from Lonnie's Trust Fund arrived Patsy opened each envelope with a shock of pleasure, but before long she was taking the money for granted. Almost without noticing it the Lyntons had slipped into a different way of life. There was a governess who lived in and taught Lonnie and Sally, which meant that Patsy had to employ a second maid to cope with the extra work. Holidays at Frinton or Bournemouth had become holidays in Brittany, and Edward's battered old car had been changed for a new one. Patsy always said that Lonnie was treated as one of the family, which was true in that what was hers was also theirs. The money was so ample that there was no difficulty about stretching the cost of a new frock for Lonnie to pay for a similar outfit for Sally, and Patsy soon lost her scruples about applying to George Osbert for extra funds to cover the cost of the annual trips to France.

As for George, he was too relieved that the arrangements for Lonnie were working successfully to query the bills he was asked to pay, but even Patsy could not ask him to cover a holiday abroad if Lonnie remained at Firsby Hall, and it was one of the things that Patsy held against Miles that he had persuaded Margot to go back on her refusal to have anything to do with Lonnie.

At first Margot had been petulant about Miles' lack of understanding about the way she felt.

'The child ought to be brought up to know something about Firsby Hall, considering it'll belong to her one day.' Miles had pointed out.

'Not a very tactful thing to say, since it won't happen until after I'm dead and gone,' Margot had drawled.

On that occasion Miles had seen that he had displeased her and let the matter drop, but by constant gentle insistence he brought Margot round to a vague feeling of disgruntlement that her sister should be profiting from Rupert's disastrous Will. Even so, he could never get her to admit that Lonnie should make her permanent home at Firsby. The most she would accept was that the little girl should spend her summer holidays with them.

By the time Lonnie and Sally went off to the girls' boarding school through which Barbara had already passed, it was an accepted thing that Lonnie should go to Firsby Hall for two months every summer. Miles saw to it that the allowance for her upkeep was transferred to Margot, while Margot turned a blind eye and pretended not to notice the way her bank balance went up every July and August.

Lonnie tried sulking about being taken away from her playmates, but Margot was blandly indifferent to her moods, and in any case she soon found that it made very little difference to the way she spent her holidays since, except when they went away to the seaside, both Sally and Guy could cycle over to visit her from their home less than two miles away.

Sally was at first thought to be too young to ride her bicycle to Firsby Hall alone, and Guy grumbled about having to escort her, but that changed when he came home from school and discovered that Patsy had sold the family piano.

Patsy said it was because it was old and ugly and took up too much room, but Guy knew that it was her way of diverting him from his addiction to music. He said nothing, but suddenly he was prepared to visit Firsby Hall every day. He took his tennis racket with him, since one of the things Miles had done was to restore the tennis court, but Margot knew that the attraction for Guy was her grand piano.

It had stood unused for so long that the first time he tried it Guy's whole body sagged in frustration. 'It needs tuning,' he said, turning away.

It was not his disappointment, but a spurt of malice towards her sister, that made Margot promise to have the instrument put in order. She had not been aware until then of how much she resented Patsy's possession of three fine children, especially now that Guy was growing up. It was so unfair that Rupert, with his looks and intelligence, should have been lost, while Patsy's commonplace brood remained.

It amused her that Guy showed signs of breaking the mould. A pianist? Who would have thought it? She began to encourage him, buying music and leaving it on the piano for him to find, changing the old gramophone which had once belonged to Rupert for a fine new one and consulting Guy as to which recordings he would like to hear.

Guy threatened Sally with sudden death if she ever told their mother that he spent two hours at the piano for every one he spent on the tennis court, which hurt Sally's feelings since, as she pointed out, they never sneaked on one another. He did not make the same threat to Lonnie because she was his ally in everything and he trusted her to keep his secret without any need to say anything about it. Fortunately, Barbara rarely accompanied them to Firsby Hall; not, that is, until the summer when Flynn Branden was staying there.

It was obvious as soon as they met that Barbara was attracted to Flynn. Who wouldn't be? Six feet tall, with golden brown hair which he kept very short but which still curled obstinately all over his head, blue eyes, a delightful smile, the fine build of a college athlete and, more than all this, a readiness to be amused and interested in everything and everyone he met.

'My dear, did you ever in all your life see anything more perfect?' Patsy murmured to Margot the first time she met him.

'Just like the hero of every penny novelette,' Margot said.

'No, that's not fair. He's got brains as well as looks. It would be a marvellous thing for Barbara. Of course, I'd hate to lose her to America, but she's been so difficult to satisfy and she does seem taken with him, doesn't she?'

'No more than every other girl he meets,' Margot said impatiently. 'All right, I admit he's a madly attractive young man. Do you think he doesn't know it? Women must have been throwing themselves at him ever since he put on his first long trousers. He's got that air of weighing them up, assessing their value. I think you should be warning Barbara not to lose her heart. She might get hurt.'

'Oh, dear, you're probably right, but I don't like to say anything to spoil her little romance and he is being very attentive.'

'She's the prettiest girl around and on the spot.'

Margot maintained her detached attitude until the day Flynn caught up with her as she was going to the churchyard to put fresh flowers on Rupert's grave. He was so sympathetic, in an unobtrusive way that did not jar on Margot's sensibilities, that she found herself talking about her dead son with a freedom she had not achieved even with Miles. She came back from the churchyard leaning on Flynn's arm and after that there was no more talk of his good opinion of himself, though Margot did think that he would be rather wasted on her niece.

The person with whom Flynn had his greatest success, though she succeeded in hiding it from everyone but Flynn himself, was Lonnie. She was fourteen and a half when they met, a thin girl all angular arms and legs, too tall for her age, awkward and selfconscious. The confiding child who had once enchanted Rupert had gone forever, but she still had the fine bone structure he had bequeathed to her, and the large brown eyes and warm colouring she had taken from her mother. There were times when Lonnie had odd flashes of beauty. Not prettiness, that was what Barbara had and would lose as she grew older, but authentic ancient beauty which haunted the mind so that people who had seen her when it came upon her were unable to forget her.

Flynn saw only a youngster with scratches on her bare brown arms and legs, too young to be of interest to him as a woman, but worth spending time on because of her vast fortune.

He was clever enough to see that the management of that money was not only the one thing they had in common, but of deep interest to Lonnie.

'No one ever talks about it,' she told him. 'I know there's a lot of it and that it'll come to me when I'm twenty one . . .'

'Or if you marry,' Flynn said.

Lonnie wrinkled her nose. 'Not very likely,' she said. 'Not for years and years. The idea doesn't interest me.'

She spoke loftily and, as far as marriage was concerned, she was telling the truth, but for the first time Lonnie had an inkling of what it might be like to be in love. Flynn, with his different way of talking, different way of looking at the world, his air of sophistication, might have been a visitor from another planet. She was dazzled by his appearance and even more by the look of deep interest he turned on her. It was a look Flynn had practised on many girls, with great effect, but to Lonnie it seemed that it was for her alone and she responded with an eagerness

71

Flynn might have found touching if he had been less self-centred.

'I know Uncle Henry made lots and lots of money,' Lonnie said. 'And he left it to . . .'

'To Rupert Humfrey, who was your father,' Flynn said easily.

'You don't know what it means to me to have someone come out with that openly,' Lonnie exclaimed. 'I know, everyone knows that it's the truth, but no one *says* anything.'

'Rupert died, having left everything to you and now here you are, a very rich young woman, worth at the last count eight million dollars.'

'That's even more than I thought.'

'The stock market's been booming. Old Henry Singleton had a shrewd eye for a bargain and he got into a whole lot of companies when they were going cheap. His estate came in at around five million when he died, but like I said, things have been going up and up.'

'How much is it in pounds?'

'Let me see . . . the last time I changed some money I got one pound for four dollars eighty-eight cents. That's too difficult a piece of arithmetic for me to do in my head. Call it five dollars to the pound, which would make your inheritance at the moment stand between one and a half and two million pounds.'

'It's too much! What am I going to do with it?'

Flynn thought her naive and lamentably ill-informed. 'You could buy works of art, endow a charity, start a racing stable, dress in diamonds and sables – and still have change left over to travel the world in your own yacht.'

'You make it sound fun,' Lonnie said wistfully. 'No one ever did that before. I suppose the other thing I could do would be to just give it all away.'

'Honey, if you're going to do that, shovel a little my way,' Flynn drawled.

'I will! It's an awful responsibility, isn't it?'

'Sure is, but there'll always be people around to advise

you. Mr Osbert and Dad now, me maybe, one day, if you choose to leave your affairs in our hands.'

'I'd like it if you were there to help me, Flynn.'

Lonnie flushed vividly, embarrassed because she thought she had sounded too eager. Hurriedly, she added, 'You're the only *young* person who's involved. The others all seem so old. When I try to get them to talk to me they sort of pat me on the head and tell me to go and play with my dolls.'

Flynn was not likely to make that mistake, not when treating Lonnie as an adult gave him such an advantage. It was the first of several long talks they had and if Lonnie was not entirely aware of the way Flynn's physical presence influenced her delight in their discussions, Flynn himself had played the game too often not to know that the kid was half in love with him. If only she had been a year or two older he might have made a serious attempt to put a ring on her finger, even though she was a plain youngster and not the type who attracted him. With all that money to gild the pill, Flynn thought he could have swallowed it easily enough and with a bit of grooming and styling Lonnie might turn out quite presentable later on.

As it was, he became a trifle bored with humouring a girl too young to be made love to and let his attention drift away to Barbara, who was the prettiest thing he had seen in England and just as keen on him as Lonnie herself.

Lonnie was too proud to betray her hurt feelings when Flynn deserted her to go to a tennis party with Barbara, but her inner turmoil made her bad-tempered and disinclined to be cooperative when Margot asked her to entertain Lou and Cissie Branden that afternoon.

Instead, she escaped into the woods without saying where she was going and, since he had no wish to take her place with the Brandens, Guy followed her, although he was to Lonnie's mind unnecessarily self-righteous about her failings as a hostess.

'Let Aunt Margot look after them,' Lonnie said. 'I'm not going to spend a sweltering afternoon sauntering round the village listening to Mrs Branden tell me how cute it is.'

'You'd have gone fast enough if Flynn had been there.'

'Flynn has more sense than to want to look at silly old cottages. I do think it was mingy of the Cottons only to invite Barbara to their party. I play much better tennis than she does.'

'You can hit the ball,' Guy conceded. 'But you don't look sweetly pretty in your pleated frock like Babs.'

Lonnie chuckled and for a moment they were united in an old alliance against Guy's older sister, but they were soon squabbling again about Lonnie's cavalier attitude towards the Brandens.

'They're your visitors,' Guy pointed out. 'It's you they've come to see.'

'I don't like going into the village,' Lonnie said flatly. 'They whisper about me, even now. And you know how awkward it is if I meet any of the Dunwells. How would you like to be caught peering at a picturesque old cottage that just happens to be where the people who thought they were your grandparents live?'

'I was forgetting,' Guy said. 'Sorry, Lonnie. I take it all back.'

'Besides, the Brandens are bores – except Flynn,' Lonnie said. 'All Mr Branden talks about is money. "Everything's booming, Miles, just booming". Didn't you love the way Aunt Margot looked when he started calling her "Margot" as soon as he arrived?'

She scrambled to her feet, looking, as Guy had hinted, a long way from a desirable guest at a sedate tennis party, her feet bare in leather sandals, although Margot had decreed that she should always wear stockings, her cotton frock a disgrace.

'I'm going to see Gran,' she said. 'You can come or not, just as you like. Perhaps you'd rather go back to the house and sneak to Aunt Margot about where I am.'

'I'll come with you,' Guy said. 'I don't want to give you away, but I don't want to tell lies about it either and I'm the first person Aunt Margot will ask when she discovers you're missing.'

When Lonnie had told Flynn that no one ever talked about her situation with her she had been thinking of the adults. Between herself and Guy, and to a certain extent Sally, there had always been total frankness. Sally was her friend, but there was a special tie between Lonnie and Guy, going back to the day when he had first put his arm round the tearsodden baby who had come to join the Lynton household. Until recently they had discussed everything together. Guy knew as much as Lonnie was able to express of her agony at losing her family and Lonnie knew all about Guy's singleminded determination to pursue a career in music, no matter what plans his mother and father might have for him.

Now Guy, with his eighteenth birthday about to be celebrated, felt that he had left his childhood behind him and most of his mind was concentrated on his battle to lead the life he wanted, so that he had let some part of his attention slip away from Lonnie. Lonnie had changed, too, physically and mentally, but her appearance was still immature. She was no longer a child, to be hugged and comforted, but neither was she anything like the girls who sometimes troubled his mind. In the past he had always known what Lonnie was thinking, now she had begun to hide her thoughts from him. Guy suspected it was because of her crush on Flynn and, when he could find time to think about it, the idea worried him.

Lonnie had not been an easy child to bring up. Patsy had sometimes said in exasperation that she only had to say it was a fine day to Lonnie to be flatly contradicted. She rebelled against everything and only Guy could unfailingly persuade her to be reasonable. He understood and sympathised with the suspicion Lonnie harboured against the world and because of that he could usually talk her out of her fits of unreasonableness. Gradually Lonnie had come to accept that she had to submit to a degree of obedience if there was to be any order in her life and until this summer Patsy had begun to think that the worst was over.

In the last year Lonnie had suddenly put on a spurt of growth, but Guy was still a good head taller than her. In spite of his obsession with music he was muscular and athletic, although his mother tried to frighten him by insisting that he was developing a stoop from bending over the piano too much. He still resembled his older sister, but whereas Barbara was undoubtedly a pretty girl, Guy would never be called handsome. His features reproduced hers with a touch of exaggeration; a thinner nose, a longer mouth and a chin which jutted forward aggressively. When he was older he would be a striking-looking man, but at the moment the strong lines of his face did not match his youthful body.

As he followed Lonnie along the woodland path it occurred to Guy that she moved as easily through the trees as her grandmother did. Guy liked Thirza, but she made him feel uneasy. She had a way of looking at you as if she knew all your secrets, which was troubling even for someone with a relatively clear conscience.

When they reached the clearing where the old wooden hut still stood, Lonnie paused.

'She's not here,' she said in disappointment.

There was a sound, too feeble to be called a shout, from near the spring of water, and then they both saw her, lying on the ground with one leg doubled under her.

They ran across the grass and Lonnie flung herself down on her knees by her grandmother's side. Thirza's eyes were shut, but the movement roused her. She looked up at Lonnie as if she had difficulty in focusing her eyes, then the vagueness cleared.

'I fell,' she said. 'Slipped on the wet grass. Never did such a thing before. Leg broken.'

Her voice faltered and her eyes closed again.

'I'll fetch help,' Guy said. 'Is there anything I can do before I go?'

The old woman's eyes opened again. 'You go,' she said. 'Lonnie . . . make tea, fetch a blanket. So cold.'

Neither of them said so, but to both Lonnie and Guy those words sounded ominous on such a hot day. Guy raced away and Lonnie obeyed her grandmother and made her a hot cup of tea. With help from her, Thirza managed to raise her head and sip it.

'Good,' she said. 'What a mischance . . . the worst thing that has happened to me since I came to live here. So . . . my time is up. I didn't expect it to come so soon.'

'Don't talk like that,' Lonnie said sharply. 'Goodness, a broken leg! That's nothing.'

'I've lain here all night, lovey. There's a fever on me. They'll put me in hospital and that'll be the end of me.'

'Don't be so silly, Gran. People go into hospital to get better. Drink some more of this tea.'

Obediently, Thirza drank and it seemed to strengthen her.

'You may be right,' she said. 'All the same, there's things I'll say to you, in case it's my last chance. There's a few pounds in the tobacco jar on the mantelpiece. Not much, but you may as well take charge of it. My old scraps of furniture are worth nothing, but I want you to promise me that if anything happens to me, now or later, you'll pack up my pink lustre tea service and send it out to your Mum in Australia.'

'Yes . . . yes . . . but don't talk like that,' Lonnie implored.

Thirza closed her eyes and went on talking in a low monotone.

'Joe's done well for himself in Australia. I knew he'd get on in the world, no matter where. But Rosa's never settled. She wanted something she's not found on the other side of the world. Refinement, an easy life, to be a lady. Having the tea set will be a comfort to her. Something that's come down through the family, and pretty, too. That'll please her.'

Her hand suddenly shot out and she grasped Lonnie's arm with hard, bony fingers.

'After I'm gone, the cabin's to be burnt,' she said. 'Promise me . . . promise!'

'But I can't . . .'

'Promise.'

'I promise,' Lonnie whispered. 'Oh, Gran, Gran, don't talk as if you were going to die. Please don't die.'

'Choice'd be a fine thing,' Thirza said with a flash of her old sardonic humour.

She lapsed into silence, a line of pain between her dark eyebrows. Lonnie, crouched awkwardly by her side, did not know what to do. She took her grandmother's hand in hers and held it and from time to time the old woman gave it a feeble squeeze, as if it comforted her to feel the touch.

'My old cat died in the spring and I didn't replace him,' she said. 'There's a young woman in the village, Lizzie Burns, who'll take my hens and rabbits and be glad of them. Six children to raise and another on the way, but she wouldn't take my advice. See to it, Lonnie.'

'Yes, yes, I will.'

'Money,' Thirza said, opening her eyes to look into Lonnie's face. 'Too much and too easy come by. You could do a lot of good with it, but I doubt you will. Having a surplus has never been my problem, so I can't advise you. You'll have to cope as best you can.'

She lapsed into a fretful muttering while Lonnie crouched by her side, growing cold and stiff on the damp grass, in spite of the heat of the day. She was still there when Guy came back with the news that an ambulance would come as close as it could and the driver was a local man who knew how to locate the cabin in the woods. He knelt down on Thirza's other side, anxious to show his concern but unsure of what to do. When he spoke to Lonnie she did not answer, but looked at him with remote eyes, as if she had retreated to some country he had never visited. She looked different: older, her immature face frozen in sorrow.

Guy tried to think of something reassuring he could say, but all he could manage was, 'She'll be all right, you know. Once her leg's set, she'll soon be up and about again.'

Lonnie shook her head, but she did not argue with him, even though she knew he was wrong. Thirza had made up her mind that her time had come and with that belief some inner source of health and strength had gone out of her.

Three days later Thirza died in the hospital she had always hoped to avoid. Lonnie was told she had developed pneumonia.

'So much for the outdoor life,' Margot said with a jarring laugh. 'One wouldn't have expected her to succumb so easily. Lonnie, I don't approve of children going to funerals. Everything will be done properly, of course. Since there's no one else to see to it, I've made the arrangements myself. Miles will attend on our behalf, and anyone from the village who cares to go to the church.'

'I shall go, whether you want me to or not,' Lonnie said.

'I forbid it.'

The look Lonnie turned on her was one of amazement that Margot should think it that easy to stop her.

'I don't see how you can prevent me unless you lock me in the nursery,' she said.

In the end Miles intervened and said he would escort Lonnie to the funeral.

'She's the old woman's only relative living in this country, as far as we know,' he pointed out.

'I had hoped to avoid reminding everyone of that,' Margot said.

'It's an old story in the village. I suppose someone has told the daughter in Australia?'

'I asked George Osbert to deal with it,' Margot said. 'Very well, if you side with Lonnie I suppose I'll have to let her go. I have no intention of being there myself, but I'll order a wreath.'

It was a meaningless gesture which Lonnie treated with scorn, just as she looked at the cross of lilies and white roses which bore her own name with surprise and a quick, painful realisation of the caustic comment her grand-mother would have made about it.

She was grateful that Guy had offered to go with her and Uncle Miles. He had been with her when she had found her grandmother stricken down, he understood something of what she felt, which was more than Uncle Miles did, in spite of the solicitous arm he put round her shoulders as they stood by the open grave.

Lonnie moved away from that sympathetic touch. She wanted to be alone, as her grandmother had been alone. Self-sufficient, not beholden to anyone, living her life with a freedom which made the restraints surrounding Lonnie seem like shackles. Golden shackles. Gran had understood about that.

As soon as the ceremony was over, Lonnie turned away. 'I'm going to walk back,' she said. 'Guy, come with me.'

It sounded like an order, but because of the special circumstances Guy followed her without protesting as he would normally have done. He had found himself unex-pectedly stirred by the funeral service. The tremendous certainty of the words had touched something in him he had not previously known to exist. Did he really believe in it – God and the life hereafter? Did Lonnie? The dead woman knew now, for certain.

'Your grandmother didn't go to church, did she?' he asked Lonnie as they went out of the gate at the back of the churchyard. 'Would all that have been what she wanted?'

'She thought everything was part of a whole and there was a pattern that had to be followed. And she wanted to be buried next to her husband. Apart from that, I don't know what she believed,' Lonnie said.

As she spoke she took off the hat and gloves Margot had forced her to wear for the service. She was leading the way and Guy realised that they were taking the path that led to the cabin in the woods.

'You've got to help me,' Lonnie said over her shoulder. When they arrived at the little hut she found the key under the stone where it was always kept on the rare occasions when Thirza had bothered to lock the door. The sudden colour of the interior flashed on them, but Lonnie could see, even though Guy did not notice it, that already there was a film of dust on the surfaces Thirza had kept bright.

She went to the tobacco jar on the mantelpiece and felt inside.

'Nearly four pounds,' she said, putting the money away in the skirt-pocket of her frock. 'That's mine. Gran said I was to have it.'

There was a wooden tea chest in which Thirza had kept her kindling wood. Lonnie turned out the sticks.

'This'll do to hold the tea set,' she said. 'Wrap the pieces up in anything soft you can find. Dusters, bits of rag, tea towels – anything.' She paused with Thirza's old cashmere shawl in her hand. 'Not that,' she decided. 'I've always liked it. I'm going to keep it.'

As they worked she said absentmindedly, 'I don't know how to send things out to Australia, do you? I'll have to get Mr Osbert to do it.'

'Is that where this is going?' Guy asked.

'To my mother. Gran wanted her to have it.'

It was rare for Lonnie to speak of her distant mother. Guy had long ago pieced together most of her story, but Lonnie's silence on the subject was almost absolute.

'Do you ever hear from her?' he ventured to ask.

'Not any longer. She used to send a birthday card and a Christmas present, but that stopped. I don't know whether it was because she lost interest or because someone told her to give it up.'

Lonnie's tone was light to the point of indifference, but something impelled Guy to say, 'It's rotten hard luck on you.'

'I don't think about it any more.' Lonnie paused with the cashmere shawl crushed between her hands. 'But I mind about losing Gran.'

'I know. She was . . . she was the most unusual person I've ever known,' Guy offered by way of comfort.

'She was like a queen. She gave me an order before she died and I'm going to carry it out. That's why I wanted you here. You're going to help me. We've got to burn this cabin.'

'Set fire to it?' Guy asked in disbelief.

'Burn it right down, so that there's nothing left.'

She had expected to have to argue with him, but to Lonnie's surprise Guy said slowly, 'It's a Romany thing, isn't it? Don't they burn the caravans of gypsies who've died?'

'I don't know. Gran didn't say. She just made me promise to see it was done.'

It was Guy who insisted on filling buckets of water and soaking the grass surrounding the hut to prevent the fire spreading. The cabin stood clear of any overhanging branches and he thought the trees would be safe. Lonnie found a can of paraffin and a bundle of old newspapers.

'Matches,' she said. 'Gran must have had some somewhere.'

'Here.'

Guy handed her the box. He helped her soak everything with the paraffin, but he let Lonnie light the matches and throw them inside.

The dry wooden walls caught easily. There was nothing of any substance to hold back the fire. The flames leapt from end to end, scarlet and gold, and a plume of smoke rose in the air.

Guy shifted away from the heat. Now that it was done he was frightened by the intensity of the fire, but exultant too, with a primitive satisfaction in the power of the blaze. He could only see Lonnie through a haze of smoke. She had moved to the other side of the hut and the flames were between them. The cashmere shawl hung from her shoulders in sweeping folds. Lit from below by the firelight her face took on an astounding maturity. She was beautiful, with a beauty that was different from anything Guy had ever seen in any other woman. In that moment she was a woman, not a child. She was what she had called her grandmother, a queen.

As he watched her, Lonnie raised her eyes from the ruins of the hut and looked at him. She made a strange gesture, half-holding out her hand and half-warding him off. Guy took one hesitating step towards her and then they were startled by a shout.

The fire had been seen. The column of smoke had brought farmworkers from the fields running to see what was going up in flames. The strange moment had gone, but it lingered in both their minds, even while they were being scolded for deliberately starting a fire that might have done untold damage in the dry heat of summer.

'It seems sort of a strange thing to do,' Lou Branden said to George Osbert when he heard about Lonnie's exploit.

'If you'd known the grandmother you'd understand,' George said.

If he spoke impatiently it was not so much because he meant to defend Lonnie's action as because he was becoming tired of the continuing presence of his American colleague. Mr and Mrs Branden and their son would be leaving soon for France and George would not be sorry to say goodbye to them.

Lou Branden had made no secret of the fact that it was the boom in stocks and shares which had enabled him to bring his wife and Flynn on this European vacation.

'I've made a killing,' he said frankly. 'We all have, those of us who were quick enough to get into the market before stocks rose to their present height. George, I've said it before, but I just have to say it again: you're making a mistake holding out against re-investing the income from the Singleton Trust in American stocks and shares.'

George's mouth tightened obstinately. So far he had withstood the pressure from his American colleague to place Lonnie's vast income on the New York Stock Exchange, and he had managed to keep Edward Lynton, who was Lonnie's third trustee, although Margot was her official guardian, on his side. He was stodgy, old-fashioned, over-cautious – all those things – and he knew that was the way the American thought of him, but he distrusted what Lou Branden called 'the quick buck'.

He could do nothing about the capital. That remained in the companies which Henry Singleton had founded or helped to found, but all the income which was not used for Lonnie's keep – and George's conscience stirred uneasily at the level of expense that had reached – went into dull, solid, British stocks of trustee status.

'I'd rather not take any chances,' he said, with a mildness that deceived Lou Branden into thinking that he could still be persuaded.

Miles could have told him that he might as well try shifting the Rock of Gibraltar as attempt to change George Osbert's mind when he thought it his duty to stand firm. Miles had, to George's way of thinking, stepped over the line in spending money on improvements to Firsby Hall and he found himself having to retrench when George dug in his heels and refused to pay for the work out of the Trust Fund.

'Maintenance, yes,' he had said. 'Good husbandry, certainly. But if you think you need new stables rather than repairing the old ones, then you will have to provide for them out of your own income. Or, I should say, Mrs Bowman's income.'

It was a reminder of Miles' status which he did not relish, especially since he knew that George had done it on purpose. George had come to regret introducing Miles Bowman to Firsby Hall. Too late, he recognised in him a man on the make. The marriage to Margot appeared on the surface to be a success, but it did not meet with George's approval, not when he observed Margot's increasing shrillness and the way she fought to retain her youthful appearance.

Just as Miles had failed to get George to pay for his ambitious new plans for the stables at Firsby Hall, so Lou Branden failed to persuade him that the rise in the American stock market was an ideal opportunity to increase the Singleton fortune.

In his exasperation he spoke his mind about Lonnie herself.

'I'd call her a handful,' he said. 'While Cissie and I have been staying with Margot and Miles we've noticed that whenever she was wanted little Lonnie was always missing. She may be going to a top school, but they certainly haven't taught her any manners. And setting that fire! Well, I'll be frank with you, George; Cissie and I had it in mind to suggest taking Lonnie back for a spell in the States, but we've talked it over and we've decided we couldn't take the responsibility of looking after her.'

'Did you mention it to Lonnie?'

'Not outright. I just asked if she wouldn't like to visit America. Sounding her out, you know.'

'That may be why she's been so difficult these holidays,' George said with a sigh. 'And the loss of her grandmother, of course. Lonnie reacts badly to any change. Certainly I don't think there can be any question of sending her to America until she's much older.'

The Brandens departed, leaving Barbara disconsolate and Lonnie relieved. Just as George had guessed, she had been on tenterhooks ever since Lou Branden had tried to find out her reaction to his idea of taking her back to the United States. Part of her had been excited, but less by the idea of visiting America than of spending more time with Flynn. If it had really come to the point she would have fought against it. Her life had achieved a routine: school, Christmas and Easter holidays at what she now called 'home' with the Lynton family, the summer months at Firsby Hall. She could cope with that, but the thought of being jolted out of that regular round and going to a strange country gave her the sick feeling in her stomach which she recognised as fear.

She was afraid of her feelings for Flynn, too. Dimly she recognised that she was too young yet to handle the violent swings of attraction and repulsion she experienced in his company and she shied away from the idea of getting closer to him, even though she believed it was something she wanted.

The loss of her grandmother was a constant nagging grief. There was no one left now. Always before at the back of her mind she had had the idea that if anything happened that was too terrible for her to deal with she could run away to Gran. Now she was alone.

Facing up to that gave Lonnie a strange poise. She became even more self-contained and very independent. Looking at the people surrounding her with cool, if biased, judgment, she decided that George Osbert could be trusted but would always be on the side of the other adults who ruled her life, the Lyntons and the Bowmans. Patsy Lynton was kind but foolish and Edward Lynton was a man who had never quite come to terms with the human race. He was kind, in a disinterested way, but anything said to him had to drop down into his subconscious to be translated into a language he understood, then he had to formulate his reply and put it into understandable words: it made for a slow conversation. Margot, Lonnie disliked and Miles she distrusted. Sally was a friend, but Barbara was hostile and always had been. Guy was her closest ally, but Lonnie became wary of friendship with him when she picked up a hint of Patsy's plans for their future.

It came by way of a sarcastic remark from Margot after Guy had been to visit one of the farms with Miles.

'Showing the young master how things are run?' she asked. 'That's what he'll be one day if Patsy has her way, you know. I wonder if Guy understands what she has lined up for him.'

It had taken Miles' quick shake of the head and frowning glance towards her to make Lonnie realise what Margot meant. It was like a piece of jigsaw falling into place, except that Lonnie meant to break up the puzzle and form her own picture.

'Your mother means to marry me off to you so that you can have Firsby Hall,' she said to Guy. 'In case you have any ideas about it yourself I may as well tell you that nothing, but nothing, would make me marry you.'

'Just as well, because I've no intention of asking you,' Guy retorted.

He was angry, but he was also embarrassed. Something had entered into his friendship with Lonnie that had not been there until the day of her grandmother's funeral, the day they had set light to the cabin and he had seen her in the firelight, looking strange and not like Lonnie at all. She disturbed him, stirring his latent sexuality. He had begun to avoid being alone with her, but his dreams were not as easily controlled and it was always Lonnie who woke him, sweating and ashamed, from erotic fantasies that bore no relation to the angular, sharptongued girl who played games like a boy and in the past would join him in any lawless escapade he could think up.

She had been such a pretty little thing when she had first come to live with them. Dimly, Guy remembered the chivalry she had aroused in him, the way he had felt that he had to protect her. It was different now. Lonnie protected herself and was very fierce about it, both verbally and, if necessary, with blows.

By October George Osbert was congratulating himself on not risking the changes Lou Branden had urged on him for increasing the Singleton Trust in the American market. Since he did not know about the talks she had had with Flynn, he was amazed to learn that Lonnie, too, was taking an interest in the Stock Exchange.

I am studying finance,' she wrote in her firm script, both bold and childlike. *'I thought I would learn about stocks and shares because I shall have such a lot of them when I'm twenty-one. I've read in* The Times *that there's been heavy trading on the New York Stock Exchange with wild swings in prices. Can you tell me what's happening to my own money? Do I own any* Steel Common, *which is one of the stocks mentioned in* The Times *as going up and down a lot in one day? I would be very interested to know what is going on.'*

There was a postscript in which George thought he recognised the sardonic voice of Thirza Seward: *'My form mistress thinks my choice of spare-time study is excentric and not in good taste.'* He was glad about the misspelling; it reassured him that he was still dealing with a child.

He wrote back meticulously, but he wished he could have heard from Lou Branden. It was at times like this that the vast distance between them was a disadvantage.

'You will have noticed the comment that the strength of British funds and other stocks in the trustee class stood out in contrast to the weakness of markets generally,' he wrote. *'I'm glad to say that all the Trust's income not required for immediate expenses has been invested in stocks of this type. As for the situation in America, I fear that there may be some losses in the capital gains which had accrued recently. However, as far as you are concerned these are only paper losses, since we have no intention of entering the market until it has steadied.'*

Lonnie was gratified by this businesslike reply. At last someone was taking her seriously. She followed the market eagerly every day and was no longer thought to be 'excentric' as the story of the disastrous crash on the New York Exchange became the most talked about topic everywhere.

The next letter she received from George Osbert was less informative than it appeared.

'I am very sorry to have to tell you that Mr Branden has died,' George wrote. *'It was very sudden and as this leaves the Singleton Trust without an American Trustee it will be necessary for me to go to New York to sort things out.'*

He might have got away with that brief note, even though it left Lonnie wondering why Flynn did not automatically take his father's place, if Edward Lynton had not been George's fellow trustee. Of necessity, George had to confide in him and from Edward to Patsy was just one short step. When Lonnie went home for Christmas she learnt the truth.

'Who would have thought it when he was staying at Firsby Hall?' Patsy said. 'You saw more of him than we did, Lonnie. What did you think of him? Did he seem like a gambler who would commit suicide?'

'Suicide?'

'Oh, duckie, didn't you know? I'm sorry, but he wasn't

a great friend, was he, and American, after all. Yes, that's why George had to go over and see to everything. I was afraid he would ask Edward to go with him, but fortunately he thought he could manage on his own. Apparently Mr Branden bought shares he couldn't pay for in the expectation of them going up so that he could sell at a profit and, of course, they went down and down and down, and when he found he was ruined . . . well, as I said, the poor man died by his own hand.'

'How?'

'Oh, Lonnie, you don't really want to know, do you? So horrid. He shot himself.'

'Was it my money he'd been gambling with?'

'He couldn't touch the capital, could he, without George and Edward consenting. But George did say the dividends hadn't been coming through as they should. He's had to pay your expenses out of the reserves he had in hand.'

Patsy meant the allowance which was paid to her, as Lonnie very well knew. As long as that arrived without any hitch Patsy was not concerned and she ended inconsequentially, 'So perhaps it was your money Mr Branden used . . . I don't know.'

'I want to see Mr Osbert.'

Patsy objected, but Lonnie was obstinate. Either George came to see her or she would go and see him. In the end, since it seemed the easiest way to satisfy her, George visited the Lyntons.

He looked tired and drawn and he eyed the festive decorations with disenchanted eyes.

'The bulk of your capital is safe,' he told Lonnie. 'From a peak of something like eight million dollars in the summer it has declined to around three million, but by anyone's standards that is a sizable fortune, and there's always the possibility that the value may recover in time. What's missing is the income for the months of August, September and October. Apparently what Branden had been in the habit of doing was buying shares in his own name, paying for them out of the income from the Singleton Trust and repaying the money when he sold out at a profit. In the end, of course, he was caught by the crash and was unable to sell to repay his theft.'

'Don't call it theft,' Lonnie protested.

'It was stealing,' George insisted. 'He would have been struck off or disbarred, or whatever they call it in the United States, and his professional life would have been ruined once it had come out.'

'So he killed himself. I wish I'd known. As far as I'm concerned, he could have had the money.'

'Fortunately, you're not yet in charge of it,' George said drily. 'That's not an attitude I could encourage, speaking as your professional adviser.'

'Will I have complete control when I'm twenty-one? Can I give it all away if I want to?'

'You can, but I hope you won't!' George exclaimed. 'After all the trouble . . .' He paused.

'You were going to say "after all the trouble it's caused me",' Lonnie said with a smile. 'Was your visit to New York tiresome?'

'I could well have done without it and the atmosphere over there was troubling. It was very soon after the crash, of course, and everyone was despondent.'

'Did you see Mrs Branden and . . . and Flynn?'

'Yes. Poor woman, I don't think she had the least idea of what her husband had been doing.'

'Nor did Flynn,' Lonnie said swiftly.

'No . . . no,' George agreed reluctantly. 'He was obviously shocked.'

Flynn had been more than shocked, he had been savage about his father's mismanagement. To George's way of thinking even a father who had committed a crime deserved more charity, but he kept that opinion to himself.

'Every effort will be made to recover the money that was stolen,' he told Lonnie.

'How?'

'Such assets as he left are up for sale. The house, for instance . . .'

'I don't want that. George, you've got to see to it. I

don't care whether you think it's in my best interest or not, I absolutely forbid you to pursue that poor, stupid woman for money that I don't need and don't want.'

Her use of his Christian name struck George almost as much as her tone of authority. Lonnie was asserting herself in an adult way for the first time. This was something different from the childish disobedience about which both Patsy and Margot had complained. She was giving him an order and it seemed to George that he was going to have to obey.

'I'll speak to the other trustees,' he said. 'But if you're adamant . . .'

'I am.'

'It's a very charitable attitude.'

'I can afford to be charitable, can't I?'

'I suppose you can, but I'm not sure I should let you condone the misuse of trust funds,' George said with a smile.

'The man's dead, for goodness sake.'

'That's true,' George admitted. 'Very well, Lonnie, I'll persuade the other trustees to waive repayment of the missing funds.'

Having won her point, Lonnie said hesitantly, 'What will Flynn do?'

'He's got good qualifications and he doesn't seem to have been implicated in the fraud. I imagine he'll join another law firm.'

In a junior position and without the prestige of being a partner; a come-down for a proud young man which George thought Flynn Branden would not relish.

'He isn't . . . you've appointed someone else to be my American trustee?' Lonnie asked.

'That was unavoidable,' George said. 'Be satisfied with taking the burden of debt off his shoulders; I can assure you Flynn will be grateful for that relief.' Again he smiled. 'You see what it is to have the power to command? Are you sure you'll want to give it up?'

'I know all about the power of money,' Lonnie said. 'It

separates people from their families, it makes nice people greedy and now, it seems, it kills.'

CHAPTER FIVE

Barbara was getting married. It was a great relief to Patsy. She had seen, all too clearly, how disappointed her elder daughter had been when Flynn Branden had gone back to America with no apparent regret at leaving her behind. Barbara had drooped and sulked and then brightened up and been hectically active, throwing herself into a constant round of dances and parties, none of which seemed to give her much enjoyment.

Now, three years after the disappointment over Flynn, she had found a nice young man and perhaps in her heart she was thankful that there had been no commitment to Flynn, considering the disgrace which had overtaken his father.

It was not quite the match her mother had hoped for, nor did it satisfy Barbara's own ambitions, but Tom had qualified as an architect, which was a very respectable profession. They would lead a suburban life, at least until Tom's talent was recognised, but Barbara seemed happy and Tom was devoted to her, so Patsy thought it would all turn out well, and even if his father was only a bank manager, Tom was very well connected on his mother's side and the cousin who was his best man would be a baronet one day.

Patsy had a tussle with her daughter over the question of the bridesmaids.

'I'm not having Lonnie,' Barbara said. 'Everyone will want to know who she is.'

'She's your cousin, who's always lived with us because her parents are dead,' Patsy said. 'That's what I've always told everyone.'

'But it isn't true and far too many people know there's a mystery about her. I don't want to hear them whispering about it at my wedding.'

Patsy was in a quandary. She had been relying on paying the dressmaker's bills out of Lonnie's allowance and it was going to be difficult to arrange that if she was not going to wear one of the bridesmaids' frocks.

Fortunately for her, Barbara took her trouble to Tom and he, with the good sense that his future mother-in-law was beginning to look upon as a real blessing, said, 'She's been brought up with you since she was a baby, almost like another sister. It'll look more strange for her not to be a bridesmaid than to have her. People will ask why she's been left out. Let her walk up the aisle with the other three and no one will notice her.'

'Yes, they will. Lonnie always gets herself noticed,' Barbara said crossly, but she let herself be persuaded and Lonnie was fitted for one of the dresses in sweetpea shades which Barbara had decided would be a good foil for her own prettiness in oyster satin.

Lonnie was seventeen, still coltishly slim, but without the angularity which had once made her limbs look like loosely assembled sticks. She had learnt to hold up her head and to walk with something of the stalking grace of her grandmother. As Barbara had said, she was noticeable. For one thing, she was half a head taller than the other bridesmaids and the deep pink chiffon of her gown draped itself over her long limbs in graceful folds which made Sally, in soft mauve, look like a bundle tied up in the middle.

There was one unexpected guest, someone Barbara would just as soon not have had at her wedding, and that was Flynn Branden.

He had called at the house unannounced only two days before the wedding and Patsy, completely distracted, had invited him before she had really had time to think what she was doing.

'Mother, how could you!' Barbara had exclaimed when she had heard about it. 'His father was a *thief*! If he hadn't killed himself he would have gone to prison!'

'Yes, dear, but it wasn't Flynn's fault and one shouldn't visit the sins of the father on the children, should one, and I was so taken by surprise I completely forgot about it when I saw Flynn again.'

The truth was that her first thought on seeing the good-looking young American was that it might unsettle Barbara. Now, seeing how appalled Barbara was looking, she thought it was because of Lou Branden's crime and told herself she should have realised that nothing would ever separate Flynn from his father's misdeeds in Barbara's mind.

'I can't take back the invitation,' Patsy said. 'It all happened in America, after all, not like a scandal in our own backyard and hardly anyone will have heard about it.'

'I don't know how he could have the gall to come and face us,' Barbara said, but she thought it inadvisable to protest too vigorously. She had put all that behind her and had no wish to remind anyone of her past folly. Flynn Branden was a swine and his father would have been a criminal if he had lived to face charges. Let Flynn come to the wedding, let him see if she cared. Tom, nice solid Tom, was worth ten of Flynn Branden.

Reassured that Barbara was not going to make a fuss, Patsy began to see the good side of having Flynn to the wedding. He was such an asset at a party; Flynn could talk to anyone and make them believe they had his undivided attention. He could help with the bridesmaids, not Sally and Lonnie, of course, but the other two, both of whom were Tom's cousins and the all-important baronet's daughters.

With this idea in her mind, Patsy was annoyed to see Flynn making a dead set at Lonnie at the reception. Lonnie was looking well, that deep pink suited her, and the little shallow crowned hat tilted to one side gave her a spurious air of sophistication.

'Lonnie, you've grown up and you're a sight to dazzle the eyes,' Flynn said.

There was no hint of embarrassment in his smile, but then Flynn had already made up his mind that he would carry off this meeting with a high hand. He was gratified by the colour that rose in Lonnie's cheeks and burned there like a signal of his continuing attraction for her.

It was the memory of her infatuation that had brought him to England when his life had reached another crisis. The first had been his father's suicide and all the complications that had followed. Some of his associates had advised him to stay put and wait for the scandal to subside since, after all, Flynn himself had been guiltless, but Flynn had preferred to throw up his position and move out.

He had found employment, helped by his excellent qualifications and references, but, as George Osbert had guessed, a subservient role did not suit Flynn's ambitions. Because he had been bored, and because he despised his employer, he had embarked on a flirtation with the man's wife, only to discover that she took it far more seriously than he did and was ready to throw up everything to marry him.

Flynn had said that rather than allow her to make such a sacrifice he himself would go away, in order to let them, as he put it, keep their heads. It was a long way from the ecstatic reaction the woman had been expecting. Soured by the realisation that she had been making a fool of herself, she had informed her husband that Flynn had molested her and Flynn had found his departure taking place more swiftly than he had planned.

At the back of his mind he blamed the Singleton Trust for his troubles. Not Lonnie herself, but the complications surrounding her which made the administration of the Trust so unusual. Even the woman who was supposed to be her guardian had shifted the responsibility on to someone else. It was the ambiguities of the situation which had made it possible for his father to fall into temptation. That, and his own greed, but Flynn did not entirely blame him for that, only for the bad judgement which had not enabled his fraud to succeed.

Taking stock of the situation, Flynn decided that his main assets were his brains, his looks and his attraction for women. Three years had passed since the summer when his teasing smile had troubled young Lonnie. She was seventeen now. Marriageable. Would she have him? Flynn thought he could capture her. Would Margot give her consent? Probably not. That was a difficulty because, as Flynn took the trouble to check, although Lonnie came into her inheritance either when she came of age or if she married before she was twenty-one, it was only if she married with the consent of her guardian. All the same, they couldn't keep the girl entirely without money and once he was sure of her he was prepared to be patient. Four years – less, more like three and a half. It would be worth the wait.

With the same gambler's instinct that had brought his father to ruin, Flynn had sold up everything he had, kissed his mother goodbye, and departed to spend the summer in Europe.

Barbara's wedding was the perfect opportunity to get himself back into the family circle. It got Barbara out of the way, too, and only Flynn and Barbara herself knew how much cause she had to complain of his treatment of her three years before. She seemed to have got over it and the man she had married looked just right, firm as the Rock of Gibraltar and never likely to give his wife any shocks – or any great pleasures, either. Flynn risked a tiny wink and a kiss on the cheek as he wished Barbara well at the reception. It was like kissing a wooden image. *So be like that, sweetheart*, he thought to himself; *you were lively enough the last time I held you in my arms*.

The memory gave a touch of mischief to his smile and that was when he encountered Lonnie. Flynn saw at once that she had improved out of all recognition. All the more reason to put his campaign in hand straight away, otherwise another man might whisk this prize away from under his nose.

'What are your plans for the future?' he asked.

'In September I'm supposed to be going to a ghastly finishing school in Switzerland,' Lonnie said. 'Can you imagine anything more ridiculous? It's only because they can't think of anything else to do with me. What I'd really like to do is to study something practical.'

'Cooking?'

'You're as bad as Aunt Patsy! I was thinking of accountancy, but everyone throws up their hands in horror at the idea.'

'It's not as if you're going to have to work,' Flynn suggested.

'That's Aunt Margot's line.'

'This is the first time a girl's ever told me I remind her of her aunts,' Flynn said plaintively.

'Then stop treating me like a child.'

'I don't think you're in the least like a child. I'm bowled over,' Flynn said. 'Do you ever get up to London?'

'Occasionally. Shopping and a matinée with Aunt Patsy and Sally, you know.' Lonnie chuckled. 'Sally hates it.'

'Could you maybe do lunch and a theatre with me?'

'I don't know . . . yes, I suppose . . . goodness, it would be exciting,' Lonnie said with a candour Flynn found both refreshing and hopeful. No other boy friends in the offing apparently.

Patsy, applied to by an excited Lonnie and a carefully offhand Flynn, was as hesitant as Lonnie had been at first.

'Perhaps, if Sally came too?' she suggested.

'Sure, why not?' Flynn said with a readiness that disarmed Patsy. 'I'll have a word with her.'

'No, I will,' Lonnie said and without a word being spoken between them Flynn knew that she meant to dissuade her cousin from accepting the invitation.

And Sally was easily persuaded, for at the same wedding, Sally, awkward, hoydenish Sally, who had never previously loved anything with less than four legs, had discovered a man who shared her obsession and their mutual delight in one another prospered all through the summer, distracting Patsy from her watch over her other difficult charge in her delight that Sally, of all people, should have captured Tom's best man, the brother of those two well-behaved cousins, the cousin who would one day be a baronet.

Thank goodness one of her children was doing well for herself. Barbara, of course, was happy with Tom, but Patsy was still dissatisfied that her pretty, ambitious daughter should have made such a lacklustre match.

As for Guy, he was totally unsatisfactory. He had disappointed his father, and only Patsy knew how deeply Edward had felt it, by refusing to take the necessary training to become a veterinary surgeon, nor did he take kindly to his mother's suggestion that he should study estate management, with Miles as his tutor.

'I wouldn't let Miles teach me to ride a bike,' Guy said.

'Don't be silly, darling; you've ridden a bicycle since you were a little boy, and horses, too, when you could. You like an outdoor life in spite of all that mooning over the piano. Surely you can see this is a way you could combine the two? Besides, Miles won't be able to carry on at Firsby Hall for ever and the day will come when Lonnie will need help.'

'Leave Lonnie out of it,' Guy said.

'Yes, but Guy, one has to think about her future. She'll need a man behind her and you've always been such good friends.'

'And always will be, if you'll leave us alone. As for combining running an estate with music . . . ! You don't have the least understanding of the amount of studying I still need to do. I can't do anything else. I've got to give my full mind to it.'

Of course, as Patsy had to admit, he did have talent and naturally they were proud of him when he gained a scholarship to the Royal College of Music, but it was so alien to everything they understood that Patsy still sometimes tried to believe that it was all a mistake and Guy would come to his senses one day.

Only Lonnie really understood the singleminded purpose that drove him, but even Guy's friendship with Lonnie did not always run smoothly. They disagreed about a lot of things, including Flynn.

'He ought not to have come to the wedding,' Guy insisted.

'Why not?' Lonnie demanded. 'If I don't hold what his father did against him then I don't see why anyone else should either.'

'I wasn't thinking of that,' Guy protested, taken aback by the way she flew to Flynn's defence. 'But he did give Babs a bit of a run around and I think it's poor taste to turn up at her wedding.'

It sounded lame, but Guy could not bring himself to voice his suspicions about Flynn's relations with Barbara. In his opinion, Flynn had behaved like a heel, and nothing he had seen of him since had improved Guy's opinion of him.

'If all the young men Barbara has flirted with had stayed at home there'd have been no ushers at the wedding,' Lonnie said. 'I think it was brave of him to come and face us.'

'I'd call it cheek rather than courage.'

'Huh! You're jealous because all the girls fell over themselves to talk to Flynn.'

'He spent more time with you than anyone else and I'm certainly not jealous of that.'

Guy broke off, baffled by his inability to put across to Lonnie the unease he felt at Flynn's reappearance and the way he had monopolised young Lonnie. Without being able to analyse it, he felt inhibited by the way the beauty that had always been latent in Lonnie had started to blossom, so that he was sometimes startled by an unexpected turn of her head or the fine line of her body as she threw up a ball on the tennis court. Other people besides Guy were beginning to be aware of Lonnie, but until Flynn came along she had appeared oblivious to it.

'I suppose Mum will keep an eye on you,' he said, confirming Lonnie's suspicion that it was because of her that he was being so fuddy-duddy over Flynn. She hardly knew whether to be annoyed or flattered.

'You know Aunt Patsy's saving me for you,' she said.

It was an old joke between them, but it no longer seemed as funny as it had once done, and Lonnie, seeing that Guy was not laughing, thought what a pity it was they were growing apart.

Shortly after the wedding Guy had his twenty-first birthday and inherited a small legacy from his paternal grandfather. Instead of doing something sensible with it, or putting it by for his expenses in London in the coming term, he decided to do a walking tour on the Continent and to take the opportunity of visiting Salzburg and Vienna.

'With your left-wing opinions about inherited wealth, don't you think you ought to give it to the poor?' Lonnie taunted him.

'I don't think a hundred pounds will corrupt me,' Guy said. 'Um . . . Lonnie, watch your step while I'm away, won't you?'

'Of course. And if you're thinking about Flynn, don't be such an old woman.'

Guy was suspicious of her airy tone – exactly the way Lonnie always talked when she was up to something – but his mind was irrevocably fixed on his trip to Austria, which he saw as an important step in his musical education, and he told himself that making Lonnie toe the line was women's work, something for his mother and Aunt Margot to handle.

Lonnie went off for her annual visit to Firsby Hall where Margot observed her friendship with Flynn, one might almost have called it a romance if Lonnie had not been so young, with equanimity and a certain malicious amusement. So much for Patsy's plan to marry the girl off to Guy. To Margot, Lonnie was little more than a child, just finding her feet in the grown up world, having her first fling and, since Margot had always liked Flynn, she thought the child was lucky to start her experiments with such a prepossessing young man.

It scarcely crossed Margot's mind that Lonnie might be hurt, nor would it have worried her if it had. The adolescent years were a time of trial, Margot remembered that all too clearly. She had spent them agonising over her lack of opportunity and she had been only three years older than Lonnie when marriage to Patrick Humfrey had set her free. Lonnie had been sheltered, Margot thought, dismissing her baby years as something she must have forgotten by now; Lonnie had been brought up as the privileged child of an affluent environment, with the prospect of a huge inheritance always in front of her. She had been expensively educated and now that she was of an age to go about in the world she never needed to shed tears over shabby clothes nor rub the toes of her satin dancing shoes with stale bread to clean them. Lonnie threw away her laddered silk stockings as carelessly as if they were provided free, she stepped out of her once-worn frocks and underclothes and left them on the floor to be picked up by a maid.

With Barbara out of the way, Guy abroad, Sally and her mother preoccupied with Sally's Bernard, and Margot carelessly complacent, Lonnie was free to meet Flynn as often as she could contrive. The only person who tried to put a brake on the affair was Miles and she had no difficulty in ignoring him.

'Do you think you ought to encourage her to go about with Flynn quite so much?' Miles asked Margot uneasily.

'He'll have to go back to America in a few weeks and it will be all over,' Margot said. 'I really can't treat the affair as anything of tremendous importance. If I forbid Lonnie to see him she'll start thinking of herself as Juliet. Fatal, my dear! No doubt she'll shed a few tears when they have to part, but at her age it will do her no lasting harm.'

'I might agree, if it weren't for the money,' Miles said, by no means reassured. 'Flynn would have a lot to gain by persuading Lonnie to marry him.'

'She can't do that without my consent.'

'Which you wouldn't give, would you?'

'You sound as if you think I might! I suppose it would be one way of getting her off my hands,' Margot said, pretending to consider. 'No, of course, I wouldn't. Seventeen! She has no more idea of what it means to be married than a babe in arms.'

She dismissed the matter, not entirely to Miles' satisfaction, and not, if the truth were told, entirely to Margot's. Until that summer she had thought of Lonnie as a child, but now she had been brought up against the fact that Lonnie was growing into a woman, and an attractive one. Jealousy stirred in Margot. She, too, had once been a lovely young woman. Now she felt herself to be growing old, with a husband younger than herself whose attention sometimes wandered. Not seriously, Miles was too cautious for that, but Margot was no longer as sure of him as she had been when they married, and the uncertainty of holding him to the close, devoted attention she craved made her suspicious of his slightest neglect. She had learnt to bear with his teasing, flirtatious manner with her married friends: when he began to extend it to Lonnie alarm bells rang for Margot. She would not have admitted it, even to herself, but somewhere deep in her subconscious was the feeling that allowing Lonnie's romance with Flynn to develop would show Miles how foolish it would be to compete against a younger, and overwhelmingly attractive, man.

Margot's suppressed jealousy would have amazed Lonnie, who thought of 'Uncle Miles' rather in the light of a grandfather.

'Dear old Miles,' she said to Flynn. 'I'm quite fond of him because he's always been kind to me ever since I was a child, but he is inclined to *pat*.'

Flynn, who had seen the lascivious light in Miles' eyes, was surprised by his own possessive reaction.

'Can't really blame him,' he said, slipping an arm round Lonnie's shoulders. 'You're getting to be so remarkably pretty.'

'Am I?'

Lonnie looked up at him, conscious of a new and intoxicating power. If she looked at Flynn like this, slowly raising her eyes, tilting her head, letting her lips fall slightly open, then Flynn would want to kiss her, just as she wanted to kiss him, all the time, with an overwhelming hunger which drove her to seek more meetings with him than Flynn thought was altogether wise. For Lonnie had totally abandoned herself to the state of being in love. She thought of nothing but Flynn, even when she appeared to be doing something unconnected with him. He was the air she breathed and the food she ate and the time they spent apart had no reality for her. It was only Flynn's caution that stopped her from blurting it all out to Margot.

Flynn had hoped to be invited to stay indefinitely at Firsby Hall, but that was rather more than Margot could bring herself to do, and so he had found an inexpensive hotel on the coast where Lonnie could easily visit him, although Flynn had not yet managed to get her to the point of going up to his bedroom to consummate the love that devoured her.

He had developed an affection for her. She was pretty enough for him to want to make love to her and Lonnie's own breathless response had already carried him a long way towards his goal. What Flynn could not quite make up his mind about was whether to come out into the open and ask Margot's permission to enter into a formal engagement. That he would be allowed to marry Lonnie quite so soon was something he did not expect, but Margot liked him, she appeared to take his pursuit of Lonnie with equanimity and it was possible that she could be persuaded to give her consent, even if it had to be for a later date. Once engaged, Flynn relied on Lonnie's own ardent nature to get them to the altar before she came of age.

When Margot invited him to dinner at Firsby Hall, Flynn took the opportunity of sounding her out. She gave him the opening by remarking, apparently at random, 'It's been so good of you to entertain Lonnie. With Sally preoccupied with her young man and Guy away she might have been at rather a loose end this summer.'

'I'm very attached to her,' Flynn said with caution. 'She's growing into a lovely girl.'

'It's only this summer that I've realised what a responsibility I've got on my hands,' Margot said, and Flynn realised that under the lazy droop of her eyelids she was watching him.

'I'm glad she'll be going away to her finishing school this autumn,' Margot went on. 'They're used to taking care of heiresses. Lonnie won't like it, but her childhood is over and she'll be chaperoned wherever she goes. No fear of fortune-hunting ski instructors or bogus noblemen eloping with any of the girls from *that* establishment.'

'Have you ever thought that perhaps the surest safeguard for Lonnie would be for her to marry young?' Flynn asked.

'Why, yes! A good, steady husband who could look after her business interests would be the ideal solution.'

Margot's agreement was so ready that Flynn was suspicious and, sure enough, she went on, 'But to marry early is one thing, to do it out of the cradle is another. Lonnie is far, far too young to be married yet, Flynn. I've never made any secret of the fact that I've found the responsibility my poor son left me a burden, but I owe it to myself, to the years Patsy and I have spent bringing her up, to allow her to look around the world a little before she commits herself. And when she does, it must be her own decision: I will never give my consent to Lonnie marrying during her minority. At least then she'll never be able to blame me for allowing her to make a mistake.'

He had been warned off. Flynn recognised it and it made him savage. If Lonnie went to Switzerland and he went back to the United States, as he must when his money ran out, then it was all too likely that her infatuation would burn itself out. By the following summer Lonnie would have spent a year in a more sophisticated environment. She might have found another man to love. At the very least she would be likely to recognise her passion for the immature thing it was. She might even come to laugh at it.

Margot had mentioned elopement. Flynn told himself that she had put the idea into his head, but the truth was he had already considered the possibility, had even looked up the marriage laws of England and found them intractable. A pity they were not in America, where several

States were more amenable to early marriage. Scotland? That might be a possibility if he could persuade Lonnie into going into hiding with him.

Margot played into his hands by warning Lonnie against him.

'I hope you're not taking that young man too seriously,' she said one day and because she was uneasy about this new, attractive Lonnie who had emerged from the awkward girl who was no rival for anyone's affections, she spoke more brusquely than she had intended.

It was the moment for Lonnie to declare her love, but remembering Flynn's warning against confiding in Margot, Lonnie merely shrugged and looked sulky, so that Margot was made even more impatient.

'Flynn is a delightful young man and quite the handsomest one I've ever known,' she said deliberately. 'But one does rather wonder how he can manage to spare the time and the money to idle away a summer when he ought to be establishing himself in his career.'

'It's a vacation before he starts a new job,' Lonnie said quickly. 'Everybody needs a holiday, especially when they've been through the sort of terrible experience that Flynn has.'

'Three years ago. No doubt his mother would have benefited too, if he had brought her with him. For all his charm, I shan't be sorry when Flynn decides to go home.'

Margot saw the way Lonnie drooped at the thought of parting with Flynn and added sharply, 'You mustn't allow yourself to be silly about him. Really, you know, you're far too young for that sort of thing. Time enough to think of lovers when your education is finished.'

'I'll be in Switzerland by September,' Lonnie told Flynn in despair. 'Will you come and visit me there, Flynn?'

'Not a chance, darling. I'll have to get back to the States and start job hunting.'

'Take me with you!'

'And get myself jailed for abducting a minor? That's no way for a rising young attorney to establish himself.'

He was laughing, treating lightly what was, to Lonnie, the end of the world.

'You don't understand how much I love you,' she said.

'I do, darling, indeed I do.'

'And you feel the same?'

'Of course.'

He kissed her and Lonnie, clinging to him, whispered, 'We ought to tell everyone, make a fuss, insist on an engagement.'

'We could do more than that,' Flynn said slowly, his hand running gently down the long line of her spine. 'Margot would give her consent fast enough if we could tell her you were pregnant.'

'No!'

Flynn was totally unprepared for the spasm that went through Lonnie. The body that had been so pliant under his hands was rigid.

'That's what happened to my mother! No, no, no! I'm not bringing a baby into the world unless I'm sure it'll have a mother and a father and a real home.'

'But, darling, I'm not going to run out on you,' Flynn protested.

'I know, I know! But I can't, Flynn, I just can't.'

'You're going to have to let me make love to you one of these days,' he said, trying to keep his voice light and teasing, although he was intensely annoyed by the closing of this promising avenue.

'I know, but not until after we're married.'

'You're telling me I ought to be prepared to wait for you. But, honey, time is one thing I don't have. Either we get something fixed up this summer or I go back to the States without you. Who knows when I'll have the time, not to mention the cash, to come over to Europe again? Do you expect me to keep my love alive with nothing to nourish it but letters? If we're parted now we'll grow away from one another. You'll forget me . . .'

'I won't!'

'That's what you think now and, God knows, I'm sure I'll never forget you, but four years is a long time to wait for a little girl to grow up.'

'I'm not a little girl!'

Flynn smiled at the bitter offence in Lonnie's exclamation.

'Then prove it by being a woman and giving yourself to me.'

'I want to – oh, Flynn, I *do* – but you must promise me, promise me faithfully, that there won't be a baby.' Lonnie hesitated. 'I know there are ways, but I can't . . . I don't know anything about them.'

He gave her his promise, but in any case that meeting was not a suitable opportunity to consummate their love and they parted with matters still in what Flynn saw as an unsatisfactory state. She was too darn young, that was the trouble. She was worse than inexperienced, she was positively innocent, and he was pretty sure he was the first man who had ever kissed her, let alone gone any further.

It was Sally, of all people, who provided him with a solution. The fact that he realised that Margot saw the invitation Sally wanted Lonnie to accept as a way of getting her away from his influence looked like the perfect irony.

'Bernard's mother has invited me to go to Scotland with them for the whole of August. You know, the Glorious Twelfth, and all that,' Sally said over the telephone in a happy rush. 'She wants you to come, too, Lonnie. You will, won't you? The thing is, I don't think she's all that pleased with Bernie falling for impecunious old me, and they've got their eye on you for his younger brother. I know he won't be of the slightest interest to you, but it'd make things ever so much easier for me if you'd accept, so you will, won't you, Lonnie, old thing?'

Nothing would have dragged Lonnie away from Sussex if Flynn had not urged her to accept.

'Scotland! Nothing could be more perfect,' he said. 'Would you marry me there, darling, would you?'

'You mean, Gretna Green?' Lonnie asked disbelievingly.

'Not necessarily. Anywhere in Scotland will do, provided we can establish three weeks' residency. Don't you see how perfect it is? There you are, respectably established with a legitimate Scottish address, and all I have to do is book into an hotel. I'll send you word where to join me and before anyone can prevent it we'll be hitched.'

'Oh, Flynn, is it really possible? How *clever* of you to know all that! Darling, yes! Of course I'll marry you, anywhere, any time.'

She was shaking all over as she flung her arms round him, overwhelmed by the realisation that the thing she wanted more than anything else in the world was going to be given to her.

Flynn toyed with the idea of pushing her into anticipating their wedding and decided it might be better tactics to postpone the full physical expression of her love that Lonnie now seemed willing to give him. It would be one in the eye for all the people who were going to query their marriage, perhaps even try to overset it, if he could say that he had preserved Lonnie's virginity until their wedding night. Not that he didn't want her; he did, quite fiercely; and the marriage was going to give him satisfaction in more ways than getting his hands on unlimited wealth.

He had become superstitious about this matter of winning Lonnie. If he could become her husband it would be like getting back his luck. Even if the vast Singleton fortune was withheld until she came of age, it would be there, waiting for them. Flynn believed that he could winkle some, at least, of the income out of her trustees so that they would have something to live on. He had no objection to working, indeed the idea of re-entering his profession with Lonnie's money behind him was welcome. He would set up his own office, take only work that appealed to him, make a name for himself, perhaps go into politics. Everything was possible, but he had to have Lonnie.

On a bright morning at the end of August when there was just a hint of the first mist of autumn in the air, Lonnie walked out of Eidart Lodge wearing the new tweed suit Patsy had thought suitable for her first visit to Scotland, with a matching garnet red jumper and a beret perched on her shining hair. She carried a raincoat over her arm, which might have been thought an unnecessary precaution on what promised to be a fine day, but Lonnie had draped it carefully to conceal the small bag she was also carrying. She had packed her sponge bag, her nightdress, a change of underclothes and a clean blouse, and with that trousseau she went off to marry Flynn.

He had prepared for the ceremony, such as it was, very carefully, making arrangements for the necessary witnesses a full three weeks in advance, giving Lonnie's address as Eidart Lodge, Blair Atholl and booking into a small hotel in Pitlochry where he could be seen to be in residence for the required period. The only thing he was afraid might go wrong was that Lonnie might lose her nerve.

There was no fear of that. Lonnie was keyed up to a high pitch of love and determination. She was going to claim her independence, she was going to shake off all the people who pretended that what they were doing with her life was for her own good: by this one stroke she was going to become an adult woman with the right to a home of her own with the man she loved.

Lonnie had hoped that Flynn would be at Pitlochry Station to meet her, even though they had had to leave the time of her arrival vague because she could not be certain when she would be able to get away without being seen. He was not there and she had to find her own way to the hotel where he had been living.

She enquired for him at the desk and to her nervous sensibility it seemed to Lonnie that the receptionist looked at her curiously.

'Will you be Miss Dunwell?' she asked.

'Er . . . yes,' Lonnie agreed, hesitating because the name sounded strange to her.

110

With the efficiency with which he had organised all the details of their elopement, Flynn had obtained a copy of her birth certificate to prove her age and had ordained that she was to be married as Eleanor Mary Dunwell.

'Your name was never legally changed, you were just called Singleton as a matter of convenience,' he had explained in one of the letters he had written to Lonnie since they had parted. 'Besides, using your real name will put anyone off the scent who comes looking for Lonnie Singleton.'

Lonnie had acquiesced, just as she now followed the receptionist meekly into the lounge where Flynn was waiting for her.

As soon as she saw him all Lonnie's nervousness fell away. He stood up, smiling all over his handsome face, and she dropped her mackintosh, her handbag, her gloves and her overnight bag and ran into his arms, not even noticing that they were not alone until the flash from a camera startled her.

Lonnie pulled away from Flynn and turned her head and the man with the big camera took another picture.

'Flynn . . . ?' Lonnie said, upset by the intrusion into their private moment of reunion.

'It's all right, darling. All part of my plan,' he soothed her. 'D'you still love me?'

'Of course I do.'

'Good. Then collect your belongings together, sweetheart, and we'll get ourselves married.'

'Just like that?'

'Sure. I've got it all arranged.'

Twenty minutes later Lonnie said in dazed disbelief, 'Is that all there is to do?'

'That's right. Just a simple declaration before two witnesses. It's called a marriage *de praesenti* and in this enlightened country it's perfectly legal.'

He left her for a moment to confer with the photographer and another young man.

'Pose for another picture, sweetheart,' he said when he came back.

'Flynn, do we have to? I thought the whole idea was to keep the marriage secret. Who are these people?'

'We need all the proof we can get that we really are married,' Flynn said. 'Come on, do as I say; take my arm and smile prettily.'

Obediently, Lonnie let him draw her arm through his, but although she tried to smile her face was anxious.

'Congratulations, Mrs Branden,' the second young man said. 'How do you feel now that you've married the man you love?'

'Oh . . . delighted, of course,' Lonnie said, totally out of her depth.

'Are you upset that none of your family was present?'

Lonnie's hold on Flynn's arm tightened and she turned to look up at him with a real smile lighting up her face.

'Flynn is all the family I want,' she said.

'Great!' The camera clicked again. 'I think that's all we need. Thanks for your cooperation.'

To Lonnie's relief they went away. 'Were they reporters?' she asked Flynn.

"Fraid so. Don't let it bother you. Like I said, it'll help to make plain that you made your decision to marry me perfectly freely.'

'Of course I did.'

Everyone seemed to take it that they really were married, which was reassuring after the stark little ceremony which had shaken Lonnie.

'I don't really understand why we need extra proof if our marriage is legal,' she admitted.

'In certain circumstances a *de praesenti* marriage might be set aside,' Flynn said with careful precision. 'But it won't be in this case.'

'How can you be so sure?'

He had nothing to go on but a gambler's instinct for probabilities. He knew, with the certainty with which his father had once known that he could make a fortune on the Stock Exchange, that once he and Lonnie were legally tied together none of the people connected with her would be likely to engage in a lengthy legal case to free her. The one thing he still had to do to make sure of her was to consummate the marriage.

Flynn looked at Lonnie speculatively, seeing how strung up she was now that the first excitement had worn off. She was still confused and worried, not entirely convinced that they were married at all.

'We'll have some lunch, and a bottle of champagne,' he said.

It took a little searching before the waitress in the dining room could discover a bottle of champagne.

'We don't get much call for it,' she apologised. Looking at them curiously, she asked, 'Is it a celebration?'

'We just got married,' Flynn said with a smile. 'Will you join us in a glass and toast our future happiness?'

'I will an' all! Here's to you!' She was still full of curiosity. 'Is it a runaway match?' she asked.

'Not exactly,' Flynn said with his easy smile. 'My wife's parents are living in Australia and, as you'll have noticed, I'm American. We hadn't really anyone to ask to our wedding.'

'D'you say so? That's sad. I'm by way of getting wed myself next spring, and we've already counted up forty-eight we'll have to invite, and that's just family.'

'I hope you'll be very happy,' Lonnie said shyly.

'Oh, aye, I dare say we'll make a go of it. Now you'll be wanting your lunch. The soup's good and then I'd recommend the chicken and maybe the apple pie to follow.'

Lonnie thought that she would not be able to eat, but unexpectedly once she had started she found she was hungry.

'No breakfast?' Flynn asked.

'Not much. I couldn't swallow,' Lonnie admitted.

He kept her glass full of champagne until she protested, 'No more! I'll be tipsy. I've only ever had one glass of champagne before and that was at Barbara's wedding.'

'Where we found one another again,' Flynn reminded her. 'Let's drink to that.'

Lonnie lifted her glass and looked at him with the same sweet confidence which had once won her father's heart.

'By this time, if Sally's found my note, everyone will know what we've done,' she said.

'You left a note?' Flynn spoke sharply and a frown replaced the smile with which he had been watching her.

'I know you said I should just walk out, but, Flynn, I couldn't,' Lonnie said. 'They might have been worried and started searching the hills for me. I didn't say where we were staying, only that I was all right and was going to marry you and I was sorry for any inconvenience I had caused Lady Ruthwell.'

The last touch made Flynn smile, in spite of himself. It sounded an odd sort of note for a runaway heiress to have left. All the same, it was a complication he could have done without.

'Were there any other passengers getting on the train when you left Blair Atholl?' he asked.

'Only one. It's a very small station.'

'The first thing they'll do when they read your note is go to the railway station and ask the ticket office clerk if he remembers you,' Flynn pointed out. 'Quite likely he'll be able to tell them where you were going.'

'I didn't think of that,' Lonnie admitted. 'But it doesn't matter, does it? We're married. It's too late for anyone to stop us.'

'Yes . . .'

Flynn wondered whether he should explain his fear that the lack of consummation of the marriage might give Lonnie's trustees just the slightest edge in having it set aside. If they could catch up with them before he could get it done, that is.

'Do you want the apple pie our waitress suggested?' he asked.

'Yes, please.'

He waited while she tucked into apple pie and cream with a schoolgirl appetite, even managed to conceal his impatience and drink a cup of the hotel's atrocious coffee, but when Lonnie told him, with an engaging grin, 'I've had too much to eat and too much wine,' Flynn pushed back his chair and held out his hand.

'What you need is a rest,' he said. 'Come up and see our room.'

Lonnie flushed and if he had not been feeling disgruntled about that unnecessary note, Flynn might have found her confusion delicious.

She went with him willingly, clinging to his arm as they climbed the polished wooden staircase.

'Just as well I've got you to hold on to,' she said. 'I might tumble down. Flynn, do you think I'm drunk?'

'Certainly not. I never let my wives get drunk on their wedding day.'

Lonnie laughed, but inside the bedroom, very conscious that Flynn was turning the key in the lock, she said in a rush, 'Flynn, have you made love to lots of girls?'

'Hundreds,' he said lightly.

'No, seriously. I want to know.'

'Two or three . . . three or four. Don't let it worry you, darling. It's of no importance.'

An unwilling recollection of her cousin Barbara slid into his mind and was dismissed. Barbara was safely married. No need to remember her.

He turned Lonnie round so that he could kiss her and she clung to him, eager and yet nervous.

'Is it going to be now?' she asked. 'I don't know what to do, Flynn.'

'I should hope not, a well brought up young lady like you,' he mocked her, but his teasing was not unkind and Lonnie felt reassured.

'Just leave everything to me,' Flynn said. 'Later on, when you're an old married lady, I'll teach you all the lovely things you can do to please me.'

He undressed her with an easy skill that made light of buttons and hooks, chuckling over the mundane underclothes revealed under the tweed skirt and fine wool jumper.

'When we've got our hands on some money I'll buy you silk undies,' he promised.

When the last garment had fallen to the floor he made her stand back so that he could look at her with the appreciative eye of a connoisseur.

'You've got a lovely, lovely body, Mrs Branden,' he said.

His own clothes were flung off with a rapidity that betrayed his growing impatience. Lonnie's candid gaze faltered, unable to sustain this first sight of a naked man.

'Don't look away,' Flynn said. 'This is me, the way I am, the same as any other man. Look at me, Lonnie.'

Lonnie obeyed him, but her face flamed, and Flynn laughed and went to join her on the big double bed he had booked for just this moment.

He was careful with her, remembering not only her inexperience, but also that over-large meal the dear girl had just scoffed. It would never do to make his young bride sick by plumping himself down on her before she had digested it.

Lonnie, totally carried away by the bliss of being with Flynn and the wonderful sensations his fondling hands aroused in her, would never have credited the degree of calculation that went into her initiation into the joys of sex. Flynn had studied his subject. He had an almost clinical understanding of the way a woman's body responded to his handling. He judged exactly the moment when he could bring Lonnie from a murmuring delight in his caresses to a wide open acceptance of his body entering hers. She cried out and he recognised a note of alarm and momentary pain, but then she clung to him with an urgency that almost matched his own and he forgot caution and thought only of his own overwhelming desire.

When he withdrew from her Flynn was not sure whether Lonnie had reached a proper climax or not. He rather thought not, but he would see to that another time. He himself had been abundantly satisfied and he looked on his marriage with even more complacency than he had before.

Lonnie lay limp and silent and when Flynn touched her

116

face he was not surprised to find that her eyelids were damp.

'All right, sweetheart?' he whispered.

Lonnie's head moved on the pillow, assuring him that all was well with her.

'Oh, Flynn,' she said. 'Flynn, I didn't *know*.'

He laughed, kissing away the traces of tears. 'It's not so good, the first time,' he said. 'It'll get better as you get more used to me.'

'Lovely,' Lonnie said contentedly. 'All the rest of our lives. We're a real married couple now, aren't we?'

'We sure are.'

He pulled the bedclothes over her bare shoulders. 'Have a rest, sweetheart. Who knows, I might find the energy to give you another lesson before we get up.'

'Mm . . . I am sleepy,' Lonnie admitted. 'I hardly slept at all last night.'

With the facility of a young animal she burrowed against him and fell asleep while Flynn lay awake by her side. It had all fallen out just as he had planned. Got you! he thought exultantly. You won't get away from me now, golden girl.

CHAPTER SIX

'I suppose you realise that since Lonnie has married without my consent she has no right to her capital until she's twenty-one?' Margot asked.

'Certainly I do.' Flynn's face expressed nothing but cool goodwill. 'I hope you'll stop thinking of me as a fortune-hunter when I tell you that all I mean to ask for is that a small income should be given to Lonnie so that she can live in reasonable comfort.'

They were all at Firsby Hall – Margot and Miles, Patsy and Edward, Flynn and Lonnie, and George Osbert, looking old and worried.

Patsy had been the first to hear of the runaway match when Sally had rung to tell her about the note Lonnie had left. Now, only two days later, they had descended on Firsby Hall, all of them appalled in various degrees by what Lonnie had done. Margot had preserved her cool demeanour, taking the news of the marriage with a shrug of her shoulders and a caustic comment about Lonnie's inherited tendency to snatch at what she wanted, but inwardly she was raging at the thought that because she had not taken Flynn's pursuit of Lonnie seriously, even though she had suspected him of trying to secure his interest with her to be followed up at a later date, it would be Flynn who would one day take Rupert's place at Firsby Hall.

As for Patsy, she was facing the withdrawal of Lonnie's allowance and, judging by her sour face, it was going to be a most unwelcome loss.

'If you ask me, Lonnie has no idea what she's done,' she said. 'George, are you serious in saying there's no way of upsetting this so-called marriage?'

'You could take it to court, or at least Mrs Bowman could as Lonnie's guardian,' George said wearily. 'My own opinion is that the marriage would stand. The ceremony may seem irregular in our eyes, but it's valid in Scotland and was properly carried out; Flynn doesn't appear to have exerted any undue influence over Lonnie . . .'

'Of course he did,' Patsy exclaimed.

George shook his head. 'She fell in love with him, that's not the same as coercing her, and they spent several weeks apart before she joined him in Pitlochry. Flynn is a young man of good standing and, as far as we know, of good character . . .'

'What about his father?'

'It was never suggested that Flynn knew about his misappropriations. The marriage has been consummated,' George said, taking up his recital of the facts they all knew already. 'And they're both adamant that there was no previous, er, liaison. I'm doubtful whether you could have the marriage overturned, especially since they're not seeking the winding-up of the Singleton Trust.

'You're a man of good sense, George,' Flynn said warmly.

'I've taken into account your own legal training. You'll have foreseen most of the objections that might be raised.'

'I'm not totally on top of the British legal system.'

'You seem to have mastered Scottish law with some success.'

'All this is quite unnecessary,' Lonnie said. 'I love Flynn and he loves me. We're married and we mean to live together. You none of you care for me, not really. Why should it matter to you what I do?'

'I brought you up as if you were one of my own children,' Patsy exclaimed. 'How can you be so heartless?'

Lonnie looked as if she would argue, but Flynn put his hand over hers and she subsided, looking mutinous.

'I think you underestimate our concern for you,' George said with a mildness that made Lonnie feel ashamed of her outburst. 'Mrs Bowman, I think you should accept the *fait accompli*, which will leave the trustees free to agree to pay Lonnie the small income Flynn has suggested.'

There was the tiniest emphasis on the word 'small' which made Flynn's eyes narrow suspiciously, but he was diverted when, after a brief pause, Margot shrugged her shoulders and said, 'Very well. I'll be guided by you. Poor Lonnie, what a singularly incompetent housewife she'll be.'

She might have let it go at that, but Flynn's complacent smile goaded her into saying, 'There's one condition. Lonnie mustn't leave England.'

'No!'

Lonnie and Flynn spoke simultaneously.

'My plan is to go back to the States and establish myself in my profession,' Flynn said.

'I want Flynn to take me to Australia,' Lonnie said.

'*Australia?*' Flynn said incredulously.

'Yes, of course. To see my mother. We've been writing to one another since Gran died. Do you realise I've got *four* brothers and two of them I've never even seen?'

'Half-brothers,' Flynn said.

Lonnie dismissed that with an irritated flap of her hand.

'Family,' she said. 'Real family. I want to get to know them.'

Margot was smiling. 'Rather a facer for you, Flynn,' she said.

'It's out of the question,' Flynn said. 'Sorry, Lonnie, but it can't be thought of for the time being. As for not being allowed to take you to the United States, I must admit I never anticipated that. It means cutting myself off from my profession and from the plans I had for a political career.'

'A future President?' Margot asked, sweetly malicious.

'Why not? At least in America that's a possibility open to anyone,' Flynn retorted. 'George, I appeal to you: is it reasonable to confine us to Britain?'

'Since you've married without Mrs Bowman's consent, she has a right to make conditions. All the same . . . Mrs Bowman, I think you've made this suggestion on the spur of the moment and perhaps you should take time to consider the consequences of preventing Flynn from working for his living.'

In the raw state of her nerves even a hint of opposition made Margot obstinate.

'Lonnie's a mere child and Flynn has hardly shown himself to be trustworthy. I think she should stay in this country where she has friends.'

'The only friend I need is my husband,' Lonnie said.

As she spoke she was struck anew by the wonder of being able to say that. My husband. She turned to Flynn and in spite of the angry scene which was taking place her lips curved in a lovely smile. For a moment they were all silenced by her radiant confidence.

The argument went on, but Margot was immovable and George, for all his attempts to mediate, was secretly in agreement with much of what she said. He was horrified by the predicament in which Lonnie had landed herself. Seventeen years old and married to a man of twenty-nine and a clever, unscrupulous man at that. Far better than anyone else he appreciated the foresight with which Flynn had planned his marriage. There was no way it could be shaken, and who could know what other plans he had made?

To test him, George said carefully, 'Of course, you understand, Lonnie, that there is no reason – and no way we could stop you – why you and Flynn shouldn't live anywhere in the world, provided you are prepared to wait until you're twenty-one to have the benefit of your inheritance. All we can do is refuse to release the capital and insist on re-investing the income until you come of age.'

'But it's so *unfair*!' Lonnie cried. 'Can't I go to Court and get someone with a bit of sense to order you to change your minds?'

'I don't want that,' Flynn said quickly, before George could answer. 'It would make a nasty smell and that might be bad for me in the future. OK, you win. Lonnie and I will make our home in this country. Just as well I like it

121

here, though I'm damned if I know what I'm going to do with myself.'

'You'll have to live on your wife,' Miles said. 'Which is no doubt what you always meant to do.'

'Don't be sarcastic or I might draw comparisons,' Flynn said. 'This situation makes Lonnie's income even more important than I thought it would be. How much will you give her?'

'You could live in reasonable comfort on a thousand a year,' George said.

'Like hell we could! I was expecting more than that even before you decided to cut me off from my own earnings.'

In the end they settled on twice as much as George had first suggested. Lonnie was to be given two thousand pounds a year out of the abundant income that came into the hands of her trustees.

'And we need somewhere to live,' Flynn said. 'If you insist on tying us down in this country then how about providing a roof over our heads?'

'I won't have you at Firsby Hall,' Margot said.

'And I wouldn't come,' Lonnie said. 'Flynn and I must have a house of our own.'

'West Lodge is empty,' Miles suggested.

In the end, Flynn was not entirely dissatisfied. They had secured an income which would enable them to live in modest affluence and a furnished, rent-free cottage in the country, although he had every intention of persuading Lonnie that they needed a *pied-à-terre* in London as well.

'I'll have to find *something* to do,' he pointed out to her. 'I'm not a country boy and I can't sit around watching the wheat grow. There must be something . . . but I'll have to get myself known. What we have to do, sweetheart, is to establish ourselves in London and make a bit of a splash.'

The splash came that weekend when the story of Lonnie's secret wedding was revealed in a Sunday paper. She would not have seen it if Flynn had not ordered a copy to be delivered to the London hotel where they were staying.

He fetched the paper from where it had been left outside their bedroom door and brought it back to spread out over the bed where Lonnie was still curled up half-asleep.

'Very satisfactory,' he said, looking at the pictures displayed on the middle pages.

Lonnie sat up and stared in horror at the photographs of herself, looking startled and, to Lonnie's way of thinking, halfwitted.

'LONNIE'S RUNAWAY MATCH'. said the headlines, and beneath: *'Secret Wedding for Singleton Heiress – "Flynn is all the family I want", Says Newly-wed Child Bride'*.

'Flynn, it's awful! Everyone will see it!'

'Why not? We're not ashamed, are we?'

'No, but . . . ugh! You should have warned me. I wouldn't have spoken to those reporters if I'd known I was going to be quoted all over the *News of the World*. I thought they were from a little local paper.'

'No point in wasting news on a local when a national paper was willing to pay good money for an exclusive.'

He was still poring in apparent pleasure over the pictures which made Lonnie crawl with embarrassment. She stared at his bent, dishevelled head and then said slowly, 'You sold the story of our wedding to the *News of the World*?'

'Sure.' Flynn looked up and caught her look of horror. 'Don't look like that, sweetie. It's paying our hotel bills. I was just about on my uppers until they handed over the cheque.'

For the first time Lonnie felt herself to be out of step with Flynn.

'I suppose we can't feel the same about everything,' she said. 'But I would have thought . . . you must have suffered in the past, just as I did, from publicity.'

She spoke diffidently, knowing that any reminder of his father's terrible death was unwelcome to Flynn. Seeing his unresponsive face, she hurried on, as if she had not meant to refer to that at all. 'I know I was very small, but I still remember being hustled out of the way of press photographers when the story of Rupert's Will came out. Having my picture in the papers still makes me cringe.'

'These reporters were extra witnesses at our wedding,' Flynn reminded her.

'Yes . . . yes, of course,' Lonnie said, but even though she tried to take it as lightly as he did, she was surprised that they felt so differently about something that, to her, tarnished the memory of their wedding day.

'First thing tomorrow we'll start looking for somewhere to live,' Flynn said, apparently oblivious to her reaction.

'We've got somewhere,' Lonnie pointed out. 'The Lodge at Firsby, though I must admit it may need quite a bit of cleaning and decorating before it's fit to live in.'

'That's our country retreat. What we need is a smart little house in town.'

'Can we afford it?'

'Sure! Why not? We're going to enter Society, you and I.'

Lonnie grimaced. 'I wouldn't know where to start.'

'Oh, come on, honey. You must have connections? What about the girls you met at school?'

'Most of them are still not 'out'. They're doing a year at finishing school, like I was supposed to, or going on to train for something. Honestly, Flynn, I hardly know anyone in London, and as for Society . . . that's not my line at all.'

'But it's going to be. What are we going to do with our time if we don't amuse ourselves?'

Lonnie thought about it, an anxious frown on her face. The only thing that had been in her mind when she married Flynn was that they would be together all the time. Vaguely, she had seen a neat house, with herself looking after it and Flynn praising her for the cooking she had still to learn, perhaps a dear little baby, looking just like Flynn, but that was something far into the future.

Faced with the realisation that Flynn had quite other ideas she was not at all sure that she was going to be able to cope.

'I thought you said you'd have to get a job,' she said.

'Yeah. That's why we've got to get ourselves known. I have to admit I never anticipated being tied to this country, but since there's no help for it I mean to make a niche for myself. Who knows, there may be a rich man out there, just looking for a smart private secretary. Or journalism – I could maybe get into that.'

Lonnie's face cleared. 'If it's to help you get established then I can do *anything*,' she said.

'That's my girl!'

They found an amusing little mews cottage in Mayfair within a week. Lonnie thought it poky, but Flynn had learnt enough about London to know that it was a good address, the sort of place the right people would be prepared to visit.

They took it furnished, at a rent that made Lonnie shudder, but Flynn didn't turn a hair.

'Look on it as an investment,' he said. 'Now, the next thing, sweetheart, is to do you over. Those schoolgirl clothes must go.'

Lonnie looked down regretfully at her flowered cotton frock, which she thought very pretty. 'It was new this summer,' she said.

'Lonnie, you're *rich*! You don't have to wear mass produced provincial rags.'

'All right. I'll go to *Derry & Toms* and see if I can find something more grown up.'

Flynn closed his eyes. 'You still haven't got the point. What I'd really like to do is take you to Paris, but since that's not possible you'll have to find out the name of a good couture house in London. And I'll go with you. I know just the image I want for you, and it doesn't include white organdie.'

'Flynn, on two thousand a year . . .'

'Don't worry. Once they know who you are they won't mind letting the bills stand over.'

'George will be cross if I get into debt.'

'George can go . . . hang himself. Sweetheart, they

haven't any power over you any more. I'm in charge now and I know exactly what's right for you.'

It seemed that Flynn knew what was right for him, too, since he went to a Savile Row tailor and ordered three new suits. Almost before she knew what was happening Lonnie found herself doing the round of the autumn dress shows. It was exciting, and she coveted some of the clothes, but it all seemed a far cry from the life she had believed she would be leading, even though Flynn was by her side, interested and critical, and very sure of what she should buy.

The new fashions were kind to Lonnie. With her long legs, slim hips and small breasts, she could wear the sleek lines and longer skirts that had just come in. Flynn made her have her hair cut and waved close to her head and immediately she looked older. She started wearing lipstick, too, and a dash of powder on her nose, which was all her clear complexion and warm colouring required.

Lonnie was pleased that Flynn approved of her new appearance even though inside she knew that she was still the same uncertain creature who had clung to him in their Scottish hotel. To Guy, returning from his walking tour to hear the stunning news of her marriage, she looked like a stranger when she opened the door of the mews cottage.

'Guy!'

The flush of delight, the spontaneous welcome, were the same Lonnie, but although Guy kissed her on the cheek and said, 'I hear I have to congratulate you,' he was shaken by the change in her.

'You're my first visitor,' Lonnie said, seizing him by the hand and leading him into the minute drawing room. 'Isn't this the dearest little house? Flynn is out – what a pity – but I'm so pleased to see you. How nice that I opened the door myself. By tomorrow I'll have a maid – honestly, Guy, I'm terrified at the idea – but, of course, I need some help. I was never terribly good at even *playing* at keeping house, as you'll remember.'

Guy ignored all this chatter. Taking her other hand in

his and making her face him he said, 'Lonnie, why did you do it?'

For a moment it seemed as if Lonnie would pretend not to understand him, then she said, 'Why did I marry Flynn? Goodness, I should have thought you would know! I love him and he loves me and we couldn't face the thought of not being together.'

'But to make a secret of it . . .'

Lonnie took her hands away from his grasp. 'Yes, well, you know what a fuss there would have been if I'd said I was going to marry him. They might have stopped me.'

'Are you happy?'

'Oh, terribly . . . wonderfully happy.'

'Flynn's good to you?'

'Of course! We've only been married a month. We're still on our honeymoon.'

Her colour rose and she avoided his eyes, but Lonnie had an idea that Guy quite understood the intense physical hold Flynn had over her.

'I do love him,' she said.

'I suppose it's all right,' Guy said. 'But I can't help wondering what your grandmother would have said.'

'Oh, Gran would have been full of good advice – and prophecies for the future! She would never have stood in the way of my happiness.'

Guy was looking unconvinced, but then he had no idea of the wonder of being married to someone you loved. At least he had the sense not to say anything more and Lonnie was grateful for that forbearance, after the waves of disapproval that had crashed round her from the rest of the family.

'Would you like some tea?' Lonnie suggested 'I can manage that. Would you believe it, Guy, it never even occurred to me until I was already married that I can't cook. Flynn's been terribly patient and we eat out most of the time though he won't take me anywhere smart until all my new clothes come home. You wouldn't believe how extravagant I've become.'

'I suppose you can afford it,' Guy said.

'Flynn says I can. I say, shall we have tea in the kitchen, as it's just the two of us?'

He followed her down the stairs into the semi-basement kitchen and Lonnie put on the kettle and set out cups and saucers. The tinkle of the spoons against the cups betrayed her nervousness.

'Lonnie, it's only me,' Guy said quietly. 'I'm not going to scold you, or criticise you, even though I don't like the way you've rushed into this marriage. If you're happy then that's all I care about.'

'I know,' Lonnie said, turning away from him to warm the teapot and throw the water down the sink. 'Everyone else was so . . . so scathing, as if they didn't think I knew what I was doing. I wish you'd been at home, Guy.'

'So do I,' Guy said.

'Tell me what you've been doing all the summer. Shall I leave these biscuits in the tin or do you insist on having them set out on a plate?'

'I've been living a gypsy existence and biscuits out of a tin are the height of civilisation to me. I've been tramping all over the place, thinking about what I was going to do with myself.'

'And?'

'I've finished my three years at the Royal College of Music and it's been suggested I should teach, but I've decided against it.'

'Are you going to starve in a garret for the sake of your art?'

'Don't laugh, it's all too likely that I'll do exactly that, but not in a garret, a rather sordid basement. I've fixed it up today.'

'Here in London?'

'Yes, so that I can go on studying with the same teacher.'

'Is Uncle Edward going to give you an allowance?'

Guy hesitated. 'I've got enough left of my grandfather's legacy to keep me going for a few months,' he said, avoiding the question because it was the withdrawal of Lonnie's allowance which his mother insisted made it impossible for Guy to be kept by his family any longer, and his father had seemed to agree.

'I'm going to have to find work,' he went on. 'But I want something casual which will leave me time for lessons and practising.'

'I wish I could help, but setting up house is frightfully expensive and my cash is disappearing fast, even though I thought it was a fortune when we first fixed it up.'

'I wouldn't take your money. It wasn't until I had to listen to Mum complaining about losing the allowance she's been drawing for bringing you up that I realised how much we'd had out of you over the years. It made me feel sick.'

'Don't you feel you had a right to it?'

'Certainly not!'

He knew that he had spoken too sharply for Lonnie to believe him. Of course he had sometimes thought of what it might have been like to be Rupert's heir, but it was not until he had had to face the realisation that Flynn would one day move into Firsby Hall and take the place that might have been his that Guy had felt any serious resentment.

It was better not to indulge in thoughts like that, not with Lonnie watching him with eyes that saw too much. There were times when she was disconcertingly like her gypsy grandmother.

'We'll always be friends, won't we?' Lonnie said.

'Of course. Whatever happens, you can count on me.'

'Not that I need anyone else now that I've got Flynn,' Lonnie said quickly. Her face was wistful for a moment. 'It would have been nice to have had just one person who was really happy about our marriage. Flynn sent his mother a cable and he had a letter from her today. He only read me a little bit of it, so I suspect she's not pleased – probably because he can't go back to America. Margot won't let George part with any of my money unless I'm living in England.'

To Guy it seemed that if Flynn was truly interested only in Lonnie then he would have taken her back to the

United States and lived on his own earnings for a few years, but he made an effort and suppressed that thought.

'You're still very young,' he said cautiously.

'I'm a married woman! By this time tomorrow I'll be an employer. When my maid and my cook come I'm going to be terribly stern with them right from the start so that they'll respect me.'

'You! You'll be taking them cups of tea in bed and begging them not to trouble themselves if they don't feel like doing the chores before the month's out!'

'I won't!'

Lonnie's protest and Guy's laughter masked the sounds of Flynn's return. He came into the kitchen and although he said it was good to see Guy and even accepted a cup of tea and sat down at the kitchen table to drink it, the easy intimacy of the reunion was spoilt. Lonnie looked selfconscious and Guy could see she regretted the biscuit tin and the milk still in its bottle. A few minutes later he said he must go.

'But I mustn't forget to give you this letter from Sally,' he said. 'Did you see the announcement of her engagement in today's *Times*?'

'No! Oh, I'm so pleased. Not that I had any doubts about it after seeing her and Bernard together in Scotland. Have they decided on a date for the wedding?'

'Not until after the New Year. I expect Sally has put it all in her letter.'

He nodded goodbye to Flynn, who did not bother to stir, and Lonnie took him up to the hall.

She lifted her face and once again Guy brushed her cheek with his lips. His hands rested on her shoulders and for a moment his grip tightened. Lonnie stiffened, anticipating that he was going to say something more about her marriage, something she did not want to hear, but Guy turned and went without another word or even a backward glance.

When Lonnie ran back to the kitchen Flynn had cleared the table.

130

'I'll just read Sally's letter and then I'll wash up,' Lonnie said.

Flynn, stowing away the milk, the sugar, the tea and biscuits, said nothing.

Lonnie perched on the edge of the kitchen table and plunged into Sally's untidily scrawled pages.

'*Dear old thing,*

'*Well, as you will have seen, I got my man at last. I'm blissfully happy, but I don't have to tell you about that do I? You rotter, you might have told me what you were up to. Did you think I would give you away?*

'*The wedding is to be in February. Mum was beginning to run round in circles biting her tail about where to hold the reception since a marquee in the garden hardly seemed ideal in the middle of winter. Fortunately, Aunt Margot has suggested moving the whole event to Firsby Hall, which Mum thinks is a wonderful idea. I can't think white satin is exactly my thing, but Mum insists and everyone, including Bernard, seems to expect it so I have given in.*

'*Lonnie, I wanted you to be my bridesmaid or matron of honour or whatever, but I may as well come out in the open and tell you that Momma Ruthwell is still not at all pleased about the way you ran off from Eidart Lodge. Calls it an abuse of hospitality and all that rot. Anyway, I've got to keep on the right side of her so I'm having to fall back on Bernard's sisters. I suggested we could economise and re-use the frocks they had for Barbara's wedding but, as you can imagine, Mum had a fit.*

'*Of course you and Flynn will come to the wedding, won't you? If I'm in London for shopping before that perhaps we can meet and you can give me the low-down on this marriage lark. Bernie has been pressing a preliminary canter on me, but on the whole I think I'll trot up the aisle in my maiden state.*'

'*Love to you and gorgeous Flynn,*

Sally'

'We're invited to the wedding, I hope?' Flynn asked.

'Yes, of course.' Lonnie decided to suppress what Sally had said about not having her as a bridesmaid. 'It's to be at Firsby Hall. If we've got the Lodge into shape by then we could stay for the weekend.'

'We'll make a push to get the place habitable. And you must offer to take in anyone who overflows from the house.' His eyes narrowed as he considered. 'Ask Sally whether her bridegroom or his best man would like us to put them up.'

'All right,' Lonnie agreed. 'Come on, I'll wash and you can wipe. It was nice to see Guy, wasn't it?'

'I suppose so.'

Lonnie touched his cheek with a wet, soapy hand. 'Don't be so disagreeable about it. I know you would have preferred me to find a dainty tray-cloth and serve tea in the drawing room, but it was only Guy. He's made up his mind to stay in London and go on with his music studies.'

'Good for him, if that's what he wants,' Flynn said. 'As long as he doesn't think he can sponge on you.'

'Guy wouldn't do that.'

Seeing that she was displeased, Flynn offered a diversion. 'Do you want to hear my news?'

'Of course. Something nice?'

'I've got a job.'

'Flynn! That's marvellous! Doing what?'

'Research assistant to an American author who's in London to work on a book. He wants information on the way the American and British legal systems have evolved.'

'How grand!'

'It pays peanuts,' Flynn warned her. 'But it's an opening. You see how right I was to insist on going to that cocktail party at the Embassy? That's where I heard about it.'

'You're always right,' Lonnie said, winding her arms round his neck. 'I've got the cleverest husband in the world, and the bestlooking.'

'And I've got the sweetest wife,' Flynn responded. 'This is the way forward for us, sweetheart. This contact could lead to others, but we have to work at it – meet the right people, get invited to the right functions. Incidentally, darling, you really must keep an eye on announcements and not miss things like your cousin's engagement.'

'I'll try,' Lonnie said.

Flynn's new employer was an internationally known writer and he received many invitations. Imperceptibly, Flynn slid into acting as his private secretary, making his telephone calls, accepting and refusing invitations, and somehow it became known that here was a personable man, in Malcolm Sainbrook's confidence, who was fun to have around and an asset at a dinner party. It was a pity he was married; on the other hand, his wife was young, beautiful and rich, and they had made a romantic elopement. They had an intangible quality, a glamour, which lifted a party and made them suddenly fashionable and sought-after.

'I feel like Alice,' Lonnie complained after an exhausting week.

'Alice who?'

'*Through the Looking Glass*. It takes all the running I can do to stay in the same place and to get somewhere else I have to run twice as fast.'

'Poor darling, are you worn out? It's gruelling, I admit, but we've been a hit, Lonnie, a definite hit. How many invitations were there in the mail this morning?'

'Five. Three dinners, a dance and the first night of a new film in aid of charity. How did we ever get on this treadmill?'

Flynn chuckled. 'Influence and our own advantages,' he said. 'I knew that once hostesses got a load of my charm and your beauty they'd want to have us to decorate their parties.'

Lonnie looked at him thoughtfully, seeing that he was genuinely gratified by their social success, and decided not to disillusion him. She saw, with surprise and a touch of indulgent amusement, that Flynn did not really understand the ramifications of English society. The people they were mixing with were bright, charming and amusing, they had money and were bent on enjoying it, but the tactics Flynn was using would never take him into the top strata. She only hoped he would never realise it and become disappointed.

As for Lonnie, the very ease with which they had been accepted made her impatient with her new friends. Not friends, she thought to herself, just acquaintances. Town people, who fluttered about like useless butterflies.

'I'm a peasant at heart,' she said out loud, which, since he had not been following her train of thought, made Flynn laugh.

'A very wealthy peasant,' he said, kissing her.

'A very poor one, as it happens,' Lonnie retorted. 'Flynn, the bills are mounting up horrifically.'

'Put them into some sort of order and I'll decide what we really must pay.'

'No need for that. One thing I can do is keep accounts.'

It was true and it had come as something of a surprise – not a shock, but decidedly a surprise – to Flynn to discover that Lonnie had a very clear idea of her financial situation. The days when she had had to ask him how much her fortune was worth in pounds were long past. She could not be expected to know all the details of the stocks and shares the trustees held for her, but she knew the main holdings and how the companies were doing. When she had once told him that she would rather take an accountancy course than go to a finishing school Lonnie had not been joking. Nor did she allow the household accounts to pass straight through her hands to Flynn, as he had anticipated. Lonnie kept tabs on what they were spending and was unexpectedly methodical in paying her bills. She was proud of her ability to keep her money affairs in order and would have been horrified to know that Flynn found it faintly irritating. Not that he had any idea of cheating her, but he had expected to keep a firm grip on Lonnie's finances, both now and, more importantly, after she came of age.

'Worrying about bills is a bourgeois trait,' he said now.

'I am bourgeois,' Lonnie retorted, laughing because she thought he was joking.

'The shops and tradespeople will give you credit – certainly your dressmaker will. They know there's plenty of money in the background and they'll be paid eventually.'

'A bit hard on them, having to wait. I think we must cut down on these plans of yours for having everything new at the Lodge. I can probably twist dear old George's arm to pay for the decorating and the new bathroom, but honestly, Flynn, the furniture is perfectly usable.'

'Shabby stuff. We wouldn't give it house room back home.'

'It's what people expect in the country. All I mean to do is have the carpets taken up and beaten and the loose covers and curtains cleaned. Once everything's clean and polished you'll be amazed how handsome it'll look.'

Flynn tilted her face up with a careless finger under her chin and kissed the tip of her nose.

'Such a good little housekeeper!' he mocked her. 'Go to Harrods and order everything new, sweetheart. If the Lodge were furnished with real antiques I'd be with you, but that heavy old stuff with no value – throw it out!'

Lonnie did not argue with him, but neither did she obey. The London house, she felt, was very much Flynn's domain, but the Lodge at Firsby was hers, part of the inheritance that would come to her one day, and she would do what she wanted with it.

She went down several times to Firsby, travelling there and back the same day and going out in the evening with Flynn, which proved an exhausting programme. She managed to recruit a couple of village women to do the cleaning, resolutely turning a deaf ear to a sly suggestion that Mrs Dunwell had been known to oblige when needed. Lonnie knew, as Flynn did not apparently realise, that her story was still of intense interest in that small community. She tried not to pay attention to the snippets of conversation she overheard.

' . . . *remember her mother?*'

'Well, o' course! We was at school together. Fancied 'erself, even as a girl.'

And always, someone saying, in wonder and disgust '. . . *all that money*!' Sometimes Lonnie fled back to London feeling as if a layer of skin had been removed from her shrinking body.

The cottage was painted, the ancient plumbing renewed, and, as Lonnie had anticipated, George Osbert agreed to pay for the renovations, but she was too proud to ask for extra help over furnishing the house, even though she was distracted by the amount of money she was spending. The carpets were taken up and floors polished, curtains and covers – good strong cretonne splashed with old-fashioned patterns of roses, very different from the plain modern designs Flynn preferred – were sent for cleaning. Lonnie did buy new mattresses and she had to stock the house with linen, china and cutlery, but everything else was retained and to Flynn's enquiries about how it was all going she returned only vague answers.

Lonnie had hoped that they might have spent their first Christmas together at the Lodge, but the new plumbing was still being installed and she had to forget that idea. Nor did Margot invite them to Firsby Hall. Instead, Patsy decided to stage a reconciliation and asked Lonnie and Flynn to join her family party.

Guy was there, of course, looking rather thinner than he had the last time Lonnie had seen him in October, and preoccupied in a strange way, as if his mind were perpetually elsewhere. Barbara and Tom came too. Barbara kissed Lonnie on the cheek and told her she was quite the wickedest girl alive, which was apparently meant to be a joke, but to Flynn she gave a look in which resentment and jealousy smouldered together, even though she smiled.

Sally was separated from her Bernard until the New Year, apart from lengthy telephone calls twice a day.

'At least it gives us a chance to have a girls' talk together,' she said to Lonnie. 'Come on – tell! Is it really as wonderful as it's made out to be?'

'If you mean making love, it's divine,' Lonnie said.

'You were a perfect beast, running off like that,' Sally told her. 'Mind you, there are times when I wish Bernie and I could do the same. All this fuss. I suppose the bliss at the end will be worth it?'

'Definitely.'

'So you haven't any dire warnings to pass on?'

'No . . .' Lonnie said slowly. 'Except . . . being in bed together isn't the whole of marriage. I suppose it was what I was mostly thinking of when I decided I had to marry Flynn, but it's not that part of it, it's the ordinary living together that's hard to get used to. I mean, always having to think what the other person will be doing so that you can fit in with their plans, and having different habits. Flynn is obsessively tidy and, as you may remember, it's never been one of my good points. He isn't good about getting up in the morning, because he likes staying up late, and I'm the other way round. I start yawning at midnight, when the day is only halfway through for Flynn. You have to adapt,' she finished lamely. 'I'm still learning.'

'I expect old Bernie and I will rub along all right,' Sally said. 'He's always wanted to be a farmer, bless him, and Poppa Ruthwell has been angelic about finding us a place. No difficulty about us getting up in the morning with six o'clock milking to be done.'

Lonnie was not sure that she had conveyed the awkwardness of living in intimacy with someone who was in many ways a stranger. Flynn could still surprise her, and not always pleasantly, but perhaps it would be better not to hint that to Sally.

Meeting Guy in the hall as she went down to dinner on Christmas Eve, Lonnie passed a hand in front of his eyes.

'Come to!' she ordered. 'You're going around looking as if you might fall over the furniture.'

Guy laughed and his abstraction seemed to disperse. 'I've been working on a difficult concerto and it runs in my head most of the time,' he admitted. 'Being deprived of a piano over Christmas is torture.'

'So you have noticed it's Christmas? I thought you'd overlooked it and here I am, your favourite cousin, wearing quite my beautifullest gown, and standing right under the mistletoe.'

She tilted up her face with her old, impudent grin, but to her surprise, instead of accepting her invitation, Guy merely brushed her cheek with his lips in the casual, meaningless way he had often greeted her.

'What's this, flirting with my wife?' Flynn asked as he, too, came down the stairs.

'Not guilty,' Guy said. 'She's flirting with me.'

'She's a baggage,' Flynn agreed, but his eyes were more watchful than his careless words conveyed.

Barbara was just behind him. As Guy and Lonnie went into the dining room she said, 'If it's kissing-under-the-mistletoe time, can I have mine?'

Flynn glanced upwards, but no one else was coming down the stairs. He would have given Barbara the same fleeting caress Guy had bestowed on Lonnie, but she put her hand on his cheek and turned his face towards her.

'Damn you, Flynn, how dared you marry Lonnie?' she whispered.

'You didn't wait for me, darling,' Flynn drawled.

'I would have done if I'd been asked. I hate you, Flynn.'

'It doesn't feel like it,' Flynn said.

His hold on her tightened, she fitted her body against his and they stood locked in a long embrace, which only slackened when a burst of laughter from the dining room broke in on them.

Barbara stirred in Flynn's arms. 'It's not over for you, any more than it is for me,' she said. 'What are we going to do?'

'Nothing,' Flynn said. 'You're reading too much into one kiss.'

'It meant as much to you as it did to me; I could tell.'

'I'll take what's on offer, the same as any man, and, sure, it's exciting to have a goodlooking woman show she finds you attractive, but I've only been married three months and no matter what you may think, I'm well-satisfied with my bargain. Don't throw yourself at me, Barbara. I'm liable to move out of the way and let you fall flat on your face.'

The brutality of it made Barbara gasp. Flynn moved away, towards the laughter and the lighted room, while she stood for a moment quite still in the empty hall and then went over to the looking glass and repaired her lipstick with hands that shook.

CHAPTER SEVEN

Because he had been absorbed in his London life and had
seen no reason to visit West Lodge in the middle of winter,
it was not until Sally's wedding that Flynn realised the
full extent of Lonnie's disobedience to his wishes.

'Lonnie, I'm furious with you,' he said, looking round
the shabby comfort of the Lodge. 'I thought I told you
to get everything new? This isn't a place we can ask people
to.'

'Yes, it is. The sort of people I like will feel at home
here.'

'Darling, I've told you before, you've got to shake off
the past. For a rich young woman you've had a most
unfortunate middle-class upbringing . . .'

'You mean I've never been taught how to spend money.
I don't see any virtue in being profligate.'

'What a word! I'm not suggesting we should have gold
bath taps, but I have a certain image to keep up and this
run-down cottage will be no help.'

'You mean your smart friends won't admire it,' Lonnie
retorted.

'They're your friends, too.'

'They visit my house, they eat my food, they drink my
alcohol – my word, they certainly do that! – but I wouldn't
call any one of them a friend. Flynn, try to understand.
The London house came ready for use. It's a convenient
place to eat and sleep, but I don't have any feeling for it.
I've worked at making West Lodge fit to live in. Such as
it is, I've made it with my own hands. It's my home, the
first I've ever had since I was taken away from my family.
Please try to like it.'

'I wish I could make you see that you set your sights
too low,' Flynn retorted. 'All right, baby, if it's your

140

dream cottage you shall keep it, but don't expect me to pretend I approve.'

He was slightly mollified when he saw that Bernard and his best man took the old chintz-covered furniture for granted, but he was not pleased that their other guest for the weekend was Guy.

'Why him?'

'It was what fitted in best,' Lonnie said, surprised by his antagonism. 'Aunt Patsy is awash with bridesmaids, not to mention Barbara and Tom, and when I went over the guest list with Margot we found that the only way she could put Guy up at the Hall was if he shared with Bernard's old aunt, which we didn't think would suit either of them, so naturally I said we'd be pleased to have him here.'

'You do realise Guy doesn't like me, don't you?'

'This weekend will give him a chance to get to know you better, then he'll be won over.' Lonnie went to him and put her arms round his neck. 'Darling, you're being an old crosspatch,' she said.

She kissed him on the cheek and after a moment Flynn put his arms round her and kissed her with something of the fervour that still made Lonnie go weak at the knees.

Lonnie wore jade green for Sally's wedding, a slim dress and matching coat in fine wool crêpe. The coat had a long scarf at the neck trimmed with silver fox at each end. Lonnie wore it with one length tossed over her shoulder and the other hanging down in front. She had a matching silver fox hat, grey lizard skin shoes and handbag and pale suede gloves. She thought she looked nice, but she did not realise, as Flynn did, that she outshone every other woman in the congregation. Only Margot might once have equalled her in elegance, but Margot was growing older and although she wore her clothes with style she no longer had the upright carriage and springing step which made Lonnie such a pleasure to watch.

The ceremony filled Lonnie with unexpected regret.

White satin might not be entirely becoming to Sally, but the look of beaming delight with which she and Bernard greeted one another as she walked towards him made up for the shortcomings in her appearance. They both spoke their vows firmly and, as she listened to the ancient words, Lonnie remembered her own stark wedding and, for the first time, felt that in some way she had been robbed. It was not that she blamed Flynn, or even that she regretted their marriage, but she did think that perhaps she, too, would have liked to have been married in familiar surroundings, in the church where her grandmother and her mother had been married. But it was her mother's marriage which had started the chain of events which had led to her own clandestine union, so it was better not to think in that way, especially after the letter she had had from Australia.

'. . . . *after all the advantages you've had I didn't expect you to throw yourself away at seventeen. As for your idea of coming to Australia, I can only say it would be better not to attempt it. I'd like to see you, of course, but the truth is, Lonnie, that we've grown too far apart. Joe never speaks about you and my life is here with him and the boys, just as yours is with this Yank you've married. Having a husband to please isn't the same as being single, as you'll discover – not that you ever gave yourself the chance to find out any different, silly girl . . .* '

Lonnie had shed tears over that letter, but Flynn dismissed it with a few careless words.

'You've got me now, sweetheart,' he pointed out. 'No sense in crying for a mother you hardly know. She's got the sense to see there's no tie between you now. Make the break and forget her.'

It was a sensible attitude, but it took no account of Lonnie's feeling of being left out in the cold on an occasion like this wedding reception, when Sally was surrounded by family, both her own and Bernie's.

Sally, her colour unbecomingly high, her wreath of

flowers askew on her head, her satin train caught up over her arm, was no one's idea of bridal elegance, but she was bursting with happiness.

'A dear girl, no doubt, but what a mess!' Flynn's amused voice breathed in Lonnie's ear.

'Sally only agreed to go in for all this fuss to please Aunt Patsy,' Lonnie said. 'Flynn, can we get away soon?'

'We ought to stay a bit longer.'

'I can feel waves of disapproval wafting towards me from Lady Ruthwell.'

'Come and make your peace with her. I've never met her and I'd like to be introduced.'

'Flynn, no!'

Flynn took her by the arm and steered her towards the bridegroom's mother. Even he could not overlook the stiffening of her ramrod back or the way her mouth tightened as he and Lonnie came up to her, but when Lonnie said, in response to a squeeze of her arm from Flynn, 'Lady Ruthwell, m-may I introduce my husband . . .', she did extend two fingers and utter a cold 'How do you do.'

Flynn took her hand firmly in his and smiled. 'You're thinking here's that fortune-hunting Yankee who carried off a girl who was staying in your house,' he said cheerfully. 'Lady Ruthwell, you have every right to feel aggrieved. The only excuse Lonnie and I can offer is that we were very much in love and being kept apart in a way we thought unnecessary.'

He dropped her hand and put his arm round Lonnie's shoulders.

'You have to admit that my girl looks good after more than five months of marriage,' he said. He turned his head to smile down at Lonnie. 'We couldn't be happier, could we, sweetheart?'

'N-no,' Lonnie said, still nervous. 'No, of course not,' she added more decidedly. 'You're a wonderful husband.'

'I'm very glad to hear it,' Lady Ruthwell said. She made an effort and added, 'It was good of you to put up Bernard and David before the wedding.'

'Glad to have been of help,' Flynn said. 'Sally and Lonnie have been like sisters so naturally she wanted to have a hand in the arrangements.'

'Quite,' Lady Ruthwell said. She appeared to catch sight of someone she knew over Flynn's shoulder, and moved away with a murmured excuse.

'Not exactly an enthusiastic response,' Lonnie commented.

'It broke the ice. Next time we meet she'll be more forthcoming.'

'The Ruthwells are very much country people; I doubt whether you'll run across them in town.'

'She's presenting those two bridesmaid sisters at Court this spring. They're bound to have a dance. Could be interesting to get ourselves invited.'

'Flynn, how do you know these things? Considering . . .'

'That I'm an American . . .'

'Yes – you've caught on to the system awfully quickly. I know far less than you do.'

'It goes back to what I've said before, sweetheart: you've been brought up all wrong. You should have been prepared to take your place in the great world instead of being hidden away so that you could grow up to marry the son of the family.'

'Flynn! Do be careful,' Lonnie said, looking round to see if anyone was in earshot.

'Don't worry, no one can hear what I'm saying in this hubbub. Come on, let's circulate.'

Flynn was better at this circulating business than she was, Lonnie acknowledged. Somehow he managed to edge up to people chatting together and insinuate himself into their conversation without giving the impression of intruding. Indeed, people seemed pleased to see him. Of course, he was divinely good-looking. Lucky old me, Lonnie thought complacently. They all think he's gorgeous, but I'm the one he married. He's pleased with me today; he likes the way I look and he likes being here at Firsby Hall. I must make more of an effort to keep up with him.

144

After all, he's entitled to expect a wife who does him credit considering how successful he is himself.

With this thought in her mind Lonnie tried to be more animated and succeeded so well that by the time she came face to face with Barbara she was armoured against her cousin's barbed remarks.

'What an exquisite ensemble,' Barbara said, looking Lonnie up and down. 'Perhaps just a little old, for you?'

'Flynn chose it,' Lonnie said, secure in the knowledge of his approval.

'Oh, of course, if *Flynn* thinks it suitable . . .' Barbara murmured with sarcastic intonation.

'He's awfully good about clothes, though his taste is fearfully expensive, isn't it, Flynn?'

Lonnie turned a smiling face to him as he came and joined them.

'I'm educating you to recognise the best of everything,' he said with an answering smile.

'Lonnie must need a lot of guidance, after marrying straight from school,' Barbara agreed. 'If there's ever anything I can do, Lonnie dear . . .'

'Thank you, while I have Flynn I don't need any other advice,' Lonnie said crisply. 'Flynn, I really think we could leave now. I'm exhausted.'

'You do look a little pale,' Barbara said.

'Yes, well . . .' Lonnie hesitated and then said no more, only looking at Flynn with mute appeal.

'Sally's gone up to change. As soon as she and Bernie have left we'll escape,' he promised her.

Bernie had left on his honeymoon and David, his best man, had departed with the other guests, but Guy was remaining until Sunday afternoon. He wished he had made some other arrangement when he saw how tired Lonnie looked after the wedding, but by the next morning she had recovered.

'I'm longing for some fresh air,' she said. 'Come for a

walk with me, Guy? Flynn has to stay in and do some writing and he'd just as soon have us out of the way.'

It was a frosty morning and every blade of grass stood stiff and white in the slanting rays of the pale sun. A thin mist had risen from the ground and hung over the fields. As they passed a frozen puddle in their path Lonnie stamped on it and shattered the ice into fragments.

'Baby!' Guy remarked. 'How old are you?'

'It's my birthday next week,' Lonnie reminded him. 'I'll be eighteen.'

Guy had nothing to say about that. To him she still seemed pathetically young.

'What's this writing Flynn has to do?' he asked.

'An article,' Lonnie said with deliberate vagueness. 'He's trying to break into journalism.'

It was one of Flynn's ventures with which she was not entirely in sympathy. Flynn was exploiting his entrée into London Society by writing for a gossip column. It made Lonnie uneasy, as if they were going to parties on false pretences. Flynn laughed at her and said that people expected to have their functions written up and even enjoyed it. Lonnie was not so sure.

Lonnie and Guy struck out towards the Downs, Lonnie striding out easily on her long legs, but not above accepting a hand from Guy when the hill became steep and the frozen grass slippery.

When they reached the top of the slope she stopped and exclaimed in pleasure. The mist below them hid the village completely. Only the tops of a few trees showed above it, like islands of vegetation in a vast white lake, which shifted and thinned, and then closed in again.

'We're alone in the world,' she exclaimed dramatically.

'Not quite,' Guy said as a sheep lumbered to its feet and skittered away right in front of him.

'Just us and a few primaeval animals,' Lonnie insisted. 'If we meet a dinosaur will you protect me?'

'Only if it's a very small dinosaur. Like that one there – see?'

A bush, looming up out of the mist, made Lonnie jump.

'Idiot,' she said. 'This is fun and I'd like to go on, but perhaps we should turn round and make for home.'

'Our nice dry cave,' Guy suggested.

'With my caveman in it waiting for me to get him some lunch,' Lonnie said. 'Let's go back through the woods. I'd like to visit the place where Gran's cabin used to be.'

The path in the chalk showed white beneath their feet. They both knew it well enough to follow it almost automatically.

'I must be careful not to slip,' Lonnie said, almost to herself.

The path through the woods was no longer as well trodden as it had been in Thirza's day, but Lonnie led the way without hesitation. The light, filtering through the mist and trees, seemed eerie to Guy and at times he almost lost sight of Lonnie even though she was never more than a few yards ahead of him.

In the clearing where the hut had stood the blackened ruin had long since become overgrown. Nothing remained but a few charred timbers, twined round with brambles which later in the year would put out leaves and conceal them completely.

'I thought I might still feel her here,' Lonnie said in a hushed voice. 'But she's gone. I wanted to tell her . . . Guy, I'm going to have a baby.'

He could think of nothing to say except, 'Are you pleased?'

'Yes, of course. Delighted. And so is Flynn. A bit scared – me, I mean. It's such a . . . a big thing to be happening. I'm not sure I'm ready for it.'

'You will be when it comes.'

'I suppose so. I wish Gran was still here. You won't tell anyone, will you? I don't want it known just yet.'

'I know Mum's a fusspot, but she has had three children of her own. She'll be sympathetic, I'm sure.'

'Yes . . . yes, of course. I'll get around to telling her soon. Margot, too, but not just yet.'

She was not yet eighteen, that was all Guy could think about as he followed Lonnie back through the trees. Not eighteen and going to be a mother. No wonder she was frightened, no wonder he felt once more that protective impulse towards her, just as he had when she was no more than six years old, as if he wanted to put his arms round her, to hold her and comfort her. Little Lonnie, who was married to a man well able to look after her, who needed no help at all from her old friend and ally.

Lonnie's pregnancy gave her little trouble after the first few queasy weeks were over. A little back ache, a certain heaviness in the legs and a strong distaste for late dinners were the only things that bothered her, and the last would have been no problem if she and Flynn had not been overwhelmed by invitations.

Lonnie went about with him until her sixth month and then she went on strike.

'I don't know what it's like in the United States, but people over here don't expect heavily pregnant ladies to go dancing,' she said. 'You go, Flynn. I know it's necessary for your work. I don't mind staying at home, truly I don't.'

The small items in the gossip column had expanded. Flynn was now 'Scorpius' of *Sun Set*, an evening paper launched by a millionaire Flynn had encountered at one of his endless parties. Employing Flynn had been a shrewd move. Flynn had a light touch with words. His column, easy to read, up to the minute, and spiced with malice, was the first thing many people read after the headlines. To begin with his identity had been kept a secret, but it had leaked out and, just as Flynn had once told Lonnie, the fact that he was known to be writing about them did not deter the fashionable world from inviting him to their houses.

He was popular, he verged on being famous, he was fun to have around. Having 'Scorpius' to one's party gave it a certain cachet. Hostesses vied with one another to get him to accept their invitations, and when his young wife retired from the scene they were by no means averse to having the handsome American on his own.

Lonnie was pleased that he was a success. At least, she thought she was. It was not quite the career she had envisaged for Flynn, but she had to agree that it suited his talents and, as he reminded her if she ever mentioned her misgivings, it was her fault that he was marooned in a foreign land and unable to follow his profession.

George Osbert thought that for a man of Flynn's mental capacity it would not have been all that difficult to qualify to practise in England, but he kept that to himself. At least Flynn was working, not sponging on Lonnie, which was what George had expected, and what he earned did help with their expensive way of life.

They began to look for a larger London house, to accommodate the baby and a nurse, and to Lonnie's relief, George arranged for Lonnie's income to be doubled and volunteered a lump sum of five thousand pounds, which enabled her to clear up her debts.

'That's more like it,' Flynn said. 'Still not a fraction of what you're entitled to expect, of course, but it'll tide us over until you can handle your income yourself.'

Lonnie would have liked the baby to be born at West Lodge, but that was something Flynn would not countenance. At his insistence she was booked to go into a smart London nursing home at the first hint of labour pains.

Lonnie often found her evenings lonely, but she remembered that she had given Flynn leave to go out without her and she tried to bear his absence with patience. It was worth it when she woke from her first sleep to feel him getting into bed beside her. His arms would go round her and his low voice would enquire, 'Who's my lovely girl, then?' Flynn rarely got any more response than a sleepy chuckle from Lonnie as she snuggled into his side and drifted back to sleep again, happy to have him with her once more.

Lonnie saw little of Sally or Guy and nothing at all, if she could help it, of Barbara, even though Barbara aspired to be one of the smart set Flynn frequented and was sometimes seen at the same parties. It was a real pleasure to Lonnie to get a telephone call from Sally to say that she and Bernard would be in London for a few nights.

'We must get together,' Sally said. 'The trouble is, we've got boring old family commitments and I've only got Thursday evening free. How about it?'

'I'd say come here, but it's Cook and Mabel's evening off,' Lonnie said. 'Flynn has to be out that night, too, so I'd certainly like some company. Can you face my cooking? I don't really want to go to a restaurant. I'm the size of a house! The baby's due within a month, you know.'

'You must come to us,' Sally said. 'Ma-in-law took a flat for the Season, because she was bringing out the girls. That's all breaking up for the summer and she's already gone off to Scotland, but the lease doesn't run out until the end of July so she's given us the run of it. You must see it! The most ghastly, over-furnished place and more rooms than we've got in our house. We can get a meal sent up from the restaurant in the basement and have a nice, cosy evening catching up on the news, such as that I'm in the same interesting condition as you.'

'Sally! I'm so pleased. What are you hoping for – a filly or a colt?'

'You may think you're the first to make that joke, but you're not. I say, what a pity about Flynn not being able to come. I suppose you have to put up with that quite a lot?'

'Mm . . . it gets a bit wearing, but on the other hand I do have him with me during the day when most husbands are working.'

'He's an amusing old thing, isn't he? I read his account of the Malrons' ball and nearly choked. So . . . we'll see you on Thursday, about seven-thirty?'

Lonnie had a pretty evening outfit which she wore to visit Sally and Bernard, a pleated silk skirt on an elasticated band and a tunic in the same amber-coloured pleated silk floating loosely over the top. Nothing could disguise her advanced pregnancy, but she managed to look graceful

150

in spite of her swollen womb and she held herself with a touching, youthful dignity.

'You look like an Italian madonna,' Sally exclaimed. 'Gosh, I hope I look like that when I'm eight months gone, but I know I'll just be a roly-poly in a flowered smock.'

'The hundred pound dress helps,' Lonnie said. 'I'll pass it on to you, Sally, if you'd like it.'

'Wow! I certainly would! Don't you want to keep it for next time?'

'Let me get over this one first,' Lonnie protested.

She settled down in one of the overstuffed armchairs with an extra cushion at her back, but shook her head at the sherry Bernard was offering her. A small, niggling pain started somewhere inside her and faded away again and Lonnie put it out of her mind, relaxing in the happy-go-lucky atmosphere which always surrounded Sally.

'Guy's coming,' Sally said. 'I thought we might as well have a foursome. What glamorous event is Flynn covering tonight?'

'The first night of a new musical.'

'I didn't know he was a theatre critic.'

'He'll be writing about who's there and what they say about it.'

When Guy arrived Lonnie thought he looked thinner than ever and as preoccupied as he had at Christmas. From the way he tucked into the food it seemed that he was in need of a square meal. Lonnie found that she had a poor appetite that evening. Everything seemed too rich to appeal to her. She pushed the food around her plate, annoyed that she was unable to do it justice and that now, when she was with friends and had the company she had often wished for during the long evenings, she was secretly longing to go home to bed. She shifted uneasily on her chair as the pain she had noticed before struck again.

An hour later, sipping cautiously at a cup of coffee, Lonnie said in a small voice, 'I'm awfully sorry, but I think I'll have to go.'

'Don't you feel well?' Sally said. 'I thought you were rather quiet.'

Lonnie caught her eye and gave a little grimace.

'Lonnie! Not the baby?'

'I don't know – I never had one before. I've had one or two pains, and the last one was . . . noticeable.'

It had had authority, that pain. It announced itself as something to be taken seriously. Not a minor stomach cramp, not a touch of wind, this was the real thing.

'It's nearly a month too early,' she said doubtfully.

'My only experience has been with mares,' Sally said. 'If you're getting regular pains you'd better be on the safe side and consult your doctor. Do you want to ring from here?'

'I'd rather go home,' Lonnie glanced at the clock. 'Flynn might be back by now. I'll collect my things and he can run me round to the nursing home.'

'I'll come with you,' Guy said. 'Bernie, will you rustle up a taxi?'

'Do you want me to come, too?' Sally offered.

'No, honestly, I'll be all right. From what they've told me it'll be hours yet before anything happens. You ring the nursing home for me and tell them I'm on my way.'

In the taxi Lonnie sat pressed into the corner, very still and self-contained.

'You're not afraid, are you?' Guy asked.

'No . . . no, I don't seem to be. Something else seems to have taken over. I'm just standing back and watching. I may feel more involved if it really starts hurting!'

He took her hand in his and they did not speak again until the taxi drew up outside the narrow house in Mayfair.

'There's a light on somewhere,' Guy said. 'Does that mean Flynn is home?'

'I hope so. On the other hand, he could have come in and gone out again. He's inclined to leave the lights on and laughs at me for going round turning them off. Better keep the taxi, just in case.'

The small house had the kitchen and servants' sitting

room in the basement, the entrance hall and dining room on the ground floor together with the staircase which led up to the drawing room and also Lonnie and Flynn's bedroom on the first floor, with two more bedrooms above. Thrown over a chair in the hall was a man's white silk evening scarf and something else which Lonnie walked past without noticing, a black and silver evening wrap which had slithered off the chair on to the floor. Guy thought nothing of it; Lonnie was notoriously careless with her clothes and it would be just like her to fling that costly garment down and forget about it.

There was a light on the stairs and one lamp on in the drawing room. Two empty glasses stood on a low table.

'Flynn must have had someone in for a drink and then gone out,' Lonnie said. 'I was hoping . . . still, he wasn't to know the infant would choose tonight to put in an appearance.'

In spite of the offhand way she spoke, she drooped with disappointment. She wanted Flynn now, she wanted him badly.

Guy's eyes were riveted to something else he had just noticed: a black suede shoe with a very high heel, decorated with a line of rhinestones, and there, by the far end of the sofa, the other one. Surely, even in Lonnie's house, a maid or someone went round picking up discarded clothing?

'Good job we kept the taxi,' Lonnie said, with determined cheerfulness. 'I've got a bag all packed and ready. I'll just pick it up.'

'Tell me where it is and I'll get it,' Guy said.

He was not sure why he spoke so quickly: the beginnings of a sick suspicion, the uneasy feeling that they were not alone in the house, a breath of perfume, someone stirring behind closed doors.

'Don't be silly! I know exactly where it is,' Lonnie said.

As she turned towards the bedroom the door opened and Flynn came out. He was dressed, but Guy noticed the details: he was in his shirtsleeves and he wore no tie:

there were shoes on his feet, but the laces were untied and Flynn was not wearing socks.

'Flynn! You are home!' Lonnie exclaimed joyfully. 'Darling, the baby's started to come. The nursing home will be expecting me by now so I'll just collect my bag and then you can drive me there – unless you'd rather take the taxi we've kept waiting?'

'Sit down, I'll get your suitcase,' Flynn said. 'Are you sure – about the baby? It's not due yet.'

'Due or not, it's decided to come. I'm . . . I'm pretty sure, Flynn. Let's go. I want to be where there are people who understand what's happening.'

She sat down on the sofa and Guy saw with relief that she had still not noticed those telltale shoes. Without looking down he edged the one nearest to him out of sight. Flynn glanced quickly at him and then away again. He realises I know, Guy thought, and he knows I'll do anything to stop Lonnie finding out at this moment.

Flynn turned away and went into the bedroom. Guy tried to believe that he was imagining the white gleam of disturbed sheets, but he noticed how carefully Flynn opened the door, just wide enough to let him through. He shut it behind him, too. Desperately, Guy broke into speech, to hide the possible sound of voices in the other room.

'Are you hoping for a boy or a girl?' he asked.

'I don't mind at all,' Lonnie said. 'Just as long as it's a nice, healthy baby. Guy, it doesn't matter, does it, coming too soon?'

'You're asking *me?*' Guy said, trying to treat it as a joke. 'You're more of an authority than I am. Perhaps you got the date wrong, even though the one thing you used to be good at was arithmetic. When I first saw you at Sally's tonight I thought you were about to give birth to an elephant.'

He kept the chatter going until Lonnie said, 'What can Flynn be doing?'

She stood up and Guy said quickly, 'Perhaps he's changing.'

'Hardly necessary. Even Flynn can't think there's a correct outfit for the expectant father taking his wife to hospital.'

She was laughing, but she was exasperated, too, worried by the delay.

To Guy's relief the bedroom door opened again and Flynn came out with the suitcase. He had pulled a thin sweater on over his shirt, replaced his socks and done up his shoes.

'All set,' he said.

Guy put his hand under Lonnie's elbow and led her out of the room. He thought they were going to get away with it, but at the top of the stairs, Lonnie stopped.

'Smoke,' she said. 'Flynn, I can smell smoke.'

'You're imagining it,' Flynn said. 'Come on, that taxi's still waiting.'

'It's not imagination. I can definitely smell smoke.' Lonnie sniffed. 'Funny smoke,' she said doubtfully. 'Guy, you can smell it, too, can't you?'

He could not only smell it, he could identify it as the aroma of a Turkish cigarette.

'No,' he said.

'The house may be on fire,' Lonnie said.

She turned back and, before either of them could stop her, she threw open the door of the bedroom.

It was Barbara. That, for Guy, was the ultimate horror. She had begun to dress and she was sitting on the side of the bed wearing a black brassière and knickers, pulling on fine black stockings. On a bedside table a Turkish cigarette smouldered in a little glass dish.

It took a few moments for realisation to hit Lonnie. She looked from Barbara to Flynn and back again and all the time the tension grew until the air seemed to vibrate.

'No,' Lonnie said at last. 'No, no, no!'

She turned to Flynn and flung out her hands. 'Not Barbara, Flynn,' she said. 'Not Barbara!'

Flynn dropped the suitcase he had been carrying and tried to take hold of her, but Lonnie struck out wildly at his hand.

'No,' she kept repeating. '*No, no, no!*'

'Lonnie . . . sweetheart, I can explain,' Flynn was saying all through her desperate repetition of denial.

Lonnie doubled up, her hands clasped over her stomach, and screamed.

CHAPTER EIGHT

She was being split in two. There was nothing in the world but pain and, far beyond the striving of her body, the agony in her mind lay in wait, ready for the moment when she would be still and it could strike again.

'Flynn . . .' she said, not because she wanted him, as the nurses thought, but trying out his name to see if it would conjure up the man she believed she had married and wipe out the image of the stranger who had betrayed her.

'You can see your husband soon,' they told her. 'Not long to go now. You're doing very well, Mrs Branden. Don't tense up again. Relax, relax . . .'

They had thought her hysterical when she had first arrived at the nursing home and had spoken to her not unkindly, but bracingly.

' . . . *very young*,' she had heard one of the nurses breathe to another, as if to excuse the state in which their latest patient had arrived.

' . . . *spoilt darling*,' came the half-heard answer.

They were indulgent towards her, as if to a child, allowing Flynn in to see her and then misunderstanding the reason why she turned from him in horror.

'You'll feel differently when you're holding your lovely baby,' they assured her. 'No point in blaming your husband is there? Be brave, it'll soon be over.'

It did not seem soon to Lonnie, but her labour was neither protracted nor complicated. If it had not been for the anguish in her mind she might almost have agreed when she was told that she was 'a very lucky girl'.

Rosemary Thirza, her names long since decided, was born at a quarter past seven the next morning.

'Just in time for breakfast,' the nurse said brightly. 'A

lovely little girl, Mrs Branden. Congratulations! Seven pounds five ounces, a very nice weight.'

Lonnie was the only patient she had ever had who did not ask, 'Is she all right?' Indeed, she said nothing and made no move to see the child. It was not until the tiny body was laid down beside her in the crook of her arm that Lonnie looked at her daughter in amazement and disbelief and was stricken by a wave of helpless love. The tiny round head with its fringe of damp hair, the little red face, eyes screwed tightly shut and mouth pursed in disapproval, the small burrowing movement the baby made, as if trying to get back to the warm familiar world it had left, all these were as wonderful to Lonnie as if this was the first baby ever born.

Tears began to run down her face. She gathered the little body closer. She was no longer a girl but a woman with responsibility for another life, and Lonnie knew one thing with a clarity that hurt: whatever Flynn might have done, the baby must not suffer.

By the time Flynn came in to see her Lonnie was composed. He hesitated in the doorway, unshaven and haggard, and still wearing the sweater and evening trousers from the night before.

'Have you been here all night?' Lonnie asked, in a voice that came out in a thin, exhausted whisper.

'They sent me away, but I didn't go to bed.'

'We've got a daughter. Did they tell you?'

She smoothed back a fold of blanket and Flynn looked down at his child.

'She's . . . so little,' he said.

'She's perfect.'

'And you? Are you all right?'

'Very tired. Too tired to talk.'

'Darling . . . I love you, truly I do.'

'Not now,' Lonnie said, closing her eyes. 'Later.'

He sent her flowers, a huge bouquet of red roses, which Lonnie looked at without any expression at all on her face. Sally came, too, with more flowers, exuberant in her congratulations and demanding to be told what it had been like.

'Absolutely ghastly,' Lonnie said. 'But worth it afterwards, just like everyone keeps telling you. You'll sail through it.'

She was amazed to hear herself, talking quite normally, laughing, even joking, just as if her entire world had not come to an end. Except for the baby. She could build a new life on her.

When Flynn returned Lonnie was sitting up, wearing a pink satin bed jacket, her hair tied back with a pink chiffon scarf. She looked like a young queen, beautiful and pitiless.

To Flynn, who had always thought he could manage Lonnie, her stillness was intimidating. As he hurried into speech he realised that Lonnie sensed his nervousness and possibly despised him for it, if she felt anything at all behind the white mask of her face.

He had thought out what he would say, but because she had thrown him off-balance it came out rushed and unconvincing.

'Lonnie, there's only one thing I want to tell you . . . I love you, I've always loved you. A moment's madness . . . a sudden temptation . . .'

'I expect you're going to say Barbara threw herself at you,' Lonnie said. 'I can believe that. What I still can't take in is that you took her back to our house and made love to her in our bedroom, on our bed. Did you plan it in advance?'

'No! I've told you . . .'

'I think you did. It was a convenient opportunity, wasn't it? The house was empty, I was out of the way. You saw a chance to enjoy your mistress, and took it.'

'No! It was a mistake to invite Barbara back for a drink, I admit that . . .'

'It certainly wasn't wise to leave the way open for her to make advances to you, considering we both know she was once in love with you and has shown that she's still jealous of you. You must have known that she'd expect

159

something to come of an invitation like that. You could have resisted, of course, but you didn't. I doubt whether you ever intended to. You don't do much without calculating the outcome first, Flynn. Including marrying me.'

'Lonnie, I swear . . .'

'Let's be honest,' Lonnie said with the detachment she had shown ever since he had arrived. 'You married me because I'm rich, or will be one day. Perhaps you were in love with me, to some extent at least. You've enjoyed making love to me – you couldn't have faked that – but I was always too young and unsophisticated for you.'

'I adored your innocence.'

'I was ignorant. An untried girl, straight from school. Why is it that I can see now that if you'd really loved me you would have waited?'

'Circumstances were against us,' Flynn said helplessly. 'Lonnie, you loved me, too.'

'Yes, I did.' Lonnie paused, looking puzzled. 'I don't seem to feel anything now, nothing at all. I feel empty. It's not just having the baby. Everything has gone out of me. I look at you and I see a stranger.'

'I'm still your husband. If you'll let me, I'll spend the rest of my life proving to you that this one slip was nothing but a moment's foolishness. Damn it, Lonnie, any other man might have done the same, given the opportunity. It's not nice, I know, but it's true.'

'I only have your word for that. I've got no experience to go on.'

'Believe me, please believe me, I never meant you to be hurt.'

'No? No, perhaps not. What I didn't know couldn't harm me. Except that it did, Flynn, it did. We've been married less than a year, but over the last few months the knowledge has been creeping nearer and nearer to me that we were not well-suited. I thought the faults were all on my side, that I had to grow up to your level, but perhaps there was always an element of deceit spoiling what should have been between us.'

'I was never unfaithful to you! I swear it.'

160

'It was your motive for marrying me I was thinking about.'

'We are suited to one another, Lonnie,' Flynn said, shying away from that. 'I've been proud of you.'

'In some ways I did come up to expectations,' Lonnie agreed.

'What are you going to do?' Flynn asked. Nothing had turned out as he had expected. He had come braced for tears and recriminations, but Lonnie's cold detachment mystified him.

'There's a new person to be considered,' Lonnie said. 'You've hardly looked at your daughter. Everything I do from now must be for her benefit.'

'Yes, of course,' Flynn said eagerly. 'Darling, we must stay together.'

'I want a proper family life for her, with a mother and a father and a settled home.'

'That's what we'll give her!'

'When I leave here I'll take Rosemary down to West Lodge.'

'With the nurse,' Flynn said.

'Yes . . . I suppose I'll need the nurse,' Lonnie said doubtfully. 'I know so little . . . I'll stay there for a time. No one will think that strange. You can come and visit us. We'll have separate bedrooms . . .'

'No!'

'Yes. Perhaps one day I might be able to bear you to touch me again, but not yet, Flynn, not yet.'

Her composure lasted until he had left her, but then Lonnie leaned back against her pillows and the tears ran down her face in a constant stream and her body was shaken with sobs, so that she gasped for breath. Now that it was over she knew that she had still been hoping for a miracle, for Flynn to be restored to her unblemished, once again the adored, unquestioned lover she had married.

She would stay with him, that was a firm decision, and not only because of her baby, but also because Lonnie could not bear to admit that all the people who had warned her against Flynn had been right. The idea of Patsy and

Margot saying 'we told you so' made her double up in shame. Twenty-four hours ago she would have defended Flynn against the world, now she had to live with the humiliation of knowing that she had been wrong. How could she have made such a terrible mistake? She had been dazzled by an accomplished charmer, helplessly in thrall to his physical attraction, and Flynn had exploited her infatuation.

Always, at the back of her mind, pushed away and unacknowledged, she had known that there was something wrong, ever since the day of their marriage. It had all been false – the running away, the careful planning, the reporters and the sale of their story to the *News of the World*. If Flynn had not been such a perfect lover she would have been angry about that, but he had always known how to get round her. Looking back, Lonnie shuddered at the times she had lain in Flynn's arms and stifled some justified complaint about his conduct or extravagance because she was overcome by the exquisite pleasure of his lovemaking.

Surely he could not have been pretending? But even as she had that consoling thought, Lonnie knew that Flynn's enjoyment of her body had been something quite separate from his equally strong determination to enjoy her money. She had been wrong about him. Right from the beginning she had been wrong, and she did not know how she was going to live with the consequences of her mistake.

Guy came towards evening. He looked almost as tired as Lonnie was beginning to feel. It was not easy to face him, knowing that he knew. It was Guy who had bundled Lonnie out of the house and into the waiting taxi, away from the scene that had wrecked her happiness.

'You were good to me last night,' Lonnie said stiffly. 'I'm grateful.'

Guy shrugged. 'Glad to know you were safely delivered. A girl, I hear.'

'Yes.'

With an effort he said, 'Lonnie, I have to know what you're going to do.'

162

'Did Barbara send you?'

'I've seen her, yes. So far I've managed to stop her from plunging into a mad confession to Tom.'

'You can tell Barbara that, no matter how much she may be hoping for it, there'll be no divorce. Flynn and I will stay together.'

'You've forgiven him?'

'I don't think I can ever forgive him. All the same, we're not splitting up.'

She was puzzled by Guy's despondency. He sat with his elbows on his knees, his hands clasped in front of him, his head bent, as if something weighed on him too heavily to allow him to look up.

'A clean break now . . .' he said in a low voice.

'No! I have to stay with Flynn so that our baby can have a settled home. Everyone thinks I've forgotten my own childhood, but I remember, Guy, oh, yes! I remember. She's going to grow up with a father and a mother.'

'Does your own happiness count for nothing?'

'Happiness?' Lonnie said, as if it were something she had only vaguely heard about. 'I'll be all right. Flynn knows how I feel. He'll go along with it.'

'I'm sure he will!' As if it were forced out of him, Guy said, 'You say you'll stay together. Does that mean you'll be living as man and wife?'

'No. I couldn't.'

'You can't live like that. Neither can Flynn.' For the first time he lifted his head and looked at her properly. 'Face facts, Lonnie . . .'

'I've done plenty of that since yesterday.'

'I've got nothing to say in Flynn's favour,' Guy said doggedly. 'In fact, I hate his guts. Barbara is my sister, after all. But you can't expect him to live in your house and be a father to your baby and not a husband to you. He'll be unfaithful and the whole messy business will start again.'

Lonnie's implacable resolve faltered. 'It's the way I feel,' she said uncertainly.

'Suppose you fall in love with someone else?'

'No! Never again!' A shiver of distaste passed over her. 'I can't imagine wanting any man to touch me again in that way – ever.'

'I daresay a good many women feel like that twelve hours after giving birth,' Guy said with a touch of humour. 'Not to mention the shock you've had.' He got up to go. 'I'm surprised you haven't told me it's none of my business.'

'I wouldn't do that because you're the only person who talks sense to me. Do you really think I should take Flynn back?'

'No. I think you should bring the whole thing out in the open and divorce him. I'd give evidence and be damned to Barbara.'

'I've told you why I can't do that. The baby . . .' Lonnie looked away from him and added in a whisper, 'The humiliation.'

'I don't like Flynn; I never have. The thought of you as his wife disgusts me. But, Lonnie, which ever way you decide to act, you're going to have to be wholehearted about it. Either a complete break or a complete reconciliation. Don't deceive yourself into thinking halfway measures will work.'

Once again tears gathered in Lonnie's eyes, but these were tears of weakness and exhaustion, not the sobs which had shaken her earlier.

'I don't know what to do,' she whispered. 'Guy, don't be hard on me. I'm so unhappy.'

Guy sat down on the edge of the bed and put his arm round her.

'My dear, sweet girl,' he said. 'I should be shot, laying down the law to you at a time like this. Concentrate on getting strong. You can grapple with other problems when you're on your feet again.'

For one moment Lonnie allowed herself the luxury of leaning against his familiar strength, then she straightened up.

'I know what you say is meant for the best,' she said. 'You've always been the one I could turn to when I needed help. You're right, at the moment I'm too worn out to make sense. All I know is that I've already told Flynn I won't divorce him and I mean to stick to that.'

CHAPTER NINE

It seemed strange to everyone who knew her that Lonnie made such a slow recovery from childbirth. Everyone, that is, but the three people who were aware of the shock she had received on the night she went into labour.

She stayed in the nursing home for a fortnight and then went down to Cogsdene with her baby and the highly-trained young woman who was to stay with her for the first few months.

'I wish you'd stay longer,' Lonnie said wistfully.

'You knew when you engaged me that six months was my limit, Mrs Branden,' the nurse pointed out. 'I special-ise in very young babies and I already have a booking for the New Year.'

'I was lucky you were free to come to me when Rose-mary decided to put in an early appearance.'

'Yes, indeed. And the same thing might happen with my next mother, so you'll have to be prepared to replace me by Christmas.'

'I'd like to look after her myself,' Lonnie said.

'You could, of course,' the nurse agreed, but she guessed from the way Lonnie sighed and shook her head that it was not a very likely solution.

There was something odd about the whole set-up: the young mother alone in the country, the husband in town. Nurse Philips liked her employer, but this isolation was not what she had expected when she took on the job. She had thought she would be based in central London, within easy reach of shops and cinemas, able to meet her friends in similar positions, not marooned in a small cottage on a country estate, and Mrs Branden's explanation that because of the baby's early arrival the new London house was not ready did not ring quite true.

Days passed without anyone calling. There was a snooty

166

woman up at the big house who had come to tea one day and Mrs Branden had taken the child up to the house for a return visit. Mr Branden sometimes came down for the weekend, but during the week they were alone and time hung heavy on their hands. Surely it was not going to continue like this for the whole of her six months' engagement?

It was a relief when Mrs Branden roused herself to suggest a trip to the coast. There was a car, it seemed, which could be had for the asking, and a chauffeur who would take them anywhere they wanted to go. While the summer weather lasted they visited Brighton and Eastbourne and all the resorts within easy reach on the south coast. All the same, it was not a lively existence.

Nurse Philips was particularly disappointed over the christening. She had attended so many that she ought to have been blasé about them, but she secretly looked forward to this first event in the lives of 'her' babies. It usually meant a party, dressing the baby up in a beautiful robe, being congratulated on the progress the child was making in her care, champagne and meeting interesting people. Nurse Philips took care to stay in the background, but it was rare for her not to be invited to the reception, even if it was only to take charge of the baby when the mother grew tired of the burden. She dearly liked a title and people who were in the news. So far the engagement with the Brandens had been a sore disappointment, even though Mrs Branden was said to be worth a fortune and Mr Branden was well-known for writing for the newspapers.

It was Lonnie's fault that her daughter's christening was so quiet. She spoke to Flynn about it one day after she had been at West Lodge for some six weeks.

'The Vicar called yesterday,' she said. 'He wanted to know whether Rosemary would be christened here. I said she would. We've fixed it for the second Sunday in September. I hope that's all right with you?'

'Well . . . yes, of course, if that's what you want,' Flynn said. 'What about godparents?'

167

'Sally and Bernard and a girl who was at school with me who happens to live nearby. Unless you have any other ideas?'

'No – I hadn't thought about it,' Flynn confessed. 'What about the other guests?'

'We'll have to ask Aunt Patsy and Uncle Edward, I suppose. Margot and Miles. Guy if he can get away.'

The unspoken name hung in the air between them.

'A few friends?' Flynn asked.

'No one else. If you're thinking of a large party up at the Hall, then you can forget it. They can come back here for a drink and a sandwich and with any luck it'll all be over before Rosemary's six o'clock feed is due.'

It seemed to Lonnie that Flynn was hesitating on the verge of mentioning another date which would normally have called for celebration: their wedding anniversary. A year ago, almost to the day, she had slipped away to join him. Looking back, Lonnie saw the girl she had been at that time as little more than a child, and a silly, headstrong one at that. She had come a long way since then. The lovely spontaneity of her love for Flynn had gone forever and she still had to come to terms with her decision to go on living with him. Lonnie had no intention of mentioning the wedding anniversary and she hoped that Flynn would see how unwelcome a reminder from him would be. The moment passed, Flynn said nothing, and Lonnie had the feeling of having won a small victory, of having imposed her will without a word being said.

Since Flynn took charge of the arrangements for the christening, his daughter's health was toasted in champagne, the sandwiches were smoked salmon and there was a beautiful iced cake. All the same, only the people Lonnie had named were present and Nurse Philips thought it a very disappointing party.

Everyone left early, as Lonnie had hoped, but that meant that the evening stretched emptily in front of her and Flynn. It was fine and warm and Flynn went out and sat on a wooden seat in the small garden with a final glass of champagne in his hand while Lonnie was inside seeing to the baby.

When Lonnie came out to join him he moved up to make room for her without saying anything.

'Rosemary's fretful,' Lonnie said. 'I think the excitement bewildered her.'

Flynn did not reply and they sat in silence for some time while the sun began to move towards the horizon.

'Are you hungry?' Lonnie asked. Flynn shook his head. 'There's cold meat and salad when you're ready for it. I don't want anything myself.'

Flynn twisted the stem of his glass round and round in his fingers. 'Lonnie, when are you coming back to London?' he asked.

When Lonnie did not reply, he went on, 'The baby's two months old. Summer's nearly over. We're inundated with invitations. What am I to tell everyone?'

'Tell them I'm feeding Rosemary myself and can't accept any invitations that keep me away from her.'

'That's an excuse for not going out, but it doesn't explain why you don't come back to London.'

'Does it need explaining?'

Flynn let that pass. 'I've moved into the new house,' he persisted. 'You haven't even seen it since it's been redecorated. Surely it would be far more convenient to install Rosemary in a proper nursery than to keep her in this poky cottage.'

'I suppose going back to a different house might make it easier,' Lonnie said. 'I couldn't face seeing *that* room again.'

Under her clear, disenchanted gaze Flynn's assurance faltered and he had to look away. 'Am I never to be forgiven?' he said. 'I've told you I'm sorry. I've tried to show you how bad I feel about having hurt you. Couldn't you manage to be a bit more generous, Lonnie?'

'Have I been ungenerous? I was worse than hurt, Flynn; I was terribly wounded. It was like having an amputation and the stump left to bleed.'

'I wish I could make you see that to me it was just a trivial incident,' Flynn said helplessly.

'Oh, don't, don't!' Lonnie said, flinching away from him as if he had hit her. 'Why can't you understand that that's what makes it so terrible to me? You didn't care – not for me nor for Barbara. When temptation was laid out in front of you, you just helped yourself, like a greedy child in a sweetshop.'

'I wish I'd never started this,' Flynn said. 'I thought we'd reached a point where you could discuss it rationally. How much longer do you need? It's useless for you to come to London if we're going to quarrel.'

'I've made up my mind that I'll pick up my life again, and I will. Give me until the end of the month and then I'll pack up here and join you in London.'

'On what terms?'

'We'll see how I feel about that when the time comes.'

'Will you sleep with me tonight?'

'No.'

Her cool finality defeated Flynn. Lonnie watched him as he walked away from her, into the house. Nurse Philips met him at the door and he paused to speak to her. Lonnie noticed the young nurse's pleased look, the way she smiled, and the way she turned her head to look after Flynn as he went past her into the house. He was still the overwhelmingly attractive man she had married, but when Lonnie looked at him she felt nothing, not even anger. The distress that had welled up in her while they had been talking drained away. She felt apathetic, without strength, just as she did most of the time these days. Nothing seemed worth doing, except cherishing Rosemary. Only with her did Lonnie still feel like a real person. With everyone else she felt transparent, as if she might fade away and never be missed.

Going back to a different house did help. It was more spacious and airy than the little Mayfair mews. Nurse Philips clearly approved of Rosemary's nursery and her own room next door. Far more the sort of setting she was used to, and there was nothing like a spell in the country to make you appreciate the lights and shops of London. She, at least, was delighted with the move to Chelsea.

'It's going to be expensive to run,' Lonnie said, looking at some of the bills that had accumulated.

'I settled what I could,' Flynn said and Lonnie, with the acute ear she had developed for the inflexions in his voice, noticed that he spoke defensively whereas in the past he would have laughed at her preoccupation with accounts.

That slight hint of weakening in Flynn's position pushed her into making a suggestion she had been thinking about ever since their talk after Rosemary's christening.

'I haven't seen a paper for weeks. Is your column still flourishing?' she asked.

'Very much so. It's not the career I had mapped out for myself . . .'

'No,' Lonnie agreed. 'I don't really like it, Flynn.'

'It serves its purpose. It amuses me and it pays quite well. It gives me a certain satisfaction . . .'

'Power.'

'You could be right about that. Power to make or mar a reputation - but only a trivial reputation. I do no real harm.'

'Except to yourself.' Lonnie leaned her chin on her linked hands and looked at him very levelly. 'Chuck it up and take me and the baby off to the States.'

'But, Lonnie . . .'

'They can't stop me inheriting when I'm twenty-one. Surely we could survive for the next two and a half years?'

'We might manage. Is that what you want? To "manage" on a restricted income in small-town America when we could be enjoying a good time here?'

'Depends on your idea of a good time.'

'I meet a lot of interesting people,' Flynn said. 'Not just the rich and titled, but people who are talented and amusing. I can drop in to see Mary Ellis in her dressing

171

room, I know Owen Nayres, Noël Coward, Jack Buchanan – and not just theatre people – politicians, writers, everyone who counts.'

'People like that make me feel young and ignorant,' Lonnie objected.

'You'll never learn to hold your own if you don't get out and about. Sweetheart, you've got a lot on your side. You're young, lovely . . .'

'Rich.'

'That, too. It counts, but the people I'd really like to see you mixing with appreciate wit and amusement even more.'

'I'll brush up on my repartee,' Lonnie said. She spoke drily, but it was the nearest she had yet come to admitting that she would start accompanying Flynn on his social round once more and he was heartened.

'It was our wedding anniversary three weeks ago and we neither of us took any notice of it,' he said abruptly.

'I remembered.'

'So did I, but I didn't dare do anything about it. You were so unyielding. Now that you've thawed a bit I'd like to give you the present I had for you.'

Lonnie took the jeweller's box he held out to her and looked in silence at the pair of ruby and diamond clips inside.

'They're beautiful,' she said at last. 'And very smart.'

She walked over to the looking glass above the fireplace and tried the effect of the clips at the neckline of her dress.

'Not what I could wear with this frock, but with something plain and dark they'll look stunning. Thank you.'

As she put the clips back in the box she said, without looking up, 'I haven't got anything for you.'

Flynn was sufficiently encouraged to put his hands lightly on her shoulders and hold her.

'There's only one thing I want,' he said. He felt her stiffen and let his hands drop. 'It seems I'm not going to get it,' he said. 'Lonnie, only a year ago you loved me enough to trust me . . .'

'Now I don't trust you enough to love you.'

'Don't play with words. You do love me. Good God, it can't have disappeared just like that! You won't allow yourself to admit it, that's all.'

'I made you an offer just now and you dismissed it without a moment's thought. I said I'd go to America with you, Flynn.'

'That's not what I want to do. I'll go back, sure, one day, but not as a struggling attorney. I want to be accepted by the upper crust, just as I have been here, and in the States that means you have to have money. When I take you to my country, honey, I want you to have the entrée to the sort of society you're accustomed to.'

'Vets and farmers and country squires. My grandmother was a gypsy and my mother was a lady's maid – have you forgotten that? Flynn, I don't belong in high society.'

'You could, if you'd only make the effort.'

'If I wanted to make the effort,' Lonnie said in a low voice. 'It all boils down to the same thing in the end, doesn't it? I have to adapt to please you, not the other way round. I thought you'd made such a sacrifice, staying in England to be with me, but it seems it was what you hankered for all along.'

'Every time we talk we reach an impasse,' Flynn said, and because he sounded so hopeless Lonnie made one more effort to reach him.

'It can't go on,' she agreed. 'One of us has got to change and I suppose it will have to be me. I'll come to your horrid parties – provided they don't interfere with Rosemary's routine.'

'Can't you put her on a bottle?'

'No.'

She spoke decisively, but she thought that it was something no man could hope to understand, her need for the communion between her and her baby which was more than just a healthy appetite and an eager little mouth tugging at her breast. In those quiet moments as she suckled her child Lonnie reached the highest level of happiness she had ever known, and she believed that

Rosemary sensed it, too, and her trouble-free progress was due to the contentment she imbibed with the milk that fed her.

'How about this?' Lonnie said, picking up an invitation at random. 'A Private View in Bond Street this evening? Are you attending that?'

'The artist's said to be a coming man. Yes, I thought I'd look in and see who was there.'

'I'll come with you. It's not much, but it'll be a start and word will get round that I'm back in town. Tomorrow I'll ring up a few people and arrange a dinner party. You must look in your diary and give me some dates when you're free.'

'We could make it a housewarming,' Flynn suggested.

'That means a larger party than I'd intended – oh, yes, why not? If I'm going to make an effort I may as well make a big one.'

The gallery was already crowded when Lonnie and Flynn arrived. Lonnie took one look at the garish splashes of colour on the walls and knew she was not going to enjoy looking at the pictures. She saw someone she knew and paused to give the answers she was to repeat endlessly in the next couple of hours: yes, she was quite well; the baby was lovely; yes, she was settled in town again, she would be letting everyone have her new address, her new telephone number, she was going to arrange a party, she'd be in touch.

'Divine pictures . . .'

'Oh, divine,' Lonnie agreed, wincing as she turned her eyes towards a field of blue intersected by jagged lines of scarlet and gold.

She stepped back and bumped into a man just behind her. 'I'm sorry . . .' she began.

'It is I who should apologise,' he said. 'I was standing close because I hoped for an introduction, but Lady Blanche did not see me. So, I will introduce myself. Alberto

Serpione. I am known always as Albi. Why do I not know you?'

He was a man of medium height, plump and sleek, probably in his forties, with an air of being totally at home in the *milieu* in which he found himself, exquisitely tailored but so much at ease in his clothes that he appeared unconscious of them. From his smooth black hair to his manicured fingertips to his shining shoes he was quite perfect and yet he had none of the contrived appearance of a dandy. His expression was mischievous, so much that of an audacious child, that Lonnie could not help smiling.

'I've been in the country having a baby,' she said. 'I'm Lonnie Branden.'

'Flynn's wife? Yes, I had heard that Flynn had a beautiful wife hidden in the country. That does not explain why we have never met before.'

'There was hardly time. We were married and we lived in London, but at first we went out very little and then . . .'

'You became pregnant. Almost you might be Italian. You're very young.'

'I'll be nineteen in February!'

'Ah, how you betray your youth when you refer to your *next* birthday, instead of the one that has gone before. Never again shall I do that. "I am thirty-five" I say . . .'

He paused to look at her with his head on one side. 'You don't believe me? No, you are right. I am forty-one. It is not a bad age. Tell me, what is your opinion of these pictures?'

Lonnie looked at him doubtfully.

'I am not the artist, nor a friend of the artist,' he encouraged her.

'I think they're pretentious rubbish,' Lonnie said.

'Good! They will sell, you understand, to those who wish to be "in the know" – you admire my perfect command of English? Yes, our fashionable friends will hang them on their walls, but you and I, who are discriminating, will go and sit on this little sofa, because already I have seen you shift from one foot to another and I think your shoes hurt, and we will talk to one another and be friends.'

Lonnie let him lead her to the yellow brocade sofa, feeling both amused and helpless. His rapid flow of talk, his slight, attractive accent, the way he put his head on one side to observe the effect of his words, all disarmed her. They would be friends, he had said. Already it seemed as if they were friends and yet she knew absolutely nothing about him. She looked round for Flynn, but he was absorbed in talk – and not paying any more attention to the paintings than she was herself.

'Do you live in London?' she asked Albi.

'Rome, Paris, London. Sometimes one, sometimes another. Perhaps this is why I missed you when you made your first début.'

'It was hardly a début. I just dipped a toe in the water and then withdrew it.'

'But now you have done your duty and had your baby – is it a girl or a boy?'

'A girl.'

'Ah, tiresome! It is all to do again.'

Although Lonnie could not help smiling at his commiserating tone, she spoke reprovingly when she answered, 'She's beautiful and I wouldn't change her for anything.'

'I see you are a devoted mother. But now you will amuse yourself a little? Do you enjoy the life of the *monde*?'

'No, I think it's boring. But Flynn . . .' She broke off, looking towards Flynn, animated and unconscious of her regard.

'Ah, yes, Flynn. So clever, so insinuating . . . I do not mean this disparagingly, you understand; he has achieved much in a short time. With you by his side he can achieve even more. What is that you are drinking?'

'Tomato juice.'

'The wine is not good, I agree – but tomato juice!'

'I have to think about my baby.'

'More and more you seem to me Italian,' he remarked. 'Your appearance, too, except that there is a fineness which does not appear in our plump little Italian women.

176

The fair ones, yes, who come from the North, but to be dark and slender, like you, that is not usual.'

'My dark colouring comes from the gypsies,' Lonnie said with a touch of bravado.

'You say? But that is interesting! Yes, I see it. You have a Magyar face.'

Lonnie doubted whether she had anything of the sort, but since the discovery seemed to please him she let it go.

'What do you do?' she asked.

'I amuse myself. You think this is not an occupation? You are wrong. I am busy, busy, busy from morning until night. Sometimes it is true I am a little bored and then I look round for a piece of work which will interest me. You, I think, will be my next project. I will educate you. You aren't educated, are you?'

'I went to school,' Lonnie said, totally taken aback.

'You can read and write and perhaps add up. You have learnt a little history – English history. Perhaps you speak French, but not well. Since you married so young you did not, obviously, attend a university.'

'Not even a finishing school, which was where I was supposed to go if I hadn't married Flynn.'

'Virgin territory! It will be a pleasure to write on this beautiful blank page. Are you free to lunch with me tomorrow?'

'Er . . . yes, I suppose . . .'

'One o'clock at the Ritz. I will give you my card because already you have forgotten my name, is it not so! All English are deaf to names.'

He stood up. 'Now we must circulate and make some remarks about these quite dreadful pictures. What will you say?'

'I think I'll say they have a dashing quality but their inner meaning eludes me,' Lonnie said.

'That is good! Yes, good! *Arrivederci*, Signora Branden. Until tomorrow.'

Lonnie made her way over to Flynn. 'Who on earth is that man who highjacked me?' she asked. 'The most extraordinary person.' She looked at the card in her hand because, of course, it was quite true that the strange foreign name had gone straight out of her head. 'Alberto Serpione. Do you know him?'

'Albi! Everyone knows Albi. Italian, of course, and appears to have plenty of money. He's got the most extraordinary reputation. Art connoisseur, bon viveur, music lover, patron of the opera . . . you name it, Albi knows something about it.'

'He's asked me to lunch with him at the Ritz tomorrow. Do you think I should go?'

'Of course. Darling, Albi really *counts*. He's not just one of the idle rich you despise; he's truly knowledgeable. Museums ask his opinion, particularly about early Italian art. I believe he's even been to Windsor Castle to advise the Keeper of the King's Pictures.'

'He says he's going to educate me.'

'Should be fascinating. What do you think of this exhibition?'

'The paintings have a dashing quality, but their inner meaning eludes me,' Lonnie said solemnly.

'Did Albi teach you to say that?'

'No, I made it up myself. Actually, I think they're awful.'

'Better not say so too loudly. The artist is Lady Blanche's lover.'

Lonnie gave a grimace of distaste. 'I hope he performs better in that capacity than he does as a painter,' she said.

'Caustic! Do you want to leave?'

'Unless you have to stay.'

'No, I've finished. I'll get a paragraph out of it, no more than that. Shall we find somewhere quiet and have something to eat?'

It was, on the whole a successful evening, except that Lonnie was on edge, sensing that Flynn wanted to bring their reconciliation to a conclusion she still resisted.

He got her home in good time and Lonnie ran straight up the stairs to the nursery.

'It's the longest I've been away from her since she was born,' she said to Nurse Philips.

'Rosemary has been asleep the whole time you've been out, Mrs Branden,' the nurse said.

As if on cue, the baby stirred in her cot, clenched her little pink fists, screwed up her face and began to cry.

'Do you think she recognised my voice?' Lonnie asked. 'Or is it just that she's nearly due for a feed?'

'I think that's most likely.'

'Greedy little horror,' Lonnie said fondly. 'I'd better change before I pick her up. Back in five minutes, Rosie-posie.'

It was one of those evenings when Rosemary behaved angelically, taking her feed with no fuss, burping up her wind with the little look of surprise that always made Lonnie laugh, and cuddling down for sleep again, pink and satisfied.

There were no lights on downstairs when Lonnie left the nursery so she was not surprised to find Flynn in their bedroom, already undressed.

'Rosemary doesn't seem to be at all upset at her new surroundings,' Lonnie said, but they both knew that she was only talking for the sake of saying something to stave off what Flynn really wanted to say.

'I thought of coming in to see her, but I wasn't sure I'd be welcome,' he said.

'I've told you that I want her to have a father as well as a mother,' Lonnie said steadily.

'But do you want a husband?'

He was still the man she had married, in spite of the disillusionment she had suffered. Tentatively, Lonnie put her hand on his arm, sensing the tenseness of his muscles under the silk, touching him as if to see whether she found it bearable. He was as goodlooking as ever, he still had the body that had thrilled her, and she had committed herself to staying married to him. Lonnie moved nearer and raised her face so that Flynn could kiss her.

'Darling, everything will be all right now,' Flynn said with a hoarseness in his voice that betrayed his mounting desire for her.

He loosened the dressing gown she had put on before

going to feed Rosemary and bent his head to kiss her neck and shoulders. The sensuous touch of his lips was not unwelcome. Her flesh remembered the pleasure he had given her in the past. She stirred in his arms and Flynn laughed softly.

'Come to bed, sweetheart,' he said. 'Be my own sweet, generous Lonnie. Love me like you did a year ago.'

Flynn fell asleep quickly after they had made love, convinced that their reconciliation was complete. Lonnie lay beside him, her eyes wide open, and her cheeks wet with tears.

CHAPTER TEN

Flynn was more than satisfied with Lonnie's progress in the world in which he had chosen to live. Tutored by Albi Serpione she gave parties which were attended by all the smart and successful, she gained an appreciation of beautiful objects and fine houses she had never had before, and her instinctive love of music was fostered by a man who knew whole scores by heart. As for her own appearance, she began to be known as an outstandingly elegant young woman.

'Never let me see you wearing yellow again,' Albi scolded her. 'For you, with the complexion of a brown eggshell, it is a disaster. In the country I permit you to be a woodland maid: greens and browns are becoming to you. In the town, you are a jewel lady – ruby, emerald, sapphire, amethyst, all these are suitable for you. Navy blue? Never! Black, yes, that is necessary.'

'Why do you take so much trouble with me?' Lonnie asked.

'It is a whim. It is Pygmalion and Galatea. You know the story? And Shaw's play, you have seen that? Then you must read it.'

If she was worried at first that Pygmalion might fall in love with his creation, that fear was soon dispelled.

'You think that perhaps one day I will pounce on you,' Albi said. 'You are wrong. I am not a pouncer, neither on women nor men.'

A year ago that pronouncement would have meant little to Lonnie, now she greeted it with a snort of laughter.

'Why ever not?' she asked.

'It is not in my nature. I have had lovers in my youth, but I did not find the process aesthetically pleasing. This is a good phrase, is it not? "Aesthetically pleasing" – which means that once the hot blood of adolescence had

181

cooled I found the heaving of two bodies on a bed less satisfying than a Mozart aria.'

'What about that Italian desire to carry on the family?'

Albi waved a hand in the air to indicate how little concerned he was.

'My nephew has the only title in the family and he is married to a very, very rich wife. It is for them to worry about producing children, which so far they have not done. As for me, I intend to spend what I have on pleasing myself while I live.'

For all his *insouciant* approach to life, Albi was a moody creature, at times excusing himself from an engagement on the grounds that he was depressed to the depths and at other times appearing so energetic and in such high spirits that Lonnie had to beg him to quieten down.

He knew all her story and was more perceptive than most people about the damage she had sustained as a child.

'It is why you are so obsessive about your own baby,' he said one day when he had called to try to persuade her to change her mind about refusing an invitation for that evening.

'No, I'm not,' Lonnie insisted. 'I told you ages ago I would never be free on a Wednesday evening. Rosemary's new nurse has only been with her a month and I can't upset her arrangements almost as soon as she arrives. We agreed she would have Wednesday afternoon and all day Thursday off each week.'

'But you have other servants. One of them could sit with the baby while you are out for a few hours, a few short hours, at this important reception.'

'Important!' Lonnie mocked him. 'You only say that because some of the Royals are going to be there. Besides, I've already refused the invitation. It would be incredibly rude to telephone now and say I've changed my mind.'

'The Ambassador would forgive you. I myself would speak to him.'

'I don't know how you contrive to be on such good

182

terms with your Embassy, considering the terrible things you say about Mussolini,' Lonnie commented.

'I say these things only in England. In Italy I am more discreet. Change your mind, Lonnie, change your mind.'

They both knew that Lonnie was not going to be persuaded. She shook her head, laughing at his insistence, as the maid announced another visitor.

'Guy!' Lonnie exclaimed, jumping to her feet. 'How nice to see you. Albi, you haven't met my cousin, Guy Lynton, have you?'

As she introduced the two men Lonnie was struck by the difference between them. Albi, so sleek and well-dressed, with his alert, birdlike glance and his nervous hands, and Guy, shabby and quiet, taking in everything and saying little.

'You must both have a drink,' she said. 'Guy, can you stay to lunch? Albi, I take it for granted that you have an engagement.'

'I am due at the Savoy in fifteen minutes,' Albi admitted. 'You may give me a glass of sherry.'

'I could stay,' Guy said. 'Would it be all right?'

'Of course. I'll ask Mavis to tell Cook.'

She looked him over critically. 'You could do with some feeding up.'

'Hard-up musicians don't eat,' Guy said flippantly.

'This is what you are doing?' Albi asked with the interest he brought to everything. 'Which instrument do you play?'

'Piano, but at the moment I'm studying composition with Dr Vaughan Williams.'

'So! You are good then. I am told he takes very few pupils and those only the very, very best.'

'It's an honour to study under him,' Guy admitted.

'And what public work have you done?'

'Nothing much. Concerts at the Royal College of Music and a bit of accompanying at recitals for other pupils.'

'Money is a difficulty?'

'It is rather,' Guy admitted. 'I work in a bookshop in the mornings and I try to get evening work when I can, ushering in theatres, washing up in a Lyons Corner House, temporary barman in a pub – that sort of thing.'

He saw the speculative glance this inquisitive Italian cast at Lonnie and added quickly and firmly, 'Lonnie knows I won't take money from her.'

'For the cost of one of my couture gowns you could have a recital at Wigmore Hall,' Lonnie said. 'Still, I know it's no use arguing with you.'

'I would like to hear you play,' Albi said. 'Would you permit this? I have a piano, a Steinway, which I play sometimes, but for my own pleasure only. It is possible I might be of assistance to you. It is my hobby, you understand, to discover what is new.'

'It's good of you to be interested,' Guy said.

'You say that as a polite way of dismissing me,' Albi said cheerfully. 'You are right to be cautious. Who has been your professor at the College? Herbert Fryer? "Uncle Sambo"? You see, I know what you call him and if you will mention my name to him you will find that he knows me, too. I am, with all my faults, a true lover of music and an occasional patron. Here, take my card. It shall be your decision whether you come to see me or not. I will not press you.'

'Do go, Guy,' Lonnie urged.

She was just a little on edge. She had hardly set eyes on Guy since the terrible night of Rosemary's birth. She knew that, disagreeing with her decision to stay with Flynn, he had deliberately kept out of her way. Seeing him brought back the memory of the scene they had both witnessed and although Lonnie told herself that she had put it all behind her, she wished she could be sure that Guy had also blotted it out of his mind.

'What I really came to tell you, in case you haven't already heard, is that Sally has had her baby. It's a girl,' Guy said.

The mention of another birth, chiming in so well with her train of thought gave Lonnie a jolt, but it faded in her delight at the news.

'That's lovely. We must drink a toast to her. Albi, I'll excuse you since you don't agree with having babies.'

'It's so disruptive,' he complained. 'All the pretty young mothers disappear into the nursery. However, since it will please you, I will drink to the good health of your new . . . cousin?'

'I couldn't possibly disentangle our relationship,' Lonnie said. 'Rosemary will call Sally "aunt" and Sally's baby will call me "aunt".'

'It is all most confusing. I must go before you addle my poor brain.' Albi drained his glass and stood up. 'I shall see you at the Wigham wedding on the twenty-first?'

'If we can find one another in the crush.'

'What will you wear?'

'The dark red Hartnell dress and jacket you chose for me with my ruby clips at the neck.'

'Good! You will present an excellent appearance.'

'You mean I'll do you credit, you tiresome man'

She held out her hand and Albi kissed it in the airy way which brought his lips nowhere near contact with her fingers.

'Who on earth was that?' Guy demanded as soon as Albi had gone.

'A friend. And, no, dear Guy, he is not anything more than a friend. Albi has been very useful to me and probably could be to you, too. His manner is a little fantastic, but he really cares about music and art.'

'Do you see a lot of him?'

'Indeed I do. Albi goes everywhere and as I, too, now go everywhere, we inevitably meet.'

'Flynn doesn't mind?'

'Certainly not. He's delighted with the way Albi has taken me in hand.'

Guy was frowning. It seemed as if he was about to say something, but he changed his mind. Instead, he commented on Lonnie's appearance.

'You look very sophisticated,' he said. 'Highly polished.'

'Thank you.'

It had not been intended entirely as a compliment. Guy was not at all sure that he liked the veneer which had been applied to the girl he had known. Hair and complexion were perfect, her thick eyebrows had been plucked into a delicate arch, lips and fingernails were painted the same clear scarlet. Her figure was perhaps a little fuller, but that if anything only added to her new maturity.

'By the time you're thirty you'll be a raving beauty,' he said abruptly.

'Albi says that, too,' Lonnie agreed. 'He says I'm beginning to grow into my face.'

From the way Guy shifted impatiently on his chair, Lonnie realised that it would be a mistake to mention Albi again.

'Tell me more about Sally,' she said.

'Yes, of course, that's why I came. She's very well and the baby, too, apparently.'

'Has Sally managed to decide on a name? Last time I heard from her she had a list a mile long.'

'Elspeth. Lonnie, the real reason I came round to see you is that when Mum passed on the news to me she said Sally was writing to ask you to be one of the godmothers and, because Mum had urged it on her, the other will be Barbara.'

Before Lonnie could say anything her maid came back to announce that luncheon was ready.

'It'll only be something light, Guy,' Lonnie said. 'I don't eat much in the middle of the day.'

She did not return to the subject of the christening until they were seated at the dining room table. Guy looked at the shining table, the heavy silver, the linen napkins and the bowl of out-of-season freesias and said nothing.

'It's going to be difficult,' Lonnie said abruptly when the maid had served them with bowls of watercress soup and left the room. 'I haven't set eyes on Barbara since . . . since that night.'

'I saw her at Christmas. She looked pretty awful. Brittle. As if she might snap in half if anyone brushed against her.'

'Poor Barbara. Funny, I never thought I'd feel sorry for her, but I do. She and Flynn had been lovers on that first visit of his to England, you know.'

'I suspected it.'

'I think she only married Tom because she despaired of ever seeing Flynn again.'

It chilled Guy to hear her talking about it so dispassionately.

'Don't you care?' he asked.

'Not about what happened in the past. It's all gone. I couldn't bear it if Flynn were ever unfaithful to me again. I've taken him back because I believe he's learnt his lesson. I don't think there's any danger in him and Barbara meeting.'

'Not to him.'

'Barbara will have to get used to seeing us together. It will be better to do it and get it over. I shall accept Sally's invitation to be Elspeth's godmother. Barbara must make up her own mind.'

Guy thought her attitude curiously hard, but since he had told her what he had come to tell her and helped her over what he had imagined might be a difficult decision, he let the subject drop.

They had a mushroom omelette with tomato salad.

'Where on earth did you get tomatoes in February?' Guy asked.

'Oh . . . imported, I suppose,' Lonnie said indifferently.

She refused the peaches preserved in brandy, but Guy could not resist them.

'If that's what you call a light meal I wouldn't mind having a full-scale one with you one day,' he said.

'You must come to dinner. Coffee? We'll have it in the drawing room, Mavis.'

The drawing room, which Guy had already seen, was fashionably pale.

'Looks as if it's been upholstered in porridge,' he commented, sitting down on one of the long sofas, strewn with cushions covered in vivid silk. They were the only touch of colour in the room, apart from the vases of spring flowers.

'Don't mock my décor,' Lonnie said. 'It cost a mint of money.'

'You've come to terms with being a rich woman?'

'I suppose I have. I've certainly learnt how to spend.'

'Doesn't Flynn come home for lunch?'

'Not very often. He has a lot of things to do.'

As he sipped hot black coffee out of the small Meissen cup she handed him, Guy was watching Lonnie and he thought he saw a shadow on her face.

'Are you happy?' he asked, and the abruptness of the question surprised him as much as it did Lonnie.

'Oh, yes.' She smiled and her look of joy dispersed the momentary impression of sadness. 'When you've drunk your coffee I'll take you upstairs to the nursery and show you why.'

They passed Rosemary's new nurse on the stairs as they went up. She was already dressed to go out.

'Just off, Mrs Branden,' she said. 'Baby is awake, but I don't think she'll give you any trouble. I'm not going away this week so I'll be back later on tonight. If you should want me . . .'

'I wouldn't dream of troubling you in your time off, Ada,' Lonnie said firmly. 'Except in an emergency, of course. Have a nice time.'

As they entered the nursery, Lonnie remarked, 'She's more homely than the first nurse I had. I wouldn't have dreamed of calling Nurse Philips by her Christian name and she almost had me signing a chit before I was allowed to pick Rosemary up.'

The nursery was light and airy, painted pale yellow, with a dado of rabbits hopping round the walls.

'This house is still a bit small for our needs,' Lonnie said. 'Most babies have a day and night nursery.'

'Most of the babies I know are lucky to have anything but a cot in a corner of their parents' room,' Guy said.

188

'I forgot you were a Socialist. All right, Rosemary is a lucky child; I admit it.' She bent over the cot and Rosemary squirmed and cooed in delight as Lonnie picked her up. 'Here she is! Come and say "hello" to your disapproving uncle, darling.'

She laughed as Rosemary bounced up and down in her arms. 'You see how delighted she is to meet you? Could you put that rug down, Guy? We'll have her down on the floor.'

Obediently, Guy spread the fluffy pink rug over the carpet and then, as Lonnie lowered Rosemary on to it and sat down beside her, he squatted down and joined them.

The baby had Lonnie's dark eyes, but there was a hint of gold in the curls which covered her head which was missing from Lonnie's brown hair. She sat on the rug, with Lonnie's hand ready to support her if she lost her balance, waving her arms in the air and producing a babble of meaningless sounds.

'She's saying "Hello, Uncle Guy, how nice to see you",' Lonnie interpreted.

'I'll take your word for it.'

'Isn't she beautiful?'

'She looks healthy.'

'There, darling! Uncle Guy thinks you look healthy.'

'Slightly overweight, perhaps.'

'She's not! Oh, well, perhaps she is, just a bit. She'll soon lose it when she starts getting about. She's quite forward for her age, don't you think? I mean, considering she was a month early?'

'She's a paragon of beauty and intelligence.'

'I think your Uncle Guy is laughing at your Mummy,' Lonnie informed Rosemary.

Seeing her with the baby, flushed and laughing, so much more like the Lonnie he had known in the past, Guy was moved to say something he had suppressed earlier.

'Lonnie, that Italian chap . . .'

'Albi? What about him? Look, she can almost catch this ball if I throw it gently.'

'Be a bit careful in your dealings with him.'

189

Lonnie sat up and stared at him. 'Why? What do you know about him? You only met him for the first time today.'

'I could be wrong. He might be taking some medication I know nothing about, but it happens to be something I've had to deal with recently – a poor devil who nearly died – and it seemed to me . . . do you happen to know if he takes drugs?'

'Of course he doesn't! Albi's a perfectly normal person. A bit exaggerated in his manner, I admit, which may have misled you . . .'

'No, it wasn't that,' Guy interrupted her. 'Think, Lonnie. Does he have swings of mood? Is he excitable one day, depressed the next?'

'Yes . . . yes, he is like that,' Lonnie admitted reluctantly.

'I thought when I met him that he was in a state of high excitement.'

'He often is. It's natural to him.'

'It's not natural, Lonnie, not in my opinion. I think he'd recently been sniffing cocaine.'

'That's *appalling*, Guy!'

'I'm glad you think so. I was afraid it might be commonplace in the circles you move in now.'

'Of course it's not. At least . . . not that I know of,' Lonnie said with the honesty that had always endeared her to Guy. 'What do you think I ought to do?'

'Nothing. It's his problem, not yours. Not mine either. But if you're ever down in the dumps and he offers you a pill or an injection or some white powder to buck you up, don't take them.'

'I won't. I suppose I ought to thank you, but I feel as if you've kicked away the steps from under me.'

'I'm sorry.'

'I rely on Albi. He tells me how to go on, which invitations to accept, who to ask to my parties, what to wear – everything I need to know.'

She turned enormous, painfilled eyes on Guy and

190

added, 'With Albi to help me I can come up to Flynn's expectations. It makes my life so much easier.'

'Oh, Lonnie, Lonnie . . .'

They were sitting close together on the pink rug. The baby had seized the rattle Lonnie had dangled in front of her and was banging it on the ground with a satisfying noise. Lonnie, feeling the careful edifice of her life crumbling beneath her, turned to Guy for comfort as instinctively as if she had still been a six year old child.

But this time Guy did not pat her on the shoulder and make soothing noises. He held her strongly and bent his head to kiss her with all the force of an ardent nature helplessly entangled in a love that was denied him.

It was as if the one piece that had always been missing from the pattern of Lonnie's life clicked into place and she saw for the first time what the design was meant to be. Guy . . . of course, Guy. He was the other half of her whole; with him she was complete. For the few seconds in which she rested in Guy's arms and his lips sought hers Lonnie was flooded with peace and joy, then she opened her eyes and reality rushed back.

To Guy it was not the revelation that it was to Lonnie and because he had long recognised his need he was the more reluctant to let her go. It was Lonnie who tore herself away from him and Lonnie who rushed into speech in a desperate attempt to deny what had happened.

'Dear Guy,' she said distractedly. 'So kind always. All the same . . . little Rosemary will be quite shocked to see her Mummy kissing anyone but Daddy, won't you, my sweet?'

With her head bent over the baby she added in a low voice. 'It must never happen again.'

'Why not?' Guy said, his mouth set in a mutinous line. 'Now that you know . . .'

'I know nothing,' Lonnie interrupted him. 'Dear God, my life is difficult enough, without any more complications. Please go, Guy.'

'If I'm nothing to you but another complication then I'll certainly go. You don't mean that, Lonnie.'

191

'I have to mean it,' Lonnie said in a low voice. 'Can you see yourself out? I don't want to leave Rosie on her own.'

'Lonnie . . .'

'Goodbye, Guy.'

She did not get up, but sat on the rug, very straight and still. He recognised the obstinate line of her mouth. Lonnie had decided on a course of action and nothing would shake her from it.

It was only after Guy had left her that Lonnie's control wavered. She bent over the baby and the tears gathered in her eyes.

'Oh, Rosie, you've got an awful fool for a mother,' she whispered. 'An awful fool.'

Because she was deeply disturbed by what Guy had said about Albi, Lonnie tackled Flynn about it that evening.

'Do you think it's true? she asked.

'I wouldn't be surprised. It's not uncommon, you know.'

'I *didn't* know.'

'There are still limits to your sophistication. I've even tried a sniff myself.'

'Flynn!'

'Don't worry. I didn't like the effect and it did nothing at all to help me write my column. I've never been tempted to have a second go.'

'Thank goodness for that. Promise me you won't experiment again.'

'Sure I'll promise you. It's just not my type of excitement.'

'Talking of excitement, are you prepared to meet Barbara if she and I are godparents to Sally's baby?'

Lonnie was pleased when Flynn hesitated and looked embarrassed. 'I could refuse,' she said.

'Don't do that. The Ruthwells are stuffy but useful. Barbara will have advance warning, just as you have. I hope we can all behave like adults.'

'I hope so, too, otherwise there might be a scene at the font.'

'Surely not. You're very scratchy tonight, sweetheart. A pity Guy spotted Albi's trouble. I can see it's upset you.'

'I don't feel I can trust him in the same way as I did before.'

'He hasn't changed, just your perception of him.'

'That's always happening to me,' Lonnie said. 'My kaleidoscope slips and the people I thought I knew turn into something different.'

Fortunately, Flynn did not take her remark seriously. He dropped a kiss on the top of her head and laughed. 'Poor baby. How was Guy?'

They were in their bedroom, changing for dinner, even though, for once, they were dining at home. Lonnie leaned forward, apparently intent on nothing but the exact line of the lipstick she was applying to her mouth.

'Just the same as usual,' she said indistinctly because of her stretched lips. 'Scruffy and tired. It's a pity he's not more presentable; I could invite him to dinner occasionally. I could use an unattached young man.'

She stood up, cool and assured once more, in a dinner gown of blue crêpe. 'I'll just go and look in on Rosemary. Pour me a drink, would you? Such bliss to indulge in a little alcohol now that she's weaned.'

CHAPTER ELEVEN

The christening of Elspeth Ruthwell passed off without any unseemly scandal. It was not held until the summer, close to Rosemary's first birthday, by which time both Lonnie and Barbara had had time to grow accustomed to the idea of meeting one another at the ceremony.

Lonnie had become much more prominent socially than she had been in the past. Her picture was frequently in the newspapers and she posed for the glossy magazines – *'Mrs Flynn Branden ("Lonnie" Branden, heiress to the Singleton fortune) with her daughter, Rosemary'*. She did the London Season with a thoroughness that earned Flynn's approval, appearing at the Chelsea Flower Show, Henley and Wimbledon, the Royal Academy Summer Show, Ascot and Goodwood, the débutantes' balls, the cocktail parties, the fashionable weddings.

She had eased herself away from her dependence on Albi, so much so that he complained half-seriously about being dropped.

'Never that, dear Albi,' Lonnie said. 'I owe you too much to neglect you. You should be proud that your pupil is able to stand on her own feet.'

'Talking of pupils, your cousin Guy has at last brought himself to play for me.'

'What did you think of him?'

'He is good,' Albi said slowly. 'As a pianist he could perhaps be in the first rank, but it is as a composer that he is really interesting. He is very, very reluctant to let me see his unfinished work – quite rightly – but he was persuaded to leave one manuscript with me so that I could study it and to me it seemed to show a truly original talent.'

'I'm so glad,' Lonnie said. 'Music means everything to Guy.'

'Everything? I think not, though it is as well that he has this consuming interest to console him. He is not a happy man. It has been said that unhappiness is good for an artist, but I think myself that to be without joy is a crippling condition for any human being.'

He was watching Lonnie closely as he spoke, but she had momentarily forgotten Albi, smitten by the realisation of Guy's burden of frustrated love. Albi put his hand under Lonnie's chin and turned her face to the light.

'Sometimes I think I see this same unhappiness in you, my Lonnie,' he said.

Lonnie jerked her head away. 'Don't be so foolish,' she said. 'I'm perfectly happy.'

'Are you? You have been, as you have just said, an excellent pupil. I have given you self-confidence, a veneer of culture and an ability to hold your own in the world in which we both live, but I have known for some time that your heart is not in it. You act your part very well, but you do not have Flynn's appetite for a worldly life. If you were both offered the choice between a ball at Buckingham Palace or a month quietly in the country, Flynn would take the glittering occasion, even though it only lasted one night, but you would tuck your baby under your arm and disappear into the trees without a backward glance.'

'That may be true, but it doesn't mean that I'm unhappy,' Lonnie said obstinately. 'I've made my choice . . .'

'And Guy, our young genius, must be content with nothing but his love of music?'

'Don't interfere, Albi. I mean that.'

'As you wish. I will say no more, except to tell you that Guy is now working for a recital. It's monstrous that he should not have had one before.'

'If only I had control of my money . . . but Guy wouldn't take it, anyway.'

'He is proud, and obstinate, and if things are as I believe, one sees that he would not want to be beholden to you. To a limited extent he will allow me to be his patron and I hope that this first small opening will lead to better concerts for him.'

'Dear Albi, you're so good,' Lonnie said.

'I am not good at all. I do only what I see is my duty. It is for you to convert Guy's family and make them support him.'

'They're not likely to listen to me,' Lonnie said.

Albi seemed so normal, as well as being kind and far too knowing, that Lonnie found it difficult to believe that he might have an addiction to drugs. And yet, studying him carefully, Lonnie could see that all was not well with Albi. He had lost weight, which did not suit him, his skin had a yellowish tinge and she noticed that he had developed a tremor in his hands. But this was not always apparent. Most of the time he seemed much as he had been, as debonair and amusing as ever.

Lonnie complained to him about having to go into the country for Elspeth's christening, leaving Rosemary behind.

'The first time we've been separated for a night,' she lamented.

'It has to come. How can you go on summer visits to your lovely English country houses unless you are prepared to allow your nurse to do her job and take care of your child while you are away?'

'I'm not doing any visiting if I can't take Rosie. We'll be spending August at West Lodge, which is a tiny cottage you would utterly despise, dear Albi.'

'But on the estate you will one day inherit,' he commented. 'It is right that you should get to know your people.'

'You make it sound positively feudal. "My people" are independent cusses who take half a day to decide whether to wish you a good morning. Now, just to show that I do still take your advice, you shall choose what I am to wear to be a godmother.'

As a result of this consultation, Lonnie appeared at the christening in a highly-becoming suit of white silk, splashed with vivid summer flowers and worn with a large picture hat.

'You look ravishing,' Flynn told her. 'Quite the loveliest girl here.'

Sally groaned when she saw her. 'I put on weight when I was expecting the baby and I simply can't get rid of it,' she complained.

'It suits you,' Lonnie said untruthfully. 'And the baby is a darling.'

'Isn't she? You must come and stay and bring Rosemary so that we can compare notes.'

The meeting with Barbara passed off stiffly, but apparently no one noticed that the two godmothers spent little time talking to one another. For Lonnie the meeting was not as significant as her encounter with Guy.

Because her resolve had not been tested in the weeks since he had taken her in his arms in Rosemary's nursery Lonnie had come to believe that by sending Guy away she had saved them from disaster and they would be able to meet calmly, as friends. She was not ready for the shock that went through her when she and Guy came face to face in the crowded marquee at the christening reception. He did not smile or speak, just looked at her, and for Lonnie the chattering crowd disappeared and they were alone. She made a gesture, as if to ward him off, and Guy took her hand in his. His touch locked Lonnie to him as forcefully as if she had clasped an electric cable.

'Don't . . . Guy, please don't look at me like that,' she said in a desperate whisper.

'As if I might sweep you up and carry you off and make love to you? Why not? That's the way I feel.'

'People will notice.'

'Good. I'd like everyone to know that I love you. That you love me.'

'I don't . . .', Lonnie said, but Guy only smiled at the feebleness of her protest, so that she began to feel angry with him.

She wrenched her hand out of his grasp. 'I'm trying to do what I think is right,' she said. 'If you really loved me you'd give me your support instead of trying to break me down.'

'I'm no Sir Galahad, darling. If I thought I could get you by going to Flynn and telling him that we love one another then I'd do it, but there's an obstinate streak in you and I'm afraid if I did anything too drastic you might turn against me. If you ever come to me it'll have to be of your own free will.'

If only he knew, Lonnie thought rebelliously. At that moment she longed to have the decision taken out of her hands, to be swept away as Guy wanted, with no regard for the consequences. But, of course, he was right – if it happened like that she would come to regret it and perhaps blame him for her recklessness.

They stood together in silence, both defeated by the violent surge of emotion that had come over them when they met and by the reaction as it ebbed away. Lonnie started like someone coming out of a dream when Flynn came up and greeted Guy.

'What are you doing these days?' he asked, making conversation because of the uneasiness he still felt in Guy's company.

'Working hard for the recital Albi has arranged,' Guy said, and if he spoke mechanically Flynn only took it as a remnant of the embarrassment that always lay between them.

'I'm coming with a massive party,' Lonnie said, taking up her social manner once more.

'Music lovers?' Guy asked with a faint smile.

'I've tried to get people who know one note from another, but I can't promise they're all connoisseurs.'

'Every ticket sold repays a bit of my debt to Albi,' Guy said. He glanced at his watch and grimaced. 'I'll have to think about going. Trains are few and far between from the local station and if I miss the next one I'll have to get someone to give me a lift to Reading to make the connection.'

'Why don't you drive back to London with us?' Flynn suggested.

He was trying to be friendly, to overcome the animosity between himself and Guy. Lonnie realised it and would have welcomed the overture if it had not meant being cooped up in a car with Guy on the long drive back to London. She willed him to think of some excuse, but after only a moment's hesitation, Guy accepted.

Lonnie saw, as she hoped Flynn did not, the way his eyebrows went up at the sight of the big Bentley they had recently bought.

'Fine car,' he said.

'She's a beauty. Handles like a bird,' Flynn said.

He was a good driver and the powerful car devoured the miles to London. Lonnie sat in front, turning occasionally to speak to Guy in the back, but there was not a great deal of conversation between any of them.

'Come in for a drink, Guy,' Flynn said as they drew up outside the Chelsea house.

Again Guy hesitated, and again he accepted.

'I'll put the car round the back, but I can easily get it out to give you a lift home, Guy,' Flynn said.

'Good of you, but I can walk from here,' Guy said.

As Flynn drove away Lonnie said, 'Guy . . . must you come in?'

'I think I should, don't you, when Flynn is going to so much trouble to win me over?' Guy's smile was mocking and he added, 'The trouble is, I'd just as soon he didn't bother: I don't want to like him.'

'You won't be able to hold out,' Lonnie said. 'Everyone likes Flynn.'

'Charm. It's a terrible gift.'

'I suppose . . . yes, you're right. To be able to get away with murder because you're irresistible, that's a difficult thing to handle without being spoilt.'

She was fumbling in her handbag, but in the end she said, 'Bother, I haven't got my keys. If you're determined on coming in you'd better ring the bell, Guy.'

The door was opened after a considerable interval by Mavis, the maid. She was not wearing her cap and apron and she looked surprised to see Lonnie.

'Madam! You've changed your mind and come back after all!'

'What do you mean?' Lonnie asked, stepping into the hall. 'We always intended coming home tonight.'

'But after the message we had . . . and you sending for the baby . . . I'm ever so sorry, madam, but we really weren't expecting you.'

Guy heard Flynn coming up behind him and stepped to one side to let him into the house.

'The baby? I never sent for her,' Lonnie said. 'Flynn, you didn't alter our plans in any way, did you?'

'Of course not. Is there something wrong?'

Lonnie was carrying her big white hat. Automatically she laid it down on a table in the hall and began stripping off her white kid gloves.

'There can't be anything wrong,' she said uncertainly. 'Explain it to me properly, Mavis.'

'A chauffeur came this morning with a message from you for Nurse. He said you were staying on a few days in the country and wanted her to bring the baby down to join you.'

Mavis looked from one to another of them and added, as if it made some difference, 'Ever such a big car it was, and he was wearing proper uniform and everything . . .'

None of them seemed capable of moving.

'Rosemary,' Lonnie whispered.

'There's been no other message, no telephone call, or anything?' Guy asked.

Mavis shook her head. 'Only what I've told you. Nurse was a bit put out at having to pack for the baby at short notice and Miss Rosemary was asleep, but she went off as good as gold and, of course, we wasn't expecting you back for two or three days or more.'

'We never sent any such message,' Flynn said. 'Surely no one else . . .'

'All the family were at the christening,' Lonnie said.

'You're quite sure there have been no letters?' Guy persisted.

'The post came, of course, and one letter put through

the door by hand. I've left it all in the drawing room, the same as usual,' Mavis replied. 'Oh, madam, I'm sorry if we've done wrong, but how could we know?'

Over Lonnie's head the eyes of the two men met.

'Let's go and look at the mail,' Flynn said. He put his hand under Lonnie's elbow and she let him lead her into the drawing room.

'Go and make some tea,' Guy said to Mavis.

'Yes, sir. Oh, sir, you don't think . . .'

'We don't know what to think yet. Make the tea.'

Lonnie was sitting on one of her pale sofas, her hands folded in her lap, perfectly still, but Flynn had begun to toss over the pile of envelopes on the desk by the window.

'An invitation . . . another . . . a couple of bills . . . your bank statement, Lonnie . . .'

He stopped and something in the quality of his silence made even Lonnie turn her head. Without speaking Flynn handed the sheet of paper he had torn out of its envelope to Guy. The message was brief:

> *'Your baby is safe. Do as you are told*
> *and she will not be hurt. Our price is*
> *£200,000. Stand by for a telephone call.*
> *Do not go to the police.'*

'Let me see,' Lonnie said.

She turned so white as she read the message that Guy thought she was going to faint, but Lonnie took a deep breath and steadied herself.

'How could they? How could anyone? A little baby,' she said distractedly.

'Money,' Flynn said. 'Two hundred thousand . . . Good God!'

'I'll pay anything, anything at all.'

'In spite of what this note says, you must call in the police,' Guy said.

'No!'

The door opened and Mavis came in with the tea Guy had ordered. She looked round, sensing drama, worried

201

about her own part in it, but not fully understanding the horror of what had happened.

'Is there . . . is there any news, madam?' she asked.

It was Guy who took it on himself to answer. 'Little Rosemary is quite safe,' he said steadily. 'Mrs Branden will explain later.'

'Yes, sir.'

Guy poured out a cup of tea and put it into Lonnie's hand, although he doubted whether she understood what she was holding, or even whether she was conscious of the maid having come in.

'Not the police,' she repeated. 'It says we mustn't. Guy, you wouldn't be so wicked.'

'Drink that tea. When you're a little less shocked you'll be able to think.' Without being asked, he handed another cup to Flynn.

'I want something stronger,' Flynn muttered.

'Better not. We all need to keep clear heads.'

'What Lonnie says is right; we can't go to the police.'

Still busy with the teapot, Guy did not answer for a minute or two, but when he had given himself the same hot drink he asked, 'How are you going to raise two hundred thousand pounds?'

'George . . .' Lonnie answered automatically. 'The money's *there*, isn't it? He'll have to release it.'

'If you approach George Osbert he'll insist on informing the police. You know that as well as I do. Better to have them in straight away. Lonnie, you're to drink that tea.'

The sharp way he spoke to her seemed to rouse Lonnie and she began to obey him.

'The house may be watched,' Flynn said.

'Possibly. Is there a back door?'

'Yes . . .'

The sharp ringing of the telephone made them all jump. For a moment they were frozen and then Flynn picked up the receiver.

'Yes,' he said. 'This is Flynn Branden. Yes, we've got your message . . . damn you! All right, all right, I won't interrupt again. Yes . . . yes . . . I understand. We need time to raise that amount of cash.'

Lonnie went to stand by his side, trying to hear what was said.

'Let me speak to him,' she whispered. 'Please, Flynn.' She took the receiver, stumbling into incoherent speech. 'My baby. Is my baby all right?'

The voice at the other end sounded mocking. 'Sure she is, Mrs Branden. And she'll stay that way if you do as you're told.'

'Is Ada with her? Let me speak to Ada.'

There was a laugh and then the receiver at the other end went down with a crash. Lonnie stood, futilely holding the dead telephone until Guy took it out of her hand and replaced it on the stand.

'What was the message?' he asked Flynn.

'Two hundred thousand pounds in used one pound and five pound notes. I'm to go to the Post Office in Trafalgar Square at twelve-thirty tomorrow and collect a *poste restante* letter which will give me instructions about the actual delivery.'

'They must have planned it well ahead.'

'Why wouldn't they let me speak to Ada?' Lonnie asked.

'Probably they're afraid she might give something away,' Guy said gently. 'I'm sure they'll be looking after Rosemary. It's not in their interest to harm her.'

'What about the Lindbergh baby?' Lonnie said.

There was no answer the two men could give her. They were all silent, remembering the little son of the Transatlantic flyer who had been killed by his kidnappers.

'That was in America,' Guy said. 'Sorry, Flynn, but it is a bit different over here.'

'Yes, sure, crime isn't as violent, on the whole, over here. About the police . . .'

'No!' Lonnie said. 'If you call in the police and anything happens to Rosemary, I'll never forgive you.'

'Sweetheart, she's my daughter, too. Guy's right; we've got to involve the authorities.'

'It's the money you're thinking about.'

'It's not! Damn it, Lonnie, that's a cheap thing to say. I care about Rosie, just as much as you do. I vote for telling the police.'

Lonnie gave an angry sob and turned away from him. Flynn looked at Guy and shrugged helplessly.

'If they do nothing else they can advise us on the best way to handle these thugs,' he said.

'I agree.'

As Flynn began to make the telephone call, Lonnie went out of the room. Worried about her, Guy followed. As he had anticipated, Lonnie had gone up to the nursery. She was standing in the middle of the room looking helpless and defeated.

'It's not as tidy as usual,' she said. 'You can tell Ada was taken by surprise and packed in a hurry. The cot, too; it's just been left as it was. She must have picked Rosemary up out of it . . .' Her voice faltered. 'My baby,' she said. 'My little baby.'

She swayed towards him and Guy put his arms round her, murmuring as if Lonnie herself had been a small child.

'She must be all right,' Lonnie whispered. 'Guy, she's all I've got.'

'Hush, darling. We'll get her back for you, I promise.'

He could hear Flynn coming up the stairs. Very gently he released Lonnie, but she still clung to him.

'The police are sending someone round, very unobtrusively,' Flynn reported. 'I'll have to go and let him in by the back door.'

'I'll do that,' Guy said. 'You look after Lonnie. Do you keep any sedatives in the house?'

'There's probably some aspirin,' Flynn said.

'No, that won't do. As soon as I've let the police in I'll go to a late-night chemist and fetch something stronger.'

'I won't take anything,' Lonnie said. 'Something might happen. I must be awake in case Rosie needs me.'

'Nothing will happen tonight,' Guy said. 'Dear heart, you must have some respite, otherwise you may collapse.'

'Stay with me,' Lonnie said.

Guy looked over her head and saw Flynn watching them.

'I could stay,' he said uncertainly.

'We'd be glad to have you,' Flynn said, but Guy knew that he spoke reluctantly.

Lonnie held on to her self-control all through the detailed questioning by the police. What was happening was a nightmare, something from which she might still wake up. Only the pain made her sure that it was really happening. The terrible ache inside her was too authentic to be a dream. Rosemary . . . little Rosie . . . her baby was out there somewhere in the hands of strangers, hard men who cared nothing for the agony of her mother or the distress of her father.

Flynn was upset, and somewhere inside her Lonnie was aware that she ought not to be surprised that it should be so. Of course he cared. He was proud of his little daughter, of her prettiness and intelligence, and the way she chuckled when he tossed her in the air.

They went over and over what had happened, detail by detail, word by word. The servants had to be taken into their confidence and questioned to find out everything they knew.

The 'chauffeur' had been a young man, in his mid-twenties, with dark hair and eyes. 'Swarthy-complexioned,' Mavis said. He had talked like a Londoner – 'A lovely deep voice, like Charles Boyer'; he had been very polite, wouldn't come into the house to wait, had sat outside in the car, except when Nurse had asked him to help with the suitcase while she carried the baby.

He was dressed in a navy blue double-breasted jacket and trousers and a peaked cap, all very correct. 'And big driving gauntlets,' she added.

'Did he take them off?' the Detective Inspector asked.

'No . . . now you come to mention it, he didn't, not at all, not even when he used the telephone.'

'He made a telephone call? You didn't mention that before.'

'I forgot. I'm in such a state, thinking what might be happening . . .'

'Yes, all right, Mavis, I understand,' the detective said patiently. 'Tell me about the telephone call.'

'He got Nurse Ada and the baby settled in the car and came back for the suitcase and then he asked if he could ring to say they were leaving, so of course I showed him the 'phone on the extension in the hall.'

'Did you hear him ask the operator for the number?'

'I wasn't paying attention. All I heard was him saying, "We're just about to leave".'

'Nothing more than that? Didn't he say who he was or ask to speak to someone in particular?'

'Not a word.'

After she had gone out of the room the Inspector remarked, 'Obviously it was a pre-arranged call with someone standing by at the other end to take it. So we know there are at least two of them in it. The point about the gloves could be significant, too. If he was that anxious not to leave fingerprints he probably has a criminal record.'

'Is there any advice you can give us?' Flynn asked.

'Get in touch with your man of business and start arranging to get the ransom together. I hope you'll never have to hand it over, but it'll be as well to be seen going through the motions. Apart from him, tell no one what has happened. At this juncture, the less publicity the better. Report to us immediately if you hear anything more.'

The long night dragged itself away and only Lonnie, deeply drugged by the pills Guy had forced her to swallow, got much sleep. Even when Guy saw her the next morning she had a drowsy, half-aware look about her and he was glad of it, knowing the sharpness of the anxiety that would attack her as soon as the effect of the sedative had worn off.

'Did you have any breakfast?' he asked.

'A cup of coffee. I can't eat.'

'Could I persuade you to go out for a breath of fresh air and some exercise?'

'No! I couldn't possibly leave the house.'

'We've got all sorts of engagements that will have to be cancelled,' Flynn remarked. 'I'd better ring my newspaper and tell them I'm ill. It's the only excuse they'll accept.'

'Don't use the telephone,' Lonnie implored him. 'Please, Flynn. Someone might be trying to get through to us.'

'If anyone rings and the line is engaged they'll try again,' he said with a gentleness that made Lonnie ashamed of her irrationality.

'Yes . . . of course,' she said. 'I'll have to pretend I'm ill, too. I can't think where I was going or who I was supposed to see this week. My diary must be around somewhere.'

'Why don't you let me handle it?' Guy suggested. 'I'm here, I might as well make myself useful. I suggest we say you've been stricken down by a case of food poisoning; that'll account for both of you being ill.'

'Poor Sally,' Lonnie said. 'If she hears about it she'll be distracted, thinking it was something we ate at the christening.'

She paused and added with a look of disbelief, 'It was only yesterday.'

Only yesterday when their main worry had been whether Lonnie and Barbara could get through an afternoon without insulting one another, only yesterday when Flynn had been on tenterhooks in case his mistress gave away their secret. It all seemed of very little importance now.

Guy worked his way patiently through Lonnie's engagements for the rest of the week, sending back theatre tickets, cancelling her appointments with the hairdresser, the manicurist, her dressmaker, a shopping expedition and lunch with another young woman and, finally, a dinner engagement for the end of the week.

'Both of them? How frightful,' the voice at the other

end of the telephone said. 'Poor Lonnie. Give her my love. I must send her some flowers. I wonder if she's heard about Albi? Whisked off to the London Clinic with an overdose of something. Accidental, of course – I mean, why should Albi . . . he's been drugging for years, silly darling. He ought to know what he can take by now. Do tell Lonnie. She's such a friend of his. If you don't think she'll find it too depressing, of course.'

Guy doubted whether even that news would get through to Lonnie, but she did say perfunctorily, 'Poor Albi. You were right about him, Guy.'

Flynn looked up from the schedules he was frowning over at his desk.

'I've thought Albi looked in a poor way for some time,' he said. 'He doesn't say much about it, but he must be worried about the way things are going in Italy. I believe the Fascists are trying to confiscate the family estates.'

'How awful,' Lonnie said without the slightest interest.

The telephone calls had passed away a little time and given them something to think about, but now Lonnie had sunk back into lethargy once more.

'If there's nothing more I can do, perhaps I should go,' Guy suggested.

'Stay until George Osbert arrives,' Flynn said. 'He might need some help in getting the money together and if Lonnie and I are supposed to be ill we can't very well leave the house. After that, yes, of course you must feel free to go.'

'No!' Lonnie said. 'Please stay, Guy, please!'

'As long as you need me,' Guy said, and Lonnie subsided.

Guy moved restlessly about the room, unable to settle into the grieving passiveness in which time drifted by for Lonnie.

'Do you mind if I talk to Mavis?' he asked abruptly.

'Ring the bell,' Flynn said.

'No, I'll go down to the kitchen.'

As soon as the door had closed behind him, Flynn said, 'There's no need for him to stay any longer.'

'He doesn't mind. And I want him here,' Lonnie said.

'You don't need to lean on Guy. You've got me.'

Lonnie did not reply, lost once more in her tormented world of imagining Rosemary lost and wanting her, crying, neglected, perhaps even hurt.

She roused herself with a jerk when Flynn said in an irritated way, 'He's in love with you, you know.'

Of course she knew, but she was not going to admit it to Flynn.

'We were brought up like brother and sister,' she said.

'No brother looks at his sister the way Guy looks at you. And what was it he called you last night? "Dear heart" – does that sound brotherly?'

'Flynn, this isn't the time to stage a jealous scene.'

'I'm not jealous. I've got no reason to be, I hope. I'm just warning you to be on your guard with Guy.'

'But to do it now, when I'm distracted with grief and worry . . .'

'I'm on edge,' Flynn excused himself. 'And it irks me the way Guy's always around when things go wrong.'

Just as well for her that he had been there on the night of Rosemary's birth, but the thought of Rosemary brought back the newer, deeper wound and Lonnie bit back the cutting retort she might have made.

Guy found Mavis and the cook sitting at the kitchen table.

'I don't know what to do about lunch,' the cook complained.

'Make it something light and I think there'll be four of us,' Guy said. 'Mr Osbert is on his way up from Sussex. Mavis, when you said yesterday that the chauffeur sounded like that film star . . .'

'Charles Boyer.'

'Yes – did you mean he had a foreign accent?'

'Not exactly, no. I'd say he was London-born, but there was something . . . he spoke sort of deeper in his throat, not up in the nose like a real Cockney.'

'That's very observant of you, Mavis. But you didn't hear him say very much, did you?'

'He wasn't chatty,' Mavis admitted. 'He gave me the message about fetching Nurse and the baby and he made that telephone call and that's all.'

'And you've told us all about that. He just said they were about to leave and then goodbye and put the telephone down?'

Mavis looked doubtful. 'He didn't say goodbye, actually.'

'Nothing at all?'

'Well . . . it might have been "cheers" or "cheerio", but it sounded more like "chow".'

'Ciao,' Guy said softly. 'I know an Italian who says that every time we meet and every time we part.'

'Italian. Yes, he did look a bit dago-ish. Swarthy, like I said yesterday.'

'I must get hold of Inspector Smith,' Guy said.

The cook glanced at the big clock on the wall. 'He's due back any minute,' she said. 'He said before midday and we're standing by to let him in by the back door, same as last night.'

Guy hurried back to the drawing room and asked, 'Flynn, the man you spoke to, are you sure he was English?'

'I thought he spoke in an American way,' Lonnie said, looking up. 'I told the Inspector so.'

'I might not notice an American accent, having one myself,' Flynn admitted.

'American! Oh, hell! I was hoping you'd say Italian.'

'A heck of a lot of Italians learnt their English in New York,' Flynn pointed out.

They put the tiny scraps of information together when the Inspector arrived, but only Guy thought they amounted to anything.

'I've got an idea,' he said. 'It's far-fetched, probably quite wrong, but I'd like to put it to you. Alberto Serpione. Drug addict and therefore in the hands of some highly unscrupulous people. Possibly experiencing money difficulties because of Fascist activities in Italy. Took an overdose yesterday and nearly killed himself.'

'Albi's my friend!' Lonnie exclaimed in horror. 'I don't defend his horrible habit, but Albi would never do anything to hurt me.'

'Did he know you'd be away this weekend?'

'Yes, he knew where we were going and why.'

'And that you were leaving the baby behind?'

'Yes.'

The Inspector looked doubtful. 'A friend of Italian origin and one word of Italian spoken by a man who was probably born in London,' he said. 'It's a tenuous connection.'

'Have you been able to trace the telephone call?'

'Unfortunately not, nor could your maid identify a photograph of some possible suspects. I'm taking her back to the Yard again for another go, but I'm not particularly hopeful.'

They were interrupted by George Osbert's arrival. Lonnie got up and went to him, holding out her hands. George took them in both of his and held them tightly.

'My dear little girl. This is a terrible business.'

'Can you get the money, George? You can, can't you?'

'Of course, of course. Though I hate to think of handing it over to men like this. It will only serve to encourage them.'

'That's how I see it,' the Inspector agreed. 'All the same, I think you'd better collect together the ransom as directed, Mr Osbert. Now, Mr Branden, it's time for you to go and pick up the *poste restante* letter in Trafalgar Square. You must go alone, but I'll have someone in the Post Office keeping an eye open to see if anyone is watching you. Bring the letter straight back here, of course.'

The letter which Flynn collected contained explicit instructions for the delivery of the ransom. It was to be packed in a suitcase and left at precisely one o'clock in the morning in a telephone kiosk in a suburban street.

Flynn was to drive away immediately after depositing the money and it would not be collected if anyone else was in the vicinity.

'Clever,' the Inspector said. 'Those quiet streets will be empty at that time of night. One of our men hanging around will stand out like a beacon. Have to go and look at the venue, but it's probably been chosen because there's no cover.'

'What about the man collecting the money?'

'A car parked down the road or round the corner. If he sees another one there he'll be off.'

He looked at Lonnie thoughtfully. 'Mrs Branden, are you prepared to do something very unpleasant and possibly useless?'

'Can't we just pay over the money?' Lonnie pleaded. 'All I want is my baby back.'

'Unfortunately, if you give in too easily you may lose the money and get nothing in return. They'll hang on to the child and up the price.'

'I'll pay *anything*.'

'That's what they count on. You want them caught, don't you?'

'I don't care,' Lonnie said. 'They can go free and have every penny I've got just so long as Rosie comes back safely.'

'So that they can do the same again to some other mother? Is that what you really want?'

'No . . . no,' Lonnie said reluctantly. 'You're right, they must be caught, but Rosie . . .' She stopped and made an effort to speak calmly. 'What is it you want me to do?'

'Visit your friend Albi.'

Lonnie went off alone on her visit to Albi. Flynn and George were out collecting the money from the Bank, the Inspector had already departed for the London Clinic and Guy, at Lonnie's earnest request, had remained in the house.

'Just in case, Guy,' Lonnie pleaded. 'Just in case there's any message.'

As she was leaving a bouquet of pink roses was delivered for her. Guy removed the card and handed the flowers to Lonnie.

'Take these with you. It'll look more natural,' he said.

She got into the waiting taxi and he saw her white, strained face looking out at him over the flowers.

At the hospital the visit had already been arranged, in the face of strong disapproval from the medical staff.

'Mr Serpione's a sick man,' the Inspector was told.

'Is he conscious?'

'Yes. Suffering . . . and he'll be worse before he's better. This isn't the time to question him about his supplier, Inspector.'

'That's not my aim – not directly. I'm concerned in another crime and the life of a small child is involved.'

When Lonnie was shown into Albi's room she was horrified by his appearance. Shrunken and yellow, he was only a shadow of his usual vivacious self. His eyes focused on her and she thought that he shrank back, then he saw the pink roses and seemed reassured.

Lonnie did exactly what she had been told to do. She walked up to the side of the bed and said, 'Albi, where is my little baby?'

The effect was far more shocking than they had anticipated. Albi threw back his head, arched his back and screamed.

The Inspector, following closely behind Lonnie, bent over him. 'Tell us,' he said. 'Come on. You know where she is. *Tell us*.'

The thin, high wailing went on and on. It brought two nurses and a doctor into the room.

'Get out,' the Inspector said. 'Yes, I know he's sick, but he knows something and he's going to talk.'

'He's my patient . . .' the doctor began.

Lonnie took both Albi's rigid hands in hers. 'Albi, dear Albi, listen to me,' she said. 'I'm your friend. I know you wouldn't do anything to harm Rosie. Tell me, please tell me, everything you know that can help me to find her.'

Albi gulped and long rigors shook his body, but he began to talk.

'Not the baby, Lonnie,' Albi said, as if he were pleading with her. 'I didn't know they meant that. I thought . . . a burglary . . . a little theft . . . you had insurance . . . but not the child, no, no, no - not that.'

'Rosemary has been kidnapped,' Lonnie said. 'Help me to get her back, Albi.'

'It was only information,' he said, still pleading with her. 'They made me tell them . . . they wouldn't give me . . . I needed it so much . . . you don't know.'

'Yes, Albi, I understand. What did you tell them?'

'When you'd be away, the domestic arrangements, the names of the servants..'

'The nurse? You told them the name of the nurse?'

'Yes.'

'And that I'd be away from Saturday to Sunday leaving Rosemary behind?'

'Yes, but I didn't know, I didn't guess . . . Lonnie you have to believe me.'

'Their names,' the Inspector said.

Albi turned his head to look at him, and they could see his body trembling under the hospital blankets.

'I know them only as Mario and Toni. They are . . .' he hesitated and then said in a terrified whisper, '*Mafiosi*.'

'The Mafia? in England? Damnation!'

'Toni . . . lived all his life in England. Mario has been in America. I know nothing more, nothing.'

'What about the kidnapping? Where are they holding the baby?'

'I don't know, I don't know. We never spoke of a kidnapping.'

It was Lonnie who asked, with a hardness she would not have thought possible, 'Then why did you try to commit suicide?'

'It was an accident,' Albi said with weak obstinacy.

'How did you get your supplies?' the Inspector asked.

'Through the Club Meraviglioso. Then the Club would no longer give me what I needed. I was told to contact Toni.'

'How?'

'I have a telephone number. In Highgate.'

'That might help. We can trace the address.'

In spite of exhaustive questioning, Albi could tell them no more.

'That's enough,' the doctor said. 'I've already let you go beyond what I think is reasonable.'

'I'll put a guard on him,' the Inspector said. 'If anyone wants to know, it's because of the drugs angle. No one gets in to see him – no one – except your own staff.'

Before she left Lonnie bent over Albi, lying white and exhausted on his tumbled pillows, and pressed her lips to his forehead.

'Poor Albi,' she said.

His eyes opened and he looked up at her with such an expression of resigned suffering on his face that she caught her breath.

'I have been so afraid,' he said. 'When yesterday I did not hear of a robbery, when you did not telephone me to say, "Dear Albi, such a bore, I've lost my ruby clips", I was terrified, terrified of what could have happened. I wanted to die. Now, I wish it more than ever. You are kind, kinder than I deserve, but my life in this world is over. Goodbye, Lonnie.'

The address in Highgate was traced and enquiries began. As the Inspector had feared, it was merely an accommodation number where a sleazy woman took messages.

'Lean on her. She'll talk,' he said. 'We've only got a few hours before Mr Branden is due to make the drop.'

She did indeed talk, to some purpose. She knew Mario and Toni, thought they were brothers, and without knowing their exact address, could pinpoint the block of flats where they lived. After that, there was no great difficulty about finding the right apartment nor in discovering that the 'brothers' had taken extra milk for the last two days.

'Not much to go on, but a useful indication,' the Inspector said.

He had another stroke of luck when the woman picked out a photograph of a known criminal and Mavis confirmed that it was the chauffeur.

'Toni Manola,' the Inspector said with satisfaction. 'Moving above his class, going in for kidnapping.'

'Will you break in and rescue Rosie?' Lonnie asked.

'We'll have to move more carefully than that, Mrs Branden.'

'But why? We know – almost certainly – that she's in there.'

'Exactly. They've got a hostage – two hostages. One false move and they might threaten to harm them.'

As he had been instructed, Flynn drove down to Croydon. He waited until exactly one o'clock and then walked quickly down the road to the telephone kiosk. There was no one about, but he noticed a car parked down the side road which had the kiosk on its corner. It was too dark for him to see whether there was anyone in the car.

Flynn put down the suitcase containing the money and walked away. It was not until after he had reversed his car and driven away, back towards London, that a man got out of the parked car and went into the telephone box. He picked up the suitcase and looked inside, then he made a telephone call, speaking quickly in Italian.

He walked briskly back to his waiting car and started it up and then, for the first time, realised that all was not going as well as he had thought. An urgent whistle shrilled, a nondescript motor car parked in the driveway of a house sprang into life, and another car, parked two turnings away, leapt forward and blocked the main road. The kidnapper zig-zagged wildly, but the two police cars, one racing up behind and one already in front of him, boxed in his car and forced it up on the pavement, crashing into the neat brick wall and hedge of the suburban house.

Lights came on in the surrounding houses, people came to the windows. The man tried to make a run for it, but he was brought down and handcuffed.

In the Highgate flat his accomplice was humming lightheartedly. It had all been almost too easy. Just as they had anticipated, the rich, foolish young woman had paid up without a murmur. Now Toni would hide up with the loot and Mario would join him later when it seemed safe. They had considered turning the screw for a little extra. Mario had been in favour of holding on to the child and demanding another fifty thousand pounds, making the pickings up to a cool quarter of a million, but Toni had disagreed and in the end Mario had decided not to risk the venture by being greedy.

He had packed his belongings and was ready to leave. The baby was asleep and so was the nurse. They had given him very little trouble, once he had established that any undue noise would lead to retaliations. The baby had cried, that was inevitable, but his neighbours were an incurious lot and he was ready to explain a visit from his sister and her child if anyone enquired.

The interval between the successful operation in Croydon and any signs of movement in the flat was nerveracking for the police. If all the lights went out they were planning to wait until Mario could be presumed to be asleep and then break in, but in the event, as they had half-anticipated, he walked out of the block carrying a suitcase and, since Toni had taken the car, waited on the pavement for the taxi he had called.

He heard footsteps behind him and turned his head, still lulled into a false sense of security by the telephone call from Toni saying that all had gone well. Even when he saw the two men in plain clothes he did not realise they were policemen, although his wary nature made his muscles tighten in anticipation of a possible attack. The hand laid on his shoulder brought a knife into his hand with one practised twist of his wrist from the sheath that held it concealed under his sleeve.

'Oh, no you don't, old son,' the policeman said with satisfaction. 'We're police and you're under arrest.'

When the police car drew up Lonnie was out of the front door and halfway down the steps before the policeman carrying Rosemary could struggle out of the back seat. Rosemary, wrapped in a blanket, was wet, hungry and bad-tempered. Lonnie held out her arms and the policeman handed over the baby, though Mrs Branden looked so white that he was afraid she might drop the bawling bundle.

Miraculously, the trembling that had taken hold of Lonnie stopped as soon as she felt Rosemary in her arms. The baby looked up at her mother, stopped crying for a moment, gulped, and then began again in earnest.

'My little love,' Lonnie whispered. 'My poor little lost treasure.'

She looked at the policeman, smiling through a dazzle of tears. 'Thank you,' she said. 'Thank you, thank you.'

Inside the house everyone crowded round – Cook and Mavis came up from the basement, George was still there, Guy and Flynn, the policemen still waiting to speak to them. For a minute or two Lonnie could not get beyond the front hall. It was Flynn who saw that she needed to get away from them all and that moment of insight gave Guy a jolt.

'Take these guys into the drawing room,' Flynn said to him. 'I'll be right down, but Lonnie and I want to take Rosie up to the nursery.'

His arm dropped round Lonnie's shoulders and she stood in its encircling embrace, oblivious to everything but the joy of holding Rosemary once more. Flynn touched his redfaced daughter's cheek with one finger and then he brushed his hand across his eyes.

At that moment Guy understood the hold that Lonnie's

marriage still had on her. He had under-estimated the strength of her love for Rosemary and he had discounted Flynn's own attachment to his child. Seeing them standing there, looking like a united family, Guy realised that there was still a bond between Flynn and Lonnie, in spite of the wrong he had done her, in spite of her realisation of the mercenary nature of his love, even in spite of Lonnie's own love for Guy.

Guy turned away, his delight in Rosie's recovery soured by the knowledge that if anything, Lonnie's resolve to remain with her husband had been strengthened rather than weakened by the ordeal she had undergone.

CHAPTER TWELVE

'HEIRESS' BABY SNATCHED!'; 'ROSEMARY REUNITED WITH
HER MOTHER'; 'SINGLETON HEIRESS IN KIDNAPPING DRAMA'
– Lonnie took one look at the screaming headlines and
fled to the country.

Alone at West Lodge with Rosemary, since the servants
remained in London with Flynn and Nurse Ada had to
be given time off to recover from her ordeal, Lonnie took
stock of her situation.

Rosemary had been kidnapped because her mother had
so much money that a pair of petty criminals had considered her fair game. More than that, at every crisis in
her life the great fortune she possessed had influenced
events against her. The loss of her first family, her restricted upbringing, the death of Flynn's father, her
marriage . . . and now Rosemary's kidnapping; all these
things had happened in the way they had because of the
Singleton inheritance.

It seemed to Lonnie that if she was ever to lead a normal
life then she must find a way of getting rid of this burden
of money. It was too much. She had, ever since she had
been old enough to understand, thought that Rupert's
Will was unjust. There was nothing she could do about it
while she was still under age, not unless she applied to
have the Trust wound up. There would be a legal battle
if she did that, because Margot still mistrusted Flynn, and
Flynn himself would certainly not support Lonnie if he
realised that once she got control of her inheritance she
meant to give it away. She would have to be patient and
wait until she was twenty-one. By that time Lonnie
thought that she would have been able to work out a plan
which would allow her to live with some peace of mind
and even to do some good in the world with the money
that had been entrusted to her.

If Flynn were sufficiently angry he might set her free. That treacherous thought slid into Lonnie's mind and was hurriedly dismissed. She could not allow herself to think like that even though, now that the horror of the kidnapping was over, the memory of the way Guy had spoken to her at the christening came back to haunt her.

He had said he loved her, said it openly in a place where anyone might have overheard him. Lonnie's lips curved in an involuntary smile as she remembered his audacity and his determination to win her. More than that, he had been there all through her ordeal, once again sustaining her in a time of anguish.

Flynn had been there, too, Lonnie reminded herself. He had taken an active part in capturing the kidnappers and he had been worried and upset by his daughter's disappearance. All the same, Lonnie knew that it had been Guy she had leant on during those two appalling days, just as Guy's was the only company she would have accepted now at a time when her need was to be alone with her lost-and-found baby.

But Guy had gone away. As soon as there was no longer anything useful he could do he had moved out of the Chelsea house and gone back to his own place, and Lonnie had been so absorbed in Rosemary that she had scarcely thanked him.

One small thing she was determined to do for him and that was to make sure that the recital Albi had arranged for him still went ahead. She employed George to discover how it stood and when he reported that two hundred pounds would be ample to cover the remaining expenses she asked him to make the payment anonymously.

'I owe him that much,' she said. 'It was Guy's quick thinking that suggested the link with Albi which helped us get Rosemary back.'

She did not say that she meant to keep Flynn in the dark about her gesture, but George understood that she wanted the payment to be made separately from her normal allowance and he kept his usual discreet silence.

The recital was to be at the beginning of September

and in the meantime Lonnie remained at West Lodge. She slept badly, waking at every noise, and getting up two or three times to make sure that Rosemary was all right. In the daytime she hardly let the baby out of her sight. By the time Flynn joined her, bringing Mavis and Cook with him, in the way they had always intended for the month of August, Lonnie was thinner and paler than she had been during the days of strain in London. It ought to have been a relief to have company in the lonely cottage, and yet Lonnie resented the intrusion into her isolation. She wanted to be alone. Just her and Rosemary. That way they would be safe.

'If it weren't for the absurd embargo on taking you out of the country I'd suggest a trip abroad to bring back some colour to your cheeks.' Flynn said. 'I dare say, if I talked to George he'd get Margot to let you off the leash for a week or two in France.'

'I don't want to go,' Lonnie said. 'I've just got Rosemary settled again. Another upheaval wouldn't be good for her.'

'You could leave her with Ada; she'll be back next week,' Flynn suggested.

Lonnie stared at him, unable to believe her ears. 'After what happened? I'll never, never go away and leave her again.'

Flynn took an irritated turn round the room, avoiding the chintz armchairs and sofa. He had never liked West Lodge. It was too small and cramped and ridiculously shabby.

'Sweetheart, you're going to have to get over feeling like that,' he said. 'What happened was terrible, sure it was. I aged ten years and I know you were devastated. All the same, let's get it into perspective. It was a badly organised, bungled kidnapping by a couple of small-time crooks who were outwitted fairly easily.'

'Next time we could be less fortunate. I think about it every time I hear a floorboard creak at night.'

'That's why you're so jumpy. Look, would you like to

sack Ada and get someone more efficient? Perhaps even hire a bodyguard if it makes you feel better?'

'Don't be absurd. And of course Ada must come back if she wants to. I couldn't get rid of her when she's just had such an awful time.'

Nurse Ada was full of remorse for her part in the kidnapping, blaming herself for something none of them had ever anticipated. She had gone with the 'chauffeur', irritated by the lack of notice that she would be taking Rosemary into the country, but lulled by his correctness, his uniform, the Daimler which had been hired for the day to produce just that reassuring effect.

She had sat in the back with Rosemary while they drove out of London in a westerly direction. When the chauffeur had pulled up at the side of a country road and asked if she minded if they stopped for a cup of coffee, since he had already driven up from Berkshire and needed a break, she had accepted without question the coffee poured out of a steaming flask and even been grateful for it. The next thing she remembered was waking up in a flat somewhere she could not identify, but which was clearly in the heart of a town, with Rosemary bawling her head off.

After that there had been hours of frightened confinement, coping as best she could with the fretful baby, tormented by the refusal of her captors to tell her anything about what was happening. To have been caught off-guard and drugged a second time, in order to prevent her raising the alarm too soon after the kidnappers had collected their loot and got away, was something that filled her with disgust.

Nurse Ada wanted to talk to Lonnie about it when she joined them at West Lodge, but she found her mistress reluctant to listen and had to fall back on the ready audience of Mavis and Cook.

Once Flynn was settled at West Lodge and the nurse was ready to take charge of Rosemary once more, Lonnie had no excuse for staying at home every day. She was persuaded to go up to Firsby Hall for dinner and managed to get through the evening with only one telephone call to make sure that Rosemary was all right. After that, Flynn coaxed her into attending the tennis parties and garden fêtes which filled the summer days in the country. When they took the baby down to the sea it reminded Lonnie all too vividly of the days she had spent without Flynn following Rosemary's birth, but she accepted that she had to put that behind her. Flynn, as far as she could judge, had behaved himself impeccably since that one episode with Barbara. If only she could have felt something towards him besides the sexual excitement he could still arouse in her.

Flynn, exuberant in his delight at the successful foiling of the kidnappers, and revelling in the publicity which Lonnie had shunned, had convinced himself that the ordeal they had shared had drawn him and Lonnie together again. The fact that Lonnie was quiet and withdrawn he put down to her nervous state and he set himself to coax her out of it.

He wanted to give expression to what he saw as their new start by making love and Lonnie, troubled in her mind but helpless, acquiesced. She told herself that she had committed herself to staying with him and Guy himself had told her that she had to go all the way with that decision, but that did not entirely explain the voluptuous abandonment of those hot August nights when she and Flynn could not sleep.

'I could eat you alive, you delicious creature,' Flynn said one night when they had flung off all the bedclothes and left the curtains pulled back to get the benefit of the cooler night air. The moon was up and shining through the window so that they lay in a pool of light, bleached and white, their limbs entangled, their hands busy, stroking and teasing, two finely tuned bodies adept at giving one another pleasure.

Lonnie shivered as Flynn ran one finger down the length of her spine. The next day she would be reluctant to remember their sensuality, but now with Flynn's body growing harder and the breath catching in his throat as he murmured love words and turned her to lie beneath him she was ready to take him for what he was, a splendid animal, a schooled and clever lover, the man who had reduced her to speechless rapture when she was still an untaught girl.

Flynn, she could see the next day, was happy, even smug about his prowess. Once she would have caught his eye and smiled at the conspiracy between them, but with the critical spirit that had come over in the last year she found herself looking away, irritated by the feeling that he was weighing up her reaction, almost as if he wanted to know whether he had given satisfaction.

'I'm going down to the village,' she announced abruptly. 'Do you want to come?'

'No, I'm too lazy,' Flynn said with a smile.

He caught her hand as she passed him and laid it against his cheek, looking up at her mischievously, once again inviting her to reminisce about the night they had passed. Lonnie paused, trying to give him the response he wanted, but when Flynn caught her round the waist and pulled her down on his lap, she struggled free.

He laughed and let her go, still armoured in his complacency. As far as Flynn was concerned, all was well with his world. Lonnie had recovered her looks and her health after what had been admittedly a very nasty experience. He was slightly bored, but he was prepared to indulge her, looking forward to an exciting round of gaieties that autumn.

'You can't think how much I'm looking forward to the day when you're free to use your fortune,' he said, apparently at random. 'Just think, darling, how splendid it'll be when we can travel. I've got great plans. What do you say to a yacht? We could hire one and cruise round the Mediterranean. No difficulty then about taking Rosemary because she can be looked after on board just as if she were in her own nursery. Isn't that a great idea?'

For a moment Lonnie was on the verge of telling him that she had every intention of getting rid of a large part of the fortune he was looking forward to sharing with her, but she had still not thought it out properly and, quite

225

apart from that, she shrank from the row there would be when she told Flynn what she wanted to do. They had just come through a terrible experience and, on the surface at any rate, they were closer to one another than they had been since the early days of their marriage. It was not the moment, Lonnie decided, to upset Flynn, not when such a long time still remained before she could carry out her plan, time which Lonnie well knew Flynn would employ in trying to persuade her to change her mind.

'Eighteen months to go,' she said. 'Maybe there'll be another crash and I'll lose it all before then.'

'Don't say that – even joking. We're going to have good times, sweetheart.'

Lonnie visited the churchyard on her way back from the village, pausing to look at the stone which marked her grandmother's grave. There were never any cut flowers on Thirza's grave because Lonnie remembered how much her grandmother had disliked the killing of flowers by plucking them, except when it was for medicinal purposes, but Lonnie had had a rosebush planted on the grave and she was pleased to see how well it was flourishing, great crimson roses with all the flamboyance of Thirza's gypsy ancestry.

Lonnie cupped her hand round one of the flowers, feeling the coolness of the petals and breathing in the fragrance that rose from its golden heart, and felt comforted. She ought not to have needed comfort; most people would have seen her as the luckiest girl in the world, but Lonnie knew that always, except when she was holding Rosemary or was completely swept away by the sexual passion of which she was vaguely ashamed, there was something missing in her life, an empty place waiting to be filled.

She saw that there was someone else in the churchyard, over by the west door by the Humfrey family vault. When she realised it was Margot, Lonnie hesitated, then she went to join her. No lack of flowers here; Margot was arranging them in a stone vase, a great mass of expensive cut blooms.

'Rupert died just thirteen years ago,' she said.

Did she bring flowers on the anniversary of her husband's death, Lonnie wondered. Somehow she suspected that Margot only made that gesture for her son.

Lonnie waited while Margot finished arranging the flowers to her satisfaction. Almost to herself Lonnie said, 'Why did he do it? Why did he saddle me with this great burden of money?'

For once Margot seemed in a mood to discuss the question dispassionately.

'I think it was his gesture of independence,' she said. 'He was very young. He never had time to grow up. He was still up at Cambridge – or should have been – when he had that unfortunate affair with your mother. If he'd stayed in America as I wanted . . . Uncle Henry was good for him; Rupert needed a father. Instead, he was off to the war, wounded . . . and almost as helpless as a baby again. I nursed him, but it irked him to be dependent on me. All the management of the estate was in my hands, as it always had been. And then he saw you, vigorous and healthy, the most beautiful child he had ever seen – he said that. He fell in love with you.'

For the first time Lonnie felt she understood the mortally-ill young man who had seen in the healthy child of his body a future that was to be denied to him.

'It was Firsby Hall he was thinking of,' she said.

'Of course,' Margot agreed. 'Uncle Henry's fortune was scarcely real to him. By the time we knew about that Rupert was too far gone for it to matter very much.'

'It was a grossly unfair Will,' Lonnie said.

'I agree. However . . . there's nothing we can do about it now.' With a touch of her old malice, Margot added, 'Patsy thought she'd redress the balance by marrying you off to Guy.'

'Yes,' Lonnie said.

'You guessed? I don't know that it would have answered. Guy has a mind of his own and with his left-wing views I doubt whether he could have swallowed the Singleton millions.'

'No.'

Margot turned to go, dusting her hands together to get rid of a few clinging leaves.

'I wasn't pleased by your marriage to Flynn,' she said. 'At least, not by the manner of it, but it seems to have answered well enough and Flynn has settled down to life in this country. Will he be willing to take on Firsby one day, do you think?'

'He can hardly wait,' Lonnie said.

'Ah.'

Margot looked at her sideways, but she made no other comment. They walked slowly towards the gate at the far side of the churchyard. The grass had been cut and little stalks worked their way into Lonnie's sandals and pricked her feet. She paused at the gate to take one off and shake it.

'Have you been happy since you married Miles?' she asked abruptly.

'Oh . . . yes. Yes, of course.'

Lonnie straightened up and looked the woman who had at last admitted to being her grandmother full in the face. As if compelled into truthfulness, Margot said, 'I was fifty when we married and Miles was forty-three. I told him I was forty-eight, but I think he always knew I'd lied. It didn't seem to matter at the time. Now, he's fifty-three and I'm sixty and the gap is wider. He needs . . . younger company, and I cling to my old friends.'

She was always so slim and graceful and beautifully groomed that age seemed hardly to have touched Margot, but Lonnie, looking at her with more searching eyes than usual, saw that beneath the exquisite maquillage her skin was tired; the lines of her jaw had sagged and in her neck the thin cords stood out. She looked her age and had finished rebelling against it.

With a flash of intuition Lonnie knew that there was another woman somewhere in Miles' life. He must have been very discreet because no hint had ever reached her, but Margot knew and she had decided to do nothing about it. Perhaps she no longer cared.

They stood together for a moment, linked by a common sorrow, two women who knew that their men had married them for what they could get out of it.

'You're happy with Flynn, aren't you?' Margot asked.

'Oh, yes! Happy enough. And there's Rosemary.'

'She's a lovely child – as you were. Thank God she took no harm from those terrible men.'

They walked on in silence until their paths parted.

'I've still got a nursery full of toys,' Margot said. 'You must bring Rosemary up more often.'

'I will,' Lonnie said.

She walked back to the Lodge and found Flynn rolling a ball along the ground for Rosemary, who tottered after it with shrieks of delight.

'I met Margot,' Lonnie said. 'Do you know, after all these years, I think she's decided to like me.'

As August began to move towards September Lonnie spent more and more time at the Hall, taking Rosemary with her to play in the garden or up in the nursery with toys that had belonged to Rupert.

'I want to leave Flynn alone to concentrate,' she explained to Margot. 'He's turning some of his experiences as an American in England into a book. He's got to get on with it because the plan is to bring it out next year when the King's Silver Jubilee will create extra interest in the United States.'

'How strangely things turn out. The last thing I would have expected when I first met Flynn was that he would become a journalist and an author.'

'I wish he hadn't. I wanted us to go to the United States and live on his earnings as a lawyer.'

They both fell silent, remembering that it had been Margot's insistence on Lonnie remaining in Britain if she was to receive any income from the Trust that was responsible for Flynn's continued presence in England.

'I was so angry about your marriage,' Margot murmured, and they both knew that it was the nearest she would ever come to admitting that she had wanted to frustrate Flynn's plans because she had been deceived in him.

Margot talked, stiffly at first, about Rupert's childhood, his days at school, his prowess at swimming and cricket and the ease with which he had acquired foreign languages.

'I'd hoped for the Foreign Office for him,' Margot said in a way that opened up vistas of embassies abroad and high-level diplomacy.

It seemed to Lonnie that after years of standing aloof Margot was trying to bind Lonnie to her. It was too late, Lonnie thought sadly. She had a certain affection for Margot and she was more sympathetic towards her than she had been in the past, but there was no longer any hope of a deep bond between them. If only she had made this effort while Lonnie was still a child. Then she would have responded, not just with warmth, but with eagerness. Remembering her starved years, when she had hungered for affection, Lonnie could still not entirely forgive Margot for her unyielding coldness.

One good thing did come out of this closer intimacy: Lonnie began to recognise in Margot's obsession with Rupert something of her own attitude towards Rosemary and to realise that she could easily develop the same smothering love for her own small daughter.

'It's hard to accept that you can love someone too much,' she said at random to Flynn one evening.

'Meaning me?' he enquired lazily.

'I was thinking of Rosemary. While she's tiny I'm sure it's right to keep her with me as much as I can, and after what happened I can hardly bear her out of my sight, but as she grows older I must try to avoid the mistake Margot made with Rupert.'

'An only child,' Flynn said significantly. 'The way to avoid spoiling Rosie is to give her a couple of brothers or sisters.'

'Not yet,' Lonnie said.

'No, of course not, it's too soon for you to have to drop

out a second time,' he agreed. 'Especially with Jubilee Year coming up when I'll need you around a lot, and then at the beginning of 1936 there'll be your important birthday.'

'Yes, I'd like to put off thinking about any more family until after I'm twenty-one.'

'Barring accidents,' Flynn said with his impudent grin.

There would be no accidents; Lonnie had learnt how to deal with that possibility. She wondered if Flynn realised how carefully she prepared against any approach from him. They would have no more children until Lonnie was sure of the ground beneath her feet once more.

'More and more I'm beginning to see how unfair Rupert's Will was,' she said.

'Not really, darling. Once it's acknowledged that you're his only child then it becomes quite logical that he should leave you everything.'

'Logical perhaps; not right.'

'You've got an over-sensitive conscience. Reverse the usual order of things and give everyone a fine present on your twenty-first birthday if it makes you feel better,' Flynn said.

'It would have to be a substantial present to make it a worthwhile gesture,' Lonnie said cautiously.

'You can afford it,' Flynn said. He stood up and stretched. 'Oof, I'm stiff. I sat over the typewriter too long this afternoon.'

'How's the book coming along?'

'Very well. It seems to flow quite easily, but I'll be glad to get back to London where I can check some of my facts.'

He stretched out his hand and pulled her to her feet.

'You'll come with me, won't you?' he said, confident of her response.

He believed that he had won her over, that everything that had ever been wrong between them had been wiped out. With an ache in her heart Lonnie acknowledged that it was logical that he should think that way. She had responded to his lovemaking with a sensuality that matched his own. It was not Flynn's fault that at nineteen she felt as dried-out as the ostrich egg Margot kept in her drawing room, gaily painted, fragile and empty.

Guy's recital took place during the first week in September. Lonnie, who had learnt a lot about organisation, collected her party together beforehand for drinks and canapés, took them to the Wigmore Hall and invited them all to supper afterwards, with the promise that Guy would be the guest of honour.

When he came on to the platform it was the first time Lonnie had seen him since the agonised hours they had spent together while Rosemary was missing. He had been avoiding her and while Lonnie believed it was necessary for them to keep apart, she was still illogically angry about that prolonged silence. He might have telephoned, she thought, while even in the same breath she knew that such slight contacts could only lead to heartache.

Lonnie and her fashionable friends were sitting in the front row. Lonnie led the applause as he bowed, looking grave and remote. She thought that he had seen her; there was just the slightest upward curve in the line of his mouth and she believed it was because her presence pleased him.

She had known that Guy played well, but was unprepared for the authority he brought to the programme, chosen to display his gifts. She had been on edge for him beforehand, but from the first note Lonnie knew that she had no need to feel nervous on his behalf.

Next to her sat one of the few men she knew who was really knowledgeable about music.

'He is good, isn't he?' Lonnie asked at the end of Guy's first group of Chopin nocturnes.

'Very good indeed. A lovely tone and exquisite phrasing. I'd be prepared to bet he'll go far. It's not only that he plays well, he's got the personality, too. Did you notice it, that frisson of excitement that went through the audience when he came on to the platform? It's what lights

232

up a performance. Another musician might play the same notes, but without that communion between player and listener he wouldn't produce the same effect.'

Lonnie had felt it, but thought it was special to her. So other people felt it too, that tingle in the air when Guy walked out amongst them. She was not surprised when another of her friends, a woman with little sense but a lot of influence through her entrepreneur husband, leaned across and said, 'My dear, he's divine! Where *have* you been hiding him?'

'Guy's a serious musician,' Lonnie said. 'He doesn't go to parties.'

All the same, he did come to her party that night and in his quiet way was a resounding success. It was only Lonnie who knew that he paid little attention to the compliments he received even though he acknowledged them politely. She was glad that she could produce one man who could offer him a discerning criticism. He and Guy stood talking together for some time, until Lonnie went to join them.

'I hope you won't mind, Lonnie, but I've just offered Guy a lift home,' her friend said.

'I'm amazed Guy has stood around allowing himself to be lionised as long as he has,' Lonnie said, smiling. 'Guy, I know you have no opinion at all of my understanding of music, but all the same you must let me tell you that you were wonderful.'

'Ah well, you know what you enjoy,' Guy said tolerantly.

'Beast! Let me tell you, I got gramophone records of everything in your programme and played them over and over so that I'd be familiar with the music beforehand.'

'Dear me! And how did my playing compare with the recorded Masters?'

'As far as I could tell you didn't play any wrong notes,' Lonnie said.

They were united in warm companionship, teasing one another, but Guy knew, under the surface, how moved she had been by his performance and the secret understanding that flowed between them gave an added satisfaction to an evening that even he, hardly daring to believe that it was true, was beginning to admit had been a triumph.

'I was so afraid the whole thing would have to be cancelled,' he said. 'You know that Albi originally took responsibility for it?'

He glanced at Lonnie, anxious in case the mention of Albi's name should distress her, but Lonnie kept her smile intact.

'Fortunately, he must have paid up before . . . before he had to leave the country,' Guy went on. 'I did have some qualms about taking his money, but in the end I decided to let the booking go ahead.'

'You were quite right,' Lonnie said steadily. 'You were entitled to this concert.'

She was glad that she had arranged for the concert to go ahead; glad, too, that Guy did not know that she had paid for it. He had had doubts about taking the money from Albi, because of what Albi had done to her, and Lonnie thought there was every chance he would have thrown it up rather than accept it from her.

Or would he? For the first time that evening, Lonnie had understood Guy's stature as a musician. No wonder he had been frustrated when none of his family had taken him seriously. Lonnie ought to have known, but unconsciously she had come to think of Guy as having his mind mainly fixed on her, and now she realised her attitude towards him had been foolishly self-centred. Guy inhabited another world quite apart from the one in which she lived, a world in which he was coming to be recognised as a leader. He was committed to music in the same overwhelming way as Lonnie was to Rosemary, and it was possible that he would be just as ruthless in fostering his talent as she would be in protecting her baby. He had needed this concert and perhaps she was wrong in thinking that he would have rejected it if he had known of her part in it.

One thing Lonnie was sure about now: as long as Guy

234

could get his hands on a piano then he had something to live for besides her, no matter how deep his frustrated love for her might be.

As Flynn had anticipated, there were many special events to mark the Silver Jubilee of King George V and Flynn and Lonnie were guests at several functions at which members of the royal family were present. Lonnie was familiar with the stories of the Prince of Wales' attachment to Mrs Ernest Simpson; she even saw her on more than one occasion, though they were never introduced. Looking at the sleek, exquisitely groomed American woman Lonnie was reminded of Margot in her younger days, but Margot had never possessed the jewels Wallis Simpson was able to wear.

'Is it true that he's given them to her, do you think?' Lonnie asked Flynn.

'So I believe. He's besotted about her. I'd give my teeth to be able to write it up, but the boss has put an embargo on gossip about Wallis and Edward. There'll be one hell of a scandal if he doesn't get over it before the old man kicks the bucket.'

'Don't talk about the King like that,' Lonnie protested.

'Sorry, sweetheart, I forgot you were a royalist,' Flynn teased her.

'Not that exactly, but I do think if you're going to have a crowned head of state then he ought to be respected.'

'Even if he takes up with a previously divorced married woman, and an American at that?'

'Edward isn't King yet. And he must know he can't marry her, so let's hope he'll be cured of his infatuation before that situation arises.'

'But suppose it's true love?' Flynn asked with mock sentimentality.

'Is there such a thing?'

'Oh, darling! What about us?'

'What indeed? When I see you flirting with Dinah

Fulton like you were last night I wonder whether you really do love me.'

'Jealous? Don't be silly, Lonnie. You know there's nothing between Dinah and me apart from a bit of light chat. Do you have to take everything so seriously?'

'Apparently I do. It's not jealousy – no, it's not that. It's more a feeling that whatever we have, you belittle it by playing up to a woman with Dinah's reputation. We both know that she's been to bed with more men than she can count and we both know that she's got her sights fixed on you. If you find yourself in an awkward situation then I hope you'll remember I warned you to steer clear of her.'

That was the first of many small clashes between Lonnie and Flynn, mostly on the same subject. Flynn was irresistible to women and in the circles in which they were moving light infidelity was taken for granted. Dinah Fulton was amazed when Flynn resisted her advances, not realising that Flynn felt Lonnie's critical eyes on him and was determined not to risk a break with her. The last thing he wanted in the months leading up to Lonnie's twenty-first birthday in February 1936 was a scandal that might lead to divorce. True, Lonnie had once said that she would never divorce him, and as far as Flynn could judge she was still in love with him, in spite of an occasional coolness and a detachment which sometimes made him uncomfortable, but if she were sufficiently enraged Lonnie was capable of throwing him out of the house and starting proceedings and Flynn had no intention of risking that.

As for Lonnie, she, too, was looking forward to her birthday, but Lonnie saw it very differently from Flynn. Lonnie was making plans and the whole purpose of the talks she was having with George Osbert was to liberate herself from the golden shackles that had crippled her life.

CHAPTER THIRTEEN

'The old King has died,' Lonnie said, going into Flynn's study and interrupting his work. 'Strange, I feel quite sad about it.'

'Should be a livelier Court with Edward on the throne,' Flynn said, pushing back his chair and standing up to stretch. 'Have they said anything about the period of mourning?'

'I don't think so. Why?'

'You'll have to go into black, of course.'

'Oh, Flynn! He wasn't exactly a close relation.'

'Even so, you'll find it's expected. Good job it's happened this month. At least it won't spoil your birthday party.'

'I wouldn't have let it do that in any case,' Lonnie said. 'Especially as it's only going to be a small family party.'

She spoke firmly because she and Flynn had already disagreed about the way she was to celebrate her important twenty-first birthday. Flynn had wanted an enormous party at the Savoy, but Lonnie had held out for an intimate family gathering and had got Margot to agree that it should be held at Firsby Hall.

'Just family,' Lonnie said. 'And George, of course, because he's been as close to me as any of my relations.'

'When you say "close" you use the right word,' Flynn said. 'Old skinflint. I'll be glad to be free of him and his moaning about extravagance.'

The past year had been a good one for Flynn. His book had been a success in America and in Britain. Some reviewers had been impatient of the facile nature of his view of life in Britain, but the great snobbish public had lapped up his anecdotes of the rich and famous, and Flynn had been clever about steering clear of comments that

237

might have caused offence in circles where he was still anxious to be received.

'I talked to you once about wanting to even up the injustice of Rupert's Will,' Lonnie said. 'I hope you took that seriously, Flynn, because I meant what I said.'

'Sure! It's like you to be so sweet and generous,' Flynn agreed. 'Not *too* lavish though, sweetheart.'

He spoke carelessly, secure in the knowledge that it would take a very large bite indeed to diminish the millions of dollars Lonnie could look forward to controlling in a few weeks' time.

'You have to think of Rosie's future,' he added, confident that that was the way to Lonnie's heart.

'I think about it all the time,' Lonnie said. 'She would never have been snatched away from me if the kidnappers hadn't thought I could afford to pay to get her back.'

'We've put all that behind us. It's not still weighing on your mind, is it?'

'I never go out of the front door without wondering whether she'll be there when I come back.'

Lonnie spoke sadly, knowing that Flynn, with his mercurial nature, had put the memory far into the recesses of his mind, just as he had forgotten his adultery with Barbara and never gave a thought to poor Albi, who had disappeared so completely that no one ever spoke his name, not even the people who had once claimed to be his closest friends.

Flynn gave Lonnie a bracelet for her birthday, a supple snake of overlapping gold scales with ruby eyes, which wound three times round her wrist. Exotic, a little bizarre, but, as Flynn had assured her, of the best and most modern design.

She had jewellery from Rosemary, too, a brooch like a daffodil enamelled in yellow and green, with a diamond raindrop on one petal. Rosemary stood close to her mother while the packet was opened. She was not quite sure what it was all about, but she knew that inside there was a

238

surprise and that Mummy would be pleased when she saw it.

'Pitty,' she said as Lonnie took out the brooch.

'Very pretty, my darling,' Lonnie said, kissing her. 'Thank you very, very much. Isn't Mummy lucky to have such lovely presents for her birthday?'

'My burfday soon?' Rosemary asked hopefully.

'Not just yet, darling. Your birthday is in the summer, when the sun shines, not in the horrid wet winter like Mummy's.'

Lonnie grimaced as the rain lashed against the windows of West Lodge.

'Dismal,' she said. 'We'll have to play indoors today, Rosie-posie.'

Lonnie had a new evening gown for her party, a gleaming slip of a dress cut on the cross in white slipper satin, with a halter neck and a lot of bare back. All her jewellery had been given to her by Flynn: the ruby and diamond clips at the neck of her dress, her ruby earrings and the snake bracelet wound round her arm.

'Fire and ice,' Flynn said in their bedroom as he shrugged himself into his jacket. 'You look gorgeous.'

Lonnie turned sideways to look at herself in the glass, admiring with the detachment she always brought to her appearance the way the gleaming satin clung to her hips and defined the long line of her thighs. She wanted to look good; it would bolster up the courage she needed that evening.

There were more presents and congratulations when they reached Firsby Hall: a clock from Patsy and Edward, a sleek cocktail shaker from Barbara and Tom, a Shetland shawl as light as a cloud from Sally and Bernard and an antique chain set with moonstones from Margot and Miles.

'It belonged to my first husband's mother,' Margot said. 'I thought you'd like to have it.'

'I love it,' Lonnie said.

George Osbert gave her a silver fountain pen.

'That's because I had to borrow yours the other day,' Lonnie accused him.

'It gave me the idea,' George admitted.

'I'm being spoilt,' Lonnie said, flushed and more gratified than she had expected because everyone had taken trouble to find something to please her. 'Guy . . . you too?'

She opened the square package and found a picture inside, a small oil painting of a gypsy caravan, very gay and colourful. A woman sat on the steps, her hands resting on her knees, her legs spread wide, and a small girl in a red skirt, with bare feet in the grass, leaned against the wheel, while a black dog with its tongue hanging out panted by her side.

'It's not exactly an Old Master,' Guy said. 'But I thought you'd like it.'

'I do.' Lonnie looked at him steadily. 'The other side of my heritage. I haven't forgotten, Guy.'

For a moment they stood slightly apart from the rest of the party.

'I thought perhaps my mother might have remembered, but she hasn't,' Lonnie said.

'My dear . . .'

'It doesn't matter. Thank you for my picture. I'll keep it at West Lodge.'

Lonnie had left the dinner to Margot and as the meal progressed she knew that it was delicious, even though she herself could find very little appetite. They drank champagne and at the end of the dinner Miles got to his feet to propose a toast to Lonnie 'on achieving her majority'.

It was Bernard who called out jocularly, with no anticipation of drawing a response, 'Speech, Lonnie, speech!'

Lonnie stood up.

'As it happens, I do have something I want to say. First of all, thank you for my lovely presents and for . . . for the support you've given me over the years, particularly Aunt Patsy and Uncle Edward and, of course, dear George.'

She paused and took a deep breath and then went on, 'I've always known that Uncle Henry was wrong to leave all his money to Rupert and, even more, that Rupert was wrong to leave it to me, and now at last I can do something about it.'

Flynn stirred uneasily, conscious that Lonnie was more in earnest than he had anticipated and that she might be planning something more drastic than he would like.

'I've talked to George,' Lonnie said. 'I can't say he approves of what I'm doing, but he has admitted that there's nothing he can do to stop me. I've asked – no, I've ordered – him to divide the entire Singleton fortune into equal parts. I'm giving one part each to you Margot, to Aunt Patsy, to Sally and Barbara and Guy; another part goes to Flynn, I'm keeping one myself and putting one in trust for Rosemary and any other children I might have. The final part I plan to use as a charitable trust.'

She looked at their stunned faces and added, 'It's the actual stocks and shares I'm transferring, so the value will go up and down unless you choose to sell out. The value has picked up since the slump and the income has accumulated and been wisely invested. If you like to think in dollars then each one of you will be a millionaire, but the rate of exchange is still around five dollars to the pound, so in pounds sterling you'll get about a quarter of a million pounds each.'

She sat down and picked up her glass, but there was nothing in it.

'Could I have some more champagne?' she asked

It was George who came round to her side and refilled her glass. No one else seemed capable of moving.

'Lonnie, you've overwhelmed us,' Miles said.

'It's generosity run mad,' Flynn said. 'Lonnie, this is . . . it doesn't make sense. Why wasn't I consulted?'

'Because I already knew what you would say. And I didn't need to consult anyone once I'd made up my mind.'

'But to deprive Rosemary . . .'

'Rosemary will have her share, and mine eventually, and yours too, if you decide to leave it to her. She'll be amply provided for. I don't want her childhood to be overshadowed by vast wealth as mine was.'

'That's it, isn't it? Just because your own childhood was unhappy . . . but Rosemary will be brought up to expect money. We can train her how to handle it.'

'That's what I am doing. I'm setting her an example to follow by giving away what I don't need.'

By a supreme effort Flynn managed to rein in his mounting temper.

'Try to think about the two hundred and fifty thousand you've gained instead of the millions you might have shared,' Lonnie advised him. 'Your own money, Flynn, to do with as you like.'

'Personally, I think Lonnie has done no more than is right,' Barbara said. She laughed in a jarring way that set Lonnie's teeth on edge. 'I can't say I expected it, but I'm prepared to say "Thank you" and take what's offered.'

Sally looked more troubled. 'I'm stunned,' she said. 'Lonnie, are you sure?'

'Absolutely. Margot, are we having coffee in the drawing room?'

Margot had to rouse herself to answer. 'Yes, I think . . . oh, yes, yes of course.' As they walked together from the dining room to the firelit drawing room she said under her breath, 'My dear, are you doing the right thing?'

'Yes. Right for me and for Rosemary and, even though he can't see it at the moment because his mind is fixed on the yacht he wanted and the unlimited funds he thought he was going to have, right for Flynn, too.'

The rest of the evening was subdued. There was only one thing on their minds and all the married couples wanted to get away and to talk about it together. What Flynn wanted was an opportunity for a resounding quarrel.

Lonnie knew that it had got to come. She had anticipated it when she had decided to make her announcement without warning him in advance. She braced herself for the coming fight and chose to go home early because she could not bear the strain of postponing it any longer.

She went upstairs to fetch her wrap and paused on the landing to look at the portrait of her father. Down in the hall Guy looked up and then went up the stairs to join her.

'If anyone still had doubts about whether you were his daughter they've had it proved to them tonight,' he said, looking at the picture. 'You've acted exactly the same way as he did. An arbitrary, pigheaded decision, taken without advice and without much thought for the consequences. Did it occur to you, Lonnie dear, that I might not want a million dollar gift from you?'

'It sets you free to concentrate on your music.'

'I've begun to make progress without the benefit of a private fortune. You're coming to my concert next month?'

'Of course. If it's against your principles to be a rich man you can give the money away.'

'I probably will.'

As they stood in silence in front of Rupert's portrait, Guy said, 'You were wrong not to tell Flynn.'

'I couldn't stand him rampaging on, trying to get me to change my mind.'

'You put a terrible affront on him, just to avoid a scene.'

'Flynn's awfully good at arguing a case: he was trained for it.'

'He's your husband. If I had a wife who lobbed such a bombshell at me in the middle of a party, I'd wring her neck.'

'I don't think Flynn will do that, being more of a gentleman than you are.'

'He's been helping himself to the brandy. Don't be flippant with him, Lonnie.'

'Oh, dear, I'd better take him home and get it over. Will it help, do you think, if I tell him I'm doing it to save his self-respect?

'No, it'll make it worse.'

'It's true, all the same. Without my millions Flynn may yet make something of himself and become a man I can respect. When he chooses to use it, he's got a brilliant mind. Yachting round the world, gambling at Monte Carlo, decking me out in diamonds – that's not the life for him, nor for me, either.'

'You're still rich.'

'But not filthy rich.'

'Try telling that to a man on the dole.'

'I knew we'd get back to Socialism. Don't forget the special fund I've put on one side. I mean to use it in ways I'm sure you'll like. Please don't quarrel with me, Guy.'

'No, we mustn't quarrel. What can I say? Except perhaps, thank you for my birthday present.'

'And thank you for mine. I love the picture.'

She had started down the stairs but turned to look back at him, outlined against the dark panelling in her gleaming white satin gown, very young and very lovely, nervous about the scene she was going to face and troubled not only by Guy's lack of enthusiasm for her grand gesture, but by his failure to say anything about their love for one another. Time was when he would have seized the chance of even such a snatched moment as their meeting on the stairs to importune her to leave Flynn and turn to him. It was the first time they had set eyes on one another for months and he had said nothing. Perhaps he had got over it.

The storm that broke over her was worse than Lonnie had anticipated. She managed to confine it to the living room at West Lodge, fearing that the servants would overhear if she let the scene take place in their bedroom. She sat huddled in one of the shabby chintz armchairs, making no attempt to defend herself against the accusations Flynn hurled at her.

She saw, now that it was too late, that Guy had been right when he warned her that Flynn would feel the affront of not having been consulted, almost as much as the loss of the fortune he had expected to have at his command after her birthday.

'What am I, your kept man?' Flynn hurled at her.

244

'Could I remind you that I've worked damned hard for the past four years to earn a living for myself? I never asked you to pay my bills, did I?'

Lonnie thought of the rent of the house in London, the cottage which had been provided by Margot, the lavish food and drink for people who were more Flynn's friends than hers and was wise enough not to reply.

'I expected that once we were free of the damned restrictions your age put on us we would share,' Flynn said. 'Damn it, Lonnie, I wanted your confidence as well as your money. How could you do this to me? Everyone saw that I had no idea what you meant to spring on us tonight. I was sick, just sick. I've never been so humiliated.'

'I'm sorry. It was because I knew you'd make this sort of scene.'

'I am not making a scene,' Flynn said with emphasis. 'I'm putting forward a reasoned argument for being treated like your husband.'

He was too incensed to sit still and the room was too small to allow him the freedom of action his exacerbated feelings required. He moved restlessly from one corner to the other.

'Lonnie, how could you, how could you?' he demanded.

'I did what I thought was right.'

'The Singleton fortune belongs – belonged – to you. You didn't cheat anyone out of a cent. Except me. You've sure cheated me.'

Lonnie uncurled her legs from under her and stood up, moving stiffly.

'Why did you marry me, Flynn? Was it just for the money?'

'Why else would I throw myself away on a kid of seventeen?'

He spoke brutally, but when he saw Lonnie flinch Flynn's hand went out towards her.

'I suppose I've always known,' Lonnie said wearily.

For one appalled moment Flynn saw himself losing not only the vast Singleton fortune for which he had served for four years, but also the portion which Lonnie had

245

allotted to him. His own money, as she had said. It was not enough, but it could be made to work for him.

'I didn't mean it,' he said quickly. 'I do love you, Lonnie. I always have. We've been good together, haven't we? If I'm angry I think I have a right to be. Could you show me any husband who wouldn't be mad as fire, knowing you've told George Osbert what you didn't see fit to confide in me?'

Lonnie looked at him oddly, almost believing that it was just the lack of confidence which had upset Flynn, but knowing him too well to be taken in by the frankness in his face. Flynn never faced one so squarely as when he was lying in his teeth.

'You should have stuck to being an advocate,' she said. 'You're desperately good at it. You do realise, don't you, that no matter how you rant and rage I won't go back on what I've done?'

'There's no chance of that, not now that lot have got the scent of money in their nostrils,' he agreed. 'You've left me with no choice but to accept it. It's going to take me a long time to get over feeling aggrieved, but in the end . . . hell, what else can I do?'

'Work with me,' Lonnie said. 'Help me with the fund I've put on one side for a charitable trust.'

'Are you joking? I've never pretended to be a do-gooder. If you want to give away even more money you'll have to do it without my cooperation.'

'I want to buy some houses,' Lonnie told George Osbert.

'More than one?' George asked in surprise. 'As an investment? I don't know that property is quite the best . . .'

'It's not an investment, not in the sense that I expect to make a profit out of it. I want nasty houses, horrid little slum places, but capable of being improved. Preferably with people living in them who are out of work, but with a skill which can be used for repairing and decorating their own homes.'

It was a departure from George's comfortable country practice to be set to buying up slum property. He went about it unwillingly, especially when he realised how closely Lonnie intended to be involved in the rehabilitation of the property.

Reluctantly, he handed over to her the details of several parcels of property of the type she had demanded.

'Goodness, can I really get them as cheaply as that?' Lonnie asked. 'Marvellous! With a quarter of a million to spend I'll really be able to do some good.'

She rejected two of the proposals out of hand. 'I'm not looking for comfortable little suburban homes. I want something dreadful.' She paused over the description of a terrace of six houses in the East End of London and George's heart sank. 'This looks right,' Lonnie said. 'I'll go and see them and let you know what I decide.'

Cherry Row had never seen a tree in blossom since it had been built, although if Lonnie had delved far enough back in the history of the area she would have been surprised to discover that there had once been an orchard on the site. The houses were eighty years old, dingy and neglected, but they had been solidly built and the fabric was sound, in spite of years of neglect. The roofs leaked and some of the floorboards were rotten, the outside lavatories had cracked pans and the cold water sinks in the sculleries sagged away from the walls, but the houses were not entirely beyond redemption.

Lonnie, accompanied by a smart young estate agent, knocked firmly on every door and asked for permission to see over the house. The squalor inside shook her, but she saw that at least some of the women were doing their best with inadequate resources to keep themselves and their surroundings clean. The fierce pride which went into blackleading a grate in a room where the paper was falling off the walls was something she could respect.

'You goin' to be our new landlord – landlady, I should say?' one woman demanded.

'I think so,' Lonnie said.

'Any chance o' gettin' our roof repaired then?' She

247

spoke roughly, suspicious of this young woman, little more than a girl, in her smart clothes.

'If I take on this property every house will be made fit to live in,' Lonnie said.

The agent stirred uneasily. Outside, afterwards he said, 'I don't want to interfere, of course, but it isn't wise to make too many promises. A lot needs doing and the rents are small.'

'So I should hope! Why have the houses been so neglected?'

'The late Mr Smart was an old man and reluctant to spend money. Not that I'm saying these houses are in really bad repair, of course.'

Lonnie grinned at him. 'Let's be frank,' she said. 'We both know they're in a shocking state. As it happens, that's just what I want. I mean to spend money putting them in order. I'll take them.'

'Your man of business . . .' the agent said, thrown off-balance by this forthright way of doing a deal.

'Mr Osbert will be in touch with you, but I can assure you I mean to buy this row of houses. For one thing, the end one being empty is ideal. I'll have that one done up first and see if I can persuade one of the other families to move into it while their house is put in order.'

As George Osbert had feared, Lonnie embarked on her campaign with all the zeal of a crusading knight, nor would she listen to anything Flynn had to say against her scheme.

'You'll be rooked,' Flynn said. 'If you put up the rents they'll say they can't pay.'

'I don't mean to increase the rent.'

'In spite of the money you're pouring into the property? Don't expect gratitude, will you? The more you give, the more they'll expect.'

'When did you ever live in a house with a leaking roof, a smelly outside lavatory, no bathroom – no hot water even? Gratitude? Good God, I should be grateful to my tenants for giving me the chance to pay back some of what I owe.'

'How long have you felt like this?' Flynn asked in bewilderment. 'You never gave me any hint that you were a raging socialist.'

'I'm not. At least, I don't think I am. But I've been worrying for years about having all that money while other people went without.'

Ever since Guy had started lecturing her about it. Better not admit to that, even to herself. He was in her mind through all the difficult weeks while she was trying to sell her idea of a rebirth of Cherry Row to its occupants.

To Lonnie's surprise her plans met with suspicion and even resistance from the people she was trying to benefit.

'No one gives something for nothing,' was the verdict in Cherry Row and they waited in sullen resentment for the catch behind the benevolence to be revealed to them.

'Is there a place nearby where I can get everyone together to talk to them?' she asked the estate agent.

'There's a room at the back of the public house on the corner.' Lonnie wrinkled her nose in distaste and he went on, 'Or the church hall at St Luke's.'

'The Vicar! Why didn't I think of him before? Surely he'll be sympathetic?'

The Vicar, a tired, middle-aged man who had struggled for years in an unrewarding parish, was as bemused as everyone else by Lonnie's enthusiasm and energy, but once he understood her purpose he was willing to give his support. Lonnie had a note pushed through the door of each of the occupied houses:

> '*I want to talk over my plans for Cherry
> Row,*' the note said. '*Can you come and meet
> me at St Luke's Church hall at three o'clock
> on Saturday afternoon? Bring the children if
> you like or they can come along later for tea
> and sandwiches at four o'clock.*'

The simplicity of the wording made the Vicar smile, but it achieved what Lonnie wanted and there was a full turn-out of tenants, both husbands and wives, at her little meeting.

The Vicar was there and the young estate agent who was going to be Lonnie's rent collector. George Osbert had wanted to come up from the country, but Lonnie had assured him that she could manage on her own. She had offered Flynn the chance to share in her new venture, but Flynn would only come if she allowed him to write it up in his column and Lonnie was averse to that sort of publicity.

'You surely aren't going to visit your slum dressed like that?' he demanded before Lonnie set out.

'The wives like seeing my pretty clothes. They'll resent it if they think I've put on something shabby to go visiting them.'

In her Hartnell suit and matching hat, with her shining hair and lacquered nails, Lonnie was as glamorous as a film star to the people who had come to meet her. They did not exactly envy her, she was too remote from them for that, but there was some impatience in the air, a feeling that she could not possibly understand their lives.

She disarmed them by the same directness she had used when writing to them.

Standing up in front of her tenants she said, 'When I was a child I inherited a lot of money, far more than I could ever use. Now that I'm twenty-one I want to put it to good use.'

There was a stir on interest. So young, and so fortunate; it was like a fairy tale.

'I've already divided the money up in a way I thought was fair, but I've kept a fund which I want to use to help people like you.'

There was another movement and this time a voice said roughly, 'We don't want charity, missus.'

'That's not what I'm offering,' Lonnie said swiftly. 'If this scheme is to work then you'll have to do your part, too.'

She fairly caught their attention when she went on, 'The houses you live in are a disgrace.'

'Too right they are,' one of the women agreed. 'We've been saying it for years.'

'I mean to repair and improve them, but I'll need your co-operation.'

'How much is it going to cost us? I'm hard put to it to pay the rent already, with my man out o'work.'

'The rents will stay the same, but from next week the money will go into a pool to pay for future repairs and decorations.'

'You mean you won't make anything out of it at all?'

'That's right. I've told you, I don't need the money. I think – I hope – that if the houses are put into good shape and the rent money is allowed to build up then they should be self-supporting in the future, barring any really bad luck.'

'There's some of us could do the decoratin' if you supplied the materials,' a man volunteered.

'That's one of the things I had in mind. Someone mentioned a husband out of work. Is there anyone here who's unemployed who'd be able to do some of the repair jobs?'

'Jesus! Sorry, Vicar. I'm a plasterer by trade, miss . . . ma'am . . . I've been out of a job, off an' on, for the last eighteen months.'

'We'll have to get the houses properly surveyed so that we know what's absolutely essential to be done. That'll mean letting men in to look at walls and . . . and drains, and so on. I hope you won't mind.'

'We're none of us ashamed of our homes,' one of the women said. 'We keep them as clean as we can, given the difficulties. I'm sure I wouldn't object to anyone coming into *my* place.'

She looked around, proud of her superior attitude.

'That's all right, then,' Lonnie said. 'I thought perhaps we could form ourselves into a company – a sort of co-operative, I suppose you'd call it – and pool any skills that might be around. Anything we haven't got, like a plumber or . . . or a roof repairer, we'll employ.'

'Trouble is, the Labour Exchange might say we were working if we were doin' it for our own benefit,' someone pointed out. 'If they docked our dole and we had nothing else coming in we'd be in Queer Street. New paint's all right, but you can't eat it.'

There were murmurs of agreement.

'But of course you'd be paid for any work done,' Lonnie said, shocked. 'There are agreed rates for that sort of work, aren't there? I don't know much about it, but there'll be someone running the scheme for me who does. I thought it would count as proper employment and you could come off the dole.'

There was such a long silence that she began to feel uneasy. At last someone said in a dazed way, 'Sounds almost too good to be true.'

'I expect there'll be difficulties, even disagreements,' Lonnie said. 'Still, with a bit of goodwill I should think we could make it work. Can anyone think of any objections to raise now?'

A timid voice spoke from the back of the small gathering.

'My husband's on the railway. He couldn't be here this afternoon because he's working. I expect he'd help where he could, but he's not much of a handyman. Does that mean we wouldn't get things done?'

'By no means. Everyone will be treated the same. The way I see it working is this: Number 6, the house at the end of the row, is empty so we'll start by turning that into a really decent place. If that was done would the people next door be prepared to move into that house so that their house could be done – and so on all down the row?'

Lonnie was unprepared for the dismayed young woman who said, 'I've asked for Number 6 for my sister. She and her husband are still living with Mum and Dad, with one baby already and another on the way. She's counting on moving into Number 6.'

Lonnie took the first of the hard decisions she had to face in her new scheme.

'I'm sorry,' she said. 'I don't see how the work can be done with families living in the houses. Having one empty

252

was what made Cherry Row ideal. Your sister can have the promise of the last house that's put in order.'

'I don't relish having to tell her.'

'A nice clean house instead of a run-down dirty one,' Lonnie urged.

She had expected more enthusiasm than she got and she admitted as much to the Vicar over the cup of tea she drank thirstily after all the talking she had done.

'These are people who've learnt to look a gift horse in the mouth,' he said. 'They need to go away and talk it over between themselves before they can come to terms with your generosity, but you'll always find them chary of expressing gratitude.'

'Gratitude isn't what I want, but a bit more excitement would be welcome,' Lonnie said ruefully.

She was glad she had thought to offer refreshments after the meeting. Going round and talking to her new tenants with a cup of tea in her hand broke the ice far more than the meeting had done and she discovered that the women, in particular, were easier to talk to when they clustered round her instead of sitting with their men. When they found out that she had a small child of her own they were even more forthcoming.

'Fancy! you must have married young,' an older woman said.

'I was seventeen.'

'Goodness, that was young. What does your hubby say to you laying out your money like this?'

Lonnie answered with apparent frankness. 'He thinks I'm crazy. But he knew I meant to do something of the sort when I divided up the money and put some on one side for . . .' She was about to say 'for charity', but just in time remembered that that was what they did not want. '. . . for helping people less fortunate,' she ended diplomatically.

'Is he rich, too?'

'He's got the same as I have,' Lonnie said truthfully.

'So he doesn't have to work for a living?'

'He does work. He writes for a newspaper.'

There was a distrustful pause and then she was asked, 'Goin' to write us up, is he?'

'Not if I can help it! This is a private arrangement between us. I don't want any publicity for it.'

On the whole, Lonnie felt that they had warmed towards her before the end of the afternoon. And the fact that she meant to take a personal interest in the progress of the work counted for a lot. They were tired of being the tenants of a cantankerous old man who never showed his face and refused to allow his rent collectors to authorise any repairs. This bright young woman with her forthright way of talking and her interest in them was something new. It would take some getting used to, but they were prepared to go along with her plans.

'See how it works out,' was the general verdict.

CHAPTER FOURTEEN

In March, just a month after the party at Firsby Hall, Guy had a concert in Leeds at which he played Mozart's Piano Concerto No.21 in C Major and a composition of his own, a *Nocturne* for piano and orchestra. The Mozart was warmly received and Guy was brought back to the platform three times to receive the applause. The audience was more puzzled by the *Nocturne*, but Lonnie noticed that the other players put down their instruments to clap and the conductor was particularly warm in the way he put his hand on Guy's shoulder and congratulated him.

She went backstage afterwards to see him. His mother and father were there and Margot. Guy looked both tired and keyed up. Lonnie, without having to be told, knew that he had driven himself to the point of exhaustion in his preparation for the concert, that he had played in a state of exultation which had lifted him above nervousness and now he was trying to cope with the aftermath.

The conductor came in behind her then and, speaking to him directly, although she did not know him, Lonnie said, 'He ought to send all these people away and be quiet.'

'Not yet. For the moment he needs the excitement, the congratulations, the reassurance that he has done well.'

Looking at her concerned face and taking in her beauty and elegance, he went on. 'I don't think we've met before. Are you a close friend of Guy's?'

'A cousin – sort of,' Lonnie said. 'Lonnie Branden.'

'Lonnie! Then I do know you, in a way. The *Nocturne* is dedicated to you, isn't it? Did you like it?'

Somehow Lonnie managed to find an answer for him while struggling to contain the joy that rose up inside her like a fountain overflowing. So much for her fear that Guy had forgotten his love for her. He had put her name on this first work of his to be performed in public.

'It was strange, haunting music,' she said. 'I don't know what to say about it. I'd like to hear it again.'

'It repays closer study. A small piece of music, but characteristic of Guy's work. I look forward with the greatest interest to his *Concerto*.'

He nodded and moved forward to speak to Guy and Lonnie noticed the warmth of his smile and his handshake, the way his hand closed over Guy's shoulder. A famous musician, a conductor of great orchestras, with whom Guy was on terms of familiarity and liking.

When she managed to get close to Guy Lonnie said, 'I thought after your London recital that we hadn't been taking you seriously enough. Now I know that even then I wasn't doing you justice. This evening you were . ... magnificent.'

Guy's eyebrows went up and he smiled his familiar lopsided smile.

'"*A prophet is not without honour* . . ." and all that,' he said. 'Whoever heard of a man's own family recognising his genius?'

'You played the Mozart beautifully, but that wasn't the most important part of the evening, was it?'

'It was a great honour but, no, for me the best thing was hearing my own work. I hope Mozart, if he's listening, will forgive me.'

For a moment they were isolated, with everyone else in the room occupied, and Lonnie murmured, 'You dedicated it to me.'

'Who else? My love.'

He was smiling down at her, serene and confident, but crackling with nervous energy. Lonnie closed her eyes, feeling dizzy, but when she put out her hand the support she found was Guy's arm, every muscle tense beneath the smooth fabric of his jacket.

'Guy, don't,' she pleaded. 'Not here, not now.'

'When?'

'Never, never!' She broke away from him and turned

256

towards the door. 'We must go,' she said loudly. 'There's a table booked for supper and I'm sure we all want to drink to Guy's success, don't we?'

Lonnie managed to get through the rest of the evening, but only by drawing on the gifts she had cultivated since her marriage. In a fountain of inconsequential chatter she drowned the desolation that must not be allowed to show, laughing and talking, keeping the party going and never, if she could help it, looking at Guy.

He was watching her, Lonnie knew that, even though she refused to glance in his direction. She sensed the moment when his excitement abated, when he began to feel the flatness of extreme exhaustion, the beginnings of the fear that, after all, he had not done as well as he had thought at the time. That was the danger point for Lonnie, when she longed to go to him and put her arms round him and reassure him.

She looked round and saw, as she had expected, that Guy had slumped in his chair, his fingers playing nervously with the stem of his empty glass, all the fire gone out of him.

'I think we ought to let poor Guy get some rest,' she said. 'Aunt Patsy, don't you agree?'

'He does look tired,' Patsy agreed. 'And I'm sure I am, after travelling all the way up here. Well, it's all been very nice and most exciting, of course. I can't say I understood that piece of yours, Guy, but other people seemed to like it, so I suppose I'm just old fashioned. At least we don't have to worry now about whether you'll make any money out of it, thanks to Lonnie.'

Guy looked up at that and once again Lonnie knew, from the amused quirk at the corner of his mouth, exactly what his reaction was to that characteristic remark from his mother. Guy tried to catch her eye to share the joke, but Lonnie looked away.

'Lonnie, you're staying at a different hotel, aren't you?' Guy asked. 'I'll see you back to it.' He glanced round and added with what Lonnie immediately recognised as rather too elaborate casualness, 'I can do with a breath of air and

I need to wind down after all the excitement, so I may go for a stroll round the town after I've dropped Lonnie off.'

Outside they discovered that it had been raining, but although the pavements gleamed wetly and there were ragged clouds chasing across the moon, the rain had stopped.

'Are your shoes up to walking?' Guy asked.

'If I skip over the puddles.'

He drew her hand through his arm and with her other hand Lonnie lifted her long skirt clear of the wet ground.

'That's better. For the last hour I've been waiting to be alone with you,' Guy said as they strolled slowly along.

'It's no use asking my opinion of the concerto. You know I haven't the technical knowledge to satisfy you,' Lonnie said, hurrying into nervous speech.

'What I want to hear you say is that you love me.'

He stopped and turned her to face him. The street was empty, not a passerby, not even a car in sight. By the light of the lamp over their heads Lonnie could see the lines of tension on Guy's face. He held her lightly, his hands just resting on her shoulders, but even through the thickness of her fur cape Lonnie could feel that touch. For the space of two heartbeats she held out, then all the pride and excitement she had felt that evening came rushing in, all the delight in his music, all her frustrated longing to take him in her arms and show him what he meant to her.

'Yes, I love you. Oh, Guy, I do, I do!'

She had scarcely spoken before Guy moved, taking his hands away from her shoulders to put his arms round her under the fur cape, holding her so tightly crushed against him that Lonnie could scarcely breathe. She wound her arms round his neck, clinging to him, her mouth opening under the force of his kiss, her hands digging into the hair at the back of his neck.

It was only when a car came round the corner, lighting them up with the beam from its headlamps, that Lonnie came to her senses. She pulled away, evading Guy's demanding hands.

'Guy . . . darling, darling, we must be sensible,' she said distractedly.

'Sensible! It's too late for that. How far is it to your hotel?'

'Just round the corner, but . . .'

'I'm coming in with you. Lonnie, you can't say no to me now.'

He was right. She had gone too far and the force of the desire that had been unleashed would give her no rest until it was satisfied. As Guy hurried her towards her hotel Lonnie tried to think calmly, to remember all the arguments she had used against giving in to their love, but it was no use, she was defeated, not just by Guy's ardour, but by her own longing for him.

As she went up to the reception desk to get her key she felt dishevelled and selfconscious, but the clerk handed over the key without apparently noticing anything unusual, even though Lonnie's fingers were so clumsy that she dropped the key and Guy had to pick it up for her.

As he straightened up he caught her eye and smiled and Lonnie smiled back, ruefully admitting the state she was in. On the far side of the open hall there were people having late-night coffee. Lonnie saw heads turned towards them, but for the moment she did not understand the stir of interest, not until one of the women got up and came towards them.

'Excuse me, it is Guy Lynton, isn't it? Oh, Mr Lynton, you must let me tell you how wonderful you were tonight. We admired you so much.'

For a moment Guy looked blank, then he murmured a word of thanks and would have moved on, but the woman put a hand on his arm.

'I wonder, would you think me quite awful if I asked you to autograph my programme? Just a minute, don't go away . . . it's right here.'

She darted back to her table and Guy muttered under his breath, 'Oh, Lord . . .'

Lonnie stood as if turned to stone. To Guy this recognition meant no more than a momentary embarrassment, but to Lonnie it came as a shock which released her from her blind unthinking flight into Guy's arms.

The woman came back, carrying not one but three programmes.

'Will you?' she asked. 'We're all so thrilled at seeing you like this.' She cast a glance at Lonnie and asked, 'Is this Mrs Lynton? Oh, no, you're not married, are you?'

Her curiosity was palpable and it was yet another warning to Lonnie. She managed to say, while Guy scribbled on the programmes, 'Guy is my cousin.'

'I expect you're ever so proud of him in the family, aren't you?'

'Yes, we are,' Lonnie agreed quietly.

She felt sick, drained of energy and quite despairing, because it was going to be impossible to get Guy to understand her sudden, irreversible change of mind.

When he turned back to her Guy saw immediately that there was something wrong.

'Lonnie . . .' he said.

'I can't go on with it.'

As she had expected Guy didn't believe her. He drew her to one side to argue fiercely, but in that brightly-lit space, surrounded by curious eyes, he was unable to use the one means of persuasion that might have brought Lonnie once more to the peak of passionate desire from which she had just tumbled.

'You've been recognised,' she said dully. 'I should have thought of it before. Your face is on posters all over the town. I can't take you up to my room.'

'Why not? What does it matter?'

'I've held out against divorcing Flynn, but I'm not so sure that, given the chance, he might not divorce *me*.'

'And a very good thing too. I'd be delighted.'

'What about Rosemary?'

'Do you think I wouldn't love and cherish her?'

'Suppose Flynn claimed custody of her?'

'He wouldn't,' Guy said, but Lonnie was not so sure.

'She's his daughter and he does love her. Even if he let

me keep her, he'd want to go on seeing her and I don't want that sort of divided life for her.'

'Once he was free perhaps he'd go back to America.'

'That could be even worse. He might insist on her going over to visit him. I'd never have a moment's peace if that happened.'

The intensity of their argument was attracting attention. Lonnie was aware of it, if Guy was not.

'Your marriage was a mistake,' he insisted. 'You know it and so does Flynn. You've paid him off. Let him take his money and go. As for Rosemary, she's young enough to adjust.'

It was too brutal. For once, Guy, exhausted but full of nervous tension, angry and hurt by her abrupt rejection, had misjudged her frame of mind, and Lonnie, recognising the ruthless strain she had always known that Guy possessed, shrank from his apparent callousness.

'If you'd ever had a child, you'd understand,' she said. 'I love Rosie . . .'

'More than you love me, it seems.'

'Please, please understand. I do love you, yes, I do, but I won't do anything that might damage her life as mine was damaged. Tonight I've been weak, but I know really that I have to put you out of my mind and you must find someone else . . .'

'Good God, do you think I haven't tried? I suffer from a crippling disability, Lonnie dear: every time I have a woman I wish she was you. I've never yet been rendered impotent, but it doesn't make for a satisfying relationship with anyone else.'

Lonnie shrank from the bitterness behind his words. The memory of her torrid summer nights with Flynn came back to haunt her and she was filled with shame.

'I'm sorry,' she said, knowing that it was an inadequate response to Guy's desperation.

'I've loved you and wanted you for longer than I can remember and now tonight, when at last I feel I've got something to bring to you . . . Lonnie, you can't do this to me.'

261

Lonnie closed her eyes, swayed now not so much by her own longing as by Guy's pain. Once again a voice broke in on her agonised indecision.

'Goodnight, Mr Lynton! So nice to have met you. We'll be looking out for your next concert.'

'Bloody woman,' Guy muttered. 'I could kill her.'

He was beaten. He knew it and so did Lonnie.

'You're going to send me away, aren't you?' he asked.

Lonnie moved her head in affirmation, unable to speak.

'You say you love me, but you don't, not in the way I thought you did.' Guy said. 'I've waited years to hear you say it and now it doesn't mean a thing. These hesitations, these fears . . . all they really amount to is that you aren't sure enough to commit yourself. If you truly loved me you'd come to me willingly without a thought for that American playboy you call a husband.'

He turned and left her and Lonnie's throat was too closed up with grief to call him back.

She returned to London the next day, quiet and selfcontained. Outwardly she was Mrs Flynn Branden, the elegant young socialite, the popular partygoer, the hostess whose invitations were eagerly sought after, but inside she was Lonnie Dunwell, crying in the dark for a love she could not have.

She went straight up to the nursery as soon as she got home, not even stopping to take off her hat and coat, and picked up Rosemary and hugged her. It was some comfort, to hold that wriggling little body in her arms and to feel Rosemary's wet kisses on her cheek.

Flynn came in search of her, holding the morning's newspaper in his hand.

'I made a mistake, not going to that concert with you,' he said. 'Seems Guy's the coming man in the music world and I've missed out on his début.'

'It was hardly that. He's played in public before,' Lonnie said, setting Rosemary down.

'But not with Barbirolli conducting,' Flynn said. 'And

what counts is what this critic has said about his own music. Was it that good?'

'It was unusual,' Lonnie said. She braced herself and added, 'He dedicated the *Nocturne* to me.'

'Hell! I could have got a whole paragraph out of that. Why didn't you tell me?'

'I didn't know until last night.'

'We'll have to keep up with him in future. When can we have him to dinner?'

'I doubt if he'd come,' Lonnie said.

'Sure he would, if you got the right people to meet him. Guy knows what side his bread's buttered and with all that money you've given him he ought to be able to afford a new tuxedo.'

'You sound so American when you say things like "tuxedo",' Lonnie said, trying to evade the issue, but when Flynn persisted she said, 'I . . . I think Guy's going abroad.'

She had spoken at random, because from her knowledge of him it seemed a likely thing for Guy to do, something she would have done herself in his shoes to try to escape the pain of being in the same town, the same country as the one whose love was denied him. She soon discovered that she had guessed correctly: Guy had gone back to his beloved Vienna.

In the months following her birthday Lonnie heard from Margot how her generosity had changed other lives.

'Miles is urging me to invest in a stud farm,' Margot told her. 'He always wanted to extend the stables here, you know, but George wouldn't countenance the cost. Now, Sally and Bernard are planning to use their share of the money to start up in Wiltshire and Miles wants to have a stake in it.'

'You don't like the idea?' Lonnie asked.

'I'm not interested in horses and I think Miles has enough to do here without getting involved in another business.'

'Then you'll turn the idea down?'

'I should, but in the end I probably won't.' Margot sounded weary. 'You know what men are like when they've set their hearts on anything. Miles will go on chivvying me until I agree. I might just as well give in easily and bask in his gratitude. Miles can be quite charming when he's getting his own way.'

It sounded so much like Lonnie's own dilemma that she could find nothing to say.

'It will give him the excuse he needs to stay away for a night occasionally,' Margot went on. 'He thinks I don't know about his mistress in Brighton but, of course, I've known almost from the time the affair started. She was a typist in George's office, about twenty-four; a peroxide blonde with a lot of bounce. George found an excuse to get rid of her and now, as far as I know, Miles supports her.

'Margot, I'm sorry . . .' Lonnie said helplessly.

'My dear, I've accepted it as something I have to bear. Miles still gives me companionship and he's a very competent estate manager. Perhaps it will surprise you when I say I have no regrets about marrying him. We had some happy years and as long as I can keep my dignity, I don't grudge him his toys. So, in the end I'll probably let him have his horses.'

'Does it always have to be like that?' Lonnie asked in a low voice.

'In my first marriage I took more than I gave. Perhaps I'm paying for that now. As for you . . . you're very young and, though it may not seem so to you, your marriage is quite new.'

'Four years.'

'That's nothing. If you and Flynn have your difficulties, it's only to be expected. I was disappointed in Flynn when he ran off with you, but I can still see that he's a charming and talented man. Be patient with him, Lonnie.'

It was all very well for Margot to dispense advice, she did not have Lonnie's cynical understanding of the way Flynn had come to terms with the division of her fortune.

As the transfers of stocks and shares came in he began to see the benefit of having money of his own. It might not be what he had anticipated, but it was substantial.

He never mentioned returning to the United States and Lonnie was no longer sure what her response would be if he did. Once she had urged it on him; now she kept quiet because she could not bear the thought of living alone with Flynn in a strange country, so far from all her friends, so far from Guy.

With her newly acquired wealth Barbara was again pursuing a social life and she had a knack of getting herself invited to the same functions as Flynn and Lonnie, more often than not without her husband.

After an evening spent watching Barbara's increasingly possessive attitude towards Flynn, Lonnie tackled him about it.

'You're not starting up that affair again, are you?' she asked.

'No, indeed!'

'It's more than I could bear.'

'I promise you, honey, that's all done with.'

Lonnie believed him, but she wondered whether Barbara was equally sure that the affair was finished.

With this doubt in her mind Lonnie was reluctant to see Barbara when her cousin called on her one day, but while she hesitated, on the verge of telling the maid to say she was out, Barbara came up the stairs to the drawing room uninvited.

'You don't mind, do you?' she said. 'I'm one of the family, after all.'

'Do come in,' Lonnie said, all sweetness. 'We'll have tea, Mavis.'

Barbara loosened her expensive coat and lit a cigarette. It struck Lonnie that she was on edge, but they both kept to small talk until the maid had brought in the tea cups and biscuits.

'No sugar or milk, just lemon for me,' Barbara said. 'I must watch my figure. These narrow fashions are dire if you put on an ounce, aren't they?'

Lonnie handed her the cup of tea without answering. Whatever Barbara had come for, it was not to talk about clothes.

Her level regard seemed to make Barbara even more nervous. The cup rattled on the saucer as she set it down.

'Tom and I are splitting up,' she said.

'I'm sorry,' Lonnie said automatically, but she was more alert than she seemed.

'It was always a mistake,' Barbara said. 'We could hardly have got off to a worse start, with Flynn turning up at our wedding. It was Flynn I really wanted.'

'Was it? Even after his father's disgrace?'

'I could have got over that, if Flynn . . .'

'If Flynn had asked you, but he didn't, did he?'

'By the time he came back it was too late and so he let himself be dazzled by your money bags. All right, you've done the decent thing about that. I'm independent now.'

'And you've decided to get rid of your husband. Are you sure you're doing the right thing, Barbara?'

Barbara lit another cigarette while the tea in her cup grew cold.

'I want something more than being a second-rate architect's wife,' she said. 'Lonnie, you know that Flynn and I love one another . . .'

'Do I?'

'You must do. You've seen us together . . .'

'Indeed I have.'

Barbara flushed, reliving the hideous embarrassment of the scene Lonnie was remembering. 'We were lovers that first time he came to England.' she said.

'I know. It's one of the things I find very hard to forgive Flynn.' The sadness with which she spoke puzzled Barbara.

'I thought he meant to marry me,' she excused herself. 'I was devastated when he went back to America without saying anything and so eventually I took Tom because it seemed the only thing to do. If I'd known Flynn meant to come back I would have waited.'

Her self-deception filled Lonnie with horror at the

disillusion that was in store for her. 'He didn't come back for you,' she said.

'If I'd still been free, you wouldn't have got him. I'd have seen to that.'

Lonnie shook her head, unable to see how she could convey to Barbara that her belief in Flynn's love was a delusion.

'Let him go,' Barbara urged her. 'There's nothing to tie him to you now . . .'

'Because I'm no longer worth millions? But Barbara, I'm still Flynn's wife and we have a child. Have you forgotten her?'

'Naturally you'd keep Rosemary. I wouldn't mind if Flynn saw her. It could all be perfectly civilised.'

'Have you talked to Flynn about this?' Lonnie asked.

'Not in so many words,' Barbara admitted. 'It's only since last night that I've made up my mind to divorce Tom.'

'He's to provide the evidence?'

'Well, naturally. He's fairly broken up about it, but he's prepared to do it decently.'

'Poor Tom. I hope he has better luck with his second wife, if it really does come to a divorce; but you're making a mistake, Barbara: Flynn won't marry you.'

'He will, he will!' Barbara stubbed out her cigarette, grinding it into the ashtray.

Lonnie watched her, trying to find a way of conveying to Barbara the hopelessness of her situation.

'When I said I was still Flynn's wife, I meant that – precisely,' she said. 'We sleep in the same bed and he makes love to me. I don't think he's entirely faithful, though he assures me he's not been back to bed with you, but we still have a marriage and I mean to keep it that way.'

Barbara tried to light yet another cigarette, but the flame of her lighter jerked so much that she had difficulty in achieving it.

'Damn you,' she said in a fierce whisper. 'I should have

known you'd hang on to him. If he turns to you sometimes it's out of frustration. It's me Flynn wants.'

'I don't think so.'

'I'm much better suited to him than you are. We share the same tastes, we've got the same ideas. You're just a mouse compared with me, for all your fancy clothes. Flynn needs me. With me by his side he could really get on. If you'd give him a divorce . . .'

'Citing you?'

'Yes! I'd even agree to that.'

'There's only one way to settle this,' Lonnie said, getting to her feet. 'Flynn must tell you himself. I've been trying to spare him – and you, though God knows why – but you're so blind, you simply won't see that Flynn is a born philanderer. He'll play up to any woman, but I'm prepared to bet the rest of my horrible fortune that he doesn't want me to divorce him so that he can marry you.'

'Flynn isn't here,' Barbara said in an uncertain whisper.

'He's working in his study. I'll fetch him.'

'No!'

'Yes. Barbara. This can't go on. Perhaps once you're convinced, you may be able to patch things up with Tom.'

She went out of the room, ignoring Barbara's protest. Outside, Lonnie leaned against the wall for a moment with her eyes closed. What had gone before had been bad enough, but the disillusionment that was coming to her cousin now was something Lonnie could hardly bear to think about.

Flynn looked up as she went into his study. He had a habit of running his fingers through his hair when he was thinking which gave him a dishevelled boyish look. He smiled at her, but Lonnie was not capable of returning that smile.

'Barbara is here and talking about divorcing Tom to marry you,' she said. 'There's no help for it, you'll have to come and see her.'

'Oh, Lonnie, must I?'

That reply alone told Lonnie everything she needed to know. Not that she had doubted the outcome. If Flynn were to leave her, it would not be for Barbara, but for a much bigger fish.

'You must,' she said.

He managed it very well. Practice, Lonnie thought; this was not the first time Flynn had given the brush-off to an importunate women. Poor Barbara.

Lonnie would have preferred to have left them alone, but Flynn took hold of her arm and propelled her into the room with him and even Barbara could not misread the fact that it was Lonnie who was reluctant to be present and Flynn who wanted her there.

Even so, it was difficult to convince her that the dream on which she had been living had no substance to it.

'It was all over a long time ago,' Flynn said. 'I'm sorry, Barbara. I've been weak and foolish, and I've behaved badly towards you – and towards Lonnie – but I've made up my mind that my place is with my wife and child and you must help me to keep to that decision.'

It was a mistake to put that hint of regret into his words because Barbara was quick to seize on it and to believe that he was acting against his true inclination, but at last it was borne in on her that Flynn might look at her sadly and speak to her gently, but he had no intention of allowing her importunity to sway him.

'You have no heart,' Barbara said in a hoarse whisper, worn out by her own frustrated anger. 'No heart at all. It was what I thought when you first let me down and then – when we met again, when you made love to me – I thought I was mistaken, that you really did care and had been driven away by circumstances, not by your own selfishness. You're a swine, Flynn, a lowdown miserable swine and I'm sorry for Lonnie. God, to think I once envied her!'

She looked round helplessly, appalled by her predicament.

'What am I to do?'

'Go back to Tom,' Flynn advised. 'I'm sorry to part with you like this, believe me I am, but in a year or two you'll thank me for it.'

'Don't be a fool. Of course I can't go back to Tom. I doubt if he'd have me.'

She stood up, pulling herself together with an effort that hurt Lonnie to see.

'I suppose you're pleased to see me humiliated,' she said to Lonnie.

'No. I've hated every minute of it. But it was necessary. Now you can get on with your real life instead of wasting it waiting for Flynn to turn to you.'

'Is that how it seemed to you?'

The bitter little smile that curled Barbara's lips was not pleasant.

'At least I can afford to live an independent life,' she said. 'And I have you to thank for that. Ironic, isn't it? I thought your money would help me to buy Flynn off you, but all it's going to do is to give me the freedom to live alone.'

Neither of them spoke as Lonnie showed her out. Lonnie was relieved when Barbara picked up a taxi straight away and drove off without a backward look.

Upstairs, Flynn had helped himself to a stiff drink. As Lonnie came back into the drawing room he looked at her with an apologetic air that grated on her because, as a reaction to Barbara's heartbreak, it seemed inadequate.

'I'm sorry you were let in for that,' he said.

'It wasn't very pleasant,' Lonnie said, speaking carefully.

'Poor deluded Barbara. There's been nothing between us, you know, not since . . .'

'Since the night Rosemary was born,' Lonnie concluded for him. 'I know.'

To Lonnie it seemed that the very air between them was chilled, so that she hugged her arms to her to stop herself from shivering. Flynn drained his glass.

'I needed that,' he said. 'A ghastly scene. Thank goodness it's over. I don't feel much like it, but I must get back to my desk.'

Already he was putting it behind him. It had been unfortunate, but he had come out of it without losing anything, certainly not his self-esteem. Lonnie was being reasonable. A little cold, but that was only to be expected. He had got rid of Barbara, who was no longer of any interest to him, and she could be forgotten. And this was the man she had chosen to live with, Lonnie thought blankly. Instead of Guy, who would give her warmth and understanding, she had this cold-hearted egotist.

If Guy had been there at that moment her rebellion against the choice she had made would have taken her into his arms regardless of the consequences, but by the time Guy was back in England Lonnie had thought again about the damage a divorce might do to Rosemary and she greeted him with nothing more than the controlled friendship which was all she allowed between them.

'Did you enjoy Vienna?' she asked.

'Not much,' Guy said. 'The atmosphere has deteriorated since I was last there. Too many Nazi sympathisers. Don't you read the papers?'

'Of course I do. Don't be rude to me, Guy.'

'Rude! Have you any idea what it feels like to have spent four months away from you and then to come back and find that nothing's changed? I worked myself into the ground and at times I managed to forget you, but now I'm back I only have to set eyes on you and I know I might just as well have stayed at home.'

They were in Lonnie's pale drawing room. Flynn was in his study. At any moment he might come into the room, especially since he had taken it into his head that Guy was a man to be cultivated.

'It hasn't been easy for me either,' Lonnie said in a low voice, but the only response she got to that was an impatient gesture from Guy. It made her angry because it seemed to her that he gave her no credit for the effort she was making to save them both from disaster.

'Tell me about your music,' she said.

'I've been composing – the time away was good for that,' Guy admitted. 'I practised, of course, and had some lessons. I was invited to give a recital at a private musical evening, mostly Jews so I suppose they'll soon be in concentration camps. I helped out a very talented violinist by acting as her accompanist when her usual pianist suddenly became unavailable, which means he was persuaded it wouldn't be wise to associate with her any longer.'

'Another Jew?'

'Of course. I nearly married her.'

'Guy . . .'

The shock was all the greater because of the way he had been speaking only a minute earlier. With an effort Lonnie held on to her control, unaware that she was clutching her arms, tightly folded across her body, holding in the hurt.

'Don't look like that. Just to get her out of the country, that's all. In the end she couldn't bring herself to leave the man she really loves.'

Lonnie let out a long breath, unaware of how much she had given away in that one moment of agony.

'Poor girl,' she said. 'Is there anything I can do?'

'I brought out some jewellery. Would you sell it and put the money in a special account, to be held for her and her family in case they ever come over as refugees?'

'Of course. But why don't you do it?'

'I may not be around.'

Before Lonnie could find out what that meant Flynn came and joined them, radiating the charm and good humour for which he was famous. His lightweight grey suit had been tailored in Saville Row and he wore it with a careless dash that made the most of his outstanding looks. By the side of him Guy looked unkempt. His hair needed cutting, his shoes needed cleaning and his flannel trousers and tweed jacket had seen better days. He was not as tall as Flynn, his features were not as regular and his expression at that moment was morose. He looked more like an out-of-work schoolmaster than a talented musician on the verge of success, Lonnie thought in mingled exasperation and affection. But it was this difficult, obstinate man who held her heart in his hand and not her fine sleek husband.

'Well, Guy! Fresh from your continental conquests?' Flynn asked.

'Hardly that.'

'I was just sick that I had to miss your Leeds concert. I hope Lonnie remembered to give you my apologies.'

'You can always rely on Lonnie to say the right thing,' Guy said, and Lonnie winced, knowing he was referring to more than her polished good manners.

'That's true,' Flynn said. 'She's a great asset. You should get yourself a wife, Guy. Now that your career has started to take off a nice, pretty girl would be useful to you. Have you been writing any more music?'

Guy's expression had become so thunderous that Lonnie was afraid of what he might say. It was a relief when he merely replied, 'I've finished the *Concerto* I've been working on for some time.'

'Great! Is it going to be performed? I'll give you a mention in my column.'

'How very good of you,' Guy said gently. 'I'm afraid it'll be some time before it achieves public performance. In the meantime, I'm going abroad again.'

'Where?' Lonnie asked, the question torn out of her.

'To Spain, of course.'

When they both stared at him in disbelief, Guy said, 'It has been reported in this complacent little country that war's broken out in Spain, hasn't it?'

'All the more reason to keep away,' Flynn said.

'I disagree. I feel it's my duty, after what I've seen in Austria and Germany, to go and fight against Fascism.'

'Guy, no!'

The protest from Lonnie was no more than a tiny whisper.

'You gave me my independence,' Guy said, and again Lonnie knew he was referring to more than the money she had shared with him. 'You mustn't complain if I use it in ways you don't like.'

'But to fight in Spain – it's crazy, illogical.'

'Not to me. I look on it as a rehearsal for the real war that's coming to Europe.'

'You really believe that?' Flynn asked.

'Since Hitler marched into the Rhineland in March anything's possible. Unless we continue to knuckle under to him – which God forbid – the day will come when we'll have to face him and fight.'

'What about your music?' Lonnie asked. 'You could be wounded – maimed for life.'

'I'll be crippled by something worse than a bullet if I don't take up this challenge. I see it so clearly. Lonnie, try to understand.'

'Challenge,' Lonnie said bitterly. 'What are you, a knight in shining armour? You're blinded by a stupid political creed. What makes you think the side you've chosen is better than the one they're fighting?'

'I've seen the damage Fascism can do. I'm volunteering to fight against Franco.'

'You're being foolish,' Flynn said. 'I don't want to sound brutal, but Lonnie's right about the dangers. Suppose you damage a hand?'

'I'm a good pianist. In fact, sometimes I'm very good. But more and more I've come to realise that my real métier is composing. I can go on doing that even with a handicap, but I have the feeling that the . . . the fountain inside will dry up if I deny what I see as an obvious duty.'

'You could be killed,' Lonnie said. She spoke flatly, knowing that nothing was going to deflect Guy from the course he had chosen.

'I'll try to survive in one piece,' Guy said.

'I suppose we have to admire your courage, if not your sense,' Flynn said. 'When do you leave?'

'In a couple of days. I came round today to say goodbye.'

Lonnie was looking at him with such desperation that Guy took pity on her and said gently, 'Could I see Rosemary before I go?'

'Yes, of course.'

Automatically, Lonnie stood up and got herself out of the room, away from her husband, who might see her distress and draw an accurate conclusion from it.

On the staircase she leaned against the wall, trembling in every limb, waiting for Guy to finish saying goodbye to Flynn.

As soon as he joined her she said, 'How could you be so cruel?'

'By my reckoning it's you who are cruel. You can't deny that you love me, you know that I love you, but you won't take the one honest step that would allow us to be together. Let me go back now and tell Flynn. Come away with me tonight.'

'When you're just about to get yourself killed? No, thank you.'

'Look on the bright side, darling – I may be lucky.'

'Don't talk in that flippant way.' Lonnie turned away. 'We'd better go up to the nursery.'

Three year old Rosemary, just in from a visit to the park, was delighted to see her uncle Guy. Her colour was high from the fresh air, her golden brown curls bounced all over her head, and she was determined that Mummy and Uncle Guy should share the dolls' tea party she had just set out.

'Love'y cakes,' she urged, waving a dimpled hand over empty plates. 'Lots of sandwiches. And cocktails.'

It was impossible not to laugh. Even Guy's sombre expression lightened as he asked. 'Where on earth did you discover cocktails, you precocious minx?'

He got no answer from Rosemary, busily pouring imaginary liquid from the miniature teapot into tiny cups.

'She picks up the most extraordinary things,' Lonnie said.

They both had to pretend to drink from the cups and then Nurse Ada intervened with a suggestion that it was time for Rosemary's real tea.

'Mummy stay?' Rosemary asked hopefully.

'Not today, darling. I'll come and tuck you up later. Now I have to see Uncle Guy out.'

And then she had to change for a real cocktail party and an evening which stretched in front of her like a path across a desert.

As they left the nursery Guy said, 'She's a beautiful child.'

'She's happy,' Lonnie said. 'I was happy when I was three years old. I don't remember it, but I'm sure I was. It was later that I found out how people can betray you, even the people closest to you.'

'It needn't be like that for Rosemary. She wouldn't be left without love, even if you split with Flynn.'

Lonnie did not reply. As she started down the stairs Guy said, 'Is there really nothing for me but an empty cup?'

She turned to look back at him, her face haunted by the memory of past unhappiness, and shook her head. Guy went down two more stairs and put his arms round her and she stood with her head leaning against his shoulder for a long moment. When Guy touched her face she let him raise her chin so that he could kiss her and they stood like that until the telephone rang in the hall below. A shiver ran through Lonnie, she pulled herself away from Guy and went on down the stairs.

The maid was coming up from the basement. Lonnie indicated the telephone and said, 'Answer it, Mavis. I'm not at home if it's for me.'

She opened the front door and let Guy out. With the maid still in the hall behind them there was nothing more they could say. Their hands clung together for a moment and then Guy turned and walked away.

CHAPTER FIFTEEN

As the summer turned to autumn Lonnie began to see some reward for the effort she had made to improve her slum property in Cherry Row. There were plenty of setbacks. She had not been prepared for the fierce neighbourly jealousies that sprang up nor for the way the women in particular watched for the slightest sign of one being given preferential treatment over another. And yet at times they stood together in a way which earned Lonnie's humblest admiration.

'You won't be down this way tomorrow, will you?' she was asked one day at the beginning of October.

'Not as far as I know, not unless you want me for something special.'

'We've heard Mosley's gang are marching this way and we mean to stop 'em. Better keep away. It'll be no place for a lady.'

'I'm not a lady, at least my husband doesn't think so since I went home with flea-bites all over my legs.'

'We told you old Ma Carter's house needed fumigating. Dirty slut, she let us all down. Worse than a gyppo.'

'Watch what you're saying, my grandmother was a gypsy,' Lonnie said.

She could joke with them now about things like that though their mixture of prejudice and goodheartedness still puzzled her, as it did now.

'I don't understand about stopping the march. What are you going to do?'

'Stand in their way. We can't any of us stomach them Blackshirts. They're coming here to annoy the Jews, trying to cause trouble. Plenty of yids around here, the streets are fair crawling with 'em, but they don't do any harm, so we're goin' to turn out to defend 'em.'

277

'You mean they're friends of yours?' Lonnie asked, a little out of her depth.

'Not so's you'd notice. Still, live an' let live is what I say. It's not that we're fond of the Jews, but we hate the Fascists worse.'

The Fascists, the people Guy was fighting against in Spain.

'I'll come and join you,' Lonnie said.

'Please yourself, but like I told you, it'll be no place for a lady.'

Lonnie stood shoulder to shoulder with her tenants and laughed with them at their rude, loud-voiced comments on the British Union of Fascists. A formidable barricade had been built across Cable Street, on the route Sir Oswald Mosley had intended to use going east from the Mint towards Limehouse, but in spite of the excitement she sensed a certain unease amongst the people she knew.

'Been a lot o' people brought in from outside,' one of them told her. 'People we don't know. Bus loads of 'em.'

'There seem to be hundreds of policemen,' Lonnie said.

'Thousands. Mosley give notice of the march, y'see, and so they say he's got a right to carry it out. Only we don't mean to let 'im.'

Mosley arrived with a motor cycle escort. He was standing up in an open Bentley, his hand raised in the Fascist salute. He made a striking figure in his jackboots and military style uniform.

'Look at 'im. Fancies 'is luck, don't 'e? What's 'e want – permission to go? Give it to 'im, quick, before 'e spoils 'is pretty knickers!'

There was some stone-throwing and signs of activity amongst the police and again Lonnie's neighbours murmured uneasily. The police were trying to push a way through Cable Street, but were not making any headway. Suddenly they made a charge, batons flailing, and were met by a hail of stones, bricks and blows from iron bars.

Lonnie, her arms up to defend her head from the miss-

278

iles thrown by her own side as much as a passing blow from a police truncheon, was pushed this way and that and found herself separated from the friends she knew. She was in the middle of a rougher element, who were determined not just to stand but to fight back with anything they could lay their hands on. She tried to get out of the crowd, but it was hopeless. All she could do, when they decided to withdraw, was to run with them, on to the next barricade. That was when she saw that they were scattering broken glass behind them.

'You can't do that!' she said fiercely.

'We fight with what weapons we can get, comrade. You ought to know that.'

'But the horses, the poor horses!'

'Fascist brutes.'

With her breath coming in gasps, half-blinded by tears and her mind in turmoil, Lonnie stumbled on. It was not what she had expected. The stand her tenants had taken, that had been honest and true and she had been glad to join in it, but what was it they had unleashed? Violence that begot violence; it was not what they had intended at all.

She turned her ankle on uneven ground, lost her balance and fell. There were legs and feet all round her, thick dirty boots which threatened to trample her underfoot. She was stifling, unable to breathe. She opened her mouth to scream in blind panic and then a hand caught hold of her by the coat collar and hauled her to her feet.

'You all right, miss?'

He was a stranger, not one of her own people. When he saw that she was not badly hurt he abandoned her. Her stockings were in tatters, her knee was bleeding, her hands were filthy and her hair was all over her face. Lonnie pushed her way to the edge of the crowd and leaned against the wall, fighting for breath.

'Mrs Branden . . . Mrs Branden . . .'

It was a man whose face was vaguely familiar, cheerful, young, lit up by the excitement that had carried her away only a short time before.

'I saw you some time ago and tried to get through to you,' he said. 'I say, you've been hurt.'

'I fell . . . I was frightened,' Lonnie said.

'Can I see you home? We've done the trick, turned them round and sent them away.'

'The police . . .'

'Poor devils, they were only carrying out their orders, and they were pretty halfhearted about it, too. I say, you do remember me, don't you? Bob Charlton. I was at school with Guy.'

'Guy,' Lonnie said, still dazed. 'That's why I did it. For Guy in Spain.'

'I've been there myself,' Bob Charlton said. 'Here, let me get you out of this.'

The crowd was dispersing now that their object was achieved. Instead of a solid phalanx it had broken up into knots of people excitedly discussing their part in the afternoon's work. As Bob led Lonnie through the less congested streets he said, 'I was wounded in Spain. That's why I came home. Didn't expect to take up the fight in London. Great stuff, wasn't it?'

Lonnie was beginning to feel more herself. 'I can't say I share your simple pleasure in a running fight,' she said. 'Still, in its way I suppose it was a victory. When you were in Spain did you see anything of Guy?'

'Rather! We fought together in the north and shared a billet.'

'He was all right?'

'He was a bit down, not relishing the fighting any more than you did this afternoon. But he was unhurt, if that's what you mean, and writing music'

'Writing music? In the middle of a war?'

'That's what we said, but you know Guy, he's an obstinate old mule – and only someone who's been to Spain knows how obstinate a mule can be. We found this house with a piano and he kept playing the same phrases over and over again until we barred him from using it and found someone who could play a tune we recognised.

Then I got a bullet in my shoulder, had trouble with it and was shipped out.'

As Bob guided her through the unfamiliar streets Lonnie, limping beside him, tried to get more out of him. He was ready enough to talk about his experiences in Spain, but Guy's name came into his reminiscences too infrequently.

'I hopped about from place to place,' Bob explained cheerfully. 'Here you are, I've got my car parked down this side alley. I'll get you home in no time.'

By the time they reached Chelsea Lonnie had almost forgotten her appearance, apart from the smart of her bleeding knee, until she met Flynn on the stairs.

'My dear Lonnie! Have you been in an accident?'

'A fall,' Lonnie said hastily. 'I must go and have a bath. My poor knee . . .'

She had hoped to avoid telling Flynn about her stand with the people of the East End, but to her horror not only did her name appear in the newspapers, but her picture as well. The name at the top of story explained it. Bob Charlton had not thought to tell her he had been covering the war in Spain for a newspaper, nor that he was in Cable Street for the same purpose.

'Brawling in the streets,' Flynn said. 'Honestly, Lonnie, you just don't have any sense of what's fitting. I'm no more a Fascist than you are, but I do draw the line at joining in a squabble between Blackshirts and left-wing rabble.'

'Just my luck to be rescued by a reporter,' Lonnie said in disgust.

'You were ashamed of what you'd done. That's why you didn't tell me about it even when you came home cut and bleeding. Were you attacked?'

'I told you: I fell down. And I wasn't ashamed. I was proud. You would have been, too, if you could have seen the way those people stood up for what they thought was right.'

Flynn hunched his shoulders impatiently and then he said something that struck a chill into Lonnie.

'They're not my people.'

'You've made your home here,' she said uncertainly.

'Four years. It's not a lifetime. I get homesick for the States, especially now with Europe in a mess, edging towards war.'

'Not war. Never that.'

'You think not? You were willing enough to go out and fight for what you believed in.'

'But not with guns, not killing people; it could never come to that.'

'I guess that's what they thought in Spain and look what's happening there.'

Lonnie shook her head, determined not to believe that there could be any resemblance between the violent events in Spain and the struggle in the rest of Europe, but she did have her doubts about the way the fight in the East End had ended, doubts she found were echoed by her tenants in Cherry Row when she visited them the next day.

'Fancy you having your picture in the paper,' they greeted her and it was obvious that they were pleased about it, as if some of her fame had rubbed off on them.

'We thought some of them from outside got too carried away,' they admitted in reply to her cautious questioning.

'The police . . . I didn't think they'd turn on us like that,' Lonnie said.

'Oh, the rozzers! That Mosley bein' one o' the nobs, they're bound to be on his side. They didn't do much harm, chargin' about with their little sticks. We had the laugh on them when they 'ad to advise the Blackshirts to go a different way, but we did think some people went too far – glass on the roads an' iron bars, an' that. We didn't want a riot, only a firm stand.'

One of the women, noticing that Lonnie was limping, asked, 'You weren't hurt, were you, missus?'

'I fell down and scraped my knee and it's stiff because I've got a bandage on it.'

She was glad she had kept her word and gone to face the Fascists with the people of Cherry Row, glad that their resistance had been successful, but Lonnie was not at all sure that she would do it again, which left her with a difficult question in her mind about just how the rise of the Fascist element could be combatted?

Lonnie took it up at a dinner party that evening. Since everyone knew about the part she had played there was no point in concealing it. She spoke out boldly, admitted that she had been disturbed by the violence that had been unleashed, and asked the distinguished politician next to her what he thought could be done.

She was wearing pale orange crêpe, cut to cling to her body to below hip level and then breaking out into assymetrical fullness like the dress of a Spanish dancer. Round her neck she wore a tiger's eye pendant on a rope of gold. She looked exactly what she was supposed to be, a rich young wife in Society with a mind that did not rise above the latest fashion, whether it was in clothes or books or music.

The Member of Parliament had heard that Mrs Branden had got herself into the newspapers because she had been in Cable Street and had dismissed her participation as a silly whim. Faced with Lonnie's honest, worried eyes he revised that opinion.

'Tom Mosley is an exceptionally able man with great personal fascination,' he said.

'I've met him and his late wife, poor Cimmie,' Lonnie said.

'Did you like him?'

'Yes . . . yes, I suppose I did. A forceful personality and I was rather timid in those days. I think he dismissed me as being of no use to him and that does rather colour one's attitude.'

'Quite. He could have achieved a great deal, but he's taken the wrong path and he's so obstinate in his wrongheadedness that I'm afraid he'll never get anywhere now.'

'You don't think his party will achieve any real power?'

'The British are too sloppy to make good Fascists. All that discipline – not our line at all. For some people, yes, it fulfills a need, but as a political force I think the British Union of Fascists is already a failure.'

'I hope you're right. I was horrified to find the police fighting on their side.'

'You don't like the Blackshirts and neither do I, but their organisation isn't illegal and their march had been sanctioned. Of course it was provocative, and of course they meant it to be, but who is to say which party shall have the right to parade and which shall not?'

'Perhaps tolerance can be carried too far,' Lonnie said.

'That's a dangerous argument, Mrs Branden,' the politician replied with a smile. 'If you think it over you'll realise it's exactly what Tom Mosley's party believe.'

'I never seem to get any farther forward,' Lonnie said. 'Whenever I try to talk about these things I just go round in circles.'

'If you really want to fight Fascism you should join one of the other political parties and support it properly. Can I sign you up for the Conservatives?'

'I don't think your record against the Blackshirts is good enough to satisfy me,' Lonnie retorted. 'And I'm not really drawn to the Labour Party, though I have been trying a little practical Socialism.'

She began to tell him about her housing scheme in Cherry Row and then her other neighbour claimed her attention and Lonnie was left feeling that she had still got nowhere in her search for a satisfactory creed to follow.

As the year wore on Flynn became more and more obsessed with the rumours about the King and Mrs Simpson. The Abdication when it came seemed to be more of a blow to him than it was to Lonnie.

'You never really thought Wallis Simpson would become Queen, did you?' Lonnie asked.

'I thought some compromise would be found,' Flynn admitted. 'But once Baldwin had made it clear a morganatic marriage wouldn't be recognised there was no hope.

A pity, because Wallis would have livened up Buckingham Palace no end.'

'Not many people in England want the Palace livened up. We'll do very well with the Yorks on the throne.'

'Dull.'

'Good. And the Duchess is a real charmer. I've been presented to her a couple of times. She had the right word for everyone and an enchanting smile.'

'You're moving in high circles,' Flynn said. 'You didn't tell me you'd met the Duchess. I suppose it was at one of those charity affairs that leave you so little time for your husband these days.'

There was not a lot Lonnie could find to say in answer to that. Her dinner table conversation with the Member of Parliament had had unexpected results. He had mentioned her to his wife as a young woman with a more serious turn of mind than he had expected and before she quite knew what was happening Lonnie found herself recruited to help provide homes for Basque children orphaned in the Spanish war.

Anything to do with the struggle in Spain could command Lonnie's attention. She knew that her motives were unworthy, but since the Basque children were benefiting from her longing for a link with the country where Guy was fighting then it seemed to her that she was doing more good than harm.

Flynn's gibe about having little time for him was all too true. Ostensibly they still lived together, but more and more they went their separate ways, Lonnie to her East End houses and fund raising for the Basque children, and Flynn to his round of social events which still provided copy for his column.

He did not like her independence. That was something that made Lonnie shiver. Flynn was jealous of the pursuits that took her away from him. The more aloof she was the more he turned to her, puzzled by this young woman who had once adored him, and who now regarded him with a detachment that was almost an insult to a man who regarded himself as an automatic conqueror.

'What's happening to us, Lonnie?' he demanded one night when they had attended different functions and returned home at different times. 'We're like strangers – and I don't only mean going out separately.'

Lonnie knew very well what he meant. He put his hand on her bare shoulder and she felt her muscles go tense, but she had slipped away from him too often and this was one night when Flynn was going to assert himself.

She submitted, but neither of them could pretend that she either gave or received any real pleasure from Flynn's lovemaking.

'If you treat me like this I'll find someone else,' Flynn uttered, his voice muffled by the pillow and his raised arm as he lay face-down beside her.

'It wouldn't be the first time,' Lonnie said.

'I'd give them all up if you'd turn to me and be as warm and loving as you were when we were first married.'

When they were first married . . . The crisis came on Lonnie without warning, a wave of hurt and disillusionment and anger with herself for the mess she had made of her life.

'Lonnie . . .'

Flynn raised himself up on his elbow as he became aware of her agonised weeping. Lonnie pushed him away, heaved herself out of bed and made for the bathroom. Flynn went after her, but she locked the door and refused to open it. She crouched on the bathmat on the floor, leaning against the bath, with only one thought in her mind: *I can't go on living like this*.

The trouble with locking herself in the bathroom was that eventually she had to go out. Lonnie splashed her swollen eyes with cold water and opened the door.

'What was all that about?' Flynn demanded, but behind his annoyance there was anxiety too.

He was worried. How strange that was and, thinking back a year or two, even stranger that she should be surprised about it.

'Everything suddenly got too much for me,' Lonnie muttered. 'I'm not happy. Flynn, we must talk.'

'Not at three o'clock in the morning after a bout of hysterics.'

It had not been hysterics, but Lonnie was too weary to argue with him. Flynn straightened the bed and she climbed in, tensing up as he joined her. If he had touched her Lonnie would have left him and gone to find a bed elsewhere, but Flynn lay with his back to her, unmoving, and eventually she dropped off to sleep.

Lonnie had meant to talk things out with Flynn immediately the following morning, but she was so tired that Flynn was up and dressed before she stirred. She woke up with a headache and a feeling of congestion round her eyes. Almost immediately Flynn came back into the room.

'A telephone call from Miles,' he said. 'Margot's ill. It sounds like a stroke. I think you ought to go down to Firsby Hall.'

Their eyes met and he added deliberately, 'A few days apart won't do us any harm. It'll give you time to calm down. I still don't know what that scene was about last night.'

'Everything,' Lonnie said.

'Yeah . . . well, that's comprehensive, but it doesn't enlighten me much. You've been overdoing it, that's obvious. Take a rest. Stay a few days at West Lodge. Maybe we can straighten it out when you get back.'

Margot was at home, not in hospital, but the pitiful, twisted wreck of a woman who lay in the big bed she had shared with two husbands was nothing like the elegant creature who had turned away from Lonnie in her childhood.

Awed by the change in her, Lonnie took her useless hand and held it. It felt cold, lifeless and heavy. Margot's lips moved and Lonnie thought she was trying to smile, but she was unable to speak.

Lonnie stayed an hour and then went back to West

Lodge, to Nurse Ada and Rosemary, who were the only people she had brought with her.

Patsy came to see her sister and cried quietly afterwards, downstairs in the drawing room with Lonnie.

'What a dreadful year this has been,' she said. 'It started well, with you giving us all that money, but what good has it done us? Guy has gone off to that awful war and not a word have I heard of him for months. Barbara's divorce drags on with nothing settled and I can't see that she's any happier for it – it's not as if she's got anyone else waiting to marry her. As for Sally and Bernard, I think they're quite mad to give up a nice farm Bernard's father found for them. Breeding race horses! They'll lose everything if they're not careful and so will Miles and it's not even his money. What will he do if Margot . . .'

She broke into noisy sobbing and Lonnie murmured soothingly and poured cups of tea, which seemed to have a calming effect.

'Everything's turned upside down,' Patsy complained. 'Fighting in the streets of London and you involved. How could you Lonnie?'

Fortunately, before Lonnie could find an answer, Patsy went on, 'Who would have thought the King would abdicate? Did you ever meet that dreadful American woman?'

'I've seen her around. Flynn knew her better than I did, but only in the most casual way.'

As she spoke his name Lonnie realised that the anguish of a few nights previously had faded. What was happening to Margot seemed more real; and more important.

'What is she really like?' Patsy asked and with an effort Lonnie realised they were still talking about Wallis Simpson.

'Very smart, beautifully groomed, very sleek. She was said to be an amusing talker. Honestly, Patsy, I can't tell you anything that hasn't already appeared in the papers.'

As Patsy dried her eyes, Lonnie asked, 'You haven't heard from Guy?'

'Not a word. You'd think he'd make an effort to write, knowing how anxious I must be.'

'I expect it's difficult,' Lonnie said, knowing from what Bob Charlton had told her just how impossible it was to get messages out from the mountains. 'I met someone who had been with him, but he'd been back in England for some weeks so his news was quite out of date.'

'You might have told me,' Patsy said.

'I will if I hear anything and, of course, I'd always be interested in any news that comes to you,' Lonnie said with such careful restraint that she realised that Patsy was paying no attention to what was really a plea for even the slightest link between herself and Guy.

Three days later Margot had a second stroke and this time she did not recover. She died quietly, with the minimum of fuss, in much the same well-bred manner as she had lived. In death her distorted features were smoothed out, revealing the noble bone structure which had been her chief beauty. Looking at her, Lonnie wished that she could feel more. There was sadness, and regret that the understanding between them in recent years could not have been achieved earlier, but the long years of rejection could not be forgotten and it was that which brought tears to her eyes, not the loss of the woman who had left it to the end of her life to admit that she was Lonnie's grandmother.

Flynn came down for the funeral and, unexpectedly, Lonnie found that she was glad of his support. He was not the man she loved and somehow she had to find a way out of the dishonest impasse she had got herself into, but there were years of familiarity between them and it still seemed more natural to take his arm than to insist on walking alone.

Rosemary was delighted to see her daddy and that troubled Lonnie. Flynn had not always been as attentive to Rosemary as Lonnie would have liked, but there was no doubt that he was fond of his enchanting little daughter. Once again Lonnie was back on the treadmill of her thoughts – leave him and deny Rosemary the company of her natural father, stay with him and deny herself the true companionship she craved. Rosemary's needs ought to come first, but was Lonnie doing her any real service by providing her with a father and mother who did not really love one another?

'I suppose I could have taken it for granted that Margot's Will would cause trouble,' Lonnie said to Flynn the day after the funeral. 'That's the story of my life.'

'Firsby Hall comes to you, there's no getting out of that,' Flynn said quickly.

'Yes, that's automatic,' Lonnie agreed. 'Unfortunately, Margot has left me the bulk of her money as well.'

'I don't see why that's unfortunate.'

'Miles expected more than he's getting.'

'Considering he's already had fifty thousand out of her to put into Sally and Bernard's stud farm . . .'

'How did you know that?'

'Miles told me himself.'

'That's probably why she's only left him an annuity. He'll have about five hundred a year from it.'

'Not bad, especially if the stud farm starts to show a profit. You won't keep him on at Firsby as manager, will you?'

'It won't be necessary because I'm getting rid of most of the land, selling to the farmers who've been tenants for so many years.'

'You'll get a lousy price.'

'They've been paying rent most of their lives and working land that didn't belong to them with no security that they could hand over to their sons. It wouldn't be right to ask them to pay through the nose.'

Flynn shrugged. 'I know better than to argue with you when it comes to bettering the lower orders.'

'A lot of those farmers consider themselves a rung above me on the social ladder,' Lonnie retorted. 'I can tell you, they don't relish having Thirza Seward's granddaughter as a landlady. They'll be delighted to be relieved of paying rent to me and they'll probably drive a hard bargain just to show that I may be Lady of the Manor in name, but I'm no better than they are in fact.'

She did the farmers rather less than justice. There was satisfaction when her plans became known and a feeling that she had done the right thing. Only Miles was appalled and Lonnie had expected that. He was dropping hints about being allowed to move back into West Lodge, but Lonnie hardened her heart and refused to listen.

'I couldn't stand it if he married his horrid mistress and brought her to live there,' she told Flynn. 'Let him find somewhere close to his investment, near Sally and Bernard, that'll be much more suitable.'

'I didn't know you knew about Miles' girl in Brighton,' Flynn said.

'Margot told me. And I suppose Miles told you.'

'He let it out one day when we were talking – "man to man" as Miles would say.'

'He exploited Margot. She said she didn't regret marrying him, but I don't see how that's possible.'

Lonnie held her breath, expecting some comment from Flynn about their own marriage, but he said nothing and, weakly, she let the moment pass. Christmas was almost on them. For Rosemary's sake, she told herself, she would avoid a showdown until after the festivities were over.

For the first time Lonnie acted as hostess at Firsby Hall. It was a subdued Christmas, but all the family who were available came to the Hall for Christmas Day luncheon. Patsy and Edward, Sally and Bernard and little Elspeth, Miles, very much the brokenhearted widower. Not Barbara. Barbara had accepted an invitation to go to Switzerland. And not Guy.

'But at least we've had a message from him,' Patsy said. 'The dirtiest scrap of paper, but it seems he was well and cheerful when he wrote.'

'May I see?' Lonnie asked.

'I haven't brought it with me,' Patsy said. 'Really, you know, it said nothing. Just what I've told you and that, if it arrived in time for Christmas, he hoped it would be a happy one. Of course, he doesn't know about Margot.'

The craving to hold in her own hands that scrap of paper with Guy's writing on it was so sharp that it was a physical pain. And he had written to his mother, not to her. Of course, he knew that she would hear about it and it was only right that he should send his message to Patsy. All the same, for one fierce moment Lonnie was angry that he had not managed something for her, too.

It was strange how natural it seemed to sit at the head of the table, to be the one who made all the arrangements and was deferred to by the servants. The Hall had never looked more beautiful. Margot would have been pleased, Lonnie thought. Everything had been done in just the way she would have liked, from the festoons of evergreen tied with red ribbons on the staircase to the pyramids of lilies of the valley forced into flower by the clever management of the old gardener who had been at Firsby ever since anyone could remember.

There was a tree for the children and presents all round it for the grown-ups. With the attention to detail Lonnie had learned in her years as a London hostess she had wrapped all her parcels in matching gold and red paper, tied with big red bows.

'Goodness, how extravagant,' Patsy commented. 'But very pretty, of course,' she added hastily. 'Your parcels make ours look dull.'

Flynn was in his element. With a flash of understanding Lonnie saw that this was the role he had always marked out for himself – master of a big house, rich enough to lead an elegant life, successful in the niche he had made for himself. He was the life and soul of the party and particularly popular with the children. Rosemary hung on his arm, jumping up and down to get his attention, colour blazing in her cheeks and her eyes brilliant with excitement.

Tears before bedtime, Lonnie thought with a wry recollection of her own nursery days. For you and me both, my little love.

For all her meticulous planning for this family Christmas and the way she held every strand of the party

292

together without seeming to exert herself, Lonnie was moving through the day in a daze of disbelief. The decision about whether or not to leave Flynn had been taken out of her hands. She was trapped. Condemned to a lifetime of running a beautiful house and being an impeccable hostess, of checking that the maids had cleaned the silver and put fresh towels in the guest bathrooms, of doing the flowers and sending out invitations to people Flynn thought important, involved in an endless round of cocktail parties and first nights, of country weekends and village fêtes and opening bring-and-buy sales. Caught by a loveless coupling on the night she had made up her mind to break free. She was pregnant.

CHAPTER SIXTEEN

Flynn was delighted when Lonnie told him about her pregnancy. She thought she caught a look of triumph on his face and could almost bring herself to admire the way he banished it and replaced it by a more suitable concern for her.

'It's great news, honey,' he said. 'Haven't I been saying for a long time we ought to have another baby? Let's hope it'll be a boy. We'll found a new dynasty – the Brandens of Firsby Hall.'

'What about Rosemary?'

'Rosemary can have her share of the money, but it's the boy who'll inherit the property, won't he? Aren't you sorry now you're selling off so much of the land?'

'No, I don't regret that,' Lonnie said. 'As for dividing the spoils, let's wait and see whether the baby does turn out to be a boy before we talk about that.'

She had recovered from her first despair and when she remembered how thrilled she had been about Rosemary's conception she was ashamed of her resentment towards this baby. Poor little unwanted scrap, what sort of child would it turn out to be? Subtly the natural forces within Lonnie began to shape her attitude. As the child grew within her she started to feel protective towards it.

She spent a lot of time at Firsby Hall during her pregnancy, walking alone in the woods and on the hills, making plans for the future. She would stand by her husband and her children and take up the role that was assigned to her by her position at Firsby. She would never become the sort of ikon of the village that Margot had been; that was not what Lonnie wanted. But she would try to do good where she could, turning her attention to the country cottages that belonged to her and the people who lived in them instead of her East End tenants.

'Are you coming up to town for the Coronation next month?' Flynn asked her in April.

'I'm rather torn,' Lonnie said. 'I could stay here and join in the village celebrations or I could take Rosemary to the street party the Cherry Row people are organising with their neighbours.'

'There'll be other parties,' Flynn said impatiently. 'The Fultons are throwing a tremendous one in Grosvenor Square, which I certainly mean to attend.'

'You know Dinah's never been a favourite of mine,' Lonnie said. 'You've decided me. I'll stay here. A six months pregnant woman will be out of place at one of Dinah's parties.'

'As you wish,' Flynn said. 'Here, I brought your mail down with me.'

Lonnie took the half-dozen envelopes with indifference, expecting nothing more than the usual invitations and perhaps a bill or two, though since she had hardly set foot in London since the New Year there could be nothing too extravagant. She ripped open one typewritten envelope and found a letter inside which she began to peruse carelessly until the name that always lurked at the back of her mind caught her attention.

'. . . very worried about Guy. I thought it might be best if you broke it to his mother. He seems to have been caught up in a squabble between two factions in our own side and we think he's been imprisoned. The trouble is, news is hard to come by and everyone denies any knowledge of him.

The only thing I can say for certain is that he's disappeared and all his belongings are still in the hotel room he was sharing in Barcelona with three of our men. Those of us who know him are doing what we can to trace him, but cautiously because if we put a foot wrong we'll end up in the same predicament.'

'Something wrong?' Flynn asked.

Unable to speak, Lonnie handed him the letter.

'I say, that sounds unfortunate,' Flynn said. 'From what I've heard, once inside a Spanish gaol and you're lucky to see daylight again. Would you like me to break it to Patsy and Edward?'

'That would be kind,' Lonnie said. 'I think I'll just go outside for a little while.'

'You're upset.'

'Yes.' Lonnie turned on him fiercely. 'It's such a *waste*.'

With an effort she controlled herself and went out into the garden. The daffodils were past their best, but the wallflowers were out all along the edge of the terrace, dark red and bronze streaked with gold. The sweet, warm scent drifted towards Lonnie over the stone balustrade. She leaned against the stone, looking out over the formal lawn, still kept meticulously as it had been in Margot's day, to the fields and dark woods beyond and, above the trees, the grey green sweep of the Downs where she and Guy had run wild together in the days of their childhood. Guy in prison, his gift of music drying up, longing for his freedom, despairing of release, wanting his own land, wanting her.

Not for one moment did Lonnie doubt that Guy still loved her, just as she loved him. She faced it, acknowledged that it was her own weakness that had separated them and turned back, dry-eyed and resolute, to take up the burden she had laid on herself, the life that the child inside her demanded she should lead. She found herself thinking that if the child was a boy then Flynn was right and she would make sure that one day he would inherit Firsby Hall. It was for his sake that she was sustaining her marriage and keeping up Firsby was a necessary part of that effort. Letting the child take it over from her one day would be a fitting end to her sacrifice.

Rosemary was still the joy of her life. The restrictions that Lonnie's pregnancy forced on her meant that she had time to spare for her little daughter. Together they went to the village fête that marked the Coronation celebrations and Rosemary drank fizzy lemonade out of the Coronation mug she was given and watched wide-eyed as a balloon with her name on it was sent off into the sky.

'A prize for the one that flies the furthest,' Lonnie

explained. 'Yours is travelling well, Rosie. Just think, someone miles and miles away will find it.'

Rosemary played hoop-la and won a paper windmill on a stick.

'It's rather young for me,' she said seriously. 'Would you like to keep it for the baby, Mummy?'

Lonnie had only just told her about the baby and Rosemary was deeply interested in the process by which it was growing inside her mother. Lonnie had a faint, painful recollection of a similar conversation with her grandmother in the woods. She had been a year older than Rosemary. That was when her world had fallen apart. It was not going to happen to her daughter.

Holding Rosemary more firmly by the hand she took her to watch the Punch and Judy.

'I wish Daddy was here,' Rosemary said.

'He's writing about the King in his coach for all those people on the other side of the world,' Lonnie said. 'You know I explained it to you.'

'I know, but I still wish he was here.'

Try as she would, Lonnie could not echo that wish. Flynn's absence all through the Coronation celebrations was a respite. It gave her time to recruit her forces, to stop gritting her teeth against his endless goodwill. Flynn was behaving so well it was almost unbelievable. His sunny good temper extended to everyone he met. The servants adored him and he was a byword in the village for his easy courtesy. Only Lonnie sensed the hollow behind the smiling mask and even she sometimes thought that perhaps she misjudged him.

They might not have control of the vast fortune he had once expected to be in Lonnie's hands, but with most of the money Lonnie had given to Margot returned to her, added to the portion she had retained and the portion she had given him, with possession of the house he had always coveted and his wife, her moodiness apparently forgotten, about to bear him the heir he confidently expected, Flynn was riding on the crest of the wave. He never talked now about going back to the United States and Lonnie decided he was enjoying the role of the English country gentleman too much to want to visit his own country for the time being.

She was big with child. The birth was imminent.

'Will the baby be born before I'm five?' Rosemary asked.

'No, I don't think it'll be until after your birthday, darling. You came early, but this baby seems to want to stay with me for his full nine months.'

'Why was I early?'

'I don't know. You've always been in a hurry, haven't you?'

'I want things *now*,' Rosemary agreed.

'Oh, darling, don't rush into everything. Learn patience.'

Otherwise you'll end up like me, my little daughter. I see myself in you so clearly.

Aloud Lonnie said, 'Goodness, it's hot. Let's go out under the trees.'

'Can we walk down to where great-grandmother had her cabin in the woods?' Rosemary coaxed.

She had always been fascinated by Lonnie's stories about Thirza and the way she had lived in a clearing in the woods with her animals.

'I suppose I can get that far if you don't mind walking slowly,' Lonnie said. 'The exercise will be good for me, but this is a heavy load I'm carrying and I can't skip along like you can.'

'I wish the cabin was still there,' Rosemary said. 'I would go and live in it all by myself and you could come and see me and have tea. Why isn't it there any more?'

'It was burnt down,' Lonnie said, her mind going back to the day when she and Guy had destroyed Thirza's belongings as she had commanded. Except the tea set she had sent out to Australia. Would she write and tell her mother that she had another grandchild? Yes, Lonnie decided, she would make that gesture, even though her

298

mother would probably not respond. She had never told her about Margot's death. It could all go in one letter and at least she would feel she had done the right thing. The cashmere shawl . . . she had saved that from the fire, too. She must look it out and the new baby could be wrapped in it, just as Rosemary had been. A lovely thing, a museum piece really, as the man who had cleaned and restored it had told her. How had Thirza come by it? Lonnie would never know now.

Thinking about these things and responding absently to her daughter's remarks as she skipped through the trees, Lonnie walked slowly along the path she had once known so well, overgrown now and sometimes difficult to follow. But the clearing when they reached it was unmistakable. The undergrowth had thickened, but the trees were still more sparse than in the surrounding woods and the misshapen outline of the cabin could still be traced. Strange how Guy had done her bidding that day. She remembered how strong she had felt, as if sustained by Thirza's spirit as she carried out the rite of her people.

Guy . . . there was still no news of him. Not all the efforts of Patsy and Edward or his comrades in the war or even Lonnie's own influential friends had succeeded in finding any trace of him since he had disappeared into the Spanish prison. He might be dead, but that was something Lonnie would not allow herself to think.

'Can I have a drink from the spring, Mummy?'

Rosemary's insistent voice interrupted Lonnie's thoughts.

'We haven't got a cup,' Lonnie said.

'Give it to me out of your hand,' Rosemary coaxed.

Not without difficulty Lonnie knelt down in front of the persistent trickle of water that still ran out of the outcrop of rock, the spring water her grandmother had loved to drink. She cupped her hand and felt the water cold on her palm. She held it out to Rosemary and her daughter lapped at the water like a little cat.

Lonnie was so intent on her that she did not know

anyone else had joined them until Rosemary looked up, startled.

'Will you give me a drink, too?'

Lonnie was dazzled by the sunlight coming across the tops of the trees straight into her eyes. Rosemary scrambled to her feet and moved away, her eyes round with surprise, and it was Guy who knelt in her place.

'Will you give me some water, Lonnie?'

'Guy . . .'

'You didn't know I was back?'

'No.'

'Let me drink from your hand.'

Scarcely knowing what she was doing, Lonnie held her cupped hand under the thin stream of icy water. Guy put his hands underneath and lifted it to his mouth. She could feel his lips moving against the palm of her hand as he drank.

When he took his hands away Lonnie tried to get up. Guy put his hand under her elbow to help her.

'Your marriage still holds, I see,' he said, with his eyes on her cumbersome figure.

'Yes.' Lonnie could find nothing more to say. The shock had been too great.

She said his name again, making sure that he was really there. 'Guy, oh, Guy . . .'

The hand on her elbow tightened for a moment. 'Yes, I'm here.'

'We had no news, except that you were in prison.'

'It was impossible to send word that I'd been released. It was done with great secrecy. I was smuggled over the border and made my way through France with scarcely a penny in my pocket. I found a British consul who helped me to get a passage on a boat out of Marseille and I thought he meant to send word home that I was on my way, but something must have gone wrong because Mum was as shocked as you were when I turned up on the doorstep last night.'

'You're so thin . . .'

'That's the result of going without food,' Guy said drily.

300

'Yes, of course . . . I know . . . we heard that conditions were bad. Guy, I can't believe it. You're safe and well and home again.'

'I find it difficult to believe myself. There were times . . . I wasn't sure I'd survive.'

Rosemary was still looking at Guy wide-eyed.

'You remember Uncle Guy,' Lonnie said encouragingly. 'He's been in Spain.'

Rosemary smiled doubtfully at the thin, dark man who had appeared like magic out of the shadow of the trees. Mummy sounded funny, as if she didn't know whether to laugh or cry, and that made Rosemary wary.

'I'll be five next week,' she said. 'Soon I'll be able to go to school.'

'I can see you've got a lot older since I saw you last,' Guy said gravely. 'So have I,' he added under his breath.

'Was it bad?' Lonnie asked.

'Bad? It was purgatory. Not just the prison, but knowing I'd been put out of action by what should have been my own side, just because I belonged to the wrong group. As for the fighting – we had hardly any guns, the wrong ammunition, no equipment, not much food. We starved and froze and fought on whether we were wounded or not, and in the end I think it's all going to be for nothing.'

'Franco will win?'

'Of course he will, with Germany and Italy behind him. What did we have? Russia – but Russia would only support the official Communist Party and I'd got myself attached to an offshoot they didn't want to recognise, so they eliminated us. I thought we were fighting for the same thing, but it seems I was wrong.'

They began to walk slowly back towards Firsby Hall.

'I understand,' Lonnie said. 'I joined in the protest against Mosley's Blackshirts marching through the East End and got caught up in a demonstration that was more violent than I'd expected. It shook up all my ideas so that I didn't know whether I'd done right or not.'

'You? Taking part in an East End rally? Tell me about it,' Guy said.

301

He sounded amused, so that Lonnie spoke defensively as she said, 'I thought I'd be fighting on the same side as you were.'

'My dear . . . I shouldn't have laughed. It was brave and sweet of you. Go on, tell me about it.'

She began to explain and to tell him about the way her improvements to the Cherry Row houses had progressed. When they reached the edge of the trees the sunlight hit them with blinding clarity.

'Will you come up to the house?' Lonnie asked.

'Is Flynn there?'

'No, he's in London until the weekend.'

'I'll come in and rest for a few minutes before I walk home. I'm a bit under the weather still.'

He was painfully thin, with deep lines etched on his face. His thick dark hair lay lankly against his skull and his eyes were dull.

'You've been ill,' Lonnie exclaimed. 'I didn't realise until I saw you in the sunlight.'

'Dysentery. It takes it out of you – in more ways than one.'

'Is that all?'

'I wasn't wounded, if that's what you mean, but I'm lost, Lonnie. My faith in what I saw as the way forward has been shaken. What am I going to do with the rest of my life?'

'Your music?'

'I kept my hands supple in prison by doing imaginary scales on a piece of wood, but that's not really a substitute for the hours of practice I should have been putting in. I haven't touched a piano yet. I don't dare.'

'You were writing music,' Lonnie said. 'Bob Charlton told me.'

'That was in the early stages, before the disillusionment began to get to me. It's eaten away something inside me. What could I write now?'

'Dirge for a lost faith?'

'That's about it, Guy admitted. 'Dum dah di dah, dum di dah di dah di dah.'

302

'Don't sing *The Dead March*, please! You know about Margot?'

'Yes. So now you're Lady of the Manor and Flynn is the Lord and has, all too obviously, used his *droit de seigneur*.'

His eyes were on her heavy body, mocking her.

'Rosie, run on and tell Mrs Edgeworth we're bringing Uncle Guy home for tea,' Lonnie said.

As soon as Rosemary was out of earshot, Lonnie said evenly, 'You told me once yourself that if I was to go on living with Flynn it would have to be all or nothing.'

For one moment she had contemplated telling him that this baby had been foisted on her on the very night when she had made up her mind to leave Flynn, but that would have been to break the spirit of the bargain she had made with herself. She would stay with her husband and bring up her children and that would be her life, as it was for plenty of other women.

'You've changed,' Guy said abruptly. 'It's not just the fact that you're so very pregnant. You've matured.'

'I've taken on a lot of responsibilities, quite apart from my own little family. I've made decisions which have been difficult and not always understood. I can stand on my own feet now.'

'I still love you, as far as it's in me to love anyone at the moment.'

'I know. But you must pick up your life again, Guy. The way you talk about your music is ridiculous. It's too much a part of you to disappear just like that. As your strength returns you'll find it will come back to you.'

'Perhaps. I can see you sometimes, I suppose?'

'I'm fixed here until after the baby's born. Come over at any time.'

He did come, but Guy had his own ways of finding out whether Flynn was at Firsby Hall and he never visited the house while Lonnie's husband was there. Occasionally Lonnie was troubled, knowing that her advanced pregnancy was protecting her for the time being, but that Guy was not likely to remain as patient with the situation once she was delivered. She thought that he did not entirely understand the strength of her resolve and she feared that he might be biding his time before testing it.

He began to look more rested and the sallowness in his face changed to a more healthy colour. The day came when Lonnie asked for tea to be served in the long room at the back of the house which Margot had called the music room.

'It's cooler in here,' Lonnie said, but she thought that Guy knew the real reason why she was using that room and why the grand piano stood open.

He got up when they had had their tea and went over to the instrument, looking at it with a mixture of fear and longing. With one long finger he picked out a note and then another. Lonnie sat quite still, almost holding her breath.

Guy sat down on the stool and spread his fingers over the keys. Suddenly he raised his hands and brought them down on the keyboard with all his force in one great jangling chord. Lonnie put her hand up to her mouth and bit her knuckles to stop herself crying out.

Guy began to play, not the music Lonnie had hoped for, but a long cascade of the scales which had rung through all the days of her childhood and driven his mother nearly mad. As the notes died away Guy hesitated, then he seemed to find the memory he was looking for and plunged into the dramatic opening of Chopin's *Third Scherzo*. As far as Lonnie could judge, he played without a mistake. She recognised that something of Guy's sadness and rebellion came through the music, but only Guy knew that he had found that work in his mind because of a recollection of Chopin composing it in conditions of utter solitude while living in a monastery cell at Valdemosa.

The music moved from the reflective passage to the forceful *coda* and then it stopped. Guy sat perfectly still, looking at his hands.

'It seems I can still play,' he said. He bent forward, tears running down his face, his body shaken by the sobs that were torn out of him.

'My dear, my dear.' Lonnie went across the room and crouched by his side, turning his head so that he could cry against her shoulder, holding his shaking body in her arms. As he began to recover, Guy pushed her away and stood up.

With his back to her, blowing his nose and rubbing his eyes, he said, 'I must start working. I played abominably. Good God! Amateur night at the Gaumont. Sorry about the histrionics. I'll be better now I've got that out of my system.'

He turned to face her, head up defiantly, and Lonnie realised that that was the last admission of weakness she was going to get from Guy.

'Will you start preparing for a concert?' she asked.

'That's a long way off. At the moment I sound like a third-rate drunk in a seedy Palm Court. It'll take a lot of work.'

'What about your own music?'

'As a matter of fact, there was a letter waiting for me from Barbirolli when I got home. It's been hanging around a long time so he may have lost interest, but he did say he'd include my piano concerto in a concert during the coming winter and wanted to know if I'd be the soloist myself.'

'Guy, that's wonderful! Do you mean you haven't answered it yet - an offer like that?'

'I thought I meant to turn it down. I suppose the fact that I couldn't bring myself to write the letter should have told me that I was going to start playing again one day. My hands – God, they're stiff. I thought I'd kept it up, but it takes more than finger exercises without keys to maintain the standard.'

He was walking about the room, talking more to himself than to Lonnie. She saw, with resignation, that he had almost forgotten she was there. The light was back in his eyes, the look of resolution, the ruthlessness which had carried him through into a career in music against the wishes of his family, the fighting spirit which would make it possible for him to succeed.

Guy stopped abruptly, standing in front of Lonnie. 'This baby - why, Lonnie, why?'

Faced with the direct question Lonnie gave him a limited version of the truth.

'I was caught unprepared one night.'

From the look of revulsion on Guy's face she knew how unwelcome he found this reminder of her relations with Flynn.

'It's properly dished us, hasn't it?' he asked.

'I've taken a lesson from my East End tenants. Some of the women have a lot to put up with, but over and over again they've said to me that they stay with their unsatisfactory husbands for the sake of the children. If they can do it, so can I.'

'You can all be martyrs together . . . how splendid for you.'

It was better not to reply to a remark like that. Apart from one passing word when they had first met in the woods this was the first time Guy had appeared to notice her pregnancy. Today he had come back to life again and now he was facing the realisation that he was further than ever from winning her. Lonnie thought of telling him of the way she had made up her mind to part with Flynn, only to be foiled, just as Guy had said, by this new baby, but the recollection was still bitter to her and it would be even worse for Guy to know how his happiness had been almost won and then lost.

'When's it due?' Guy asked. 'Soon, I presume?'

'Next week. I'm pretty sure it'll be on time.'

'I may not be here.'

'There's no reason why you should be,' Lonnie said deliberately. 'Go and get on with your life, Guy, and leave me to manage mine.'

He took both her hands in his and stood holding them loosely.

'Even without giving me what I want you've been more help to me than anyone else. Without you I might have broken down completely.'

'I doubt it. You're tougher than you seem and there's

something in you – call it a creative spirit – which demanded to live. You only needed time.'

'And your healing touch. Do I have to say goodbye, Lonnie?'

'I think it's best. Goodbye, Guy.'

James Humfrey Branden was born punctually on the exact day when Lonnie had been told to expect him.

'A boy!' Flynn said. 'I knew it'd be a boy. Isn't he a great little fella?'

His delight was so great that Lonnie felt faintly aggrieved on Rosemary's behalf. For the first time she realised that while Flynn thought his little daughter was cute and her prettiness and intelligence pleased him, his attitude towards her had always been coloured by the memory of the night she had been born. Towards this new baby he had no such reservations and, besides, James Humfrey was the son and heir he had always wanted.

It was Flynn's idea to give the baby the family name of Humfrey.

'If he wanted to, he could hyphenate it when he grows up,' he said.

Lonnie agreed gravely that the infant squawling in the bassinet in which his grandfather had once lain could, indeed, saddle himself with a double barrelled name one day if he so wished, and she had to admit that it was something that might well have pleased Margot.

James was by no means as placid a baby as Rosemary had been. It occurred to Lonnie that for all the trauma attending her birth, Rosemary had been a longed-for baby, whereas Lonnie had carried James with rebellion in her heart. Perhaps she was being fanciful, but because of this thought, Lonnie was patient with James' strong-willed demands for attention.

'We ought to ask Guy to be one of his godparents,' Flynn said.

'Oh, I don't think . . . Guy is such a busy person, now that he's taken up his music again,' Lonnie said.

'Sure he is, but he could spare one day out of his schedule,' Flynn argued. 'Guy's a coming man, honey. This concert with Barbirolli is going to put him right on the map. He's being talked about. Even the fact that he went to Spain hasn't done him any harm, in publicity terms.'

'Poor Guy. He'll hate having that exploited,' Lonnie said, striving to speak lightly. 'You can ask him, if you want, but I think he'll refuse.'

She never knew what Flynn said to Guy, but it must have been persuasive because, to her surprise, Guy agreed to be James' godfather.

It was the day of the christening before she found out why.

'I'll do anything that gives me a hold over you,' Guy said. 'You can hardly refuse to let me see my godson now and again. One of these days your marriage is going to break down and then I'll be there, waiting for you to turn to me, as you should have done years ago.'

'Guy, that's wickedly unfair to me. I've made up my mind to do what I think is right and you ought to respect that decision instead of trying to undermine it.'

'Why should I respect a wrongheaded decision? You belong to me and one day you're going to admit it.'

'I don't belong to anyone except myself,' Lonnie said fiercely. 'This is a ridiculous conversation to be having in the middle of a christening party. Stop it, Guy.'

She looked across to the other side of the room, to where Flynn was cradling his infant son on one arm and holding a glass of champagne in his other hand. James was wearing the Humfrey christening robe, embroidered silk and fine lace, and the long skirts hung down over Flynn's arm.

'I've absolutely no grounds for breaking up my marriage,' Lonnie said in a low voice. 'Flynn is a model husband these days.'

'Yes, isn't he?' Guy said thoughtfully. 'Do you know that poem of Housman's – "*And miles around the wonder*

308

grew, how well I did behave"? Do you think he'll be able to keep it up?'

Lonnie moved away without answering. It was too disturbing, to feel herself under siege like this. Guy had recovered more than his health in the weeks since she had last seen him; he had gained in assurance and his whole personality had a new force. In the past he had accepted her ruling on their relations, but now his determination to win her frightened Lonnie. She made up her mind to stay close to Flynn, not just on that day, but in the weeks ahead, going up to London with him instead of staying in the country as she preferred, playing the hostess and pleasing him by attending all the parties to which he was invited. She would get some new clothes, start reading the newspapers again, buy the new novels, see the recent plays and films, go back to being the Society lady with her photograph in the glossy magazines. And none of it was what she wanted.

In spite of her reservations, Lonnie did get enjoyment out of the social round on which she embarked. The people with whom she mixed were bright and amusing and she could more than hold her own with them. She got back her slim figure and once again began to be noted for her elegant appearance. By the time Guy's concert came round in November Lonnie was back in the swim.

Lonnie knew that Patsy and Edward would be at the concert and that Sally and Bernard were coming up from Wiltshire, but she made no attempt to join the family gathering. Instead, she collected together a party of ten to attend the concert and invited them all to dine with her and Flynn at the Dorchester afterwards.

She wore a long-sleeved dinner gown of sapphire blue with a silver fox stole round her shoulders and the sapphire pendant Flynn had given her when James was born.

'Look after it,' Flynn said, only half-joking. 'If things get any worse we may find ourselves hocking your jewellery.'

There had been a slump on the New York Stock Exchange and Lonnie knew that Flynn was worried. She had never asked what he had done with the securities she had transferred to him, but she suspected that he had switched into more risky ventures and might now be in deeper than she was herself with her more conservative investments.

She put it out of her mind, confident that she had more than enough money for her own needs and for her children. If Flynn played ducks and drakes with his private fortune, then that was his worry.

The Queen's Hall was full. That was Barbirolli's name, packing them in even though the major work of the evening was a modern work by an unknown composer and a British composer at that. The musical world might be buzzing with the rumour that here was a major new talent, but the average concert-goer was suspicious of anything outside the known classics and it was a tribute to the great orchestra and its conductor that they had turned up in such numbers for a work they had not heard before.

The concert opened with Mendelssohn's *Hebrides* overture. That was conventional enough to satisfy anyone and played with a fine vigour.

Lonnie had not known how nervous she was until Guy actually appeared on the platform, far more than she had been for his earlier recital and for his concert in Leeds. He looked remote and unsmiling, quite different from his usual self, just as he had the first time she had seen him perform.

He gave a cursory bow, as if the audience had no reality for him. He sat down at the piano and gave a nod to the conductor. Lonnie felt a pain in her hands and realised that she had been pressing her long nails so hard into the flesh that she had a row of indentations across each palm.

Remembering the strange little *Nocturne* Guy had played in Leeds Lonnie had expected the piano concerto to be difficult to understand, but the music was unexpectedly accessible. True, the rhythmic pattern was complex, and must have been fiendishly difficult to play, but there was none of the dissonance Lonnie associated with modern music. In the first movement there was a faint thread of a tune which Guy had given to the horns and which she wanted to hear again, but although a snatch of it was repeated by the strings, it disappeared as the movement rose to a crescendo and ended. The second movement opened with the piano playing alone against a background of soft drum beats. It was unusual, and very effective, a lonely sound with a touch of menace, which was reinforced as the full orchestra joined in, and then the violins took up the melody in quite a different way and Guy at the piano joined in this new variation as the mutter of the drums died away. It was not happy music. Lonnie, concentrating hard, could hear the sadness in it in spite of the lyrical nature of the string passages. Her wish to hear more of the tune in the first movement was granted when the third movement was reached. There it was, that hint of a tune, developed into a soaring melody which Guy had given first to the woodwind and then took up himself, developing and embellishing it, until finally the full orchestra swept it into a resounding climax.

The clapping started as soon as the last note died away. Lonnie could feel herself smiling all over her face, even though there were tears in her eyes, and her hands smarted she was clapping so hard.

'That was great!' Flynn exclaimed. 'I mean, it wasn't just good, it was *great!* For heaven's sake, who would have thought it?'

'Since when have you been a music critic?' Lonnie flashed at him.

'Never mind the music, I know success when I see it. Listen to the audience. Guy's a raving hit. And I may not be a critic, but I liked that piece. Everyone liked it. Some of it was sort of strange, but even those bits were interesting. Lonnie, isn't there any way you could persuade Guy to come to our party after the concert?'

All I have to do is ask him, Lonnie thought. This unusual man, this fine musician, this possible genius, will come if I call him, and I'm not going to do it.

'Guy has other commitments,' she said. 'Sorry, Flynn,

311

but you couldn't expect him to ditch Barbirolli just because his cousin asks him to dinner.'

'I guess not. But we must have him round soon.'

'Soon,' Lonnie said, purposely vague.

She suddenly felt tired, worn out by her nervousness beforehand and by her intense participation in the music during Guy's performance. And there was still the symphony to come.

'Couldn't we leave now?' Flynn suggested.

'It would be discourteous,' Lonnie said. 'We ought to stay to the end.'

'Can't we go round behind and see Guy?'

'He'll be exhausted. I think he'd be more grateful to be left alone tonight.'

'You know him best,' Flynn conceded. 'I'd just like to shake him by the hand and congratulate him. It must be quite something to be called back four times for a first performance of something the pianist has written himself.'

Following this success Guy began to be in demand and spent much of his time touring the country and even appearing on Continental concert platforms. He sent Lonnie postcards from each town where he appeared, always with the same message – 'Yours ever', 'Yours, as always' and his name. Conventional enough, except that she knew he meant it to be taken literally.

How long could it go on? Lonnie felt sometimes that her own resolution must break, especially when Flynn's sunny good temper began to fray. He became moody and preoccupied and, since she could see no other reason for it, Lonnie guessed that his losses in the current American slump were troubling him. He volunteered no information and she did not ask, mainly because she had no idea what she would do if Flynn asked her to help him with more money.

He was particularly fractious when Lonnie revealed that she had bought a second row of houses and was doing them up in the same manner as those in Cherry Row. It took up a lot of her time, all she could spare from the baby and Rosemary, not to mention her various committees and the entertaining she undertook for Flynn. She had a busy life and she tried to tell herself that it was a useful one, but there were times when she rebelled against the emptiness at the centre of her existence. In those moods only the children kept her under the same roof as Flynn. Gradually the wild longing for freedom, and for Guy, would subside and she would remember all the other people who depended on her and take up the burden of her days once more.

It was during one of these fits of disenchantment that Lonnie received a letter which brought back memories she would have preferred to forget.

'Poor Albi is dead,' she told Flynn.

'I don't know why you say "poor Albi",' Flynn responded. 'The swine treated us badly enough.'

'He suffered for it. Anyway, he's dead now and it seems he wanted to make some amends. He's left Rosemary a piece of jewellery. Quite an important piece, by the sound of it.'

'Lucky Rosemary. What is it and how much is it worth?'

'This letter's from a firm of lawyers in Rome and they say that it's an aquamarine, pearl and diamond necklace – sounds rather pretty – and if I'd rather have the money on Rosemary's behalf they have a client who'd buy it for five thousand pounds.'

'Don't sell without an independent valuation.'

'I don't want it to be sold. I'd like Rosemary to have it.'

'The money would be more useful.'

'It would be Rosie's money and would have to go into her trust fund,' Lonnie pointed out.

'I never suggested different. Maybe you're right and jewellery will hold its value better than investments. I haven't been lucky in that line just recently.'

So he was going to tell her, in spite of her efforts not to know.

'Have you burnt your fingers?' Lonnie said, speaking with a carelessness that had nothing to do with the sick feeling in her stomach.

'I'm a trifle scorched.'

Lonnie took a grip on herself and said steadily, 'I'm not going to fund your losses, Flynn.'

'Did I ask for a handout?'

From his wounded look one would never have thought that that was just what Flynn had had in mind.

'My articles on the Coronation sold well, so I can get by,' he went on. 'I'm just warning you to go easy with the way you throw your money into those housing schemes, because if you run short you can't look to me to bail you out.'

CHAPTER SEVENTEEN

'Do we know someone called the Marchesa di Sessiliogni?' Lonnie asked.

Flynn looked up from his letters to answer her. 'We don't, but we'd like to. She was Kat Kettlewell, two or three marriages back, and what she inherited from her grandfather makes the Singleton fortune look like peanuts – even before you started giving it all away.'

'Her secretary telephoned from Claridge's to say she'd like to come round and see me this afternoon. I can't think why.'

'What time? I'd like to meet her. She's been high on the scene in Rome and Paris, but I don't remember her visiting London. Could be a useful contact.'

'She's coming at four.'

'Tea time,' Flynn said. 'I would have thought cocktails were more in Kat Kettlewell's line. OK, I'll be around. Let me know when she arrives.'

The woman who was shown into Lonnie's drawing room that cold December afternoon had none of Lonnie's inhibitions about flaunting her wealth. She was dressed entirely in black and Lonnie's eye was sufficiently well-developed for her to register the couture line of Schiaparelli at a glance. An absurd tall hat was balanced on one side of her tawny hair, her skin was gleamingly suntanned, she wore very bright lipstick which matched her long fingernails and she glittered discreetly with diamonds in her ears, on a brooch at her throat and on her fingers.

She was about thirty-four, as Lonnie knew from Flynn's swift research into their guest: poised, glamorous, extrovert and with a forthright manner which Lonnie found herself liking.

'I guess you're wondering what the heck I want with you,' the Marchesa said. 'I've brought poor old Albi's

315

necklace over for you. He made me promise to bring it in person, perhaps because he knew I wanted it myself and would look after it better than if it came through the mail. I always travel with a private detective to guard my jewellery and the insurance I carry would more than have compensated if I'd lost it on the way.'

'How very kind of you,' Lonnie murmured automatically as she took the rubbed velvet case the Marchesa was holding out to her. As she opened it she exclaimed, 'Oh, what a pretty thing!'

'Isn't it? I want it, Mrs Branden. What'll you take for it?'

Lonnie had discovered a note inside the case and was too preoccupied to answer her for a moment or two.

> 'My dear Lonnie,
>   I am sending you my last present.
> I hope I am right in thinking it will
> prove to be what you need.
> Goodbye.
>
>   Albi.'

It puzzled her because, as she pointed out to the Marchesa, the necklace belonged to her daughter, not to her.

'Sure, but you could sell it on her behalf. I'm prepared to give more than the first figure I named. Let's see, I'm not used to thinking in pounds. I offered five thousand pounds, didn't I? I'd raise that a couple of thousand, I guess.'

'It's not a question of money,' Lonnie said. 'Albi felt he owed my daughter a debt and this is his way of repaying it. I want to keep it for her until she's grown up. If you like to wait until Rosemary's twenty-one then she may be prepared to let you have it.'

'I'll be a withered old hag past wearing pretty necklaces by that time. I can see you mean what you say, so I won't tease you. It's a pity because I'd set my heart on that necklace.'

'Have it copied,' Lonnie suggested.

'It wouldn't be the same. It's a family piece, you know. Belonged to Albi's grandmother, who was my late husband's mother's sister.'

'Your late husband?'

'I've been a widow the last three months.'

'I'm sorry,' Lonnie said.

'No need to be. Guglielmo and I had just about reached the end of the road and I was at my wits' end to see how to get free, considering he was a real fervent Catholic. You'd think I would have had more sense after my two previous fiascos, but I was just hypnotised by his olde worlde charm and the title and the palazzo and all that.'

'Er, yes,' Lonnie said.

'Two divorced and one dead. I begin to feel like your Henry Eight.'

To Lonnie's relief the door opened to admit the tea trolley and, with it, Flynn. The look of surprise on his face as he registered the Marchesa's presence was a masterpiece of acting, but his delighted smile as Lonnie introduced them was sincere; the Marchesa was just the sort of woman he admired and, of course, it helped that she was American by birth. As the Marchesa said, they were both expatriates.

'Don't you ever get homesick, Flynn?' she asked. 'Look, drop this Marchesa business, will you? I'm still Kat Kettlewell, in spite of my three marriages, and I mean to go back to my maiden name and put the past behind me. It tickled me for a time to have a title, but when you come down to it "Kettlewell" means more in the States than "Sessiliogni", which nobody can say anyway.'

'I had to stick around in England because Lonnie's affairs required it,' Flynn said. 'And then I got myself into a line of business which made it necessary to be based in London. Now that the Coronation is behind us and things are a bit flat, I might think about a trip back home.'

'Europe's in a mess,' Kat said. 'To begin with I didn't mind Mussolini, but he's got above himself lately and I can't stand that jumped-up little man in Berlin. They're

317

brewing up trouble between them and I'd just as soon be on the other side of the Atlantic when the storm breaks.'

Lonnie was pouring out tea, but she looked up at that and asked uneasily, 'You don't really think there's any possibility of war, do you? I have a cousin who insists it's only a matter of time.'

'Looks that way to me,' Kat said. 'Milk but no sugar in my tea, thank you. Is your cousin in politics or a diplomat or something?'

'No,' Lonnie said. 'He's spent a lot of time abroad and that's the impression he's brought back.'

'Lonnie's talking about Guy Lynton, the pianist and composer,' Flynn said.

'Really? He's your cousin? I'd certainly like to meet him.'

The Marchesa took an address book out of her handbag – black leather with gold corners, and Lonnie had no doubt that it was real gold, as was the little pencil attached to the book.

'Can you give me his address and telephone number?'

If Flynn had not been there Lonnie might have pretended forgetfulness, but he knew that she had the address of the flat Guy had recently taken in Knightsbridge. She was cross with herself for having mentioned Guy's opinion of the European situation.

'I didn't realise Guy's success was known in Rome,' she said.

'I heard him play in Paris and he wowed them in the aisles,' Kat said. 'I had his name in my mind because Albi had spoken of him. Albi had a great admiration for him.'

'He arranged Guy's first recital,' Lonnie said. 'Poor Albi. Did he . . . was he ill for a long time?'

'He couldn't keep off the hard stuff, not for long. In the end the family put him into a nursing home and the nuns looked after him. They said he made a religious end, but they always say that. If you ask me he died laughing, because my husband went first and since I'd failed to produce the required heir, Albi got the title and went out as the Marchese di Sessiliogni – the last thing he'd ever expected. Are you sure you won't change your mind about that necklace, Lonnie?'

The way Kat spoke of Albi irked Lonnie. She smiled and shook her head at her last question and this time Kate apparently recognised the finality of her refusal.

'In that case, I'll be on my way,' she said. 'Thanks for the tea. My secretary will be sending out invitations for a party or two while I'm in London and I hope to see you then.'

'We'll be delighted,' Flynn said. 'Let me see you out.'

Lonnie could hear them laughing on the stairs. She opened the jewel case and touched the necklace gently. Flynn would probably want her to wear it herself, but Lonnie would never do that. The necklace could go into the Bank and perhaps by the time Rosemary was old enough to appreciate it the memory of her kidnapping would have faded sufficiently for Lonnie to be able to look at it without shuddering.

Kat Kettlewell moved out of Claridge's and took a house in Berkeley Square having, apparently, decided to settle in London for a time although Lonnie had had the impression that she had intended her visit to be merely an interlude before returning to the United States. Flynn and Lonnie saw a lot of her. She rarely gave a party to which they were not invited and Lonnie was annoyed to find herself thinking that she must have a new gown whenever she went to dine with Kat. Why did she feel this need to compete? Flynn obviously admired Kat, but that ought not to matter, considering that Lonnie had decided she was no longer in love with him. All the same, she did not like to see Flynn making a judgement between them and coming down on Kat's side.

The other thing that annoyed Lonnie was that Kat had taken up Guy and Guy had allowed it to happen. He, too, was invited to her parties as a matter of course. His other engagements did not always allow him to accept, but when they did he appeared to have no objection to being lionised by Kat.

'Do you like her – really?' Lonnie asked him abruptly

one evening when they stood isolated for a moment in the ballroom of the Berkeley Square house. Kat had announced that she was going to 'do the Season' and was starting it off by giving a dance for the débutante daughter of aristocratic but impoverished English friends who were only too thankful to allow Kat to bear some of the cost of launching Jennifer into the world.

'Certainly I like Kat,' Guy said, answering Lonnie's question. 'Why? Don't you?'

'Yes, of course,' Lonnie answered unconvincingly. 'She makes me feel steamrollered, that's all.'

'I know what you mean,' Guy agreed. 'I don't allow her to ride over me, and she respects that.'

Lonnie watched Kat as she danced. She was wearing creamy satin and looked like a statuette in bronze and ivory. She was not really beautiful, but who noticed that when she was so glowing with vitality? She was dancing with Flynn and they made a striking pair, both tall and well-made, both animated and given to easy laughter. Once again Lonnie failed to find a reason for her unease. They were not having an affair, she was almost sure of that, but there was something between them, a spark that was missing now from her marriage.

She gave an involuntary sigh and found Guy watching her with an expression she could not fathom.

'I'm not jealous,' Lonnie said quickly.

'Of course not. Why should you be? You care very little for Flynn and he cares even less for you. Why should either of you be jealous of the other?'

'He's still my husband.'

'You know what I think about that, but I suppose we can't very well discuss it here.'

'We can't discuss it at all,' Lonnie said. 'Guy, don't be difficult.'

'When I think of the months I've allowed to go by without even mentioning that I love you . . . all right, Lonnie, I won't say another word. Will you dance with me?'

Lonnie shook her head, but Guy was not in the mood

to be denied. He put his arms around her and guided her on to the floor and unless she made a scene there was not a lot Lonnie could do about it. She let her feet move into the rhythm of the dance and her body relax in Guy's hold. The insistent throb of the music united them like one heartbeat. In a moment of forgetfulness Lonnie looked up and smiled and Guy's arms tightened around her.

Lonnie looked away. She mustn't give herself away, not openly, here on the dance floor. She had been strong for so long, denying the love between them. If Flynn saw them together now and guessed he would make her life a misery and all her months of lonely denial would be wasted.

'I don't think I want to dance any more,' she said.

Guy moved to the edge of the dancing crowd without making the protest she had expected. Glancing up at him, Lonnie saw that he looked strained, almost grim.

'You're right,' he said. 'Dancing together is a mistake. Would you like a drink?'

They moved towards the buffet and stood, side by side but not touching, with glasses of champagne in their hands which neither of them really wanted.

'I may go abroad again,' Guy said.

'Not Vienna! You won't go there, now that the Nazis have taken over in Austria, will you?'

'I don't know where I'll go. I've only just this minute made up my mind that I've got to get away. I'd take off tomorrow, but I'm committed to recording the piano concerto.'

'And you've got a broadcast next week. You're pleased about that?'

'Of course, but I mean to make composing my main occupation and, thanks to you, I don't need concert engagements to keep myself alive.'

'So I did do some good?' Lonnie asked.

'I suppose so. No, that's not fair. I ought not to be so grudging. Generosity like yours is always rewarding in the end. As far as music is concerned, I'm fulfilled in a way

I never thought would be possible. But I'm eaten up with frustration because I can't have you as well.'

Lonnie looked at him helplessly, invaded by the same despair that set bitter lines on Guy's dark face. His unhappiness was more than she could bear, and yet the remedy demanded so much from her that she did not know how to frame the offer of comfort that trembled on her lips.

There was a small sharp sound, curiously audible even in that crowd, and then Lonnie was conscious of shards of glass on the floor by her feet. Guy stood looking intently at the thin broken stem of the glass he had been twisting in his strong, musician's fingers.

'Something had to snap, I suppose,' he said. 'And a champagne glass is of no great importance. Your gown is splashed. Do you want to go and get it sponged off?'

Lonnie moved away without answering. She did go and dab ineffectually at her chiffon gown, glad of the excuse to be alone for a few minutes. Her hands shook and she felt icy cold. She had come within a breath of throwing up everything and telling Guy she would go away with him. How could she have let her control slip like that? How could she have forgotten, even momentarily, the careful edifice of her life, her two dear children, her resolution to keep her family together? Guy was right, he must go away and until he did she must try not to see him, not at all, not even in company.

Her visits to Firsby Hall were the only thing that kept Lonnie going all through the rest of that arduous spring season. It was the one place where she felt real. Everywhere else she acted the part of Mrs Flynn Branden, tireless socialite, philanthropist, good hostess, delightful guest, a support to her husband and a loving mother to her children. The last at least was true. The children were her delight and her reason for living and nowhere more so than when she could take them off to Firsby and romp around the house and grounds with them.

Lonnie sometimes regretted that Firsby Hall was so accessible. Flynn liked to invite guests for the weekend and enjoyed showing off the place to them. It seemed to Lonnie that Kat, for one, must have known many grander and more beautiful country houses, but Kat seemed to enjoy herself at Firsby, taking easily to the quiet country life and spoiling the children with expensive presents.

James, just taking his first tottering steps, was too young to appreciate the cost of the scaled-down model car in which he could not yet reach the pedals, but there was an acquisitive gleam in Rosemary's eyes whenever she knew 'Auntie Kat' was going to be a visitor which Lonnie found distinctively unattractive.

'You really mustn't spoil them like this,' Lonnie said, watching Rosemary wobble down the drive on her gleaming new bicycle.

'They're such pets,' Kat excused herself.

They were not pets, they were human beings and it was not Kat who had to correct them when they were overexcited and above themselves, Lonnie thought grimly, but she managed to stop herself from pointing out that Kat saw the best of them when they were giving her hugs and kisses in return for their latest presents.

All the same, she was irritated enough to say to Flynn as they were dressing for dinner, 'Considering she's had three husbands and seems devoted to children, you'd think Kat would have gone in for a family of her own.'

Lonnie nearly added 'instead of poaching mine', but was thankful she had bitten it back when Flynn said, quite casually, 'Didn't you know? Kat can't have children. It's common knowledge that she chased all over Europe trying every gynaecologist and every clinic she could find, particularly when she was married to the Marchese. He was desperate for an heir and when he died without one the title went to Albi. Now that Albi's gone it's defunct and all Kat's treatments were a waste of time.'

After that Lonnie tried to feel more charitable towards this woman who had everything except the blessing of the children she had wanted. Kat never spoke about it and Lonnie respected that reticence, but now that she knew Kat's secret she recognised the hunger in the other woman which pushed her into buying the affection of her friends' children.

Lonnie was unsure about the relations between Flynn and Kat. Flynn appeared to be highly satisfied with life, even though he still grumbled about the money market situation. On the surface, he and Lonnie appeared to live in complete amity; they even slept together occasionally and only Lonnie knew how she despised herself for the sensuality Flynn could still arouse in her and how she sometimes cried into her pillow afterwards because of what she saw as a betrayal of the love that should have been given to Guy.

As spring turned to summer, Flynn made fewer and fewer demands on her. Lonnie was uneasy, sure that there was another woman in his life and guessing that it must be Kat. If they were having an affair then Lonnie had grounds for a divorce and there were times when she thought that was the only solution. Was this the 'present' which Albi, with a last flicker of his mischievous spirit, had sent her? If so, it was not working out quite as he might have intended.

What Lonnie shrank from was obtaining the evidence. Unless Flynn volunteered information, and if he did Lonnie knew they would have to conceal their collusion from the Divorce Court, it would mean hiring a private detective to follow the erring husband and his mistress. If they stayed together at an hotel then it might be possible to obtain proof of their adultery, but Lonnie doubted whether they would be so indiscreet, nor did she think Flynn would take Kat back to their own house, not after his experience with Barbara, and Kat's own servants would never betray her, she paid them too well.

Lonnie watched the way Kat and Flynn glowed when they were together and continued to hold her tongue, not realising that Flynn might construe her dignified silence as further proof that she would never consent to a divorce.

Only once did Lonnie nerve herself to say, 'Flynn, what is there between you and Kat?'

'Friendship . . . admiration. Kat's what I always wanted you to be.'

'If she's your ideal then I could never measure up. You see a lot of her.'

'So could you if you didn't have so many other interests.'

'I need to have interests outside the social whirl otherwise I'll be nothing but your shadow. I've worked hard to keep our marriage together and sometimes I wonder whether it's worth it when I see you chasing after another woman.'

If Flynn had said openly that he loved Kat and would marry her if he were free then Lonnie had reached the point where she would have accepted that there was nothing more she could do to keep them together.

Instead, he shrugged his shoulders and said, 'I go around with Kat because it's a pleasure to be with her. She's got the vitality of ten. Everything's fun for Kat. If you don't like it then try to spend more time with me yourself.'

When August came round Kat gave up her London house and started a round of country visits, including a week at Firsby Hall with Lonnie and Flynn. She seemed to be impervious to Lonnie's reservations about having her as a guest, although she must have noticed that the invitation had been given by Flynn.

She lay out on the terrace in one of the long basketwork chairs which Margot had introduced, basking in what was, for once, a flawless English summer day.

'This surely is a lovely place,' Kat remarked.

'It's not for sale,' Lonnie said, able to joke about it because this was one thing Kat was quite unable to buy, no matter how great her wealth.

'Don't worry, Lonnie honey, a house in Europe is the last thing I'd buy right now.'

For a moment, on that peaceful, sunny day, Lonnie did not grasp her meaning and then she realised that Kat was thinking about the deteriorating international situation. Since the Germans had marched into Austria in March there had been increasingly strident demands for the return of the Sudeten Germans in Czechoslovakia to their 'homeland' and it was beginning to look as if this might blow up into real trouble.

'The time has come for us Yanks to go home,' Kat said. 'What do you say, Flynn?'

'I agree,' Flynn said, but it never occurred to Lonnie that he meant anything more than that it was the right time for Kat to return to America.

Even when he turned to Lonnie and said, quite casually, 'I've been meaning to talk it over with you,' she still did not understand what he meant.

'I know it'll be a wrench to leave Firsby Hall,' Flynn went on. 'But perhaps we could let it, so that we'd know it was being looked after. That way you'd keep a foot in the old country in case we ever wanted to come back.'

'Come back?' Lonnie could only repeat the words in stark disbelief. 'You don't mean . . . you can't mean that you want to live in America?'

'Yes, of course. I always meant to go home one day and, as Kat says, this is the time. I certainly don't intend to get caught up in European war.'

Watching her appalled face, Flynn said softly, 'Think how often you urged me to do just what I'm now planning.'

'That was years ago,' Lonnie said.

She was aware of Kat watching them, apparently relaxed, but tense beneath the careless manner. Lonnie wished she would have the tact to go away and let her talk over this development with Flynn in private. Of course he was right: she had wanted him to go back to his own country. Over and over again she had offered to go with him, to endure any hardship the loss of her income might mean to him. But that was a long time ago, when she had first loved him, before she had totally lost faith in him, before she had realised her love for Guy.

Guy . . . where was Guy? Somewhere on his travels, giving concerts abroad with only vague rumours of success wafting to England occasionally, keeping out of her way, grimly giving her a chance to salvage the marriage he despised. If there was a war, Guy would fight, and she would be on the other side of the world, isolated from her home, her friends, her relations. It was a deprivation Lonnie could not bring herself to contemplate.

'This is my home,' she said, trying to speak steadily. 'I can't leave it. And what about my work? I can't desert my tenants and the people who depend on me.'

'That's very highminded of you, but you'll feel differently when the bombs start raining down,' Kat said. 'Think of the children. Don't you owe it to them to take them to a safe place?'

Lonnie shook her head, trying to clear her mind. It had come on her so suddenly. There must be arguments she could use to convince Flynn that they had to stay in England, but she could not marshal them while her thoughts were in turmoil, nor was it something she wanted to discuss with Kat.

'I don't want to go,' was all she could find to say.

'I don't know why it should seem to be such a shock to you,' Flynn said. 'You begged and pleaded with me . . . but, there, we won't go into that now. Just make up your mind to it, Lonnie. I plan to book passages for us before the end of September.'

'Flynn, you must be out of your mind. Even if I meant to go – which I don't – I couldn't be ready as soon as next month.'

'You could if you tried. What do you have to do? Give George a power of attorney, pack your bags, pick up the kids and leave.'

'Flynn's right, Lonnie,' Kat said. 'The sooner you get out, the better. Now don't look daggers at me, honey. I don't want to get mixed up in a row between you and Flynn, but do remember Flynn has right on his side. Any father would want to see his children safe. And, after all, the kids are American.'

'American?' Lonnie said. 'But they were born here.'

'American father. They can claim a US passport when

327

they need it and, believe me, that's a very useful thing to have.'

It seemed to Lonnie that Flynn and Kat had united against her and there was nothing she could do to dent the armour of their assurance that they were in the right.

'Lonnie, I'll ask you one more time and then the subject's closed for the time being,' Flynn said. 'Will you come to America with me in September?'

'No,' said Lonnie. 'I won't.'

CHAPTER EIGHTEEN

'What's this story Mum's been feeding me?' Guy demanded. 'Is it true that Flynn's going to America without you? What's happened? Have you separated at last?'

'Guy, I'm so glad to see you. Where have you been?'

'Scandinavia. Come on, put me in the picture.'

He was deeply tanned, as if he had spent long hours in the open air and, as usual when he was excited, he blazed with nervous energy.

'When you're like this I feel I'll get an electric shock if I touch you,' Lonnie said.

'Try. I can promise you a shock all right. Come on, Lonnie. Don't keep me waiting. Is this the end of the line for you and Flynn?'

'I suppose it must be. I've refused to go to America with him, even though he's asked me over and over again. He's booked a suite on the *Queen Mary*. He's even written to me.'

Without waiting to be asked, Lonnie held out Flynn's letter. She watched Guy's face carefully as he read it and when he started to frown she sighed in relief.

'You see it, too,' she said. 'It's false, isn't it? He doesn't really want me to go with him. He's just going through the motions. It's been niggling at me ever since he first sprang the idea on me – out of the blue and in front of Kat. It felt *wrong*.'

'Kat? Is she sailing at the same time?'

'Yes Don't ask me if they're lovers. I think they are, but I've got no proof.'

'Kat would be a sore temptation to Flynn,' Guy said. 'All that money, plus her pep and vitality, and a yen for the kind of life Flynn enjoys. I wonder what she sees in him?'

'He's attractive to women.'

'Attractive men are ten a penny for the Kat Kettlewells of this world. She could have Flynn for breakfast and throw him away with her grapefruit rind.'

'She's been married three times. Perhaps she's got into the habit,' Lonnie said drily.

'I'm glad you can joke about it,' Guy said.

They were in the drawing room of Lonnie's London house. Guy had been too restless to sit down and now he stood over Lonnie and, taking both her hands in his, drew her to her feet. She looked at him steadily and then, of her own volition, moved forward and put both her arms round his neck. As their lips met Lonnie allowed herself to think that here, at last, was the happiness she had been denying herself for so long. She clung to Guy with a fierceness that made him laugh out loud as he raised his head.

'Will you marry me when you're free, gypsy girl?' he asked.

'If I'm free,' Lonnie said, moving away from him. 'Even if I can prove that Flynn and Kat are sleeping together, it's going to be difficult to get myself a divorce on the other side of the Atlantic.'

Guy bent to pick up Flynn's letter, which had fallen to the floor unheeded.

'This is a very carefully constructed letter,' he said. 'It sounds false to you? Of course it does! It's not a letter from a husband to his wife, it's a document written by a lawyer, intended for use in court. Flynn has pleaded with you – and the right is all on his side – to follow him to his home country, which you adopted when you married him, and to take his children out of harm's way. You mean to refuse. That puts you in the wrong. I would guess that Flynn means to claim that you have deserted him. He'll find a place in the United States where divorce is easy, tell how he asked you to accompany him, produce Kat as a witness, plus the correspondence, and hey presto! he'll be a free man.'

His reasoning was logical, and yet Lonnie could hardly take it in.

'Why be so devious?' she asked.

'You've made it clear in the past that divorce is out as far as you're concerned.'

'All the same . . . we've drifted a long way apart during this last year. I've hung on because Flynn never gave any indication of wanting us to part, but if he'd told me that he wanted to marry Kat I wouldn't have stood in his way, not any more.'

'Flynn couldn't have known that,' Guy pointed out. 'Not unless you told him.'

He saw that Lonnie was still unconvinced and added, 'Perhaps, for some reason, he wants to be the innocent party. I wouldn't have said that Kat was exactly puritanical, but possibly she didn't want to appear in a divorce case.'

Lonnie made an impatient gesture. 'Half the people I know have been divorced on manufactured evidence. Flynn would know there was no need for Kat to be named.'

'I give up, but I'm sure I'm right. Flynn means to get himself a divorce as soon as the *Queen Mary* docks, then he'll marry Kat and live happily ever after on her millions. What really interests me is what we're going to do?'

'Will you come and live with me at Firsby Hall?'

'Will I . . . ? Lonnie, you don't do things by half, do you? My darling girl, you know I'd live with you in a tent if that was what you wanted.'

He held her at arm's length and looked down at her searchingly.

'It's not just because you're angry with Flynn, this sudden capitulation?'

'Partly,' Lonnie admitted. 'If he wants to behave like a corkscrew, then let him, but I'd rather be honest about what I want to do. I've held out against giving Flynn grounds for divorce because I was so afraid he'd claim custody of the children, but if he's going to divorce me anyway . . .'

Her face changed and she clutched Guy's arm, frantic in her sudden realisation of what was going on.

'The children! Guy, the *children*. That's the gift Flynn can take to Kat. The thing she wants more than anything else in the world and can't have. Kat will never bear a child. Do you see? She can't have children of her own, so she's going to take mine.'

Lonnie was shaking from head to foot, so shocked that she could scarcely stand.

Very carefully, Guy guided her to a chair. 'When does the ship sail?' he asked.

'This evening. I don't know the time.'

'And where are the children?'

'At Firsby.'

Guy picked up the telephone and asked for the number. It took a minute or two to get through. Lonnie said nothing, but sat looking at him, her eyes huge with fear.

When Guy put down the telephone Lonnie already knew the answer, but she said, 'Tell me.'

'Flynn picked up the children this morning, saying they were going to Southampton to see him off. The nurse wanted to go with them, but he said it wasn't necessary.'

'I must stop him. Guy, I must! How quickly can we get to Southampton?'

'I'd like to consult George before we do anything else.'

His conversation with George Osbert was crisp and to the point. Guy was smiling when he put the telephone down.

'George is snorting like an old war-horse going into battle,' he said. 'He's been wanting to get the better of Flynn for years.'

'The only thing that matters is to get the children off the ship,' Lonnie said.

They were both thinking of the same thing: the crisis over Czechoslovakia. The situation had reached such a critical point that the British Prime Minister had flown to Munich to negotiate personally with Adolf Hitler.

'If Mr Chamberlain's mission to Munich is a failure we may be at war by this time next week,' Lonnie said. 'After that, if Rosemary and James are on the other side of the Atlantic, what chance have I got of seeing them again, perhaps for years and years? Flynn thought of that, of course. Damn him, he's always been too clever for me.'

'He's over-reached himself this time,' Guy said, sounding so confident that for a moment Lonnie was almost comforted. 'George is applying for an injunction to stop him taking the children out of the country without your permission. He's getting in touch with the shipping company to say that the ship isn't to be allowed to sail with Rosemary and James on board.'

'Will they listen to him?' Lonnie asked.

'George thinks they'll put the whole party ashore, just to be on the safe side,' Guy said, not revealing that George was by no means as confident as he made him sound.

One more telephone call and then Guy said, 'The boat train left twenty minutes ago. We'll have to drive. Come on, my car's downstairs.'

Lonnie snatched up a coat, but she had no hat and no gloves and when she opened her handbag she discovered it was the one she had emptied that morning when she had changed her clothes.

'Money,' she said.

'I've got plenty,' Guy said. 'And, thanks to you, I've indulged in a rather good new car. Once we're clear of London I'll let her out and we'll just have to pray there are no traffic cops about.'

He drove with dash and skill, weaving in and out of the traffic when necessary, consuming the miles in a powerful rush when the road was clear. They spoke very little. Only occasionally, when they were held up, Guy's fingers played on the steering wheel and he muttered impatiently.

'Are you hungry?' he asked as they approached Basingstoke.

'I don't think so. Don't stop,' Lonnie said.

A few minutes later she roused herself to say, 'I'm sorry, I'm being selfish. I mustn't make you go without food just because I can't eat.'

Guy raised his hand to glance at the watch strapped to his wrist.

'We can spare ten minutes or so,' he said. 'I'll stop at the next suitable place.'

When it came to the point, Lonnie was not sorry to get out and stretch her legs and visit the ladies cloakroom of the small country hotel where Guy had pulled up. When she came out he was waiting for her.

'I've got a flask of tea and some sandwiches,' he said. 'We'll eat as we go. Feeling better?'

'More comfortable,' Lonnie admitted.

For the first time since they had set out she was able to smile.

'Good. We're going to succeed, you know. We'll reach Southampton in time and then I have to ring George to find out what to do next.'

They sped on, with Guy holding a roast beef sandwich in one hand. Lonnie bit tentatively at her own sandwich and found that, because she was reassured by Guy's confidence, she was able to eat it.

'You were with me when Rosemary was kidnapped,' she said. 'You're always around when there's a crisis in my life.'

'We belong together,' Guy said. 'I want to be with you always. I'm not easy to live with, Lonnie. The music takes possession of me and I opt out of ordinary life. You might find you can't bear living with a husband who's only half-aware of you at times and overwhelmingly demanding at others.'

'Six hours a day practice, I know,' Lonnie said with resignation. 'I can bear anything if we're together. It's taken me long enough to admit it, but I've known for years that I ought to give up the lie I was living. If it hadn't been for James . . . he was an accident, but a very precious one. Guy, I don't think I can live, not even with you, if I lose James and Rosemary. Go faster, please go faster.'

'Steady, darling. There's no point in running ourselves off the road. I'll get you there in time, I promise you.'

The outskirts of Southampton slowed them up. Guy stopped at the first public call-box he saw and Lonnie sat in the car, consumed with anxiety, while he spoke once again to George.

'We are going straight to the docks, aren't we?' she asked as Guy got back into the car. 'Please, Guy, I must see Rosie and James.'

'One more call, darling. George has fixed up for us to see some legal bloke – a Justice of the Peace or magistrate or something – who'll issue an order to prevent Rosemary and James sailing. No use going to the ship and finding we have no authority.'

'I'm their *mother*.'

'And Flynn is their father. Be patient, darling. We've got plenty of time.'

He glanced at his watch again and realised that what he said was by no means true. It was getting close to sailing time and Guy knew that visitors would be sent ashore well before the ship was due to depart.

Fortunately, George had done his work with characteristic thoroughness. A strong-featured, middle-aged man was waiting for them.

'Mrs Branden?' he said. 'Get back in the car. I'm coming with you to serve the notice myself. We've precious little time to lose and I'm known at the docks. Without me you might have difficulty in getting through the gates.'

Visitors were beginning to come down the gangplank when they arrived at the ship, turning to wave to the friends they had been seeing off. The sailor on duty at the foot looked startled as the urgent party of three hurried towards him.

'The "Visitors Off" has been announced,' he said. 'Sorry, sir . . . madam, you're too late, unless you're passengers.'

'I'm going to fetch my children,' Lonnie said and pushed past him, running up the slatted wooden gangplank, stumbling in her desperation to get on board.

She never looked behind her, but when she reached the deck she was aware of the two men following her. After that it was all confusion to Lonnie. She had never been on a large ship before and she had not been prepared for the size of it, for the long sweep of the decks, the flights of stairs, the corridors full of doors, behind any one of which Rosemary and James might be waiting in bewilderment.

'Steady, Lonnie,' Guy said. 'We've got the cabin number. This way.'

The suite Flynn had taken was spacious. At the back of her mind Lonnie registered that Kat must be paying for it. The two children were in the State Room, James sitting on the floor with the beginnings of the fierce frown on his face that Lonnie knew meant that he was hungry and about to tell the world of his need for food, and Rosemary, not quite at ease, tired of looking out of the porthole at the bustle on the quayside and ready to join James in tears at any moment.

'Mummy!' she said, grappling Lonnie round the waist, fierce in her relief. 'It's a very *big* ship and you weren't *here.*'

'I'm here now,' Lonnie pointed out, and Guy marvelled at the calm that had come to her now that she had the children to deal with.

'I've told Daddy over an' over, I can't go to America because I haven't said goodbye to Mackintosh and Wobbles.'

Mackintosh was the puppy she had been given for her last birthday and Wobbles was her pet rabbit.

'Isn't Daddy silly?' Lonnie said. 'Of course you're not going to America. You're coming with me. Goodness, I don't know what to give Wobbles for his supper. What does he like?'

'Lettuce and things,' Rosemary said. 'Is James coming, too?'

'Of course.'

'He's got a new nurse. She said he was a fine laddie. She's gone to get some mushy stuff to eat because I told her he was going to start yelling. I'm hungry, too.'

James, finding that his signs of distress were getting no attention, opened his mouth and began to roar. Lonnie picked him up and James gave a gulp before going on with his protest at being kept waiting.

'Poor little man, you're wet through,' Lonnie said.

The door opened and the nurse came in with, as Rosemary had said, James' supper.

'Feed him and change him,' Lonnie said. 'Then I'm taking him off the ship.'

Up to that moment she had ignored Flynn, but behind her conversation with Rosemary she had been aware of the talk going on between him and the other men. When she had handed over the baby, Lonnie turned to look at him. He was flushed and angry and she saw that he was going to try to talk his way out of the situation.

'Where's Kat?' she asked.

'In her own State Room.'

'If she wants children so badly she ought to learn how to deal with them,' Lonnie remarked. 'I don't want to talk here so we'll go and join Kat.' She cast a meaning look towards Rosemary, all eyes and ears. 'Rosie, stay with Nurse and be a good girl. I'll be back in a minute.'

They found Kat, surrounded by the suitcases her maid had not yet unpacked, making a telephone call. She glanced over her shoulder and saw Flynn in the doorway.

'Lots of people we know on board, darling,' she said. 'I'm fixing up a party.'

She saw Lonnie behind Flynn and caught her breath, putting down the telephone while someone at the other end was still talking.

'Rather more people on board than you thought,' Lonnie said. 'I'm here to take back my children and I'd like it understood that under no circumstances will I ever part with them.'

'We'll fight,' Kat said. 'Flynn has a right to remove his children to a safe place. He doesn't want to risk them being caught up in a European war. What's wrong about that?'

The Southampton lawyer intervened. 'You haven't heard the latest news,' he said. 'Mr Chamberlain has landed at Croydon. He's done a deal with Herr Hitler which, he says, promises "peace in our time".' He permitted himself a thin-lipped smile. 'I doubt if it'll last that long, but for the moment the threat of war has been averted.'

'Flynn still wants to bring up his kids in his own country,' Kat insisted. 'Flynn, put your foot down.'

'I'm hamstrung,' Flynn said. 'This order prevents me taking the children out of the country without the consent of the court.'

'There are two things you can do,' the lawyer said. 'You can leave the ship, come back and fight your case, or you can sail and leave the children with their mother.'

'Damn it, Flynn, you know how keen I am to have the children,' Kat said. 'Let's get a good lawyer and fight every inch of the way.'

Flynn looked at her with a curious, twisted smile.

'Not so long ago I was as good a lawyer as you could hope to get,' he said. 'We haven't got a case, Kat. Lonnie is a devoted mother. With the worst will in the world, I can't say anything against her character. If we'd managed to get them over to the States and war had broken out and my divorce had gone through as I planned, Lonnie would have had one hell of a job to get them back. As it is, I don't think there's a chance of custody being given to me.'

'You've got no backbone,' Kat said in disgust. 'I want Rosie and James as well as you. A whole family, not just a new husband. God knows, they come two a penny.'

She spoke brutally, deliberately wounding him, and it was only Lonnie who heard the desperation behind her words.

'There are many, many children waiting to be adopted,' she said with a gentleness that surprised the three men. 'Couldn't you give your love to some homeless waif who needs it?'

'I want Flynn's children. I know their pedigree,' Kat said.

'You're not talking about prize animals,' Guy said in disgust. 'Lonnie, is there any more to be said? Flynn

338

accepts that he can't take the children with him. It's time we got off the ship.'

He was surprised and not altogether pleased when Lonnie turned to Flynn again.

'Will you be coming back to England?' she asked.

'I doubt it.'

'Will you and Kat get married?'

Flynn glanced at Kat, who was sitting with her chin in her hand and her face averted.

'I suppose so.'

It seemed to Lonnie that for the first time Flynn was facing the possibility that if Kat was not going to get the complete package she thought she was buying, she might not want him at all. Because she knew him so well she saw his confidence waver and the dismay that swept over him.

'Flynn, you said it yourself just now,' she said urgently. 'You were a first-rate lawyer. You could be again. Save yourself before it's too late.'

Flynn stared at her, not wanting to understand her meaning, then he lifted his hands in a strange gesture, as if they were linked together.

'Golden shackles,' he said. 'I wish to God I'd never set foot in England.'

'I wish you well, Flynn.'

'You're too damned charitable. You always were. I couldn't cope with it. Get out, Lonnie. You've beaten me and I don't particularly want to see you around any longer.'

As they filed away down the long passageway, Lonnie put her hand up to her face.

'Lonnie, for goodness sake, you're not upsetting yourself over Flynn, are you?' Guy asked in exasperation.

'Of course not,' Lonnie said, but she had to turn her head away to hide her tears. It was something Guy would never understand, that in spite of her relief at being free at last she could still feel an aching regret for the young love she had lavished on Flynn. If Margot hadn't made them stay in England . . . but it was too late to start

339

thinking like that and in any case it was Flynn who had tied himself down by his refusal to forego the enjoyment of her money. It was over, and she was glad that it was over.

Fortunately, Guy was diverted by the business of removing the children from the ship.

'Ideally, I'd like to take them home,' Lonnie said. 'But it's too late. Can we find a small hotel for the night? I'll have the children in my room.'

'What about me?' Guy muttered rebelliously.

'Your turn will come,' Lonnie said.

'I hope that's a promise,' Guy retorted, but he had started to smile and he found them very adequate accommodation for the night.

When they drove back to Sussex the next day Guy seemed more preoccupied by the reports of Mr Chamberlain's return from Munich than anything else.

'I find all the rejoicing nauseating,' he told Lonnie.

'Surely you want peace?'

'Not peace at any price. We're going to have to pay for this, Lonnie. You made a stand once, to stop Mosley and his thugs marching through the East End. That's the only way we're going to put an end to Hitler's demands.'

'Perhaps he'll be satisfied now.'

'Not him. Next time he'll be more aggressive and even more sure of getting his own way. The only thing we've gained is time and I hope we use it to re-arm.'

They were talking with difficulty, since Lonnie was in the back of the car trying to amuse Rosemary on the long journey and to appease James' fretfulness at the upset to his routine. By the time they reached Firsby Hall she was exhausted, not just by the journey but by her distress the previous day.

'Go and rest,' Guy said. 'I'll stay with Mum and Dad. When you feel ready we'll meet and talk.'

By the following day Lonnie had at least one of the answers she needed. She telephoned Guy and asked him to walk through the woods and meet her near her grandmother's old cabin.

It was the second day of October, a golden autumn day with a clear blue sky above and a haze of mist on the horizon, as warm as summer but with a hint in the air of frosts to come. The leaves still hung on the trees, slowly turning colour. As Lonnie walked a few drifted down, twisting in the still air, and carpeted the path she was following.

Guy was already waiting for her by the burnt-out shell of Thirza's cabin. Lonnie held out to him the wireless message she had received.

' "*Divorce proceedings will go ahead as intended. Flynn and Kat*",' Guy read. 'It sounds as if they're staying together. I'm surprised. I thought she meant to ditch him.'

'Better for Flynn if she had,' Lonnie said. 'Perhaps I'm wrong. Perhaps they love one another. At any rate, it seems that I'll be a free woman as soon as Flynn can shake himself clear of me.'

'You'd better consult George, to make sure the divorce is valid in this country.'

'Yes, I must do that,' Lonnie agreed with a sigh.

'Are you still regretting the past?'

'I'll always do that, but I'm ready to put it behind me. A profound mistake, made when I was too young to know what I was doing. It was bitterly hard to admit that all the people who told me that, were right. Perhaps that's why I persevered for so long, trying to make something of a marriage that should never have happened, not in the way it did. I was as rash as my mother before me. I wonder if I'll be able to stop Rosemary from repeating the pattern?'

'Are you going to let me be around to help you?'

'Of course. It's going to be difficult, explaining to Rosie that Flynn won't be coming back and that you are going to be my husband. She'll be puzzled and upset, but at least she won't be as bereft as I was when I was a child.'

'Poor little scrap,' Guy said with a smile. 'My heart went out to you then, just as it does now.'

For the first time since their meeting they turned to one another and kissed. With Guy's smiling lips brushing hers,

Lonnie murmured her love to him, and then he caught her to him so fiercely that her mouth felt bruised.

She struggled to free herself and Guy's hold slackened.

'How long have I got to wait?' he said in her ear. 'Lonnie, I love you so much, so much.'

'I said I'd take you to live with me openly at Firsby Hall and I meant it at the time, but I've had a fright, Guy. If Flynn could have found something to say against me it might have swung the balance towards allowing him to keep the children. I can't live with that possibility hanging over me. We can't live together until we can get married.'

Guy gave a sigh that was more like a groan.

'It could be months. It's more than I can bear. As long as there was no hope, I managed – somehow. But now that I know you're free of Flynn, even if there's a legal tie between you, I want you so much that it's burning me up. I can't work. You come between me and my music.'

'Guy, Guy!' Lonnie put up her hand and stopped his mouth. 'My darling, we can't live under the same roof, but I don't mean we can't be together. If we're very careful, very discreet . . .'

'A hole in the corner affair? That's not what I want.'

'Nor me. But think, Guy, think what I've got to lose.'

Guy leaned his forehead against hers, his eyes closed, and drew a deep breath.

'I know,' he said. 'And I've got so much to gain, if I'm patient. But it's hard, my darling, it's very hard.'

'Come and sit down,' Lonnie said. 'There's a fallen log over there.'

She led him through the grass to the far side of what had once been the clearing in the woods. The shadows were beginning to lengthen across the grass and the sun was turning from gold to red. They sat on the log with their arms round one another, not speaking, until Lonnie turned her head and put her lips to Guy's mouth.

She was wearing a jersey with a silk scarf round the neck and a full, gathered woollen skirt. Guy's hand felt for the edge of her jersey and crept up inside, until he could touch her breast. Lonnie gasped and shuddered. She lifted her mouth blindly, seeking the solace he could give her.

Feeling her nipples, hard against his hand, and the way her body strained towards him, Guy said, very softly in her ear, 'Shall I tumble you in the grass, my nut brown maid?'

'Yes,' Lonnie said. 'Oh, yes, Guy.'

She twisted out of his arms and pulled the jersey over her head, flinging it on the ground. The long thick skirt followed. This time she spread it carefully and sat on it, holding out her arms.

Guy knelt for a moment in front of her and then he laid her gently back amongst her discarded clothing. Something had been released in Lonnie that she had never known was in her. She was fierce with him, as demanding as a queen with a subject lover, and Guy matched her wild abandon, freed at last from the restraint he had put on his passion, carried away into a world where there was no reality but their striving bodies and the delicious languor that fell on them as at last they separated.

They lay for a long time, dreamily silent, until the chill evening air made Guy shiver. He raised himself on his elbow and looked down at Lonnie, drowsing in the crook of his arm, her hair wild, her eyes drugged with the surfeit of their loving.

'I'm scratched all over and I don't know whether it's from sticks and stones or from you, you hell cat,' he said. 'So you love me?'

'It seems I do,' Lonnie agreed, taking up his light, mocking tone. She sat up, half-delighted and half-ashamed. 'Whatever got into me?'

Guy gave a ribald snort and she tapped him half-heartedly with her hand.

'The spirit of the woods,' he suggested. 'Do you know your old legends? I felt like one of those sacrificial youths, forced to mate with the priestess queen before she killed him.'

'Forced?' Lonnie said. 'You seemed willing enough to me.'

'That was because you had me under your spell. Come on, darling, we must get dressed or you'll catch cold. Besides, it's too disturbing, seeing you sitting there like that.'

Lonnie felt around and began to pull on her clothes.

'Guy, it was as good as I thought it was, wasn't it?' she asked, with her voice muffled by the jersey as she dragged it on over her head.

'The earth definitely moved,' Guy assured her solemnly. 'We probably caused an earthquake in San Francisco and an eruption of Mount Etna.'

'Do you feel better?'

'Better? I'm a new man. Oh, Lonnie, you wonder! I'm delirious, I'm crazy. I think I'll go home and write a symphony.'

'Wouldn't it be wonderful if you did? I'd be so proud.'

She stood up, a little uncertainly. 'My legs don't seem to want to hold me.'

'Hang on to me, darling. I'll walk you home.'

He helped her to smooth her hair, laughing when she murmured distractedly that she must look a sight.

'You look like what you are, a wicked, wanton gypsy,' he said.

'Should I feel ashamed?'

'Certainly not. I won't allow it. You're my bride-to-be and we've plighted our troth in the good old-fashioned way, that's all. Half the local children were got in the hedgerow, if the truth be told.'

'As I was myself,' Lonnie said. 'I understand better now what drove my mother. When I went to Flynn I was completely inexperienced . . .'

'Don't speak of him,' Guy said, touching her lips with his finger. 'The future belongs to us.'

'The whole of the rest of our lives,' Lonnie said. 'Guy, it's too good to be true.'

'Don't say that. Accept the gift of our love and be

344

thankful. I've belonged to you the whole of my life and you've belonged to me. We were parted for a time . . .'

'Too long . . . and it was my fault.'

'Now at last we're where we should always have been.'

'I've discovered something so precious I don't know how I could have lived without it for so long, the joy of giving my love to a man I can trust completely. You are myself, I know you through and through, mind and body. I didn't know it was possible to feel so . . . complete. We'll always be together, won't we, Guy?'

Guy looked up at the clear, untroubled sky, deep blue with one star bright above them. Somewhere in the distance there was a throb in the air as an aeroplane passed over the coast towards London. For a moment he was visited by a recollection of the turbulent world and his experience of war in Spain, then he put the thought away from him.

'Always,' he said.